CW00495584

White is the coldest colour

John Nicholl

Published in 2015 by FeedARead.com Publishing

Copyright © John Nicholl

The author or authors assert their moral right under the Copyright, Designs and Patents Act, 1988, to be identified as the author or authors of this work.

All Rights reserved. No part of this publication may be reproduced, copied, stored in a retrieval system, or transmitted, in any form or by any means, without the prior written consent of the copyright holder, nor be otherwise circulated in any form of binding or cover other than that in which it is published and without a similar condition being imposed on the subsequent purchaser.

A CIP catalogue record for this title is available from the British Library.

White is the coldest colour is entirely fictional, but draws on my experiences as a child protection social worker, manager and trainer. During my career I was faced with case after case that left me incredulous as to the harm sexual predators chose to inflict on their victims. The book reflects that reality.

The story is set in 1992, a more naïve time when many found it extremely difficult to believe that a significant number of adults posed a serious risk to children.

The book includes content that some readers may find upsetting from the start.

It is dedicated to survivors everywhere.

Chapter 1

Thursday 9, January 1992

The video featured two middle-aged men wearing nothing but black leather bondage hoods, who were eagerly assaulting an eight-year-old boy with shoulder-length russet brown hair parted in the middle. Their blows gradually increased in severity until their victim slumped unconscious and bleeding. He hung there, suspended by twisted arms, with his head dangling towards a white-tiled floor stained with intermingling bodily fluids.

As the film came to an eventual blood-spattered conclusion, fifty-eight-year-old Dr David Galbraith wiped himself with a paper hankie taken from a box kept next to the desktop computer, discarded the soiled tissue in a waste paper basket to the right of his desk, switched off the television, and ejected the tape from the VCR.

He returned to his seat, balanced his gold metal-rimmed reading glasses on the bridge of his nose, opened the olive green cardboard file on the desktop in front of him, and began perusing the contents… The cellar provided an excellent production studio, both functional and aesthetically pleasing. It wasn't quite perfect, of course; the family kitchen didn't provide the ideal access point. And forcing the Welsh oak dresser aside on each and every occasion was an unfortunate necessity. But, nonetheless, its development was something to be proud of. And only utilising professional assistance on a strictly cash basis from like-minded contacts made absolute sense. Security was everything.

Lining the walls with eight inches of highly efficient soundproofing foam was truly inspired. Even the most piercing and prolonged screams couldn't be heard in the rest of the house, or anywhere else for that matter. It was entirely practical, as was the stainless steel medical trolley. Where else would he keep the various tools of his trade?

He actively controlled his breathing and closed his eyes for a second or two, before opening them slowly and refocussing on his notes… And what of his plaything? How did the process begin? It was important to pin down the specific details; important to identify the precise moment in time. Ah, yes, he first saw the little bastard at the Gwyn children's home, and decided immediately that he provided suitable project material if the opportunity arose. And of course, fate smiled on him.

Dr Galbraith turned the page... He was driving the Daimler in the direction of Caerystwyth, and despite the poor visibility he spotted the little bastard walking, head bowed, in the opposite direction. That was worthy of a symbolic pat on the back if anything was.

Whether or not to abduct the little bastard wasn't an easy decision to make. He knew it was risky. Maybe he became complacent and gambled with his freedom? And what if he'd been caught? It just didn't bear thinking about.

The doctor bit his lower lip hard, and resisted the impulse to shriek as the pressure in his head escalated exponentially: pounding, booming, compression and sound that made him twist and blink and squirm and pant for breath... The long game would have been a much safer option. Why the hell did he deviate from such a well-established and successful protocol?

He repeatedly clenched and relaxed his fists... At the end of the day, the opportunity to make fantasy reality was just too good to ignore. That was reasonable, wasn't it? His actions weren't entirely irresponsible. He'd entertained numerous guests over the years without even a hint of police attention. All right, he hadn't abducted a child before, that was a first, but he'd taken a minute or two to weigh up the pros and cons in his mind before acting. The country road was predictably quiet; he hadn't seen another car for at least ten minutes or more, and even in the unlikely event that one had come along at an inopportune moment, what would the driver have seen in those few brief seconds anyway? It's not as if the little bastard struggled.

The little bastard recognised him as soon as he braked, reversed, and wound down the window with an electric buzz. He appeared impressed by the car. Why wouldn't he be? And the appalling weather certainly helped. The little bastard took little persuasion to jump into the front passenger seat despite his usual diffidence. Yes, he complained somewhat, and started asking infuriating questions once he realised they weren't travelling in the direction of the children's home. But, he was still a powerful man. It wasn't difficult to knock the little bastard senseless.

Dr Galbraith laughed, head back, throat taut, Adam's apple protruding… What a glorious moment! He'd felt omnipotent, as if he could get away with anything. And who knows, maybe he could have. There was no room for doubt that day. No invasive, incomprehensible cacophony inside his skull to make his life a fucking misery.

Transferring the little bastard to the car boot was an excellent idea. Utilising the Persian rug to facilitate his journey from boot to cellar was a stroke of genius. And Cynthia didn't suspect a damn thing. Not that she'd have dared ask any unwelcome questions anyway.

Carrying the little bastard down the twelve cold grey concrete steps proved easy enough. Throwing him to the tiled floor was virtually effortless. It only took one punch to bring him back to semiconsciousness, before administering the fast-acting psychoactive drug. And it worked quickly. But then it always did.

Good old Sherwood only took about twenty minutes to arrive. All he had to do was make the call, say they had a guest waiting, and he came immediately. The fool must have driven at breakneck speed. What the hell was the man thinking?

Sherwood paused momentarily when he saw the dark blood pooled around the little bastard's head. Why did the man entertain such regrettable doubts? If only he'd learnt to embrace his true nature, things may have worked out differently.

Dr Galbraith frowned… And he had to do much of the work himself. He had to pull the little bastard up by his hair, and slap him in the face, again and again and again, until he eventually regained consciousness, and supported his own weight. He had to push the little bastard hard against the cellar wall and hold him there by the throat. He had to order Sherwood to secure the little bastard's wrists in the black steel manacles above his head. He had to force the feeding tube up one of the little bastard's nostrils, down his throat and into his stomach. Coming to think of it, he addressed the majority of necessary tasks without significant assistance. He could almost certainly manage the entire process unaided if required.

What the hell was he thinking? A man of his elevated status and superior intellect shouldn't be burdened with manual labour. That was the role of the followers, rather than the visionaries.

But, was he doing Sherwood's memory a disservice? The man wasn't totally useless. He stripped the little bastard off and hosed him down with the high pressure washer; he held his head still like an attentive staff nurse, he fetched the high-calorie intravenous fluid and attached it to the drip stand, and he made the coffee afterwards. Now, that was something Sherwood was good at. Maybe at some point in the not-too-distant future he should consider a suitably pliant replacement. It was certainly worth considering.

Dr Galbraith broke into a smile that lit up his face… Sherwood was so disappointed when told that producing the first video would have to wait for another day. The man never did understand the need to maintain meticulous records despite his social science background. It was another of the simpleton's insurmountable failings.

His smile evaporated as quickly as it appeared… It was something of a shock when the little bastard's heart stopped after just ten days. But at least the process was immortalised on film for future reference.

Sherwood hadn't taken it well, of course. It seemed guilt could be a terrible burden for those who indulged such pointless emotions. What was it he said at the time? He thought they'd gone too far. He thought they'd crossed a line. And maybe he was right. What use was a dead child?

Dismembering the body proved a surprisingly demanding process. But at least the surgical skills learnt in medical school, had finally been put to good use. And keeping Sherwood on side was an onerous task. All the fool had to do was hold the little bastard's head and limbs still. How hard could it be? Was it really necessary to throw up constantly and howl like a hungry baby?

The floor was soiled to such an extent that it was difficult to tell the original colour of the tiles. And the stench! At least Sherwood cleaned up fairly effectively after a great deal of animated cajoling: will you stop throwing up, man? Use the damn bleach, unblock the drain, you've missed some. Come on, Richard, you've missed some! It may well have been easier to clean up and bag the damn body himself.

And then came the grim aftermath. Fantasy-offending-remorse-fantasy-offending-remorse: a depressingly predictable pattern. But this time was different. Sherwood tried to minimise his responsibility. He spouted some mindless crap about loving children too much. The man was a childcare expert, he was a relatively intelligent man, he'd read the relevant text books, he understood the theory from an academic perspective. He must have known that was utter shit. Surely not even Sherwood could be that deluded?

And even after all that, he tried to help the man despite the obvious inconvenience. He showed him the four videos, which at the end of the day spoke for themselves. In reality they weren't so very different. It was blatantly obvious, but for some inexplicable reason it needed saying. What more could he conceivably have done? He'd even shared that he too experienced occasional nagging doubts in the early days of his offending, all those years ago. All right, it may have been more to do with a fear of arrest than a crisis of conscience, but for a time, in the early days of their relationship, he had hoped that Cynthia may change him. Perhaps if he'd chosen an emotionally stronger woman she'd have steered him along a different path. Maybe if Cynthia had spawned boys rather than her two nauseating female brats, he'd have understood what it was other parents felt for their offspring. But, no, no, the bitch couldn't even get that right.

It beggared belief. How could an apparently intelligent woman be so consistently stupid? And Sherwood wasn't much better. If a respected doctor such as himself could abandon any semblance of a conscience, learn to fully embrace his true nature, and view life and death from a purely Darwinian perspective, why the hell couldn't Sherwood do likewise? That was the one thing which may have saved him. Was there really a need for that endless self-indulgent soul searching? What was it Sherwood said on the subject? That the burden of guilt was overwhelming. That there was no escaping the dark world he'd played his part in creating. What the hell was that about?

And despite everything, he'd utilised his therapeutic skills in an attempt to help the man. He'd explained why they did what they did. Why Sherwood did what he did. That he was facing his true self for the first time, with no room for his usual rationalisation, self-deception or denial. But, Sherwood's guilt became even more entrenched. He insisted that Gareth's death was a watershed moment. Gareth! He actually used the little bastard's name, and claimed he'd never offend again as a result of his death.

Dr Galbraith slammed the palm of his right hand down on his desktop… Claiming he'd talk to the authorities rather than harm another child was an abomination. Sherwood became an intolerable liability at that precise moment. Something had to be done. It really was as simple as that.

Two days passed, and Sherwood was still maintaining his laughable position. The man even turned down the opportunity to attend a gathering of the ring. He hadn't missed a meeting for years. That was far too significant a development to ignore. Enough was enough. Providing the paracetamol was an act of human kindness.

He sat Sherwood on that ghastly bohemian red leather settee of his, poured one tot of single malt whisky after another down his ungrateful throat, and handed him the tablets one at a time. He even did that for the man before repeatedly reinforcing his feelings of guilt and remorse: 'You've done terrible things, Richard. You will never overcome your guilt, Richard. You will harm other children, Richard. Death can be a welcome release, Richard. It needn't be painful, Richard.' It was something along those lines. Anyway, whatever his choice of words they had the desired effect. That's what mattered. And liver damage wasn't such a bad way to go, was it? Why concern himself? Sherwood was better off dead. There seemed little purpose in further pondering such inconsequences.

Dr Galbraith removed his spectacles, closed Gareth's project file, and was instantly back in the present. He ran a hand through his neat black hair, rose easily from his seat, pulled up his pants and trousers, and tucked his shirt-tail into his waistband with both hands… It had been too long, far too long, and no amount of reminiscing would sustain him, however dedicated his approach.

He took a GP referral letter from an inside pocket of the bespoke navy blue single-breasted suit jacket hanging on the back of the study door, removed it from its ivory envelope, returned to his seat, unfolded it carefully, and reread it for the sixth time since receiving it the previous morning… The little bastard was the past, and a new project was essential if the pressure in his head were to become even remotely manageable.

He blinked repeatedly as a single bead of sweat ran down his forehead and found a home in his left eye… It was looking hopeful. His new patient was the correct gender and within the required age range. He had to be worth a look, didn't he?

He closed his eyes again and nodded once, confirming the conclusion of his ruminations… Yes, yes, of course he was. New projects made life worth living.

Chapter 2

'Will you read to me, Mummy?'

'Oh, Anthony, it's well past your bedtime. What will the teacher say if you fall asleep in class again?'

'Just a few pages, Mummy, please. I'm feeling sad.'

'Come here, cariad, and give your old mum a hug.'

Anthony buried his head in the warm orange wool of her jumper.

Molly disentangled herself from her son. 'Now then, cariad, into bed with you, and I'll tuck you in nice and snug. I've put your teddy and a nice warm hot-water bottle under your quilt.'

'Just a few pages, please. I don't want to be on my own.'

'Okay, just five minutes. But then it's time for sleeping.'

Molly Mailer picked up the paperback and began reading.

'Is Dad coming to see me on Saturday, Mummy?'

Molly closed the book and rested it on the small glass-topped bedside cabinet.

'No, cariad, Dad can't make it this weekend.' She rubbed the top of his head tenderly with the palm of her hand, leant forward, and kissed him on the forehead. 'Shall I read the story now?'

'Why can't he come, Mummy?'

'I explained, cariad. He's going away for the weekend.'

'With his new friend?'

'Yes, cariad, with his new friend!'

Anthony sat up and frowned. 'It's all my fault.'

Molly hugged her son tightly. 'How many times do I have to tell you, cariad? It's not your fault. It really, really isn't. Mum and Dad both love you. Dad still loves you. Now, under the quilt with you, and I'll lie down on top of the bed to keep you company until you fall asleep.'

A few moments later Anthony curled up into a ball, hugged his teddy bear tightly to his chest, and started snoring quietly.

Molly rose stiffly from the bed, silently cursed her aching lower back, and tiptoed out of the room: ever so slowly, ever so carefully… Please don't wake up, Tony. Please don't wake up.

She gritted her teeth and grimaced as she stared into the large oval bathroom mirror on the wall above the heated towel rail, focusing on the inevitable signs of ageing, cruelly highlighted by the glaring, excessively bright florescent light above her head… It wasn't good. She looked tired, she looked jaded, and she looked older. There was no denying it, however tempting it was to try.

She took a deep intake of breath through her nose, and exhaled slowly and gradually through her open mouth… That's what single parenthood did to you. The separation had taken its toll.

She sighed, rubbed her bleary eyes with the back of one hand, and headed downstairs… Any attempts at beautification, however seemingly necessary, would have to wait.

Molly shuffled into the kitchen on tired legs and switched the kettle on… Anthony was finally asleep, and Siân was out again. Why not make the most of the free time whilst she had the opportunity?

She slumped into an unforgiving kitchen chair, rested her elbows on the pine table, and cradled a large mug of her favoured peppermint tea, sweetened with an overgenerous helping of Welsh honey, in both hands. She closed her eyes and tried to relax as the rising vapour warmed her face… Should she head up to bed to enjoy her Lesley Thomas? It was tempting. No, she was going to have to wait up to let Siân in. That was if she bothered coming home at all.

Molly groaned loudly and took a calming gulp of the fast-cooling liquid… Would it be sensible to give Siân her own key? It would definitely make life easier. But, was she really old enough for that kind of independence? Yes, no, yes, no? It wasn't easy making decisions when you were used to a partner acting as a sounding board. Why not sleep on it?

She yawned and fought to stay awake, but after about fifteen minutes of good intentions she capitulated, rested her head on the kitchen table, and slept.

Molly woke with a start, and stared at the kitchen clock… Twenty past twelve. Oh, not again, what did the thoughtless girl think she was doing? She was only fifteen, for goodness' sake.

She hurried into the cottage's tiny hall with its ancient faded red-tiled floor, grabbed the house-phone from its wall-mounted cradle next to the front door, and sat on the bottom step of the stairway, which creaked noisily under her weight. Molly stilled herself and listened intently… No sound of stirring from Anthony's room. Thank God for small mercies.

After a minute or two's cautious silence, Molly went to dial. But then it dawned on her… Who was she going to ring? Siân hadn't shared details of friends for months. Was ringing arbitrary parents at half past twelve in the morning really such a good idea? All she could do was wait, worry, and hope for the best.

Molly flopped back into the same unforgiving kitchen chair and wept. Deep, all-consuming sobs caused her chest to heave repeatedly as she gasped for breath… Should she ring her mum again? It was about an hour later in Majorca, but she badly needed to talk. Why not? Mum wouldn't mind her calling. She never did.

Molly waited for what seemed like an age before finally hearing her mother's familiar voice say, 'Hello,' in melodic Welsh tones, tinged with a barely decipherable but unequivocal hint of Spanish.

'Molly? It's about half one in the morning here. What's wrong, love?'

'Sorry, Mum, just the usual stuff.'

'Sorry to hear that, love. But half past one? Can't we talk in the morning?'

There was a moment's silence before Molly began weeping without words.

'Oh, Molly, things can't be that bad, can they?'

'Not great to be honest, Mum.' She paused, and then added, 'I wish Mike hadn't met that tart.'

'I know, love. I know. Give me a second; Dad's sleeping. I'll pick up the phone in the lounge.'

'Hello, Molly?'

'Yes, I'm still here, Mum.'

'Right, love. Tell me all about it.'

'Siân's out again. God only knows where. I just wish she'd tell me where she's going, or at least give me a call to say she's safe. It's not much to ask, is it?'

'Siân's a teenager, love, you weren't so very different at that age, to be honest.'

'Yeah, I suppose you're right, Mum. But it's not easy on my own.'

'I know, love. Now, tell me. How's Anthony doing?'

Molly shook her head slowly and frowned. 'Tony? Where do I start?'

'That bad, eh?'

Molly swallowed hard before responding. 'Oh, Mum, he's changed. He's clingy, he's wetting the bed most nights, and he's even started taking a teddy bear to bed again. Mr Snuggles! Can you believe that? He's seven not four. I thought those days were long gone.'

'It's understandable, love, in the circumstances.'

'He just stays in and plays with his bloody Lego. Anything to avoid mixing.' She paused for breath and continued. 'He asks me about Mike constantly: is Dad coming today? Can I see Dad on Saturday? Will Dad play football with me? I try to be patient, Mum, but he asks the same bloody questions every single day. I'm struggling, Mum. The other morning he threw an entire bowl of cornflakes across the room when I told him Mike couldn't make it this Saturday. There was one hell of a mess. And, then he went completely to pieces: stamping about the kitchen with tears streaming down his face, snot everywhere. It was like the terrible twos, but worse. It s-seems never-ending.'

'He's at that age, love. He's missing his dad. I know it's not what you want to hear, but these things don't sort themselves out overnight. I wish I could be there with you, love, but, what with Dad's kidney problems…'

'I know, Mum.'

'Have you told Mike about all this?'

‘I’ve tried talking to him, but we just end up arguing. I miss him, Mum. He says he’s sorry and wants us to get back together, but he’s still living with that woman. It makes me so bloody angry.’

‘I know, love. But don’t give up on him just yet, eh. You two were together for a long time.’

There was a moment’s silence as Molly wiped away her tears. ‘There’s something I haven’t told you, Mum. I saw them together.’

‘Really? When was that, love?’

‘Before he left. She’d sent him naked photos. I found them hidden in his sock drawer. Let’s just say they didn’t leave anything to the imagination. There was no escaping reality after that. He let me down, Mum. He let the kids down. I really trusted him. I hate him sometimes.’

‘I know, love.’

‘I didn’t tell him what I’d seen at first. I tried to live with it for the sake of the kids. But it gnawed away at me. I sat outside the bank one lunchtime and waited until they eventually came out together. Oh, Mum, she is so very young: figure hugging clothes, immaculate hair and make-up, long legs, high heels and a ridiculously short skirt. And, so pretty. It made me feel totally redundant.’

‘That must have been awful, love. But, you’re far from useless.’

‘They walked straight past my car, and turned into Merlin Lane. I followed them a couple of minutes later and found them in the Scala. You know it, Mum, that nice Greek restaurant we used to visit on special occasions.’

‘I remember, love.’

‘He was sitting opposite her on a table for two with his back to me.’ Molly laughed despite herself. ‘I was lucky if he bought me a bag of chips. I just stood and watched them at first, without saying a word. But then Mike leant across the table and kissed her.’ She paused, contemplating the past. ‘The pig complained bitterly if I tried to hold his hand in public.’

‘How did he react, love?’

'Some garbage along the lines of, it wasn't what it looked like. I threw a glass of red wine in his face and told him to move out. He told me a few days later that he moved in with her that evening. The worst thing was telling Anthony.'

'Why haven't you told me all this before, love?'

'Things become more real somehow, when you talk about them.'

'Yes, I know what you mean.'

Should she tell her? Yes, why not? There was nothing to lose. 'You'll be pleased to hear that there may be some light at the end of the tunnel, Mum.'

'Well, thank goodness for that, love. Tell me more.'

'Tony's teacher rang me. She said he'd regressed.'

'I can't say it sounds too positive so far, love.'

Molly smiled, but the expression quickly left her face. 'I talked to Dr Procter, Mum. You must remember her?'

'Of course, she was my GP for years.'

'I thought she may prescribe Tony something to cheer him up a bit. But no, she's referred him to the child guidance clinic. She said it's got a good reputation. I thought you may disapprove?'

'Not at all, love, any idea how long the waiting list is?'

'Not really, Mum, but you know what the NHS is like. It'll probably be months.'

'Well, at least you're on the list, love. It's good news. But you need to let Mike know what's happening. Ring him, try to stay calm, tell him about the appointment, and tell him you still care about him. Because you do, don't you, love?'

Molly smiled thinly. 'I suppose you're right, Mum. Thanks for the chat. Give my love to Dad. I love you, Mum.'

'I love you too, Molly. Kiss the children for me. Now, it's late. Try to get some sleep.'

Chapter 3

Cynthia Galbraith rose at 5:30 a.m. on Friday 10, January, as she invariably did on days when her husband was working. She showered, dressed in an immaculate white silk dress, carefully styled her caramel-blonde hair and skilfully applied her make-up, taking care to look her best. She suspected that her husband would treat her efforts with utter indifference; nonetheless, she reminded herself, she had to keep trying.

After one last anxious peek in the dressing table mirror, Cynthia hurried downstairs, ensuring not to make even the slightest noise that may prematurely disturb her husband's slumber… He wouldn't be ready to get up until seven o'clock, and she'd need every available second to prepare for his eventual appearance.

Cynthia rushed into the kitchen and began preparing breakfast in line with Dr Galbraith's particular requirements… Every detail mattered.

She placed a choice of two high-fibre cereals on the large stripped oak table, lining up the boxes so that each was exactly parallel with the other. She added an exquisite French Chantilly porcelain plate, a matching cup, saucer and bowl, a solid silver spoon, a jug of full-cream milk, a bowl of dark muscovado sugar, and a silver gilt toast rack, that she would fill with his preferred white toast at the correct time. Next, she poured chilled freshly squeezed orange juice into a nineteenth-century crystal wine glass, placing it precisely one-inch from the right side of the plate. Cynthia used a stainless steel twelve-inch ruler to ensure she got the distance exactly right, and checked the measurements time and time again… He'd be disappointed if she got it wrong. That could mean punishment, and the ruler had a sharp edge.

Cynthia entered the hall and tensed inexorably as she heard the shrill tone of the doctor's alarm clock permeating the air… He was getting up. It wouldn't be long until he came downstairs. She had to get a move on.

She raced back into the kitchen and switched on the toaster, double-checking that it was set to her husband's precise required setting… Too light, or too dark, and at best, he would refuse to eat it.

She checked again to ensure that everything was on the table and in its correct position… It had to be perfect. Nothing less was acceptable. A white linen napkin! How could she be so stupid?

She hurriedly took one from a dresser drawer and held it up in the light of the kitchen window, confirming it was clean and totally crease-free. She took a deep breath, sucking the oxygen deep into her lungs… Thank God, immaculate. Surely it was good enough?

Cynthia switched on the percolator and added her husband's favourite fine ground Columbian coffee. Finally, she took two free-range eggs, three rashers of unsmoked Danish bacon, organic plum tomatoes and button mushrooms from the larder fridge located next to the range cooker, and laid them on the shiny black granite worktop.

She moved to the centre of the room and turned slowly in a circle, surveying the entire kitchen with keen eyes… There had to be something she hadn't done correctly. There was always something.

Cynthia checked the clock for the umpteenth time that morning… Time was running out at an alarming rate. She had to start cooking.

Dr Galbraith awoke in unusually good spirits for a man who didn't particularly like mornings. He threw back his duck-down quilt, leapt out of bed with an easy athleticism that belied his age, and paused for a moment on the landing en route to the bathroom to appreciate the glorious enticing aroma of high quality bacon and coffee wafting up the sweeping stair case… Was it worth heading down for breakfast? Cynthia was, he had to acknowledge, an excellent cook, although of course it would never do to tell her that. He was hungry, that was certainly true, but did he really want to see the obnoxious bitch with all that entailed? Did he need the distraction? He had options, naturally. He could order her out of the kitchen, and eat alone and in silence. That was worth considering. But she'd gone to a great deal of effort to prepare everything in line with his instructions. The bitch always did.

It would be amusing to ignore her efforts and grab a sandwich on the way to work.

The doctor grinned at the thought, but rejected the idea almost immediately… What the hell was he thinking? He needed adequate sustenance to sustain him on such an important day.

Dr Galbraith dropped to the bathroom floor and began doing press-ups: one, two, three, four… The bitch's psychological disintegration had been a glorious triumph.

He grinned, and rubbed the sweat from his eyes with the back of one hand: fifteen, sixteen, seventeen… Where oh where had the happy young law student gone? It had taken a little longer than anticipated to break her spirit completely, but he shouldn't be too hard on himself. Her abusive childhood had been to his advantage, but there were numerous obstacles that he had perhaps underestimated. By the time of their meeting she'd moved on to achieve an active social life, a wide circle of friends, and hobbies and interests. It posed a formidable challenge. And Cynthia possessed spirit. She'd left more than once in the early years of their relationship, before being persuaded back with unkept promises. Such things were never easy, particularly where a more intelligent subject was concerned. But, difficulties or not, his methods had worked. That's what mattered. That was something to be proud of.

He glanced sideways, admiring his reflection in the mirrored wall tiles: eighty-four, eighty-five, eighty-six… The constant criticism, the never-ending fault-finding, the denial of pleasures, and the occasional physical punishments had proven an extremely effective strategy.

Ninety-eight, ninety-nine, one hundred! He sat bolt upright on the bathroom floor… How would he summarise the demise of her self-worth and its consequences in his thesis? He had to use the right words, the correct phrases, if his peers were to fully appreciate his observations.

The doctor rested his stubbled chin on the palm of one hand, and visualised the words appearing on the page. But then it hit him in the gut like a physical blow… It was important work, certainly, but could he really spare the time at such a crucial juncture? Shouldn't he be focusing his attention entirely on Anthony Mailer? Of course he should. Of course he should! The thesis could wait. The bitch wasn't going anywhere.

Dr Galbraith showered, luxuriating in the sensual pleasure of the hot water warming his skin… Come on, man, focus, focus. Time was getting on.

He stepped out of the cubicle and dried quickly with a large, fluffy, pink bath towel, before throwing it to the floor next to the bidet… Right, come on, man. Time to shave.

He stood at the sink, stared at his reflected image in the illuminated magnifying mirror, and used a Victorian mother-of-pearl cut-throat razor to precisely shape the slightly greying sideburns that framed his well-proportioned face. Next, he used a silver-mounted mock turtleshell comb to coax his fashionably styled short hair into place, and to create a perfect side parting with copious amounts of shiny white Brylcreem hair wax. He stood there, staring into the shaving mirror for almost three minutes and admired his reflection… Come on, man, get on with it, get on with it. He'd wasted enough time already.

The doctor returned to his opulent bedroom to get dressed. He put on dark blue boxer shorts, black knee-length socks, and chose a white Italian cotton shirt from a choice of six perfectly ironed by Cynthia the previous evening. The shirt was followed by a dark grey single-breasted suit comprising a forty-four-inch chest jacket, and trousers tailored to fit his trim thirty-three-inch waist. There were large holes cut in both trouser pockets, big enough for a hand to fit through. The suit was one of several high-end Savile Row business suits hanging in his spacious fitted wardrobes… Off the peg items just didn't meet his required standards.

Next came highly polished black leather-soled slip-on shoes festooned with bright silver buckles, and a pair of solid 18 CT gold cufflinks in the form of handcuffs, that never failed to amuse him. The final touch was a silk tie with a brightly coloured cartoon logo on the front. He adjusted the Windsor knot repeatedly until it was perfect… The tie was a stroke of absolute genius. He was a genius. What other explanation was there?

He made one final superfluous adjustment to the knot… Anything that helped engage the little bastards and gain their trust, however seemingly insignificant, was an undoubted bonus.

Dr Galbraith descended the stairs and approached the kitchen, where Cynthia was standing at the AGA putting the finishing flourishes to his meal. She turned, met his accusing gaze, and forced a brittle smile as he entered the room.

'Good morning, dear!'

'Is it? Are you sure, Cynthia? Are you really sure?'

'Sorry, dear!'

He took a pristine white cotton glove from a drawer next to the Belfast sink, and strolled casually around the kitchen, running a forefinger across various surfaces… Spotless. She was learning. The bitch was learning.

'Is everything all right, dear?'

'Why the hell isn't my breakfast ready?'

'Take a seat, dear. I'll pour your coffee and serve your full English in a second.'

'Why do you assume I want coffee?'

'You always have coffee, dear.'

'Do I?'

'Well, I thought…?'

'You thought? Is that really such a good idea?'

Cynthia opened her mouth as if to speak, but then closed it again, unable to find the words.

Dr Galbraith glared at her with a sardonic expression that withered her fragile soul. 'Just serve my bacon and eggs, girl. Perhaps you can get that right.'

She took a step backwards on unsteady legs, and looked down as the yellow urine pooled on the tiles around her feet.

Chapter 4

Dr Galbraith unlocked the doors of his metallic black Daimler sedan, and jumped into the driver's seat with a self-satisfied expression on his angular face. He took a moment or two to appreciate the car's lavish interior and smiled broadly before starting the engine… He'd earned it. It was nothing less than he deserved: a warm, sumptuous haven of supple grey leather and polished walnut. A man of his accomplishments and elevated status deserved such luxuries.

The doctor turned the ignition key and the 4.5-litre V12 engine roared into life… It was a good sound, a reassuring sound that pleased him.

As he drove the eighteen miles from his home to the South Wales Department of Child, Adolescent and Family Psychiatry where he was employed as a consultant child psychiatrist, he happily anticipated arranging Anthony's initial appointment… Anticipation was a part of the pleasure. Not as pleasurable as it had once been, possibly, but still agreeable. The waiting had become more difficult; he had to acknowledge that. But things shouldn't be rushed this time, whatever the temptation. He'd made that mistake once before.

He shook his head aggressively and tapped two fingers repeatedly on the steering wheel… Maybe he wouldn't be so lucky the next time.

The doctor's head was instantaneously filled with violent vibrating sound that made him wince. He closed his eyes for a fleeting moment, trying to ignore the pain, and then quickly reopened them, suddenly aware of the morning traffic… Come on, man. Get a grip.

He punched the windscreen hard with a clenched fist and felt slightly better… Focus, man, focus, stick to the plan. Stick to the fucking plan. He'd get his hands on the little bastard. He just had to be patient.

Dr Galbraith exhaled slowly with an audible hiss… If he wasn't going to blow this he had to act on his experience, remember what he'd learnt over the years, and put those skills to good use. He'd come a long way since his first impulsive hurried offences and the inevitable anxiety that followed. Every knock on his door, every passing car, every phone that rang, had left him close to panic in those early days, all those years ago. The fear of arrest had been all-consuming at times. He'd fought against his base impulses, and actually considered stopping for a time. What was he thinking? What the hell was that about?

He flinched, and vigorously massaged his throbbing scalp with one hand whilst manoeuvring with the other... And why did he bother pondering the evolution of his inclinations? All that research and nothing significant to show for it. All those books. What a waste of time and money! As a child psychiatrist he theoretically understood the often insurmountable harm that men of his ilk inflicted on their victims. Of course he did. But what did it matter? He no longer felt any concern for their suffering. That was the crux of it. If he'd become an immoral creature, devoid of conscience empathy and virtue, so fucking what? He enjoyed his pastime, and the subject was worthy of scientific study. That's what counted. There was no room for sentimental angst. What more did he need to know? All that mattered was silencing the victims, effectively concealing any evidence, and not getting caught.

The doctor squealed like an over-enthusiastic cheer leader as the discordant din in his head gradually subsided... And, hadn't he done his job well? He'd avoided detection for almost thirty years, and nothing needed to change. Not if he reverted to his tried and tested modus operandi and slavishly stuck to it. Not a fucking thing!

Dr Galbraith parked in the clinic's quiet car park next to his secretary's aged red Mini Clubman and turned off the Daimler's powerful engine... Right. The moronic bitch had arrived early.

His entire body tensed and twitched... Fucking typical. The bitch had an irritating habit of doing that. What was it with the woman?

He stilled himself, met his steel-blue eyes in the rear-view mirror, and addressed himself in the style of an alpha male sports coach or military drill instructor, 'Game face. Mask on. Come on, man, mask on.'

Dr Galbraith tried desperately to ignore the resurgent pressure and deafening din inside his skull as he locked the doors, and strolled across the car park as casually as possible in case she was watching.

He stopped at the entrance briefly before entering the clinic, and drew repeated urgent gulps of cold Welsh morning air deep into his lungs… His anger was building. It wouldn't be easy, but he had to control it. The vile bitch would be there: sitting at her desk, flabby and sweating, stinking of stale body odour, doused in cheap pound shop perfume, and spouting some mindless crap as soon as he opened the door. How the hell was he going to cope with it this time? It would be therapeutic to ram her repugnant yellow teeth down her damn throat.

He smiled sardonically… How good would that feel? One day he'd make the bitch suffer. But, like it or not, now was not that time.

He grimaced as a sudden stabbing pain jolted his brain on entering the small reception, which also served as his young secretary's office… He'd been successfully conning people for years. Why the hell should that change now?

'Good morning, Doctor!'

'And a good morning to you, Sharon!' He paused, cocked his head to one side at an approximate forty-five-degree angle and studied her for a second or two. 'Have you done something different with your hair, my dear girl?'

She looked down at her desktop, avoiding his gaze. 'Oh, nothing special, Doctor, I just washed it before work and put a few curlers in.'

'Well, whatever you did, my dear girl, you look marvellous.'

She smiled warmly and self-consciously adjusted her fringe with chubby fingers.

Dr Galbraith looked her up and down… The moronic bitch was as malleable as warm putty. 'Now then, Sharon, first things first, there's no clinic this morning as I recall; no patients for us to worry about. Why not make us both some coffee?'

She nodded. 'One heaped spoonful of Nescafé, a splash of semi-skimmed, and one sugar?'

'Exactly right as always, my dear. I'll be in my office.'

She called after him as he walked away. 'How about a biscuit?'

He snorted disdainfully… The greedy bitch was looking for any excuse to fill her repugnant face again. Maybe a trough would be a suitable birthday gift. 'Not for me thank you, my dear. I enjoyed an excellent breakfast. But why don't you have one?'

Sharon switched on the kettle and frowned: sullen, dejected... Had he forgotten her birthday? It wasn't like him.

She spooned coffee granules into two mugs, added milk and finally sugar: one level spoonful for the doctor as per usual, and three heaped for herself, whilst waiting for the water to come to the boil.

Dr Galbraith entered his seemingly unremarkable magnolia office, adjusted his recently acquired black leather swivel chair, and sat at the modern veneered desk he'd located directly against the rear wall, avoiding any barrier between himself and prospective victims. He moved a flowering Christmas cactus aside, and picked up the silver-framed black-and-white photo of his wife and two young daughters. He held it out in front of him in both hands, stared at it for several seconds and smiled contentedly... He must ensure he referred to the portrait when first meeting the little bastard and his needful family.

Dr Galbraith placed the photograph back on his desk and slowly scanned the room with eager eyes... Was everything in its place? Was everything as it should be? The poster covering the glass panel in his office door could do with some additional Sellotape. That was a job for Sharon. Surely the incompetent bitch could manage that much.

He shook his head vigorously... It beggared belief. Why the hell were all the women in his life such a burden?

Dr Galbraith manoeuvred himself to the centre of the room in his chair and examined the room's only window... That pleb at the garden centre had been surprisingly knowledgeable despite his youth and obvious limitations. The elaeagnus bush had grown significantly faster than he could have hoped, and the thorns formed an excellent barrier. He really couldn't have made a better choice.

The doctor rose from his seat, pushed the chair back in the direction of his desk with a flick of his right foot, approached the window, adjusted the blinds and peered out... He still had a reasonable view of the car park without the fear of potentially interfering external onlookers. He'd need to strategically trim the bush at some stage, but that could almost certainly wait until spring.

He turned away from the window, surveyed the room for one final time, and smiled… It was an undoubted triumph. One more thing to be proud of.

Dr Galbraith opened Anthony Mailer's file and read slowly, taking his time, and carefully considering each word… The little bastard had blamed himself for his parents' break up and had developed various behavioural problems as a result. His mother had accepted the family doctor's offer of specialist help.

He sat back in his chair and stretched his arms high above his head before lowering them slowly and deliberately… It wasn't a complex scenario. Far from it, in fact; if he were of a mind to help, he could. Of course he could. If the little bastard had been a girl, he would have provided an excellent therapeutic service. If he was a little older he would have done likewise. That was entirely reasonable, wasn't it? Of course it was. What the hell did it matter if he used a few boys for his own purposes?

The resurgent pressure began to build again… Why the hell was he forced to keep his true nature secret from the world at large? He helped the vast majority of children he saw. That was to his credit. People should be grateful for that.

The doctor's thoughts were suddenly interrupted by his young secretary tapping on the door with the point of her scarlet court shoe, and entering his office with his mug of coffee in one hand and the clinic's appointments diary in the other.

'Come in, my dear girl. Come in, and make yourself comfortable. I neglected to wish you a happy birthday earlier, and so I will do it now. Is it eighteen or nineteen this year?'

She giggled bashfully. 'Oh, you know I'm older than that.'

He grinned… The repulsive bitch looked nearer to forty than twenty. 'Well, you don't look it, my dear. Now then, to business; when's the next free appointment?'

Sharon sat at his side, opened the diary, flicked through the pages, stopped, continued, and then stopped again. 'Not until the twenty-seventh, I'm afraid, Doctor.'

He stared at the floor fleetingly, and then slowly raised his eyes, fixing her with an intense look that she struggled to decipher. 'There's nothing sooner?'

Was there a degree of anxiety in his voice?

She urgently reopened the book and frowned. 'I'll take another look, Doctor, but you really mustn't overdo it. You've been looking tired recently, and you've been getting those terrible headaches of yours. Didn't you say you were planning a holiday?'

Keep control, man, keep control, indulge the interfering bitch. 'That is not your concern, young lady. The children have to come first. You know that. If I don't help them, who's going to do it?' He tapped the desktop repeatedly with his right index finger. 'Now, come on, diary.'

Sharon sighed… He was such a caring man. If only there were more like him.

'There is one cancellation on Friday the seventeenth, Doctor. That's half past ten a week today, but I'm sure you mentioned a dental appointment.'

Dr Galbraith visibly relaxed… A week was too long. But it seemed there was no viable alternative. 'No, no, Sharon, that will have to do. It will have to do. Please ensure the appointment letter is sent out first class this morning. This particular child is in crisis. The Mailers need my urgent help.' He stood, pointed towards the door, and smiled engagingly. 'Do you hear me, girl? Get it done please.'

She left the office promptly, her body quivering like a pink blancmange with each step… If the doctor could be so very dedicated, then so could she.

Dr Galbraith opened Anthony's file for the second time that morning, and reread the general practitioner's letter repeatedly before pushing it aside a few minutes later… How could the stupid bitch take so long to type a few miserable lines of script?

He cleared his throat and shouted, 'Is the Mailer letter ready, Sharon?'

'It's nearly done, Doctor. Do you want the entire family to attend?'

Oh for fuck's sake, it was the little bastard's first appointment. Why the hell did she always need to ask? 'Yes, please, Sharon, a standard initial appointment letter: the mother, the father and the two children.'

'I'll have it done in five minutes, Doctor.'

He rubbed a hand over his chin… A damn chimp could type faster. 'Thank you, my dear.'

She shook her head as she started typing… What was the hurry this time? Sometimes, he was too dedicated for his own good.

Dr Galbraith sighed loudly and screwed up his face. 'Where the hell is it, Sharon?'

'I'm typing as fast as I can, Doctor.'

Focus, man, focus. Too harsh, far too harsh, placate the bitch.

He actively calmed himself before entering her office. 'I apologise if I appear somewhat irate this morning, my dear. But it really couldn't be more urgent.'

Sharon finished typing a second or two later, her fleshy bust heaving with the effort of it all. 'That's it, done!'

'Thank you, my dear. I'll check the contents in my office.'

Dr Galbraith sat at his desk and held the letter out in front of him, accommodating his long-sightedness, rather than making use of his reading glasses. He began reading but struggled to concentrate despite the contents' usual captivation… He was doing the right thing, wasn't he? It was a fair question in the circumstances. He usually made a point of avoiding children who enjoyed close family ties. Why the hell was this time any different?

He clawed at his scalp and desperately tried to ignore the invasive crashing symbols in his mind… Was it really a wise move? The risks were high. What if the little bastard said something to the wrong person? What if that someone actually listened to him and acted on his allegations? It just didn't bear thinking about.

He blinked and twitched and sweated and paced the floor, as the escalating racket threatened to overwhelm him completely… He'd made exceptions in the past. Of course he had. When it had suited him. He'd taken risks, but they were considered risks. That was the essential caveat. A man of his intelligence and expertise could handle such complications. Of course he could. And the little bastard was well worth the additional effort.

Dr Galbraith felt suddenly calmer… All he had to do was think things through and stick to a plan. Manipulating the little bastard would be easy enough. He was good at it, and had to remember that. It was just a matter of how. The father was an obvious vulnerability. And if that failed, which seemed highly unlikely, there were other viable options. Of course there were. He'd undertaken the task on numerous occasions without any significant issues arising. How many boys was it at the last count? Was it ninety-seven, or ninety-eight? Either way it was something to be proud of. What the hell was he worrying about? His methods had worked before and they would again.

He returned to his seat just as Sharon knocked on the door and entered without waiting to be asked. 'Would you like me to post the Mailer letter at lunchtime, Doctor?'

Dr Galbraith beamed. 'That will not be necessary, Sharon. You've done an excellent job. Thank you, my dear girl.'

She blushed crimson. 'Are you sure, Doctor? You did say earlier…'

'I'm grateful, my dear. Extremely grateful, but I'm about to leave for a meeting. I'll post this one myself on the way.'

She smiled contentedly as he took a faux crocodile-leather wallet from the inside pocket of his suit jacket, opened it theatrically, and handed her a crisp ten-pound note. 'Happy birthday, my dear girl, please treat yourself to something nice for lunch. And don't rush back. You deserve it.'

She gushed, and decided to ignore the fact that there was nothing marked in his diary… He really was a wonderful boss, and unbelievably generous. His wife really was a lucky woman. 'Will I see you after the meeting, Doctor?'

She was hoping the answer was yes, but she didn't receive a response. Dr Galbraith waved exuberantly as he rushed from the clinic and headed towards his car. His mind was focused on other things.

Chapter 5

WPC Jane Pritchard glanced knowingly at Alan Garret, her child protection social work colleague, and refocused on the nervous, nine-year-old, somewhat overweight boy they'd been interviewing at one of the county's two social services video interview facilities for almost an hour.

After a moment's silence she leant towards the boy, and took the lead in line with her joint investigation training. 'Just so we're clear, Dewi. You're saying you were assaulted by a male doctor as well as your father?'

The boy stared at the floor and remained silent for a second or two before nodding reticently and saying, 'Yes' in a faltering voice.

'How many times did it happen?'

'Just the t-time I told you about.'

Alan Garret nodded. 'You're doing really well, Dewi. None of this was your fault. It's important to remember that.'

WPC Pritchard lifted a hand to her face, brushed her auburn hair away from her eyes and smiled. 'That's right, Dewi. I know this isn't easy, but it is important. Do you need a tissue before we carry on?'

She reached out holding a paper hankie taken from her handbag, but withdrew her hand when he didn't accept it. 'No?'

The boy wiped away his tears with the sleeve of his grey jumper and shook his head.

'Okay, then we'll continue. When did it happen?'

'Last s-summer, before I was taken into care.'

'Do you know which month it was?'

He shook his head… How was he supposed to know that?

'Was it at the start of the school holidays, in the middle, or at the end?'

'At the start, I think.'

'But you can't be sure?'

'No.'

'Where did it happen?'

'In a white room.'

'A white room? Can you tell us more about the room? Any details at all would be helpful.'

'It was covered in white tiles, like a bathroom.'

The officer frowned, oblivious to her expression. 'Anything else?'

'There weren't any windows.'

'What, none at all?'

'No.'

'Do you mean they were boarded up, or something?'

'No, there just weren't any.'

'Had you ever seen the room before?'

'No.'

'Were you ever taken there again?'

'No.'

'This is an important question, Dewi. Please think carefully before you answer. Do you know where the room is?'

'No.'

'Can you describe the building it was in?'

'No, I didn't see it.'

She paused momentarily, searching for an appropriate question… This was not going well. He looked ready to bolt for the door. 'Well, if you didn't see the building, how did you get to the room?'

'My father took me there.'

'And you didn't see the building?'

The boy dabbed at his face with a damp woollen sleeve… She didn't believe him. Why didn't she believe him? 'Dad blindfolded me as soon as we were in the car.'

The officer visibly relaxed and the tension left her face… Maybe she should be more trusting. 'Ah, now I understand. Where did you start the journey?'

The boy blinked repeatedly… Perhaps she did believe him after all. 'Dad woke me up in bed at home and took me to his car.'

'Do you know what time it was?'

She must believe him, or why ask the time? 'No.'

'Was it light or dark?'

'Dark.'

'Can you remember how long the journey took?'

He lifted a hand to his face, covering his eyes. 'Not really, I just remember being scared.'

'Was it a short journey, or a long journey?'

'A long journey.'

'More than an hour, or less than an hour?'

Why did she keep asking? Please let her stop. 'Less, I think.'

Dewi's entire body tensed involuntarily, and the officer decided not to pursue the matter further. 'That's really helpful, Dewi, but I need to ask you some more questions about the man.'

'I've already told you what he did!'

He was close to panic. Why wouldn't he be? How would she feel in the same circumstances? 'We don't need to talk about that again, Dewi. But, I need you to tell us anything that can help us find out who the man is, so that we can arrest him.'

Dewi relaxed slightly and sounded slightly more confident when he said, 'Okay.'

'Why do you think he's a doctor?'

'My father said he was.'

The WPC paused… Was it too much to ask for? 'Did your father ever say the man's name?'

'Yes.'

She attempted to mask her excitement. 'What was it, Dewi? Can you remember?'

'The doctor made me take some medicine when we got there. I felt sleepy.'

'Try to think, Dewi. Take your time, please.'

She wanted an answer. All he could do was try his best. 'I think it may have been Dr Griffiths.'

'Are you a little bit sure, or very sure?'

He looked disappointed, almost despondent. 'I can't remember what happened very clearly. But I'm sure his name started with a G.'

'Definitely a G?'

'I think so.'

She hid her disappointment as best she could. 'Do you know what kind of doctor he was, Dewi?' She regretted the question as soon as she asked it, and wasn't surprised when the boy replied, 'No,' with a bewildered expression on his face.

'All right, Dewi. Not many more questions left. What did the man look like? Let's start with his hair. What hair colour did the doctor have?'

The boy's eyes narrowed to virtual slits. 'Dark'

'Black or brown, is that what you mean?'

'Yes, but I'm not sure which, sorry.'

'That's all right, Dewi. We just want you to tell us what you remember, nothing more. How long was his hair?'

That was one he could answer. 'Short, like mine.'

She smiled. 'That's helpful, Dewi; how tall was he?'

'Taller than my father.'

The pencil-thin middle-aged social worker rose to his feet. 'I'm six-foot-two inches tall, Dewi. Was the man shorter or taller than me, or about the same height?'

'About the same height, but he looked a lot stronger.'

Alan Garret sat back down, and the WPC grinned momentarily despite, or perhaps due to the obvious tension. 'Why do you think he looked stronger than Alan?'

'He was bigger, like a wrestler on the telly.'

'Big fat, or big muscular?'

The boy raised his arms, as if momentarily flexing his biceps. 'Big muscular.'

'That's really helpful, Dewi. Is there anything else you can tell us about the man? Anything at all?'

'Not really.'

'What about his eyes? Do you remember the colour of his eyes?'

‘Blue.’

‘You’re sure?’

Why ask again? He’d answered the question once. ‘I think they were blue.’

‘But you’re not sure?’

The boy shook his head.

‘No?’

His breathing became more laboured. ‘Not really.’

She silently admonished herself… Too much pressure; she was pushing too hard. ‘If you’re not sure of the answer, Dewi, it’s fine to say so. Just say, I don’t know. Don’t try to guess.’

‘Okay.’

‘Did you ever tell anyone else about the man before telling your foster mum last night?’

‘No, never.’

‘Not even your mother?’

His eyes filled with tears and his chubby face reddened. ‘She knew all about what my father did to me, and she didn’t help. She didn’t stop him. Why would I tell her?’

She checked her watch, and looked towards the social worker who nodded his silent agreement… The boy had had enough. It was time to bring matters to a close. ‘All right, Dewi, I understand. We’re almost finished, but there is one more thing I need to ask you. Is that okay?’

Oh, God, not more questions. ‘I suppose so.’

The WPC smiled softly and nodded. ‘Dewi, I have to ask you why you didn’t tell us about this man the last time, when you told us what your father did to you.’

‘I was too scared.’

‘Are you saying you were more scared of the man, than of your father?’

He stared at the floor and said, ‘Yes.’

Jane Pritchard frowned. ‘Why? After everything your father did to you.’

‘My f-father said the doctor would kill me if I ever said anything.’

It was too late to stop now. She had to ask. 'And you believed him?'

Dewi took a blue Ventolin asthma pump from a trouser pocket and inhaled two urgent puffs of the drug into his lungs before saying, 'Yes.'

What could she say to that? What the hell was wrong with these people? 'Sometimes adults say things to frighten children, to stop them getting the help they need. You're safe now, Dewi. You do understand that, don't you?'

People kept saying he was safe. Perhaps it was true. 'Yes.'

He didn't look convinced. Why would he be? He'd been let down all his life. 'That's good to hear, Dewi. Is there anything else you want to say, or anything you want to ask either of us before we bring the interview to an end?'

Dewi rose from the beanbag and adjusted the tight waistband of his trousers. 'Can we get something to eat on the way back to my foster parents' house? They wouldn't mind.'

WPC Pritchard turned to the social worker… Why wouldn't he comfort-eat after what he'd been through? Maybe she'd do the same thing. 'Do you mind providing the transport, Alan? I need to label the tapes and start writing the transcript as soon as possible.'

Alan Garret stood, smiled broadly, and guided Dewi towards the door. 'Come on, young man. I'll give your foster parents a ring to see if they can meet us at McDonalds for a burger.'

As they walked towards the stairs, WPC Pritchard called after them. 'Alan, is it okay if I use your office to give my inspector a ring? I could do with some privacy.'

'No problem, Jane, I'll speak to you soon.'

Jane Pritchard completed the practical tasks required of her by the rules of evidence, and headed downstairs to the kitchen for a quick cuppa before making her call… It had already been a long stressful day, and a few minutes to herself was one small luxury she planned to make the most of.

She took a shortcake biscuit from a tin decorated with a stereotypical highland scene, and nibbled at it, savouring the rich buttery texture as the kettle slowly came to the boil. She sat at the small Formica table and tried to think about something other than child protection; *anything* other than child protection, but her naturally conscientious nature overrode her desire for some quality time. She swore silently under her breath, gobbled down the remainder of the biscuit, and pushed her mug to one side before heading to Alan Garret's untidy office, piled high with unread Social Work Today magazines on every conceivable surface.

She only had to wait for a few seconds before a control room officer, whose voice she didn't recognise answered the phone.

'Hello, this is WPC 458, can you put me through to DI Simpson's office please?'

'Will do, Jane. I think he's in.'

'DI Simpson.'

'Hello, sir. It's Jane Pritchard. I'm sorry to bother you.'

'No bother, Constable. What can I do for you?'

'I could do with some advice, sir.'

'Why aren't you talking to Grav, he's your local DI?'

'Inspector Gravel's on leave, sir. And I understand you have overall responsibility for child protection for the force area.'

Trevor Simpson laughed. 'Ah, yes, Grav said something about going to Bournemouth with his missus. Silver wedding celebrations.' He laughed again. 'I believe his mother-in-law went with them.' He checked his Rado watch. 'Right, Jane. How can I help you?'

'I've just undertaken a joint interview with a nine-year-old boy named Dewi Williams, sir.'

'Yeah, I know the case. Grav mentioned it. Any new developments?'

'Sir, the boy told us that sometime during the summer months he was blindfolded by his father and taken by car to an unknown venue, where he was assaulted by a man he believes to be a doctor. He's given a sketchy description of the abuser and of the location, but the details of the room sound dubious.'

‘You’ve done the right thing in contacting me, Jane. But, is the boy a reliable witness?’

‘I’ve got absolutely no reason to think that he’s making any of this up, sir. He’s been reliable in the past. He was taken somewhere, I’m sure of that, but from what he said I think it likely he was drugged.’

‘Right, Jane. Get the transcript of the interview completed, send it over to me this afternoon, and I’ll take a look at it. Talk to your DS and contact his counterparts in the other two child protection units. Ask them if there’s been any other mention of a doctor, or of children being taken to a venue that matches the boy’s description. Give the social services child protection team managers a ring, and ask the same questions. Let me know if you have any joy. I may well pay the father a visit at Swansea nick. Grav mentioned that he’s appealing the length of his sentence. That should provide me with some leverage. I’ll have a chat with Grav as soon as he’s back and get him up to speed if I think there’s anything in it.’

‘Thank you, sir. I’ll get it done.’

Chapter 6

Molly received three letters on Monday 13, January. She sat on the stairs, discarded the two brown envelopes, and urgently opened the white one… Could it be an appointment letter from the clinic? Here's hoping it was. But, surely not! After all, only a few days had passed since she'd spoken to Dr Procter.

Molly unfolded the letter, and held it out in front of her, taking advantage of the unseasonable winter sunshine streaming through the leaded glass panel in the front door… *The Department of Child, Adolescent and Family Psychiatry.* It was an appointment letter. How about that!

She crossed the middle and index fingers of her right hand and perused the contents… How long would the wait be? Several miserable weeks at best, probably months. But no, unbelievably, it was only four days away.

Molly smiled, rose from the step with a new energy she hadn't felt for some time, and danced in a small circle with the letter held high above her head in one hand… What a great service. The GP had said Dr Galbraith was good. It looked as if she was right.

She left the appointment letter propped up against a mock art deco silver-plated photo frame on the sideboard in the dining room for safe keeping, and ascended the stairs to wake her children. Anthony had slept through the night for the first time in several weeks, and was already wide awake. Molly examined his bed, trying not to be too obvious… It was dry. What a relief! Should she praise him? Should she draw his attention to it at all? Yes, it felt like the right thing to do.

Molly looked at Anthony, meeting his eyes, and smiled warmly. 'Well done, cariad. I'm proud of you. I'll call at the Spar to buy you some sweets for when you get back from school.'

Anthony dressed in the clothes laid out at the bottom of his bed by his mother earlier that morning. He pulled on his favourite pair of Wrangler blue jeans, a bright yellow cotton tee-shirt, and a warm green and white woollen jumper with a large red dragon motif on the front, before running towards the bathroom to empty his bladder. He almost made it, but not quite. When he shouted, 'Mum!' with obvious urgency, Molly rushed into the bathroom and saw the dark wet patch on the front of his trousers. She bit her lip determinedly rather than say something she knew she would later regret and forced a reluctant smile. 'Don't worry, cariad. It's not your fault. I should have told you to go to the toilet before getting dressed.'

Anthony nodded sheepishly, but didn't say anything… The brief triumph of the dry bed was well and truly over.

Molly's eyes moistened as she placed clean clothes on Anthony's bed for the second time that morning. She helped him out of his soiled trousers, pants and socks, wiped her tears from her face with a cotton sleeve, and struggled to regain her composure. 'Have a warm shower, cariad, it'll make you feel better. Get a move on though, Siân will want to use the bathroom once you've finished.'

Molly listened for the reassuring sound of the electric shower pump before approaching Siân's bedroom door. She raised her hand to knock, but before she had the opportunity to act on her intentions, she heard Siân shout, 'I'm already up, Mum. It's not easy sleeping what with the racket you and Tony make.'

Molly thought, same old Siân, but simply said, 'Sorry, love. I'll see you downstairs…' There was no point in inviting an argument.

After getting dressed, Anthony followed his mother downstairs for breakfast. He sat at the kitchen table, and chose to ignore his older sister as she entered the room a couple of minutes later. Siân was never particularly communicative in the mornings, and today was no different, as she sat in virtual silence eating a bowl of sugar-free cereal.

Anthony raised his eyes from his much-loved Sugar Puffs, and turned to Molly, who was buttering some wholemeal toast on a worktop next to the electric cooker. 'Is Dad coming tonight, Mum?'

Molly sighed… Here we go again. 'Not tonight, cariad, but you'll definitely see him on Friday. He's coming to the doctor's with us. I'll be ringing him to arrange it as soon as you two are at school.'

Anthony beamed, and began eating his cereal with renewed gusto.

Siân didn't say anything in response to the news, but she hurried from the kitchen, retreating to the isolation of her teenage bedroom to await the school bus… There were more important things in life than enforced family reunions.

Siân left the cottage first, and shouted an unenthusiastic, 'See you later,' before closing the front door, and running down the path towards her bus, which was about to leave without her.

Molly thought, one down, one to go, and encouraged Anthony to finish his second bowl of Sugar Puffs, whilst absently checking to ensure he had everything he needed for his school day… She wasn't looking forward to contacting Mike, but needs must.

Molly held her son's hand tightly in hers and encouraged him out through the front door towards the bus stop, conveniently located almost directly outside the cottage on the same side of the road. It was a bright winter morning, but despite the sunshine, a penetrating January chill caused them both to shiver uncontrollably as they stood, waiting together on the twinkling tarmacadam pavement. Almost immediately, a familiar diesel growl permeated the air, and the school bus appeared from around a bend in the road, half-full of rowdy, chatting, laughing primary age children.

Molly rubbed the top of Anthony's head and smiled. 'Right then, cariad. On you get. Your friends are already on the bus. I'll see you later. Try and have a good day.' She walked closely behind him, patted him on the back as he got on, and waved energetically until the vehicle eventually disappeared into the distance.

Molly hurried back into the cottage, grateful for the comparative warmth that met her at the front door. She paused momentarily in the hall, considering picking up the phone, but quickly decided on another comforting hot drink before making the call. She switched the kettle on, placed a herbal teabag and a large spoonful of local honey in a favoured mug, poured in the boiling water, and stirred vigorously, causing a small amount of the scalding liquid to spill onto the worktop. Molly swore loudly… Housework could wait.

She turned on Radio 2 and sat at the kitchen table, thinking the music and chatter may help her relax. But she quickly concluded that she was simply putting off the inevitable. She approached the sink, added a few drops of cooling tap water to her tea, and drained her mug, savouring the intense sweetness at the bottom… In her mother's wise words: it was time to bite the bullet.

Molly picked up the phone, dialled her husband's direct office number, and waited whilst tugging repeatedly at her mousey hair with her free hand… How should she begin the conversation? Perhaps an assertive approach was best. Or possibly not? Maybe persuasion rather than coercion was advisable. At the end of the day, whichever approach she adopted, Mike would be surprised she'd rung at all.

She was seriously considering placing the phone back on its receiver and ringing again later in the day to allow sufficient time for another cathartic discussion with her mother, when she heard her errant husband's infuriatingly chirpy phone voice at the other end of the line. 'Hello, Mike Mailer speaking.'

'Hello, Mike. It's Molly, we need to talk.'

'Molly, what is it? Is there something wrong? Has something happened to one of the kids?'

'Relax, Mike. It's nothing like that, no need to panic. But, we do need to talk about the children.'

'You had me worried for a minute, Mo. I'm a bit busy at the moment, to be honest. Can I give you a ring after work?'

'Oh, be fair, Mike, when was the last time I rang you at the bank? I'd really like you to make time to talk now. They're your children as well as mine. Or have you forgotten that small fact?'

Mike tightened his grip on the phone. 'Give me a second, Molly. I'll close the door.'

'You do that.'

'Hello, Mo. What's this about, love?'

'Love? I think that ship well and truly sailed when you moved in with that tart.'

'Now look, Molly. I really haven't got time for this shit now. If you've got something meaningful to say, please spit it out.'

Molly paused, swallowing her words… Try to stay calm, don't get personal, tell him you still care about him. Wasn't that what her mother had advised?

'Molly? Are you still there?'

'Hold on, Mike. Can we start again? I really don't want to argue. We've done enough of that for one lifetime. I'm not going to pretend I'm not still seriously pissed off with you, but the children need to come first for a change.'

'Fair enough, you're right. What's this all about, love?'

She chose to ignore the platitude this time… Where on earth should she start?

'Molly? I've got work to get on with. Are you going to tell me what this is about or what?'

'Yes, of course I am. That's why I rang. Things haven't been easy since you left. It's hit the kids hard. They miss you, Mike. Particularly Tony. Siân goes her own way. I hardly see her these days, to be honest. But, Anthony! It's like he's mourning a death.'

'What do you want from me?'

There was a moment's silence… Should she tell him? How would he react? Yes, why not? What was there to lose? 'I miss you, Mike. Despite everything you've done. I still love you, God help me.'

'Mo, I'm sorry. How many times do I have to say it? If I could turn the clock back I would. Honestly I would. But I can't, can I?'

'What do you take me for, Mike? You're still living with that fucking woman. End it, move out, and maybe we can talk about the future.'

'Thanks, Mo. That's good to hear.'

'Don't think it's going to be easy, Mike. If you're serious about this, I need action, not more empty words. I don't think you understand just how bad things are here. You're not here to see it, day in day out like I am. I need help, Mike. We need help as a family.'

'I hear what you're saying, Mo.'

Molly took a deep breath… It was now or never. 'I've spoken to Dr Procter about Anthony. I didn't know what else to do.'

'Really? Can she give him something?'

'Give him something? It's not nearly that easy, Mike. The doctor's arranged for us to see someone at the child guidance clinic. That means you, me, and the children. The appointment letter arrived this morning.'

Mike cursed silently under his breath. 'Are you sure the doctor wants to see us all, love?'

'Yes, Mike, I'm sure. Very sure! I couldn't be more sure. That's how it works. You need to pick us up at ten o'clock on Friday morning. That's this coming Friday! If you're serious about us getting back together at some point in the future, you will do this for me.'

Mike sighed… Washing his dirty laundry in front of a pseudo-scientific stranger was not his idea of fun. But at the end of the day, if there was a chance of reconciliation he couldn't afford to jeopardise the opportunity. 'Fair enough, love, I'll be there on time, guaranteed.'

'I don't want to be late, Mike. This is important.'

'I said I'd be there on time, Mo, and I will be. Now leave it there, please.'

Molly put the phone down and walked towards the lounge, deep in thought… She'd got her own way as expected, that was true. But for some reason it felt a rather hollow victory.

She sat on the brown faux leather settee facing the lounge window and the unkempt garden beyond, and wiped a tear from her cheek… Mike was a waste of space, but he should be *her* waste of space. She wanted him back, there was no denying it. But it wasn't going to be easy to trust him again. If he actually left the tart instead of just talking about it, that would be an excellent start.

She smiled fleetingly… Life could be better. It could be a lot better, but at least now Anthony was going to get the support he needed.

Chapter 7

Dr Galbraith sat at his desk, frantically turning the pages of his personal diary: Tuesday 14, January. The 14, January… Oh, for fuck's sake, another child protection case conference. Why the hell did the system dedicate so much time and effort to such a tedious task? What were the misguided fools thinking? That was one question he couldn't answer; but what he did know was that it was a tragic waste of his valuable time. Where the hell was that invitation letter?

He opened a desk drawer and foraged through the contents… Where the hell had he put it? Ah, yes, yes, his in-tray, it was still in his in-tray.

The doctor unfolded the notification letter and accompanying papers, and spread them out on his desktop in front of him. He took his reading glasses from an inside pocket of his dark grey pinstripe jacket, and perused the contents… Four-year-old twin sisters; alleged sexual abuse, no unequivocal medical evidence supporting the girls' video statements, an ineffectual mother targeted and befriended by a predatory paedophile employed as a secondary school music teacher prior to his arrest, the mother supporting the alleged abuser. No surprises there, he'd chosen well. It all seemed straight forward enough, nothing unusual. What was the alleged perpetrator's name? Gary Davies? Gary Davies? The name rang a bell for some reason.

He closed his eyes, searching his busy mind… Ah yes, Davies. He was a member of the ring. An inconsequential member, certainly, but still a member. That counted for something. He'd seen him at various gatherings over the years.

Dr Galbraith took a well-thumbed notebook from his brown leather briefcase, and referred back to the letter… Who was in the chair? Mel Nicholson: senior child protection social work manager?

He opened his notebook and referred to his hand written notes… Nicholson? Nicholson? Ah yes, he'd met the interfering busybody on a course a few years back. He was one of those idiotic egalitarian, save the world, black and white, good and evil merchants.

The doctor turned the page and continued reading… Nicholson had moved to Devon to work for the NSPCC a couple of years back. He'd obviously returned to Wales. Probably promoted. That was worthy of note.

And who else was attending? The usual miserable plebs, no doubt. More misguided simpletons dedicated to an utterly pointless endeavour.

He examined the list of attendees… Ah, yes, Detective Inspector Roy Thomas. Wasn't his bitch wife expecting the last time he'd spoken to him? R-S-T… Yes, there he was: Roy Thomas. He was correct, of course; no surprise there. The little brat should be about three months old by now.

Dr Galbraith checked the clock… He should have allowed himself more time. His organisation wasn't what it was. Time to make a move.

The doctor placed the notebook back in his briefcase and locked it, before putting the key in the inside pocket of his jacket for safe keeping. As he walked across his office towards reception his head was aching, the pressure was building, but he repeatedly reminded himself that he had to maintain the deception if his plan were to become reality… It was becoming harder; every day it was harder.

Dr Galbraith smiled humourlessly at his secretary. 'I'm attending a child protection case conference at the social services resource centre in Caerystwyth this morning, my dear girl. I will leave the clinic in your very capable hands. Dr Rosie Higgins will be here this afternoon to help me with the backlog. She's a good doctor, and I'm sure you'll like her. I will see you in the morning, my dear. Have a good day.'

The doctor parked the Daimler half on and half off the curb, and rushed towards the entrance to the resource centre to intercept Mel Nicholson, who was about to enter the building. 'Mel, is that really you, my dear boy? Marvellous to see you again. Devon, wasn't it? NSPCC, if I recall correctly?'

Nicholson shook the doctor's hand firmly. 'Good to see you, Doc. Plymouth, I was based in Plymouth.'

‘Good to have you back on board, old man. Their loss our gain, so to speak. Promotion?’

‘Yeah, I’m heading up child protection services for the local authority. It’s good to be back in Wales.’

‘Quite right. Quite right.’ He pushed up a jacket sleeve and checked his gold Cartier wristwatch. ‘Better make a move, old man. I didn’t have an opportunity to read the papers, pressure of work and all that. Any idea who’s in the chair?’

‘That’ll be me.’

‘It’s a terrible world, dear boy, a terrible world. But, I’m sure you’ll do a marvellous job.’

Dr Galbraith entered the conference room in the style of a film star navigating the red carpet: a wave here, a smile there. He approached DI Thomas and patted him robustly on the shoulder. ‘Congratulations, old boy! Boy or girl?’

The inspector beamed. ‘A boy: Gareth, after the rugby player, but please don’t tell the wife that.’

The doctor laughed exuberantly. ‘Our secret, old boy!’ He raised an open hand in the air. ‘Oh, I can see our chairman wants to make a start. I’d better take my seat before I’m reprimanded.’

Nicholson, as he was generally known, opened the meeting by introducing himself, and asking the attendees to do likewise. He explained that the purpose of the meeting was to decide if the children were at risk, and if they were, to agree a multi-agency child protection plan. Before requesting individual contributions he reminded Davies that he was still subject to police caution. Anything he said could be used in evidence.

At the mention of the police, Davies shuffled uneasily in his seat and glanced furtively in Dr Galbraith’s direction, repeatedly attempting to meet his eyes. The doctor looked away on every occasion… What the hell did the idiot think he was doing? Too obvious, far too obvious! He would help him, of course he would. That was expected of him as a fellow ring member. But now was not the time. There’d be ample opportunity when he met the moronic bitch mother, and provided therapy to her hideous daughters.

Nicholson facilitated the conference with an efficiency born of experience. Within the hour, the girls' names had been included on the 'at risk' register. It had been agreed that they would return to the care of their mother, on the condition that they had no further contact with Davies. A comprehensive risk assessment would be undertaken by child care social workers, and Dr Galbraith would provide appropriate therapy.

The doctor stifled a laugh… If the cretins thought the girls were adequately protected, they were kidding themselves.

Dr Galbraith approached Davies in the car park as he strode, head bowed, towards his estate car. He introduced himself flamboyantly, as if meeting Davies for the first time, shook hands, and handed him a business card with words of reassurance written on the back in blue ink. He gave Davies a knowing nod, and quickly turned away to approach the mother, who was standing a few yards behind them, trying to be as inconspicuous as possible. Dr Galbraith addressed her quietly, in contrived soft reassuring tones. 'Hello, my dear, try not to worry, these conferences don't always get it right. The reasons children say such things can be far more complex than the average person appreciates. They may have seen something inappropriate on television, or be recounting nightmares for example. And, to be honest, it's not unusual for well-meaning but misguided social workers to put ideas in children's heads. They sometimes ask leading questions, as do the police. It can be all too easy to jump to the wrong conclusions. That may well be the case with regard to your daughters. Bring the girls to see me at my home at half past four this afternoon. If errors have been made, as I suspect they have, I'll have you all back together before you know it. I've given Mr Davies my card with the address and contact details.'

The mother looked at the ground as she spoke, only raising her eyes for an instant before quickly refocusing on the tarmac. 'Thank you, Doctor. I just couldn't believe Gary had done the awful things they said he had. He's the best thing that's happened to me in a long, long time. I just want the girls home with us. We both do, don't we, Gary?'

Davies nodded his eager agreement.

Dr Galbraith took her hand in his, squeezed it gently, and then shook it. 'They will be, my dear lady. They will be. Now, I must get on. We will sort out this unfortunate misunderstanding before you know it.' He smiled warmly. 'I look forward to seeing you this afternoon.'

Chapter 8

WPC Jane Pritchard arrived early for her shift on Wednesday 15, January, and eventually tracked down DI Trevor Simpson in the police canteen, where he was engaged in mundane morale-sapping conversation with a junior colleague. She bought herself a cup of predictably unappetising tea, and slowly approached his table. ‘Hello, sir. Have you got five minutes? I’ve completed the enquiries you required.’

‘Take a seat, Jane. Do you know DS Halfpenny?’

‘Yes, sir, we were at the training college together.’

‘You all right, Jane?’

‘Yes, not bad, thanks, Joe.’

DI Simpson took a sip of his hot coffee and frowned. ‘If you head off and get on with the Wilson robbery, Joe, I’ll catch up with you later in the day.’

‘Will do, sir.’

‘What’s the news, Jane?’

‘I’ve spoken to everyone concerned, and it seems a white room has featured in at least three investigations over the years.’

‘You’ve got the details, I presume?’

‘Yeah, there was a young lad of six in August 1984. Similar story really: he alleged he was taken to a white room by an uncle.’

‘Any mention of a doctor?’

‘No, sir, and the case didn’t go anywhere. No forensic evidence, and the child’s account contained significant inconsistencies. A child psychiatrist put the allegations down to nightmares at the time, and that was the end of it. But given what we know now?’

‘You may well be right, Jane. Any idea who the psychiatrist was?’

‘No, sorry, sir, but I’m sure I can dig out the file and find out.’

‘Don’t worry about it; it’s not of any consequence. What’s next?’

‘There was a boy of five in June 1987, and a boy of four in May 89.’

'Different families?'

'Yeah.'

'All boys?'

'Yeah.'

'Anything that helps us?'

'Not really, sir, nothing that identifies the location. The men were suspected of sexual offences, and the kids' names were placed on the child protection register. But, same old story: insufficient evidence for prosecutions as far as the CPS were concerned.'

'I think we're going to have to revisit this lot, Jane. I don't believe in coincidences. Were all three children local?'

'Yeah, they all live within a five-mile radius of Caerystwyth.'

'I'm guessing the white room's probably in the same area. Sorry, Jane, I'm just thinking out loud. Anything you haven't told me?'

'The six-year-old mentioned being filmed.'

'Ah, that makes sense.'

'I thought so, sir.'

'Any mention of a doctor?'

'Afraid not.'

'I want you to write a full report and get it to me as soon as possible, Jane. There's got to be something in it.'

'I'll get it done today, sir.'

DI Simpson shook his head. 'What's wrong with these people?'

'I hope you don't mind me asking, sir, but you said you may speak to Dewi's father at some point?'

'You can leave it with me, Constable. Get that paperwork to me as quickly as possible.'

Chapter 9

Anthony didn't like Thursday mornings. Thursday mornings meant English, Welsh and mathematics: three lessons he didn't particularly enjoy. Miss Larkin somehow succeeded in making English and Welsh bearable, but he found geometry utterly excruciating. Anthony listened at first, trying to grasp the complex concepts, but he quickly concluded that his teacher may as well be speaking a foreign language he couldn't begin to understand. He glanced repeatedly at the clock above the door as the lessons progressed, and wondered why the hands were moving so slowly. When lunchtime eventually arrived, he felt as if a burdensome physical force had been lifted from his chest, and he smiled spontaneously for the first time since arriving at school that morning.

Anthony chose pork sausage, baked beans and chips for lunch: one of his favourite meals. And for the first time since his father's departure, he gulped it down, eager to escape to the schoolyard to play football with his friends. The game went well: he scored a goal, which was unusual for him, and his side won. Anthony walked back to the classroom when the bell rang, thinking that Thursdays weren't so bad after all.

Anthony found the afternoon's music and art lessons far more enjoyable than the morning's academic tedium. To his surprise, he'd recently begun enjoying both drawing and painting far more than previously. He wasn't sure why, but splashing paint around on paper somehow made him feel better. He painted a picture of his family: his mother, his father, his sister and himself, standing outside the cottage on a warm sun-drenched summer day. For some reason he couldn't comprehend, he painted his father much larger and in brighter colours than the rest of the family. Miss Larkin pointed it out, asking why the man in his painting was so big. Anthony replied, 'It's my dad,' but said no more than that.

Miss Larkin gave a sigh of relief when the much-anticipated bell that signalled the end of the school day, rang out loudly in every part of the modern open-plan building. She stood at the front of her class, surveying her domain with obvious pride, and said, 'Stand, put your paints away, pour the dirty water into the sink and wash the brushes before going home.' Once the children had completed their various tasks, she smiled, and added the same familiar instructions she issued every afternoon: 'Walk, don't run, and remember your homework.'

Anthony was particularly keen to show his mother his watercolour as soon as he arrived home, and double-checked that it was safely in his bag, before rushing out of the classroom as fast as it was possible to walk without actually running. Most of the children did likewise, and were outside talking excitedly with friends; but Anthony waited alone and in silence for the bus to arrive. When it eventually turned up about five minutes later, he boarded last and sat at the front, rather than join the rest of the boys at the back.

Molly was watching from the kitchen window when the bus appeared in the street amongst clouds of dirty soot-black diesel fumes. She opened the front door as it came to a gradual stop, and waved as Anthony disembarked with his bag clutched tightly in one hand, and the painting in the other.

Molly buttoned her brown woollen cardigan against the winter chill, and met Anthony at the path's half-way point. 'Come on, cariad. I've made you a nice big mug of hot chocolate.'

Anthony followed his mother into the kitchen, took off his coat, hung it on the back of a chair, placed his schoolbag in a corner, and held up his picture in full view.

'That looks like a nice painting, cariad. Can I have a look?'

Anthony smiled eagerly, and handed her his picture. Molly held it out in front of her and studied it… It portrayed the four of them, that was obvious, but why was Mike so very large? Did the fact Tony was missing his father explain it? Possibly. Maybe it was something else to ask the psychiatrist.

'Do you like it, Mum?'

'Get some sticky tape from the drawer, cariad.'

Molly smiled warmly as Anthony handed her the Sellotape. As she displayed the picture on the pantry door she was praising Anthony's artistic endeavours, but thinking about the impact her errant husband's infidelity had had on them all… Anthony needed more help than she could give him. The child guidance clinic was a welcome beacon of hope.

Siân arrived home about ten minutes later, and went straight to her bedroom without speaking to either her mother or brother. Molly gave her a short reprieve, and then called to her from the hall. 'Tea's almost ready, love. We're all going to eat at the table for a change. I need to have a chat with you both.'

Siân didn't reply, but she appeared in the kitchen just as Molly was placing three plates of spaghetti bolognese topped with generous helpings of grated cheddar cheese on the kitchen table. Molly smiled at her daughter and pulled out a chair before saying, 'Sit down, love. Is water okay?'

Siân nodded unenthusiastically.

'What about you, Tony, milk or squash?'

'Orange squash, please, Mum.'

Molly handed her children their drinks and joined them at the table. 'I wanted to remind you both that we're going to the clinic in the morning.'

Siân frowned in an exaggerated teenage manner. 'Do I really have to go, Mum? Anthony's the one with the problems, not me!'

'We've already talked about this, Siân. The doctor wants to see us all. Please, love!'

Siân chose not to reply, but Molly noted she hadn't said no.

Anthony grinned sheepishly as a length of pasta fell from his mouth and onto his jumper. 'Can I watch telly now, Mum?'

'Finish your food first, Anthony. Surely you can wait that long?'

He said nothing more, but gulped down the remainder of his meal at breakneck speed.

Molly shook her head and smiled thinly. 'Off you both go. I'll do the washing up tonight. But tomorrow I want some help.'

Molly put Anthony to bed a little earlier than usual and read to him for approximately twenty minutes before saying, 'I need to telephone Dad, cariad. You get off to sleep. It's a big day tomorrow.'

'Dad is definitely coming, isn't he, Mummy?'

'Yes, cariad, definitely!'

Anthony beamed. 'I scored a goal today, Mum. I'm going to tell Dad about it.'

'Did you, cariad? That's brilliant! Dad will be pleased. You'll be able to start going to rugby training again soon.'

Anthony's smile evaporated from his face.

'Now then, cariad, eyes closed and off to sleep with you. I'll leave the landing light on just for tonight. Goodnight, Tony.'

'Goodnight, Mum!'

Molly sat on the bottom step of the stairs and dialled Mike's number. She was very much hoping that Tina wouldn't answer when she heard Mike say, 'Hello?'

'Mike, it's Molly. I just wanted to make sure you hadn't forgotten about tomorrow morning.'

'Of course I haven't forgotten, Mo.'

'Please make sure you're not late, Mike. We need to be there before half past ten. It's the first appointment. I want to make a good impression.'

'I know that, love. I'll …'

'You promised to speak to Siân, Mike. The doctor wants to see us all. I've already explained that to you.'

'Slow down, love. I said I'd speak to her, and I will. Is she in?'

'She's out somewhere. Hopefully, she'll be back at some point. I'll ask her to ring you if and when she finally turns up. See you in the morning, Mike. Please don't be late.'

Molly put the phone down before he had the opportunity to respond, and shook her head regretfully… Be more patient, you daft woman. What had her mother told her? Conversation as opposed to monologue. It was sound advice. Mike was trying. Not hard enough, but he was trying.

Siân eventually arrived home when Molly was about to give up on her and head to bed for the night. Molly met her at the back door, and was relieved that she was sober and, wonder of wonders, communicative. She decided that in the circumstances it was best to ignore the time… There were bigger fish to fry.

'Hi, Mum,'

Molly forced a transient smile. 'Hi, love, Dad wanted you to ring him before bed.'

'Is it about tomorrow, Mum?'

Molly nodded. 'Yes, love, it is.'

'I'll go if you want me to. I do care about Tony. You do know that, don't you?'

'Of course I do, love.'

'Sorry about earlier, Mum.'

Molly smiled, this time spontaneously. 'Thanks, love. Come here and give your old mum a hug.'

For once Siân didn't pull away.

Chapter 10

Trevor Simpson peered into DI Gravel's disorganised office and grinned. 'How was Bournemouth?'

The forlorn expression on Grav's face rendered any further discussion on the subject entirely unnecessary, but DI Simpson chose to pursue the matter nonetheless. 'I hope the mother-in-law enjoyed herself.'

'Look, Trevor, unless you've got something useful to say, I suggest you fuck off and let me get on with some work.'

DI Simpson guffawed loudly, and decided not to bait his friend any further despite the temptation. 'No, seriously, there is one thing I wanted to mention, Grav.'

'Come in, Trevor. Pull up a seat. Got time for a quick coffee?'

'Tea, please, milk, one sugar.'

Grav swivelled in his seat, reached down, and switched on a kettle in a dark corner behind him. 'Right then, Trevor. What have you got for me?'

'You know I'm heading up child protection for the force?'

'I do, Trevor. I was just glad it wasn't me the brass asked, to be honest.'

'Yeah, I know what you mean, Grav. Look, while you were away, I've had Jane Pritchard making some enquiries for me.'

'I thought you were non-operational?'

'I am in the main, Grav, but needs must. Jane needed some advice, you weren't available, and it progressed from there.'

'Fair enough, Trevor, what have you had her doing?'

'She interviewed a young lad who mentioned being taken to a white room, where he alleges he was sexually assaulted by a man he believes to be a doctor.'

'Could be an unused hospital building, or the like?'

DI Simpson nodded once. 'Could be, I guess. It was Dewi Williams, you handled the case.'

'Of course.'

'It seems it wasn't only his father.'

'Oh, for fuck's sake!'

'I've had Jane ferreting about to see if there's been any mention of a white room or a doctor in other similar cases.'

'Any joy?'

'Yeah, nothing definitive, but there may be something in it. I'd like to pursue matters further with Jane's help, if that's all right with you?'

'Knock yourself out, Trevor.'

DI Simpson stood and drained the dregs of his tea. 'I was planning on paying Dewi's father a visit at Swansea nick this afternoon.'

'Simon Williams? Good luck with that. He's an obnoxious cunt at the best of times. Did you know he's appealing his sentence?'

'Yeah, you mentioned it before your leave. I may well be able to use it.'

'It's got to be worth a try, Trevor. Let me know how it goes.'

It took DI Simpson just over an hour to make the approximate forty-mile journey to HM Prison Swansea in the Sandfields area of the sprawling Welsh seaside city. He parked his red Mondeo in Oystermouth Road, directly below the high Victorian granite walls, opened the driver's door, and hurriedly made his way to the main entrance, just as the increasingly foreboding grey skies began to fill the air with icy drizzle that threatened to turn to snow at any minute.

The stout sanguine middle-aged guard on the door quickly checked the inspector's name off against a list of expected visitors, before enthusiastically waving him through, rather than engaging in the potentially lengthy security procedures that could potentially accompany such visits.

DI Simpson made his way through the prison's familiar corridors to interview room three as instructed, and waited with increasing impatience, while a burly prison officer escorted an extremely reluctant and orally obstructive Simon Williams from the sexual offenders unit.

DI Simpson remained seated behind a small rectangular table when the two men finally entered the brightly lit room a few minutes later, and gestured to the prisoner to take a seat opposite him. As Williams sat in brooding silence the inspector turned to the guard, who was standing just inside the door. 'I don't need you to stay, thanks, mate. I'll give you a shout when I'm finished, if that's all right with you?'

'Yeah, no probs, ring the bell on the wall behind you when you're done.'

DI Simpson rested the palms of both hands on the grimy tabletop, and stared directly at Williams, who held his gaze momentarily before suddenly looking away. 'I hear you're not particularly enjoying your stay here, Simon. Accommodation not up to your required standard?'

Williams shifted uneasily in his seat. 'What the fuck do you want?'

'Were you expecting room service, gourmet food, or a spa facility possibly?'

'Just get to the fucking point!'

'I need some answers, and you're going to give them to me, Simon.'

'Am I fuck!'

'I hear you're appealing the length of your sentence, Simon. Be a shame if the Court of Appeal somehow got the idea you're being uncooperative.'

'You're not going to do me any favours whatever I tell you.'

'Well, you're right there, Simon. I wouldn't piss on you if you were on fire, to be honest. But I'll promise you one thing: I'll do everything in my power to make your life a total misery if I don't get the information I came here for.'

Silence.

'Am I not speaking English, Simon?'

Silence.

The DI grinned. 'Oh, it's going to be like that is it? How would you feel about moving out of the nonces' wing? See what life's like amongst the rest of the prison population. You know who I'm talking about: the hard men who can't be at home to protect their kids from scum like you.'

Silence.

‘We’ve been talking to your son, Simon. He had some very interesting matters to tell us about things you haven’t been charged with yet.’

The remaining colour drained from Williams’ pasty prison face. ‘You can’t do that.’

‘Oh, I think you’ll find we can, Simon. Are you seeing any chance of an early release disappearing before your very eyes? Magic, eh! Perhaps another four or five years is a more likely outcome.’

‘What do you want, you bastard?’

‘Now, now, Simon, no need for that.’

‘I’m waiting.’

‘You took your son to a white room, Simon. Do you remember that?’

Silence.

‘He was assaulted in that room by a man you referred to as, Doctor. Anything you want to tell me, Simon?’

‘Fuck all.’

‘Videos were made.’

‘Like fuck they were.’

The DI stared at him incredulously. ‘What’s the denial about? We know it happened, Simon. You took him from your home, you blindfolded him during the car journey, he was drugged. Stop pissing me about, man. Do you really want to stay here for another ten years or more?’

Williams looked as if he may throw up at any moment. ‘What are you asking me?’

‘Do I have to spell it out for you, Simon? Where’s the room? Who’s the doctor?’

‘No fucking way!’

‘So you confirm they exist.’

‘Fuck off. I didn’t say that.’

‘Oh, you did, Simon. You did.’

‘I’ve got nothing more to say.’

‘Who’s the doctor? Where’s the room? Two simple questions. Just two answers, and I’m gone from your life forever. No more charges;

no unhelpful chat with the judge, no hateful prisoners kicking the shit out of you at every opportunity. It seems like a good deal to me.'

A single tear ran down Williams' cheek as he focused on the ceiling.

'So you'd prefer to stay here a spell longer, rather than give me the information I want?'

Williams closed his eyes tightly, and slowly nodded three times. 'I'd happily do another ten years, before I'd grass up that bastard.'

'You sound as if you actually mean that, Simon? Think, and think hard. What you decide now is going to shape your life for a long time to come.'

'I want to go back to my cell.'

'I'm going to give you one final opportunity, Simon. Make no mistake, I won't be coming back here again unless it's to charge you with further offences.'

Simon Williams rose to his feet and yelled, 'I want to go back to my fucking cell,' his voice reverberating with raw emotion.

DI Simpson swivelled in his chair, reached out to ring the bell on the wall behind him, and stood to leave. 'Careful what you wish for, Simon. It's going to be a long stay. If you have a change of heart, pick up the phone. You know where to find me.'

Chapter 11

Molly Mailer's radio alarm clock sounded at precisely 7:00 a.m. on Friday 17, January. She listened with only passing interest as the DJ announced the next track with an enthusiasm that seemed at odds with the time of the morning, and rolled over, pulling the warming duvet tightly around herself against the penetrating morning frost. She closed her eyes briefly, telling herself unconvincingly that another five minutes in bed wouldn't do any harm, but all too soon she accepted the inevitable and reluctantly dragged her weary body out of bed. Molly stretched, yawned expansively, and hurried to the bathroom, keen to freshen up before her teenage daughter got up… If Siân got there first it would inevitably be a frustratingly long wait.

Molly washed her hands and face with Simple unscented soap and water, brushed her teeth for a full two minutes, and ran a brush through her sleep tangled mousy hair. After a second or two staring into the wall mirror, she inexpertly applied some subtle pink lipstick, in a valiant but ultimately unsuccessful attempt to boost her flagging self-confidence. She could quite happily have gone back to bed at that point to hide from the world, but her internal voice told her to stop feeling sorry for herself, and to get on with the day ahead… It was an important day. Anthony needed help. They all needed help. Hopefully Dr Galbraith was the man to provide it.

Molly decided to enjoy a cup of her favoured herbal tea before waking her children… She could do with the brief reprieve, and it wouldn't do them any harm to get some extra sleep. Why not put the radio on in the kitchen and make herself a hot drink?

She placed a peppermint teabag in a mug, poured in the boiling water, spooned in an overgenerous helping of honey, agitated the bag with a tarnished teaspoon, and added a few drops of cold water from the tap before checking the clock. She took a large gulp, reluctantly put the mug to one side, and decided that waking her children couldn't be put off any longer after all.

'Time to get up, you two. Dad will be picking us up in an hour. Breakfast will be on the table in five minutes.'

Anthony shouted, 'Thanks, Mum,' and suddenly appeared from his bedroom fully dressed. Molly chose to ignore the predictable mumbled complaints emanating from her teenage daughter's bedroom… Siân's reaction could have been a lot worse given the circumstances.

Molly allowed Siân another ten minutes before finally heading back upstairs and knocking repeatedly on her bedroom door. 'Are you up, love? The bathroom's free.'

'Do I really have to go, Mum?'

Molly took a deep breath, and began counting to ten… Be patient, Molly. Be patient. 'The doctor wants to see us all together, love. We talked about this last night, didn't we? I really haven't got time for this now.'

'All right! All right! I get the message.'

Molly put four slices of white bread in the toaster, switched on the kettle for the second time that morning, and placed two boxes of cereal and a carton of fresh milk on the kitchen table. Anthony loved sugary cereals, but Siân had begun eating muesli with skimmed milk every morning, as part of a New Year resolution to lose weight she didn't need to lose.

Molly filled a glass with cold water from the tap, steadied herself, and took a large refreshing gulp… Should she ring Mike? What if the tart answered? She may do without that this morning, of all mornings. Was Mike really capable of forgetting such an important appointment?

She took another swig of water… He was a useless git sometimes. It really could happen if his mind were focused on other things.

The phone rang and rang before Molly finally heard Mike's familiar voice say, 'Hello.' Molly closed her eyes and said a silent prayer of thanks that Tina hadn't answered. 'Do you remember you're picking us up for the clinic at ten, Mike?'

'I haven't forgotten, Molly. I was getting ready when you rang.'

'So it's Molly this morning, is it? What happened to Mo or love? I suppose that bloody tart's listening. I wouldn't want you getting into any trouble.'

'Please, Molly, not now. I will talk to her about us, I swear.'

'Sorry, I missed that, Mike. You seemed to be whispering.'

'Molly, just leave it, will you! We can talk later, after the appointment if you still want to. Do I need to bring anything?'

'No, Mike, just be on time for once in your life.'

'Right then you two. Have you had enough breakfast?'

Anthony had just finished his second bowl of Sugar Puffs and was enjoying a glass of chilled apple juice from the fridge despite the winter weather. 'Can I watch television, Mum?'

'Yes, I suppose so, cariad, but please be quick. Dad's picking us up for the doctor soon. What about you, Siân, fancy a cuppa?'

Siân rose from the table and tossed a teabag into her mug without reply.

Molly noted the length of her miniskirt… It was one more battle that was best postponed. Siân was cooperating, and for now that was enough. 'Take what you need for school, love. Dad can drop you off after the doctor.'

'What's the doctor actually going to do, Mum?'

Molly paused before responding. 'I don't really know to be honest, love. Dr Procter didn't really say very much about that. But I'm sure Dr Galbraith will help sort things out. Come on, love, finish getting ready. Dad will be here in about ten minutes.'

Siân looked pensively towards the floor. 'He's not bringing that tart with him is he, Mum?'

Molly couldn't help but smile. 'No, love, the tart won't be coming.'

Mike Mailer parked his shiny, new, Arctic white Ford Escort XR 3 convertible sports saloon outside the detached Welsh stone cottage he had shared with his wife and children. He'd borrowed the full cost of the car by taking advantage of an employees' preferential loan rate from the bank, after Tina persuaded him that it was high time he prioritised their needs above those of Molly and the children. Mike had serious misgivings at the time, and was badly regretting capitulating… What the hell was Mo going to say when she saw the car for the first time? He hadn't been as forthcoming with money for the kids as he should have been due to the loan repayments. Whatever she said, it wouldn't be pretty. And what would he say in response? What could he say? He was in the wrong. That was blatantly obvious to anyone.

Mike turned off the engine… Should he knock on the front door, or just sound the horn and wait?

He went to open the car door, but changed his mind almost immediately and pressed the horn hard three times… He just couldn't face going into the building that had so recently been his home.

A few seconds later Molly left the cottage, followed by Anthony and finally Siân, who was dragging her feet at the back. Mike felt as if the swords of Damocles were hanging over him as his family walked down the fragmented concrete path towards his recent extravagance. He got out promptly, and opened both doors before ushering his children into the somewhat cramped rear seats. He took a deep breath… Maybe he could avoid a row, but probably not. Who was he trying to kid? There was a shit storm coming his way. 'You're all looking smart this morning.'

Anthony smiled, Siân didn't respond at all, and Molly fixed him with an accusing glare that left him in absolutely no doubt how she felt… At some point in the not-too-distant future he was going to cop it big time. It couldn't be avoided in the long run, but it would be avoided for now.

Mike turned the key, the engine burst into life, and they began their journey with everyone sitting in apprehensive silence. He repeatedly tried to engage his children in conversation, but it seemed no one was in the mood to talk. It took just over twenty tense minutes to reach their destination. There were only two other cars in the car park when they arrived, and ample room for the convertible. Mike parked alongside Dr Galbraith's luxury limousine and quipped, 'Nice car, bet it's the doctor's,' in a final unsuccessful attempt to lighten the pervasive mood. No one moved an inch until Molly said, 'Let's go you lot. We don't want to be late. Out you all get.'

Dr Galbraith watched from his office window as the Mailers walked across the car park. He looked at the family, but only truly saw Anthony. He focused on his potential victim as if he were witnessing the greatest sight of his life… Short ginger hair, a little off putting possibly? But, no, no, the style suited him. And he was tall for his age. He was slim. Those had to be good qualities, didn't they? Yes, yes, of course they were. Of course they were. He'd do just fine.

He pressed his face against the blinds with his nose touching the glass… Come on, you little bastard. In you come. In you come.

Molly eased open the heavy door leading into the clinic's brightly lit reception and walked in sheepishly, with the rest of the Mailer clan following close behind. Sharon Breen, who acted as both secretary and receptionist, stood up behind her desk and smiled warmly. 'You must be the Mailer family. Please take a seat. Dr Galbraith shouldn't be too long. He doesn't like to keep his patients waiting.'

Molly said, 'Thank you,' the brief exchange was over, and silence reverberated around the room.

After five minutes the Mailer family were still waiting in various states of nervous anxiety. Sharon looked up from her desk with a smile of genuine regret. 'I'm really sorry about this. He shouldn't be too much longer. He must be doing something really important.'

Molly acknowledged her warm-heartedness with a forced, quickly vanishing smile, but didn't reply.

In reality, Dr Galbraith wasn't doing anything at all except waiting, and watching the seconds tick by on the wall clock above his desk. He made a point of never seeing a family until exactly ten minutes after their appointed time had elapsed… He hated every excruciating minute, but it reinforced his importance, and therefore his power. The sacrifice was probably worth it.

He checked the clock against his Cartier, straightened his cartoon tie, pulled up the zip of his trousers, waited for his erection to subside, and cursed the repetitious throbbing in his head… Only eight minutes had passed, but could he wait another two? Why was he struggling so badly? He'd always managed the anticipation in the past. What had changed? Why the hell couldn't he do it now?

The doctor blinked repeatedly and wiped the sweat from his brow with a shirt sleeve, leaving moist stains on the cuff… Was he losing his touch? No, no, of course he wasn't.

He ran a hand through his short black hair and rose to his feet… He could no more wait another two minutes than two hours. The little bastard was special. That must be it. What other explanation was there?

Dr Galbraith closed his eyes momentarily in silent meditation… Come on, man. Focus. Game face.

He opened his office door, stood facing the family, smiled, introduced himself, and shook each of their hands in turn. 'Welcome, welcome. Marvellous to see you all. Please accept my sincere apologies for keeping you waiting. Unavoidable I'm afraid; something of an emergency. I'm certain Sharon, here, has been looking after you. Please join me in my office. I'm sure we'll all have an extremely productive morning.'

Dr Galbraith watched with eager attention as the Mailers entered his office… The bitch mother took the lead as she had on arrival. That was well worthy of note. No doubt he could use it to his advantage.

He sat in a chair he'd positioned close to the centre of the room, and beckoned the family to sit in chairs placed in a semicircle, so that each one was facing him. The doctor's chair was larger and higher than the others.

Molly sat to the immediate left of the doctor, with Anthony next to her. He hurriedly pulled his chair closer to his mother, and clung tightly to her arm. Mike sat to the right side of the doctor, with Siân immediately next to him. When they were finally settled in their seats, Dr Galbraith spoke up, clearly enunciating each word. 'You may have noticed the video camera and microphones.' He pointed flamboyantly to the wall-mounted camera high in one corner of the room and to the two sensitive black microphones on each of the walls. 'I find it particularly helpful to record all appointments and the majority of therapy sessions. I have a similar set up in the therapy room which I will show you later. It's an essential part of the process. So you've no objections, I presume?' His tone strongly suggested it was a statement of fact rather than a question.

The family members looked at each other sheepishly, but nobody said a word.

'Mrs Mailer, I assume you're in agreement?'

Molly nodded meekly.

Dr Galbraith smiled… Of course he hadn't lost his touch. What the hell was he worrying about? Things were already going his way.

The doctor remained silent for a second or two before elucidating his thoughts. 'Let's start as we mean to go on. Mr Mailer, you move to sit next to Mrs Mailer. Siân, you stay where you are, my dear. Anthony, you can sit nearer to me.'

Both parents thought this a very odd start to the appointment, but neither vocalised their thoughts: Mike for want of an easy life, and Molly not wanting to seem in any way uncooperative in the interests of her son's wellbeing.

Anthony stared at Molly with tears welling in his eyes. 'Mum, I want to sit by you.'

Molly scowled unconvincingly. 'It'll be all right, cariad. Listen to the doctor. I'm only here next to Dad.'

As Molly rose from her seat with the intention of comforting Anthony, who was sitting on the very edge of his chair with tears rolling down his freckled face, Dr Galbraith raised his right hand in the style of an assertive police officer stopping traffic. He reached behind him, opened his desk drawer, and took out a white paper bag of sherbet lemons. He stood facing Anthony's chair and offered him a sweet. Anthony looked away, met his mother's eyes, and shook his head reluctantly. The doctor sat, moved his seat forward, took a single sweet from the bag, unwrapped it slowly, popped it into his mouth, and sucked it in exaggerated style, which amused Anthony despite his tears.

'Mmm..., delicious, absolutely delicious!' He held the bag out for the second time. 'Go on, take one. Take one. You won't be sorry.'

Anthony took one, but didn't unwrap it.

Dr Galbraith took three sweets from the bag, and handed one to Molly, Mike and Siân in turn. 'Come on, let's all have one. I can't resist them.' He sat without speaking until each of the family opened their sweets, put them in their mouths and started sucking. He placed an open hand on Anthony's shoulder and held it there for a second or two. 'That's more like it. What do you say, Anthony? Nice, eh?'

Anthony nodded, and grinned for the first time since arriving at the clinic.

The doctor did likewise. 'What do you say, Mum? Nice?'

Molly looked at Anthony... He was grinning. He seemed more at ease. He obviously liked the doctor. The strange psychiatrist with his unconventional methods really did seem to know what he was doing.

'Mrs Mailer?'

Molly smiled, and said, 'Lovely.'

Dr Galbraith laughed. 'Quite right, Mum. Quite right.'

Neither Mike nor Siân really knew what to think, and remained silent.

Dr Galbraith smiled at each of the family members in turn. 'Right, we must get on. Let's make a start. Your general practitioner, Dr Procter, has asked me to see your family because Anthony here needs my help. He needs my urgent help. You may be wondering why, if that is the case, I have arranged to see you all here this morning?' He paused for a second or two, as if carefully considering his subsequent choice of words, and continued, 'Experience has taught me that in the vast majority of cases, it is best that I meet the patient's immediate family in order to gain a proper understanding of the child's problems. If I fully understand the family, the particular complex dynamics involved, I understand the child.' He paused again, and in a contrived manner intended to suggest his words were of no great significance, added, 'I will of course need to see Anthony on a one-to-one basis at some point in the near future if therapy is to be successful.'

Molly's anxiety at this proposition showed clearly on her face.

'Let's not worry about that for now, Mrs Mailer. Nothing to worry about, nothing whatsoever. Rest assured, we will get to know each other properly before then.'

Molly still didn't respond, but it was glaringly obvious from her anxious expression that her concerns hadn't been adequately alleviated.

Dr Galbraith met her eyes and broke into an engaging smile. 'Oh come, come, Molly. It is all right if I call you Molly, isn't it?'

Molly nodded reticently… She was warming to the good-looking doctor and his unusual methods.

'Let us proceed. I read Dr Procter's referral letter with interest, and have a good basic understanding of the facts. It would be extremely useful, however, if each of you were to outline the events that have lead you to my door. In your own words, so to speak.'

For the next hour or more, Dr Galbraith asked each family member considered questions in turn, building up a comprehensive detailed history of all events leading to Anthony's behavioural issues. When conversation stalled, or threatened to become heated, Dr Galbraith smoothed the conversational wheels with a smile, empathetic words, or the enthusiastic offer of another sweet.

At the conclusion of the process Dr Galbraith stood and smiled, focusing primarily on Molly. 'Thank you all for your contributions. You've all done marvellously. You should all be very proud of yourselves. Mr Mailer, or should I call you Mike? I appreciate that you are not finding this process easy. You are in the firing line, so to speak. Feelings of guilt are never easy to bear' He laughed. 'Given some of your verbal statements, nonverbal gestures and facial expressions, I strongly suspect that you doubt the value of psychiatry, and are here more to please your wife than wishing to fully engage in the therapeutic process. Not to worry. It is of no real consequence. It is to your credit that you are here at all.'

Mike grinned sheepishly and nodded… The doctor had it spot on. Perhaps there was more to this than he'd thought.

'Molly, my dear, I believe you've found the morning somewhat cathartic. A significant part of you has enjoyed telling your story. Getting it off your chest, so to speak. Nothing wrong with that, my dear. Nothing whatsoever! You have been hurt, of that I have no doubt. You have had to deal with emotive feelings of abandonment, anger and disappointment, while continuing to care for your traumatised children. Such things are never easy. It is to your credit that you are prepared to forgive your husband, subject to specific conditions of course. Conditions that are yet to be fulfilled.' He smiled. 'Forgiveness has a great capacity to heal even in the most difficult of situations. Your obvious commitment to Anthony's wellbeing and his necessary treatment will pay undoubted dividends in due course. Thank you, my dear.

Siân, my dear girl, I'm sure you'll agree that at your age parents have a tendency to be highly embarrassing at the best of times. All this personal stuff must have been truly excruciating for you. You want your brother to get better, that is clear to me, but you will no doubt be delighted to hear that I will not need to see you again. Having you here today has been very helpful indeed. Thank you, my dear.'

The doctor grinned at Anthony, handed him another sweet, and then addressed the entire family. 'Anthony's case is extremely complex. When parents decide to live apart, a young child can often feel as if their small world has been turned upside down. And, of course, it has been. It is a condition I like to refer to as separation anxiety. Anthony is at an age when family breakdown tends to be particularly traumatic. He is struggling to accept his father's departure from the family home. That is obvious to us all. It will undoubtedly help him to express his sadness to a trusted authority figure in a safe environment, and to make sense of his feelings. I will help him do that. Anthony, you need to understand, is filled with confusing conflicted emotions that I will explore with him in a secure therapeutic context.

Molly, my dear, you will no doubt be pleased to hear that you are already doing most things correctly. Anthony feels safe in your care, and as a result, you are inevitably on the receiving end of his acting out behaviours. Try not to worry about that. Easier said than done, I appreciate. But as the therapeutic process progresses, things will gradually improve. There may well be a deterioration in his behaviour in the short term, of course. But, if that is the case, it is of no real concern.'

Molly smiled nervously and shifted uneasily in her seat.

Dr Galbraith reciprocated, and adopted a pensive expression. 'How can I best explain it? Ah yes, yes, it's a bit like shaking a bottle of fizzy pop, and then taking the top off.' He laughed. 'One hell of a mess at first, but then things calm down very nicely. I'm sure that will be the case with Anthony. It will take time, of course. I am in no doubt about that. But, it is absolutely essential that Anthony completes the entire course of treatment. I really can't stress that requirement enough.'

The doctor turned to Anthony. 'I can only apologise for all that adult stuff, young man. Nothing to worry about. Nothing whatsoever! You've been through a tough time, my boy. But things will get better from here. Think of me as your friend. Someone you can talk to about absolutely anything that is worrying you. We will meet here, or sometimes at my home.'

Molly stiffened, and met his gaze. 'Your home?'

Dr Galbraith turned to face her. 'I see patients at my home on rare occasions if I consider they need more of my time than the clinic's busy schedule allows. It may or may not prove necessary in Anthony's case.'

Molly nodded nervously… Was Tony one of those children?

The doctor refocused on Anthony, who was becoming increasingly bored as the session progressed. 'So, you see, Anthony, we will get to know each other extremely well.'

Dr Galbraith paused briefly and smiled. 'I'll show you all the therapy room in a short while. But there is one important matter I wish to address first.' He took a grey cardboard folder from his desktop, and handed an individual sheet of typed paper to each family member. 'What you have in front of you is a therapeutic contract that confirms all our commitment to fully engage in the process for Anthony's benefit. Let me talk you all through it:

1. Mr and Mrs Mailer will ensure that Anthony arrives for each appointment on time;
2. Anthony's appointments will be prioritised above all else;
3. Mr and Mrs Mailer agree to follow the treatment plan;
4. Mr and Mrs Mailer agree to therapy sessions being video recorded when deemed appropriate by Dr Galbraith;
5. Mr and Mrs Mailer agree to Anthony being seen at any venue deemed appropriate by Dr Galbraith;
6. Mr and Mrs Mailer will ensure that Anthony completes his entire course of treatment;
7. Dr Galbraith will meet Anthony's therapeutic needs to the very best of his ability.

I'm sorry if all this appears extremely formal, but experience has taught me that it is essential that we all properly understand the crucial nature of the intervention. I have had several cases in the past where parents have not been fully committed to the process, sometimes with tragic consequences.' He smiled from ear to ear. 'Having talked to you all this morning, I am sure you will not be one of those unfortunate families. Do you all understand? Now is the time to say if there is anything at all that requires clarification.'

Molly and Mike both nodded their silent agreement.

'Okay, it seems we're all singing from the same hymn sheet, so to speak. I'll collect those from you, and we can all sign the original copy.' He handed Molly a clipboard and pen. 'If you sign first, my dear, and then everyone can do likewise?'

Molly was about to sign, but hesitated.

Dr Galbraith blinked repeatedly as the pressure in his head suddenly escalated and made him flinch… What the hell was the bitch thinking? 'Is there something worrying you, my dear girl?'

'I was just wondering what is meant by other venues.'

'Oh, that's nothing to worry about, my dear. I may need to see Anthony at school for example, or at the consulting room at my home as I mentioned earlier. And, once a year, in the summer months when it's warmer, I take a group of boys camping with other like-minded colleagues. It's a therapy we call intermediate treatment. It proves surprisingly effective; we all have a marvellous time. But, we mustn't worry about that at this early stage, must we, Molly?' He laughed. 'We won't be camping in the Welsh winter. It's far too cold for that.'

Molly signed, followed by Mike, Siân and finally Anthony, who wrote his name in unjoined script.

Dr Galbraith took the clipboard and pen from him, and signed the agreement with an exuberant flourish. 'Thank you, Anthony. You've done an excellent job, young man. I will ask Sharon to make personal copies for each of you to take away with you. Now then, let me show you the therapy room before we arrange another appointment.'

The doctor stood up immediately, proactively avoiding any further discussion, and approached the therapy room, located just a few feet from where they all sat. When they were all crowded together at the entrance, Dr Galbraith pointed out the single red light above the door. 'When therapy sessions are underway, they must not be disturbed under any circumstances. I really can't stress that enough.'

After pausing to emphasise the point in his usual excessively exuberant manner, he finally opened the door. The room was brightly painted in a cheery primrose yellow, and had colourful cartoon murals on each of the four walls. There were large navy blue beanbags and various toys scattered around the floor. A high-tech video camera was mounted high in one corner of the room, and a video player and television set were positioned on the back wall opposite the door. The guided tour only took a couple of minutes, but served his purpose of bringing the session to a timely end without further potentially unhelpful questions.

The Mailers followed Dr Galbraith into reception where Sharon was still working away at her desk. She looked up and smiled engagingly. 'What can I do for you, Doctor?'

Dr Galbraith raised himself to his full six-foot-two-inches. 'Now then, Sharon my dear girl, Anthony here needs another appointment as soon as possible.'

Sharon turned the pages of the appointments diary. 'There's nothing until half past ten on the thirty-first of this month, I'm afraid, Doctor.'

The doctor shook his head vigorously, desperately attempting to clear his mind and think more clearly… Focus, man, focus. Get a fucking grip.

He forced a scarcely credible smile. 'That won't do. It won't do at all.' He glared at Sharon with pleading eyes. 'There has to be an earlier appointment?'

Sharon shrunk back into her seat with a startled expression on her face.

Too urgent, man. Far too urgent; the atmosphere in the room had changed. There was an undeniable tension in the air. Sharon had visibly stiffened. That wasn't good. It wasn't good at all. Was he in danger of blowing it? He had to say something. He had to rescue the situation. Say something, man. Come on, say something. 'I apologise if I seem somewhat irate…' Not a bad start.

He grinned anxiously, appearing slightly manic. 'Anthony here needs my help. He needs my urgent help…' Hadn't he said that before? Focus, man! For fuck's sake, focus. 'I don't want to delay therapy if at all possible. It wouldn't be in Anthony's interests. Look again please, Sharon. We can't let this young man down.' He relaxed as the pressure in his head subsided slightly… He'd done well. He was back on track.

Sharon turned the pages urgently. 'I'm very sorry, Doctor. There really is nothing else free. I'm afraid you're booked solid.'

He grimaced as his facial muscles tightened inexorably, and a violent stabbing pain exploded in his head… Two fucking weeks was too long. Far too long.

He mopped his forehead with a clean white linen handkerchief taken from a trouser pocket, and felt his heart pounding in his chest, and the blood surging through his veins… Surely they could hear it. No, that made no sense. The mask was slipping. Get them out. Get them out as quickly as possible. 'In that case, Sharon, the thirty-first will have to do. It will have to do. I'm sure you will keep a close eye on our patient before then, won't you, Mum?'

Molly smiled and nodded with renewed enthusiasm… If the doctor thought it so very urgent, perhaps Tony needed more help than she'd realised.

Dr Galbraith spoke for one last time as the family were about to leave, 'I won't need to see you all next time. If you bring Anthony along, Molly, I will see you together very briefly, and then it would be extremely useful for me to spend some time with Anthony alone. I will look forward to seeing you in two weeks' time.'

Molly put her arm around Anthony's shoulder and guided him towards the exit. 'Thank you, Doctor. We'll see you then.'

Dr Galbraith smiled as the all-consuming booming in his mind reduced to a barely perceivable throb… He hadn't lost his touch. He was well on course. He was back in control. The bitch mother didn't suspect a thing. 'You're very welcome, my dear. I'll look forward to it.'

Traffic was surprisingly quiet on the return trip. Mike dropped Siân off at her secondary-school en route as planned, and before very long he was parking the convertible directly outside the Mailer family cottage. Each of them had been somewhat preoccupied with their own thoughts during the journey, and nobody said very much at all, with the exception of Anthony, who was just glad to have both his parents in the same place at the same time.

Mike exited the car first, and immediately rushed around the rear to open the passengers' side door… If he got under way quickly, he just might avoid annoying Mo more than he already had. He probably wouldn't get away with it, but it had to be worth a try. 'Get a move on, you lot. Out! I need to get to work.'

Molly knew exactly what he was doing, but decided to let it slide… Further point scoring could wait for another time. The day had been stressful enough already.

Chapter 12

'I know you've been interviewed on video before, Donna, but I'll quickly recap what we're going to be doing. We're undertaking a further interview due to the new things you told Alan at your foster home. Is there anything you want to ask either of us before we make a start?'

Eight-year-old Donna Bevan shook her head and said, 'No.'

'Right then, Donna. Go into the interview room with Alan and make yourself comfortable. I'll switch the recording equipment on in the control room I showed you last time, and join you in a minute or two. Okay?'

Donna nodded reticently, entered the small eggshell blue-painted rectangular room with its wall-mounted video camera and self-levelling microphones, and sat on a large purple beanbag stuffed with polystyrene beads.

Alan Garret sat opposite the young girl, noticed she was trembling, and smiled warmly… Kids shouldn't have to go through this shit. 'She won't be too long, Donna. You know how this works by now. As soon as Pam joins us, she'll say who we all are for the tape, and then ask you about what happened. It's important not to feel pressured to try and answer any questions you don't know the answer to. Just say I don't know. That'll be fine. You may be asked about anything you say today in court if any of the men are prosecuted. You do understand that, don't you?'

The girl's facial muscles tensed as she broke into a frown. 'Yes, I remember.'

WPC Pam Forsyth entered the room, closed the door behind her, and sat immediately next to the experienced social worker on the low level, black fabric two-seater settee. She proactively met Donna's eyes, smiled and nodded. 'All right, Donna. If you're ready we'll make a start.'

The eight-year-old girl shifted uneasily on her beanbag, forced a thin smile, and said, 'Okay' in a quiet voice resonating with obvious emotion.

'It's 3:23 p.m. on Friday, 17, January 1992. Present are: Detective Constable Pam Forsyth, Alan Garret, child protection senior social work practitioner, and the interviewee, Donna Bevan, d.o.b. 11, January 1985. Is there anything at all you want to ask us before we make a start, Donna?'

The girl closed her eyes and quickly reopened them. 'No thanks.'

'If I said I was wearing a red dress, would that be the truth or a lie?'

'A lie.'

'And if I said I was wearing a blue jumper, jeans and trainers, would that be the truth or a lie?'

The girl smiled again, slightly more convincingly this time. 'The truth!'

'It's very important that everything you tell us today is the truth, Donna. Do you understand?'

She nodded and said, 'Yes.'

'Then we'll get on. Am I right in saying that at approximately half past seven yesterday evening you told Alan that you were assaulted by several men in addition to your father?'

The girl's reply was barely audible.

'It's important to speak a little louder, Donna. Did you say, yes?'

Her response was a little louder this time. 'Yes.'

'That's much better; I could hear your answer nice and clearly that time.'

'Okay.'

'We will need to talk about the details of what they did to you later, Donna. But first of all I want to ask you some other questions about what happened. If you need to take a break at any time, just say.'

'Okay.'

'Can you remember how many men assaulted you, Donna?'

'A lot!'

Alan Garret took a deep breath, taken aback by the girl's haunted expression… Was she really capable of continuing? 'Take your time, Donna. I know this isn't easy.'

Pam Forsyth met her eyes. 'Alan's right, Donna. Take your time. There's absolutely no rush. We can take as long it takes.'

The girl's breathing became more erratic. 'Okay.'

'How many do you think?'

'I don't know.'

'Less than five or more than five?'

She raised her knees and lowered her head, appearing smaller. 'More than five!'

'Less than ten or more than ten?'

She hugged her knees tightly to her chest and closed her eyes. 'More, I think.'

'But, you can't be sure?'

'No.'

'Sorry, Donna, I didn't quite hear that.'

'No!'

'When did these things happen, Donna?'

'It's been happening for as long as I can remember. It only stopped when I went to live with my foster parents.'

'How old were you the first time it happened?'

'I can't remember. Very small, I think.'

The WPC frowned. 'How often did it happen, Donna?'

'A lot!'

'Every week, or every month, or every year?'

'Depends.'

'What do you mean by that?'

'Sometimes it happened every week when men came to the house. But we were only taken to the farm about two or three times a year.'

'When you say we, who exactly do you mean?'

'Me, my brother and sister, and lots of other children!'

The WPC took a deep breath. 'We will talk more about that later, Donna. But I need to understand a little bit more about how things happened first. Is that all right?'

She shook her head despondently. 'I suppose so.'

'Can you tell us more about the farm?'

'Dad used to take us to the pet club.'

Where the hell was this going? 'Pet club?'

'That's what the doctor told us to call it. Everyone called it that.'

'Who's the doctor?'

Silence.

'Do you know the doctor's name, Donna?'

Donna looked at the floor and whispered, 'Yes.'

'What is it?'

'Do I have to say?'

Come on girl. This matters. 'It would be very helpful if you could, Donna.'

'What if he finds out I've told you?'

The poor girl's absolutely terrified. 'We can make sure you're safe, Donna.'

'I'm not sure.'

'You're not sure of his name, or you're not sure if you should say?'

She shook her head slowly and deliberately, and squinted as the afternoon sun broke through the clouds and filled the room with winter sunshine. 'I'm not sure if I should say.'

The WPC adjusted the dark blue curtains. 'This is really important, Donna.'

She didn't respond for a second or two, and then whispered, 'Dr Galbraith,' ever so quietly.

'Did you say Dr Galbraith, Donna?'

Silence.

'We need to be certain what you said, Donna.'

Silence.

'Did you hear what Donna said, Alan?'

'No, could you say the name again, Donna?'

Silence.

The WPC reached forward and touched the girl on the shoulder. 'Say the name again please, Donna.'

The young girl raised two fists to her face and closed her eyes tight shut.

Should she push it? Should she ask again? No, she may clam up completely. 'Was the doctor at the farm?'

Donna lowered her hands but kept her eyes closed. 'Yes, always, he told everyone what to do.'

'Like a boss?'

'Yes, like a boss.'

'Was he one of the men who assaulted you, Donna?'

She opened her eyes and shook her head vigourously. 'No, he only ever hurt the boys.'

It had to be worth a try. 'Do you know the doctor's first name, Donna?'

Silence.

'You never heard anyone call him by his first name?'

'No, everyone called him, Doctor.'

'Could you tell me what he looked like?'

She grimaced. 'Yes, I t-think so.'

Time to move on. She was in danger of blowing it. 'That's good, Donna, we'll come back to that later.'

'Okay.'

'Who else was at the farm?'

'Lots of grownups and other children!'

'Were there men and women, or just men?'

'Mostly men!'

'Could you tell us who the adults were? Do you know their names?'

'I know some of their names.'

'That's good, Donna, I'll ask you about each of them in turn in a short while. But I want to ask you some other questions first. Is that all right?'

'Yes, I suppose so.'

‘Do you know any of the other children, Donna?’

‘My brother and sister were always there.’

‘Did bad things happen to them as well?’

A tear ran down the young girl’s cheek as she replied in the affirmative.

Alan Garret moved nearer to the edge of the settee. ‘Do you need to take a break, Donna?’

‘No, I want to finish.’

Pam Forsyth nodded. ‘All right, Donna. We’ll carry on for a while, and then stop for a drink and a biscuit when you’re ready. Is that all right with you?’

‘Will you talk to my brother and sister like this?’

‘We’ll need to talk to my sergeant and Alan’s team manager first. But I’m sure we will interview them either tomorrow or on Sunday.’

‘Okay.’

‘You said other children were at the farm?’

‘Yes.’

‘Could you tell us any of their names?’

‘Some.’

‘That’s really helpful, Donna; I’ll ask you more about that in a little while and we’ll make a list.’

‘Okay.’

‘Do you know where the farm is?’

‘No.’

‘How did you get there?’

‘We were all taken in the back of a van or a big lorry.’

‘Do you know what kind of van it was?’

‘It was white.’

‘Anything else?’

‘No.’

‘What about the lorry?’

‘I only saw the inside of the lorry, and it was always dark when they shut the door.’

‘Where did you start the journey?’

‘Dad used to put tape over our eyes before taking us somewhere in his car to meet the others.’

‘And you don’t know where that was?’

‘No.’

‘So, your father used to take you somewhere, and then you went in the van or lorry with the other children?’

‘Yes, we were all crammed in. It was horrible.’

‘Did you ever take the tape off your eyes when you were on the journey?’

‘Yes, once.’

‘Did you see where you were going?’

‘No.’

‘Why was that?’

‘The windows were all covered up at the back of the van, and there weren’t any in the lorry.’

‘Ah, I understand. How long did it take to get to the farm?’

‘I’m not really sure. But it was quite a long way.’

‘About how long do you think?’

‘I suppose about half an hour.’

‘What happened when you arrived at the farm?’

‘One of the men would open the doors and tell us to get out.’

‘They told you and the other children to get out of the van or lorry?’

‘Yes, and they hit us and shouted at us if we didn’t move quickly enough.’

‘You’re doing very well, Donna. Tell us what would happen next.’

‘We used to be taken into a big building.’

‘What sort of building was it?’

‘We called it the barn.’

‘That’s very helpful, Donna; would you recognise the barn if you ever saw it again?’

‘Yes, but why are you asking that?’

WPC Forsyth winced… The question was insensitive. She had to choose her words more carefully. 'You won't ever be taken there again, Donna. I just need to know if you'd recognise the place in photographs for evidential purposes after we find it.'

Donna wiped a tear from her cheek. 'Yes, I think I would.'

WPC Forsyth silently admonished herself for the ill-advised use of investigative jargon. 'Do you remember what I said when I explained what evidence is the last time you were interviewed, Donna?'

'Yes, I remember.'

'That's good, Donna, I just want to ask you one last question before we take a break.'

'Okay.'

'This may seem like an odd question. But were you ever taken to a white room?'

The young girl looked at her quizzically and said, 'No.'

'What, never?'

'Never.'

'Thank you, Donna. Let's take a break now and go downstairs for a drink.'

Chapter 13

Helen Frost, Mel Nicholson's bright and efficient admin officer, immediately recognised the caller's high-pitched voice with its musical West Country tones. 'Hi, Karen, it's Helen. Hold on. He's here somewhere.'

'Thanks, Helen.'

She peered out through the office door and shouted loudly down the corridor. 'Mel, Karen's on the phone!'

Nicholson, who was in the kitchen making coffee, called back, 'Tell her to hang on. I'll be there in two minutes.'

Helen sighed. 'He won't be long, Karen.'

Karen Smith, a social services department childcare team manager, sounded unusually irate. 'I heard him, Helen. Tell him to get a move on. It's urgent!'

Helen passed on the message and her boss trotted down the corridor. He knew Karen well and had learnt to respect her judgment… If she said it was urgent, it was urgent. 'Karen, it's Mel. What's up?'

There was a brief silence before Karen spoke. 'You're not going to believe this, Mel. I think we've got a paedophile ring operating in the area.'

Nicholson swallowed hard. 'You think we've got a paedophile ring operating in *our* area?'

'Okay. If you want to be pedantic about it. We've got a paedophile ring operating in *our* area. Is that clear enough for you?'

'Hold on, Karen.' He turned to his assistant who was organising some files in a grey steel cabinet next to his desk. 'Helen, I need some privacy. Close the door on your way out please.'

She sensed that something serious had happened and left without complaint or comment.

'Karen, it's Mel. Are you alone?'

'Yeah.'

'What exactly have you got for me?'

'Are you sitting comfortably?'

'What?'

'You weren't a Jackanory fan then?'

'Karen!'

'Sorry, Mel, just trying to stay sane in a mad world. We've been working with a family with three kids: two girls of eight and six, and a boy of four. We applied for place of safety orders after the alleged rape of the eight-year-old girl by the father. She said the mother was also involved. All three children are with foster carers pending care proceedings.'

'Where's the father now?'

'He's remanded in Swansea prison pending trial.'

Nicholson scratched his head. 'When you say the mother was involved, what exactly are we talking about?'

'It's not great to be honest, Mel. The eight-year-old said her mother held her down to facilitate the assault. She even supplied the condoms he used.'

'How's the investigation progressing?'

'We've already undertaken further joint interviews with each of the three children. They've described being sexually assaulted by multiple adults: sometimes alone and sometimes along with other children.'

'All three of them?'

'Yeah, I'm afraid so.'

'Not just by the father?'

'By their parents, several members of the extended family, and others.'

'Others?'

'Family friends, acquaintances, strangers!'

'Were they able to name any of the other children and abusers?'

'They were, Mel. Quite a few as it happens. The investigation's been ongoing for several weeks already, but it's only now we're realising the scope and organised nature of what's going on. It took some time for the kids to feel safe enough to start giving details. Not surprising really, when you think about it. It's growing all the time. It's big, Mel. I should probably have contacted you sooner.'

Nicholson spoke in a barely audible whisper. 'Don't say any more for now, Karen. I'll be with you in about twenty minutes.'

Nicholson drove the sixteen miles to the team manager's office far faster than usual despite the increasingly inclement winter weather. Karen already had a cup of warming, strong, black coffee waiting for him when he opened her office door. 'Have a seat, Mel, where do you want me to start?'

'I'm not in any hurry, Karen. Take your time. Give me the entire picture.'

'It's horrendous, Mel. I've never heard anything like it. Once the three Bevan children started talking, they really started talking. Alan Garret, my senior practitioner, and Pam Forsyth from the police were focusing on the father initially, but then there was mention of an uncle. It all came to a head on Friday. The oldest girl started talking about other adults, and subsequently her younger siblings confirmed her disclosures over the weekend. If what they've said is accurate, and we've got absolutely no reason to think it isn't, a great many children and numerous offenders are involved. It's not like anything I've dealt with before, Mel. We've already got the names of seventeen children. And they're only the ones the Bevan children know by name.'

'And they've named some of the abusers?'

'A few, and they've described others.'

'Anyone we know?'

'Yeah, I've started going back over the files. Some of the families involved have got a long history with the department. A lot of things make sense now. I don't know how we missed the links for so long, to be honest.'

'Don't beat yourself up, Karen. Hindsight tends to make things seem a great deal clearer than they were at the time.'

'Mel, there's one more thing I need to discuss with you.'

Nicholson laughed, but his expression portrayed his concern. 'Just when I thought I'd heard it all.'

'Do you know David Galbraith, the psychiatrist?'

'Dr Galbraith, yes, of course I do. Do you want him to work with the Bevan kids? I can talk to him for you, if that helps?'

'The two oldest children have named him, Mel.'

'Named him?'

'He's a part of the ring, Mel.'

'What? That sounds highly unlikely.'

'He's an abuser, Mel. The children have named him. They've given accurate descriptions. They've given details of offences against several young boys. He's one sadistic bastard by the sound of things.'

'Galbraith?'

'Yes, Mel, Galbraith!'

'For fuck's sake, I've heard it all now. He's the last person I'd have suspected.'

Karen rose from her chair. 'Time for another coffee?'

'Please.'

Nicholson sat back in his seat desperately trying to compose himself… He'd thought he could no longer be shocked. He'd been wrong. But, like it or not, he was the operational head of the county's child protection services. It was time to step up and assume the lead however uncertain he felt inside.

Karen soon reappeared balancing two mugs of coffee and a plate of chocolate digestive biscuits on an old battered tin Guinness tray. Nicholson thanked her profusely, ate two digestives ravenously, and attempted to exude an air of confidence he didn't feel. 'Right, Karen, this is what we need to do: firstly, and this is important, we need to keep this on a need to know basis. Don't talk to anyone unless we agree to it in advance. I'll get the director up to speed straight away, and talk to Trevor Simpson later today. Do you know him?'

Karen shook her head and took another biscuit from the plate.

'He's my opposite number in the police. He's sound. Knows what he's talking about. We need him involved.'

'Okay.'

'We need to arrange an initial planning meeting as soon as is practicable. Grab a pen, and I'll give you a list of who needs to be there.'

Karen picked up a clear plastic Biro and glanced pensively at her boss.

'It's the usual suspects really: the police, education, health, legal, ourselves and any other key agencies directly involved. I don't want the foster carers there. It wouldn't be appropriate in the circumstances.'

'Makes sense, Mel.'

He stood up and spoke as calmly as he could manage. 'I'll leave it with you, Karen. We can use the children's resource centre. It's as good a venue as any. Let's get together this afternoon; after three if at all possible, or tomorrow morning at the very latest. Tell everyone it's urgent, and ring me if anyone has a problem attending. I'll have a quiet word if necessary. Let me know as soon as you've got a time. I'll get off now and let you get on with things.'

'Will do, Mel. Thanks.'

'You're welcome. I'll speak to you shortly.'

Nicholson found an empty room and rang the director of social services before leaving the childcare team office. His day was about to get a lot more interesting. The phone was answered by Sheila Hoyle, the director's officious, often overbearing secretary, who acted as a self-appointed gatekeeper between her boss and the rest of the world. It was a role in which she excelled, and it took Nicholson a full two minutes to convince her that his call couldn't wait… How many times did you have to say something was urgent?

The director was somewhat prickly when he first spoke, but he rapidly changed his attitude when Nicholson explained the reason for his unexpected call.

Approximately twenty-five minutes later Nicholson was back at social service headquarters, and knocking reticently on the director's office door. Roy Evans was sitting expansively in a brown leather swivel chair behind a large Victorian walnut desk when Nicholson entered his excessively spacious office. He got straight to the point. 'This sounds serious, Mel. Give me the entire picture.'

As Nicholson outlined the relevant facts, the director became visibly less relaxed with each new revelation. 'Right, Mel. You've got my attention, how do we take this thing forward?'

'We'll get a planning meeting together as soon as possible. Karen Smith is already making the necessary arrangements. It's going to be a complex investigation, but the quicker we get on with it the better. There's a great many children in need of protection.'

Roy Evans cocked his head at a slight angle, and held his chin between the thumb and first two fingers of his right hand. 'That sounds fine as far as it goes, Mel. But I want you to set up a dedicated team to deal with this investigation and nothing else. I want Phillip Beringer to manage it for us. He's got the necessary experience and cool-headed temperament for the job. Have a word with him for me, and take him to the planning meeting. The two of you need to work out how many social workers you'll need to proceed. We can transfer them from their current teams as needed. Give some thought to who the best people are and give me a provisional list for final approval. You can involve yourself as you see fit, but keep a watching brief. I want daily updates at four each and every afternoon. I haven't got your child protection experience, Mel, but I've been in the job long enough to know that this case is likely to define our careers for good or bad. I don't want this to be another Cleveland. Make certain you keep me in the loop. I don't want any surprises.' He scratched his nose with a manicured fingernail. 'Have you talked to the police yet?'

Nicholson paused for a second to clear his head before replying. 'Not as yet, but once we've finished here I'll head to my office and make some calls.'

'Fair enough, Mel, that does it for now. Get it done.'

Nicholson hurried to his office at the other side of the 1960s concrete building, and hurriedly peeled a yellow post-it note from the wall above his desk. He screwed his eyes up, squinting hard, struggling to decipher Helen's terrible scribbled handwriting. He smiled… It was good news. Things were progressing quickly. The planning meeting was arranged for three o'clock that afternoon, and everyone required would be attending.

Come on, Trevor! Answer the frigging thing.

'DI Simpson.'

'Trevor, it's Mel. I've got something for you.'

'Hi Mel, good to hear from you. I was planning to give you a ring myself at some point today. Things seem to be heating up a bit.'

Nicholson laughed. 'That's one way of putting it.'

'You kick off, Mel, and we'll proceed from there.'

The inspector listened patiently as Nicholson outlined the basic facts. When he eventually stopped speaking, DI Simpson remained silent for a moment, lost in thought, before finally saying, 'Yeah, I've been told much the same thing at this end, Mel. But David Galbraith? Pam seems pretty certain that the Bevan girl named him, but I've viewed the tape; I couldn't hear the name. He's always seemed all right to me, to be honest. Do you really think there's anything in it?'

'It seems so, Trevor. The two younger siblings corroborated Donna's allegations on Sunday.'

'They're very young, Mel; I wouldn't want to rely on their evidence.'

'Let's wait and see what people have to say this afternoon.'

Nicholson had to make three calls before finally tracking down Phillip Beringer at a child protection investigation training course at a local hotel, where he was presenting a lecture on the assessment of risk. Beringer listened intently as his old friend summarised the morning's events.

'The director wants me to manage it?'

Nicholson laughed to lighten the obvious tension. 'He does, Phillip. Fuck knows why. I tried to talk him out of it, but there you go.' He paused for a response that didn't materialise. 'Are you still there, Phil? Are you up for it?'

Beringer ran a hand through his sparse greying hair… He wouldn't be attending any more courses for a while. Saying no wasn't really an option. Not if he was serious about a future promotion and a better pension. 'Why not, Mel, it's not as if I've got anything else to do.'

'Nice one, Phil, I thought you'd done a runner for a second or two.'

This time it was Beringer's turn to laugh. 'Don't think I didn't think about it. Are you doing the driving this afternoon?'

'Yeah, I'm giving Helen a lift; she's taking the minutes. I suppose I may as well pick you up too. I've got to make sure you actually turn up somehow.'

'Thanks, Mel, I'll try and get hold of a crash helmet from somewhere. See you later.'

Chapter 14

Nicholson opened the planning meeting with introductions, more for Helen's benefit than anything else, and advised the attendees what they were there to do. After a lengthy discussion that left several of the professionals wishing they were virtually anywhere else, the way forward was finally agreed. Phillip Beringer would head up the new dedicated social work investigative team, and would have day-to-day lead management responsibility. DI Simpson would head up a similar dedicated police team, and would liaise directly with Beringer to facilitate joint action as and when deemed necessary. Beringer would similarly liaise with the council solicitors and two local consultant paediatricians. DI Simpson would do likewise with the Crown Prosecution Service. Nicholson would act as a consultant: a sounding board and source of advice to everyone involved.

When it came to discussing the alleged involvement of Dr Galbraith, the tension in the room was virtually palpable. Several attendees expressed their grave concerns, arguing that the South Wales Health Authority should be formally advised of the situation with a view to his suspension. DI Simpson silently tolerated the impassioned arguments for a time, before eventually rising to his feet. He held both hands out in front of him with his fingers spread wide and bellowed, 'I do not want Galbraith warned. I do not want him to have the opportunity to warn other suspects. I do not want to give these people the opportunity to destroy evidence. I do not want them to have the opportunity to silence witnesses. I understand your anxieties, really, I do. But this is a complex, high-risk criminal investigation. A criminal investigation! If we act prematurely there is a very real risk we will blow it. If that happens, many more children will ultimately suffer.' He paused for a moment, meeting the eyes of each potential dissenter in turn. 'Make no mistake. If any of you break confidence, if any of you says a single word that potentially compromises this enquiry, I will arrest you for attempting to pervert the course of justice. This is high-pressure, high-risk work, people. Live with it!'

After a period of stunned silence a paediatrician asked what several of the attendees were thinking. 'What about surveillance?'

DI Simpson smirked dismissively. 'It's a nice idea, but that's all it is. There are over three hundred of these people in this county alone. And those are just the ones we know about as of now; the number's growing all the time. As much as we'd like to, we can't watch all of them. And, even if we did watch Galbraith, what would we actually watch? We can't watch him when he's at home with his daughters. We can't watch him when he's with his patients. We can't watch him when he visits friends' homes. We have absolutely no idea where or when the ring meets, or how often. It could be months before the next gathering. What use would surveillance be, even if I had the resources? Which I don't, by the way! It would make us all feel a little better. But that's all it would do. Look, people. Twenty-six children have already been identified, others will inevitably follow. There are numerous adults involved. I'm going to need every available officer. This is going to take time to get right. If we try and rush things or overstretch our resources, we'll inevitably make mistakes. Nobody wants that. I certainly don't. When we do arrest these people, I want to make it stick. There is absolutely no point at all in pulling them in and then letting them go again without charge. That would achieve precisely nothing. The second we have enough for successful prosecutions we'll be knocking on their doors. That I can guarantee.'

Chapter 15

Phillip Beringer slurped the creamy head from his fourth glass of Irish Guinness, and handed Mike Mailer another pint of the local Buckleys Bitter Ale. The two men met every Wednesday without fail for an overly competitive game of squash, inevitably followed by an hour or two at one local bar or another. The Caerystwyth rugby club was a much favoured watering hole. Beringer had been the best man at Mike and Molly's wedding, and they had asked him to be a godfather to Siân a few months later. He was flattered by the request, and happily acceded without hesitation despite his wavering faith.

Beringer grinned. 'There you are, you miserable sod.'

'Cheers, Phil.'

'Do you know what, Mike? I watched a documentary the other night about inmates on death row in Texas. None of them were as miserable as you are. What's up?'

Mike took the last Embassy cigarette from a packet of twenty, struck a match, lit the tip, and sucked on the filter hungrily, savouring the nicotine hit as the life-sapping fumes filled his lungs. 'Who the fuck are you, my mother?'

Beringer laughed. 'One of the many down sides of being a social worker, and believe me there's quite a few, is that virtual strangers seem to think they have the God-given right to unburden themselves whenever they choose. And yet we've been mates for years, and you tell me fuck all. Why don't you drop the macho bullshit and tell me what the problem is?'

Mike Mailer shook his head discontentedly and quickly downed his pint. 'How long have you got?'

'As long as it takes, Mike. As long as it takes.'

Mike approached the bar, ordered another two pints to oil the conversational wheels, and returned to his seat. 'It's this business with Molly and the kids. It's doing my head in. I sometimes wish I'd never met Tina, to be honest.'

'But you did, Mike. That's what comes of thinking with your dick.'

'Yeah, very helpful! Do any of your clients ever come back for a second appointment?'

Beringer grinned. 'You're going to have to decide what it is you really want, Mike. You can either think it through logically, weigh up the pros and cons, or listen to your gut. Knowing you as well as I do, I suspect you'll find the latter method a lot more reliable.'

'It's difficult, Phil. I never intended to leave Molly in the first place. I never planned to move in with Tina. It just happened.'

'What a load of crap! Things don't just happen, Mike. You're not some flotsam subject to the ebb and flow of the tide. You made choices at every stage. You're still making choices.'

'Yeah, but if Molly hadn't found out…'

'For fuck's sake, Mike! She did find out. You need to grow a pair and take responsibility for what you've done. If you're serious about Tina, tell Molly that. Make it crystal clear, and let her get on with her life. If you're not, if you're serious about trying to get back with Molly, then do something about it.'

'I've told Molly I'm sorry time and time again.'

'I wonder what planet you're on sometimes. What would you say if it were the other way around? What if it were Molly living with some other bloke and telling you she was sorry?'

'Have you seen Tina? She is a very good-looking girl. The sex is going to be hard to give up.'

'Do you love her?'

Mike stubbed out his cigarette, placed the tips of his fingers together as if in prayer, and rested his elbows on the table, carefully considering his response. 'It's lust. I don't love the girl.'

'Do you love Molly?'

Mike finished his beer. 'Yeah, yeah, I suppose I do.'

'Do the words cake and eat it mean anything to you?'

Mike's face reddened, and he laughed hoarsely. 'Yeah, I know. I've been a prat.'

‘You’re not going to hear me disagreeing with that particular conclusion. Molly’s a cracking girl; you’ve got two lovely children. Wasn’t that enough?’

‘I guess it should have been, but…’

‘There’s no but, Mike. You’re not some kid in college. You’re a father with responsibilities. They don’t deserve the shit you’ve been giving them. How the hell do you expect Molly to think you’re serious about you two getting back together when you’re still living with the woman you left her for? Think about it, for fuck’s sake.’

‘I know, Phillip. Honestly, I know.’

‘Well, do something about it then. Stop being so fucking ineffectual.’

Mike shook his head slowly. ‘I will.’

‘How are the kids?’

‘How about another pint?’

‘How are the kids?’

‘They’re still playing up, if you must know. Molly’s arranged for us to see a psychiatrist, of all people.’

‘What, you and the children?’

‘Yeah, of course, us and the children. He’s a child psychiatrist.’

Beringer felt his facial muscles tighten as he frowned. ‘Who’s the doctor?’

‘Are you all right, Phil? You look like crap all of a sudden.’

‘His name, Mike?’

‘Galbraith, David Galbraith, what’s it matter?’

‘Has Tony actually seen him yet?’

‘Yeah, he’s got a second appointment this Friday, as it happens. Mo’s going in with him this time. I’m just providing the transport. I can’t see the point of it all myself, to be honest. Mo’s already said that Tony’s more his old self again. I’m only going along with it to win a few Brownie points.’

Beringer felt physically sick, his mind racing… Think! If Anthony’s mood had improved, it wasn’t too late. Nothing had happened yet, but, it would. It definitely would. What the fuck could he say without breaking confidence and potentially jeopardising the investigation?

He stood up without speaking, ran out of the pub and threw up against a wall in a dark corner of the car park... What could he say? Time to think. He needed time to think.

Beringer reappeared a few minutes later, looking pale and drawn, with tears welling in his eyes. 'I'm feeling like shit, Mike. Must be something I ate. I'm going to have to make a move, mate.' He downed the dregs of his pint to wash the remaining vomit from his mouth. 'Look, Mike, before I head off, I just wanted to say that it's highly likely that Tony's mood and behaviour has improved because you and Molly are on speaking terms again. It's got fuck all to do with the doctor. Tony needs time, Mike, not a head doctor.'

'We've been mates a long time, Phillip. Is there something you're not telling me?'

Should he tell him? Siân and Anthony were his godchildren, after all. No, it was potential career suicide. 'Kids get labelled, Mike. These things can follow them for their entire education. He needs his family. It really is that simple. I'd seriously think about knocking it on the head, if I were you. I just want what's best for Tony, that's all.'

'I'm not arguing with you, Phil. But, Mo?'

'Do you want me to talk to her?'

Mike nodded enthusiastically. 'Yeah, thanks, Phil. Sounds like a plan. It's appreciated. She's not going to listen to a word I say.' He checked his watch.

'It's only twenty to ten. Fancy another pint before you go?'

'Not for me, thanks, mate. It's time I headed off to get some shut eye. I'll speak to you in a couple of days to see how things are going.'

Beringer drove home with unnecessary haste despite being well over the drink-drive limit. When he eventually arrived at his third floor town centre flat, he made a mug of strong milky instant coffee with two large spoonfuls of white sugar, in a short-lived attempt to sober up. He sat at his kitchen table, trying to get his thoughts together… Could he convince Molly that the clinic wasn't a good idea? She could be an extremely stubborn woman when she wanted to be. She'd take a lot of convincing, but it had to be worth a try. There was nothing to lose and everything to gain. He had to give it his best shot.

Beringer staggered into his lounge and picked up the phone before dialling Molly's number… He wouldn't be able to live with himself if Galbraith abused his godson. His old friendships were well and truly on the line.

The ringtone sounded for what seemed like an age before Molly picked up the receiver and said, 'Hello.'

'Hello, Molly. It's Phil. Have you got time for a quick chat?'

'Are you pissed?'

'What a question! It's nice to talk to you as well. No, Molly, honestly, I've had a couple of pints with Mike, but that's all.'

'If this is some pathetic attempt at marriage guidance on behalf of that weak-willed mate of yours, you can tell him to leave that tart before talking to me about the future. He must think I'm a complete idiot.'

'He does want you back as it happens, Molly. But I'm calling about Anthony's appointment with Galbraith.'

'What about it?'

'You know I love Tony, don't you?'

'I'm tired, Phil. If you've got something to say, just say it and let me get back to the television.'

'I don't think it's a good idea, Molly. I really don't think Tony needs that kind of intervention.'

'You've got no idea what he's been like, Phil. He needs help. The doctor's making his case a priority.'

Beringer blew the air from his mouth with a barely audible whistle. 'I work with children like Tony all the time, Molly. It's what I do day in, day out. He just needs some consistency and reassurance about the future. That would better come from you and Mike than a stranger, however well-qualified. I can't make it any clearer than that.'

'I'm not so sure, Phil. The first appointment went a lot better than I could have hoped. I've seen positive changes in Tony. I don't know what the doctor did exactly, but whatever it was, it seems to be working.'

Beringer closed his eyes and searched for an adequate response… This wasn't going his way. 'I don't think it's got anything to do with the clinic, Molly. If Tony's mood and behaviour has improved as much as Mike said it had, there's no way that's down to one appointment at the clinic. You and Mike seem to be addressing your differences at last. I'm certain Tony's responding to that. Just give him time. That's all he needs.'

'I'm not so sure, Phil. I wasn't persuaded about going myself at first. But it really seems to be helping. The doctor's a really nice guy. A bit odd I suppose, but he really seems to care about his patients. What harm can another appointment do?'

'Promise me you'll give it more thought, please.'

'I don't know what this is about, Phil. But, if it means that much to you, yes, I'll think about it. Now go and sleep it off.'

Chapter 16

It was chilly in the Mailer household at 6:30 a.m. on a frosty Welsh winter morning, and the central heating wouldn't be coming on for another half hour. Molly shivered against the cold, and hurriedly pulled on one of Mike's old, red replica, Wales rugby shirts and an unfashionable pink cardigan bought cheaply in the local market the previous week. She crept across the landing, holding her white Dunlop daps in one hand, and after a brief bathroom visit, headed downstairs to make herself some much needed breakfast. Molly had slept somewhat fitfully after Beringer's phone call, and concluded that a mug of sweet peppermint tea and a large bowl of sugary Kellogg's Frosties were entirely justified in the circumstances.

She sat at the kitchen table trying not to think about the next morning's appointment, trying not to think about the phone call, and attempting to relax.

But she couldn't stop her mind racing… Had Mike put Phil up to it? He never did have a very high opinion of psychiatry or the people who required it. 'Psychobabble for needy people', wasn't that what he'd called it when one of his colleagues saw a psychologist after a mugging? But, if that was the case, why had Phil been so willing to support him? He was a therapist himself, wasn't he? Not the same as the doctor, but similar. Was there something more to it? There had to be, surely. He'd sounded genuine. Or was she overthinking it and in danger of becoming paranoid? There was only one way to find out, and she needed answers.

Molly picked up the phone in the hall and dialled Mike's number… What was she worrying about? If she woke her sleeping husband and his new love, that was all right with her.

Molly swore silently under her breath when she heard Tina's chirpy girlish voice at the other end of the line. She grimaced, and spoke through gritted teeth, trying her utmost to sound suitably confident and assertive. 'I need to speak to Mike. It's his wife.'

'He's still asleep, Molly. I'll ask him to ring you later. Was it really necessary to phone so early?'

Molly bit the tip of her tongue, resisting the temptation to yell a stream of heartfelt insults… How could anyone be so very irritating? 'It's urgent, Tina. Just get him. Now, please.'

'Molly?'

'And a good morning to you as well, Mike. Tina sounded a little put out. I hope I haven't disturbed your domestic bliss?'

'Why have you rung, Molly?'

'I've had Phil on the phone last night, talking about Tony. Did *you* put him up to it?'

'What? No! We had a game of squash after work as usual, but we didn't talk about Tony.'

'You never were a very good liar, Mike. You might want to try being honest for once in your sad life. He was obviously pissed when he rang. How stupid do you think I am? Don't answer that by the way.'

'We had a couple of pints after the game. That was all.'

'Really? A couple? I'm sure you did, Mike. Now, what about Anthony?'

Mike listened intently for a second or two, confirmed that Tina was in the shower, and spoke in a quiet whisper. 'Look, Mo. I told Phil about the clinic.'

'So, why the denial?'

Mike sighed. 'Phil sounded genuinely concerned. That's the truth! I just didn't want you thinking that his call was down to me.'

'So what exactly did he say?'

'Um… something about children being labelled. He said it can follow kids when they go up to secondary school.'

'Anything else?'

'That any improvement in Tony's behaviour can't be down to one appointment at the clinic. I tend to agree with him to be honest, Mo. What did the doctor actually do after all? He talked, asked questions and handed out a few sweets. What did that achieve?'

‘Anything else, Mike? Anything at all?’

Should he say anything more? Phil had probably told her anyway. Of course he had. She was asking questions she already had the answer to. ‘He said that Tony was feeling better because we’re talking again.’

‘Yeah, Phil said much the same thing to me. But, I’m not so sure, Mike. Why the sudden change in Tony? The more I think about it… the doctor must have helped. What other explanation is there? He seems like a different boy. I’m not saying Tony’s been the perfect child since the appointment. I wouldn’t want that anyway. But he does seem happier. He really does. And Dr Galbraith seemed to think that he needs more help, not less. He said it’s urgent. Why would he say that if it wasn’t true? What if I cancel, and Tony gets worse again? He obviously likes the doctor. Why not give it another go?’

‘Look, Mo. Phil should know about this stuff. But if you think it’s a good idea, I’m happy to go along with it.’

‘Anything for an easy life, eh, Mike?’

Mike scratched his head… She had it spot on as usual. Was he really that predictable? ‘It’s not like that, Mo. I just trust your judgement, love.’

‘You are seriously winding me up, Mike. Just pick us up in the morning if you can spare your precious time. And don’t even think about being late.’

‘Bloody hell, Mo. I won’t be. See you in the morning.’

Chapter 17

Phillip Beringer dragged himself out of bed at 8:40 a.m. on Thursday 30, January. He cursed crudely, forcefully threw his box of herbal sleeping tablets across his bedroom, and headed downstairs to ring in sick for the first time in over three years, feigning a severe migraine.

After a brief bathroom visit he headed to the kitchen to fetch some breakfast, and sat in the lounge-cum-dining room in his striped flannelette pyjamas. He drank semi-skimmed milk from the carton, and chewed on a half-cooked piece of stale toast that he'd smothered in Marmite, from the distinctive bulbous glass pot balanced precariously on the grubby arm of his armchair.

Beringer gulped down the last of the milk, casually propelled the remaining bread crust across the room into a wastepaper bin located immediately next to the gas fire, and rose stiffly from his chair to switch on the television. He stood in front of the screen, pressed various buttons and reviewed the available channels, before quickly deciding that nothing on offer was going to distract him for very long. He switched the set off and picked up the phone… He'd been listening to other people's problems for years. Where were they when he needed someone to talk to?

He placed the phone back on its receiver… Should he ring anybody at all?

Beringer balanced on a three-legged stool next to the phone for almost five minutes, trying to make a decision… What if Molly decided to take Anthony to his appointment despite his advice? It was a significant possibility. She seemed far from convinced by his argument. Perhaps he should have another word with Mike? No, that was completely pointless. It was Molly who made the decisions when it came to their children. He'd given it his best shot. But was that good enough? Was doing nothing more and living in hope really a viable option?

He stood up and kicked the stool over with the ball of his bare foot… Like fuck it was.

Beringer picked up the phone again, and tapped the handset repeatedly on his thigh… He'd already ruled out talking to Nicholson. Talking to someone within the area was always going to be potentially risky to the investigation, and to his career for that matter. What about someone from his old college days? He was still on speaking terms with one or two of them.

He weighed up his limited options… What about Bernie? He was in child protection in the north of England somewhere. He was a down-to-earth sort of bloke with a lot of relevant experience. They'd got pissed together a few times in the old days as young men, when blissfully oblivious to the future realities of the professional lives they'd so naïvely chosen. He may be worth talking to. Why not give it a try? There weren't any other obvious candidates.

Beringer took his contacts book from the windowsill below the lounge window and flicked through the well-thumbed pages until he eventually located Bernard Gormley's work number.

'Good morning, can I speak to Mr Gormley, please?'

'I can put you through to the duty social worker, if that helps.'

'It's a personal call. I'm an old mate of Bern.'

'Who shall I say is calling?'

'Phillip Beringer.'

'Thank you, Mr Beringer. I'll see if he's available.'

'Hello, Phil, it's Bern. You're a blast from the past.'

'Yeah, it's been a while, Bern. How's the wife and kids?'

'Good, thanks. Are you still living the single life?'

'Yeah, I'm afraid so, mate. Who'd have me?'

'You've got a point there, Phil.'

'Look, Bern, this isn't a social call.'

Bernard Gormley laughed. 'Yeah, I guessed that much, Phil. What can I do for you?'

'I could do with some advice. Have you got five minutes to talk?'

‘As long as you need.’

‘Bern, this has to be on a strictly confidential basis, yeah?’

‘Goes without saying.’

‘We’re investigating a paedophile ring. It’s big. Everyone’s under a lot of pressure.’

‘And?’

‘The police are looking to make coordinated arrests in the not-too-distant future. We’re doing everything we can to prevent any of the suspects getting any clue of what’s coming. You know, for obvious reasons.’

‘And you’re having to live with various kids being at risk while the investigation continues. Not an easy thing to do.’

‘No, it’s not, Bern. But it’s become more personal than that.’

‘What are you talking about?’

‘One of the suspects is a child psychiatrist.’

‘Oh, for fuck’s sake.’

‘It gets worse, Bern. A close mate of mine’s son is due to see the bastard tomorrow. I’m the boy’s godfather.’

‘Oh, that’s bad! Does the boy match the victim profile?’

‘It seems so.’

‘And you haven’t said anything to either of the parents? I’m not sure I could just stand by and let things happen.’

‘I’m not just standing by, Bern. That’s why I’m on the fucking phone. I’ve already tried to influence the parents in the direction of cancelling the appointment, but the mother still seems keen. She’s the sort of woman who’s hard to derail once her mind’s set on something, if you know what I mean. I don’t know what the hell to do next, to be honest. Obviously I want to tell them, but if the doctor gets even the slightest hint that something’s up, the consequences for the investigation could be dire.’

‘You’re not wrong there, Phil, but…’

‘But what?’

‘You need to use your imagination, mate. Get creative.’

‘I’ve spent most of the night trying to get creative, Bern.’

‘How will they get to the appointment?’

‘By car, but what the hell’s that got to do with anything?’

‘How many have they got?’

‘What, cars?’

‘Yeah, that’s what I asked you.’

‘Just the one!’

‘Disable the engine, smash the windscreen, syphon the petrol. Do something. It’s got to be better than doing fuck all.’

‘Really? You’re telling me to vandalise the man’s car?’

‘That’s what I’m telling you.’

‘What’s that going to achieve? Even if they don’t get there, the mother’s likely to arrange another appointment.’

‘I’m not saying it would resolve the situation long term, Phil. But it may just buy you some time.’

Beringer shook his head. ‘And that’s the best you’ve got?’

‘That’s the best I’ve got.’

Chapter 18

Dr Galbraith woke with a start on Friday 31, January. He'd spent the night sleeping intermittently in the recliner chair in one corner of his study next to a faulty radiator, and he was cold, stiff and tired. He stood, raised both arms in the air to stretch his back, yawned loudly, and smiled… Was today the day? It could be. It was something to aim for. But he had to be careful. He shouldn't rush things.

The doctor showered and shaved before dropping to the bathroom floor and doing seventy-five rapid press-ups, which left him only slightly out of breath. He jumped athletically to his feet and admired his reflection in his magnified shaving mirror before heading towards his palatial bedroom to get dressed.

He chose a Prince of Wales check suit made from an exquisite lambs' wool cloth, a pristine white Egyptian cotton shirt, and a highly polished pair of black leather Oxford brogues. He finished the outfit off with his favoured gold cufflinks, and a brightly coloured cartoon tie adorned with a sporting logo, which he considered Anthony would almost certainly appreciate. He stared into a framed mirror hanging to the side of the king-size bed in the light of the window and adjusted his hair, carefully coaxing the precise side parting into place. Finally, he swept nonexistent fluff from both shoulders with a cherry wood clothes brush. Dr Galbraith looked in the mirror for one final time, drinking in his image, and decided that he looked truly wonderful. He left his bedroom, slammed the door behind him, strode purposefully across the landing, and descended the stairs two or three steps at a time.

Dr Galbraith sat at the kitchen table, actively ignoring Cynthia who was standing next to the range cooker cleaning and recleaning a spotless granite worktop. She was still cleaning the same worktop when he finally finished breakfast about twenty minutes later.

The doctor stood and glared at the back of her head. 'I initially thought that you'd actually managed to do a reasonable job of preparing breakfast, for once in your miserable life.'

She steadied herself, and slowly turned to face him. 'Initially, dear?'

'The position of my glass was two millimetres out of place.'

'I checked twice, dear. I used the ruler. I'm sure…'

He took a step towards her. 'Are you calling me a liar?'

'No, of course not, dear. I would never…'

'Two millimetres isn't acceptable. I shouldn't have to tell you that.'

Cynthia fought to control her trembling body; she fought to control her bladder, and she searched for a response, any response that may placate him… Say something, Cynthia. Say something. 'I'm s-sorry, dear. I'll do better. I promise I'll do better. Have you g-got everything you need for w-work, dear?'

He approached her slowly, placing his face only inches from hers, and spat his words, spraying her face with buttery yellow saliva. 'Don't pretend you care about my work, bitch.'

'But I do care, dear.'

He swivelled his head and glared towards the door. 'I can hear your fucking brats crying. You would be well advised to sort them out before I do.'

The couple's two young daughters were standing, ashen-faced and weeping at the top of the stairs when Cynthia reached the landing. No one spoke, but Cynthia smiled softly, and gestured to them to come to her. Both girls walked forward and hugged her tightly with eager arms. Cynthia held them close, shielding them from their cruel world, until they heard the front door slam shut a minute or two later. She forced a thin smile and spoke in a hushed whisper. 'It's not Daddy's fault, girls. I must try harder. We all must.'

Dr Galbraith sat back in the driver's seat, red-faced and panting hard. He took slow, deep, deliberate breaths as the pressure in his head mounted… Think, man, think. Picture the scene: the little bastard hanging there, helpless and at his mercy. That's it, that's it, make it big, make it bright, make it loud.

He squirmed and twitched and sweated and struggled to relax as the pounding gradually subsided and became bearable… That's it, that's it. Now all he had to do was make fantasy reality.

Dr Galbraith mopped his brow with the sleeve of his jacket… Stay positive, man, stay positive. At least now he could move his project forward. Not as fast as he would like to, certainly. But, forward nonetheless. The little bastard would soon be within his grasp. Albeit for only an hour, and with his ghastly, interfering bitch mother hovering somewhere in the background like a foul odour. Today was not the day he'd live out his ultimate fantasies, he had to accept that. But it would bring that day nearer. That was something to be grateful for. Something to celebrate. Something to be proud of. A sweet sorrow, so to speak. Today, however frustratingly, he would have to be satisfied with whatever he could get away with.

The doctor arrived in the clinic's empty car park much earlier than usual. He secured the vehicle with the click of a button, and smiled as he made his way across the car park… At least his moronic bitch secretary wasn't in work yet.

He strode into the clinic's reception and entered the four-digit-code into the burglar alarm control box with unneeded haste… It felt good to be standing in the empty room, avoiding the usual ritual of good mornings and other nauseating mundane pleasantries with his needy secretary. One day he'd tell the obnoxious bitch exactly what he thought of her.

He clenched his fists, before consciously relaxing his hands… One day, yes, one day.

Dr Galbraith darted from room to room, repeatedly checking that everything was ready: video camera, yes; video recorder, yes; new videotape, yes; television, yes; and microphones, yes… Everything in its place and working perfectly. Things were well on course. Just one more thing to organise.

He lowered himself to the floor of the therapy room and urgently arranged several children's videos on the shelf immediately below the television. He ensured that all but one were suitable only for very young children: Postman Pat, Noddy, Paddington Bear, Play School, and the like… Yes, yes, they were ideal.

He picked up a Best Goal compilation, discarded the tape behind him for later disposal, and took an unlabelled videotape from his briefcase, before putting it in the case and placing it back on the shelf with the others. He relaxed momentarily and smiled… It was a simple technique. One he'd used many times over the years. But, he couldn't be too careful. There was always an element of risk and no room for complacency. Staying focused was everything.

Dr Galbraith sat at his desk and repeatedly reviewed the plan in his mind—point by point, again and again and again… Was following the tried and tested process he'd utilised so many times before, giving him the temporary illusion of a self-control he no longer possessed? He had to be sure everything was right. He had to avoid any potential pitfalls. Think, man, think!

'Good morning, Doctor, you're an early bird today.'

He checked the clock… Oh for fuck's sake. The bitch was early. Why today of all days?

He pictured her bloody and dying, and smiled… Game face. Come on, man, game face. 'And a good morning to you, my dear girl! Is that a new blouse you're wearing?'

Sharon giggled like a self-conscious schoolgirl. 'What, this old thing? No, I've had it for ages.'

'Well, it looks marvellous, my dear.'

Sharon beamed.

Gullible bitch. 'I need you to perform an errand for me a little later, my dear girl. After you've welcomed Anthony and his charming mother to our clinic. Nothing too strenuous of course. Simply delivering an urgent report to the social services in Swansea for me. It will take you an hour or so I expect, nothing more.'

'When exactly would you like me to take it?'

He grinned and adopted a relaxed persona, sitting half on and half off one corner of her desk. 'Let's not worry about that for now, my dear.

I'll let you know nearer the time. Why don't you make us both a nice cup of coffee to start our day properly?'

Sharon frowned… Something wasn't right. It wasn't particularly warm in the room; why was he sweating? His shirt was sticking to his body. And why was his left eye twitching? He was usually so composed. Should she say something or ignore it? Yes, of course she should. They were friends, after all. 'Are you all right, Doctor? You look a little red in the face. Can I get you something?'

Get a grip, man. The bitch is onto something. 'Nice of you to notice, my dear girl. Nothing to worry about. You know I don't like to complain. I suspect the girls brought some winter virus or other back from school. It's inevitable at this time of year I'm afraid.'

'You must look after yourself better, Doctor.'

Yes, yes, he was doing well. Keep it up, keep it up. 'The entire family has gone down with it. Poor Cynthia was in a terrible state when I left the house this morning. I really hate to leave her like that. Now then, how about that coffee you were about to make us?'

'You sit there and try to relax, Doctor. It won't be long before the Mailers arrive.' She picked up her handbag and went to open it. 'Would you like some Solpadeine? I'm sure I've got some in here somewhere.'

'No thanks, my dear girl. Just a coffee will be wonderful.'

The doctor slumped at his desk, staring at the clock, watching the second hand, and willing it to move faster. He fantasised, but this time it failed to alleviate his escalating distress. He clawed at his scalp with short clipped nails and clamped his cupped hands over his ears… If he didn't get his hands on the little bastard soon, the consequences to his wellbeing could prove insurmountable.

Chapter 19

Mike Mailer had taken full advantage of the opportunity for a lay in, and finally dragged himself out of bed at 9:12 a.m. He put on the previous day's pants, socks, shirt and tie, and one of his two low-budget supermarket work suits, before casually running an electric shaver over his face on the way to the bathroom.

Mike checked the Seiko divers' watch he'd received as a Christmas gift from Molly two years previously… Nearly half past nine. Time for a quick coffee and a piece of toast smothered in peanut butter and strawberry jam if he got a shift on.

Mike left the flat about twenty minutes later, in the certain knowledge that he was cutting it fine… But, then he always did. That was his way, and there was nothing wrong with that.

He reached into one trouser pocket, then another, and finally found his car keys in the right inside pocket of his pinstripe polyester jacket… Sod's law. Why was it always the last pocket you looked in?

He clutched the keys tightly in one hand, and began jogging the hundred yards or more along the shiny wet pavement, to where he'd finally found an adequate parking space for the XR3 the previous evening. As he approached the car he spotted a flat tyre, then another, then another, and then another… Bastard vandals! They'd been slashed. That was going to cost him. High-performance tyres didn't come cheap.

Mike checked the time… Fuck it!

He turned on his heels, and began sprinting back in the direction of the flat.

Come on Mo, answer the bloody phone, girl.

'Hello.'

'Hello, Mo. It's Mike.'

'Where the hell are you?'

'Some jealous bastard's slashed all the tyres on my car.'

'So you're not on your way?'

'I've only just found out; literally five minutes ago, love.'

'If this is some pathetic rouse to avoid your responsibilities, I'll kick your arse for you.'

'No, straight up, Mo. I'm totally gutted.'

'Well, what the hell do you expect me to do now? There's no way we're getting to Anthony's appointment on time, is there?'

'I'm really sorry, Mo. But, what do you expect me to do about it?'

'Think of something.'

'Well, why don't you order a taxi?'

'I'm completely skint, Mike!'

'I'll give you the money.'

'Oh, really, that'll make a nice change.'

'Don't be like that, Mo. I'm trying my best here. Why don't you contact the clinic and explain you're running late? You can always arrange another appointment if you have to, but you never know your luck.'

'Right, I'll ring the clinic. You order a taxi and get here as fast as you can.'

'You want me to arrange a taxi from here?'

'Yes, Mike, I've got about fifty pence in my purse. Now get on with it please.'

Mike began searching through the yellow pages for the number of a local cab firm, while Molly contacted the clinic and tried to sound as conciliatory as possible when Sharon answered the phone with a cheery, 'Hello.'

'Hello, it's Mrs Mailer, Molly Mailer, Anthony's mother. I'm afraid we're running late. I've got a taxi on the way, but there's no way we can be there on time.'

'I'm sorry to hear that, Mrs Mailer. The doctor has gone out of his way to accommodate your son. Would you like me to send out another appointment?'

‘I am so very sorry. We would have been there by now, but some idiot damaged my husband’s car tyres. As I said, there’s a taxi on the way to pick us up as I speak. Would it be possible to ask the doctor if he can still see us?’

‘Well, I really don’t think…’

‘Please, Sharon, just ask him. I’d really appreciate it.’

‘Oh, I suppose I could, just this once. I’ll speak to him and give you a call back.’

‘Thank you so much. But, do you mind if I hold on. I’m expecting the taxi at any second.’

‘I’ll be as quick as I can, Mrs Mailer. But no promises.’

Dr Galbraith was standing facing the window when Sharon entered his office. She couldn’t put her finger on why, but there was an almost tangible tension in the air when he turned and asked, ‘Who was on the phone?’

‘The Mailer family are running late, Doctor. Shall I rearrange the appointment?’

He suddenly felt light-headed, and the room became an impressionist blur of bland colours. ‘You stated that they’re running late, Sharon. That suggests they still intend to attend today?’

Sharon hurried towards him and took his arm. ‘I think you’d better sit down, Doctor. You’re looking terribly pale.’

He shifted uneasily in his seat, closed his eyes, and pinched the bridge of his nose tightly between forefinger and thumb. ‘Is the Mailer boy coming today, or not?’

‘Well, yes, they’re trying to get here, but…’

Dr Galbraith’s relief was virtually overwhelming, and he struggled to contain his burgeoning excitement before responding. ‘I will see them as soon as they arrive, Sharon. If I have any further appointments booked for later today, please ring around and cancel them.’

The red Citroen BX taxi cab pulled into the clinic’s car park approximately twenty-five minutes later, and stopped directly alongside the doctor’s Daimler. Mike hurriedly wound down the front passenger side window while Molly and Anthony disembarked, and said, 'Do you want me to come in with you, Mo? It's no problem at all if you do.' He waited for an answer with bated breath... Please say no, Mo. Please say no.

Molly thought for a second or two, and quickly concluded that it wasn't time to roll out the welcome mat just yet. She turned to face him and shook her head. 'No need to panic, Mike. The doctor just wants to see me and Tony this time. But, I want you and the taxi back here in exactly an hour. Okay?'

'That's great, Mo, I'll see you then.'

Molly broke into a mirthless smile... Mike was nothing if not predictable.

Dr Galbraith watched from behind his office blinds, as he had two weeks previously... No, no, no, what the hell was the damn father doing there?

He turned away from the window and fought the impulse to vomit... Things couldn't go wrong now. Not now, not when he was so close.

The doctor threw open his office door, and ran past his stunned secretary in the direction of the car park. As he burst outside into the bright winter sunshine he saw the taxi driving away with Mike still ensconced in the front seat. He stopped dead in his tracks, acutely aware of the ludicrous nature of his actions and the negative impression they may give... What the hell was he doing? What could he say? How could he explain himself this time?

Dr Galbraith closed his eyes, quickly reopened them, and screamed, *get a grip, man*, inside his head. 'Ah, what a shame! I was very much hoping to have a quick word with Mr Mailer before he left.'

Molly smiled nervously. 'He'll be back in an hour if you still need to speak to him.'

Dr Galbraith patted Anthony on the back with the palm of his right hand... Had he gotten away with it? It seemed so. 'Not to worry. How are you, young man? I've been awaiting your arrival. I have a rather nice box of Quality Street in my office drawer with your name on it, if your mum's agreeable? What do you say, Mum? Can Anthony have some chocolates?'

Molly replied in the affirmative and followed Dr Galbraith into reception with Anthony's hand in hers.

'If you both take a seat in my office, I'll have a quick word with Sharon here, and be with you very shortly.'

'Sharon, my dear girl, that report I mentioned earlier is in the out-tray. Now would be an excellent time to deliver it.'

'I could send it by special delivery, Doctor.'

'I thought I'd made it perfectly clear that it has to be delivered today!'

She averted her eyes and stood to leave.

Dr Galbraith smiled warmly… The needy bitch. 'Your efforts are much appreciated, Sharon. Please ensure you enjoy a nice lunch before you return. You deserve it, my dear. Now off you go. It can't wait a second longer.'

She smiled tentatively, collected the document, and headed for the exit.

Dr Galbraith buttoned his suit jacket to conceal his burgeoning erection before joining Molly and Anthony in his magnolia office. He sat facing them both, but spoke directly to Molly. 'It's truly wonderful to see you again, my dear girl. But there is absolutely no need for you to stay. Anthony will be fine in my care. Absolutely fine. You can collect him in precisely an hour.'

The doctor stood, opened a desk drawer, and took out the aforementioned box of confectionery. He allowed Anthony to choose a chocolate first, and then returned his attention to Molly, who was about to leave. 'Take a handful before you go, my dear girl. Go on, take some. Why not treat yourself? What do you say, Anthony? Should Mum take some sweets before she leaves us together?'

Anthony smiled and nodded twice… If spending an hour talking to the doctor meant eating sweets and helped get his dad home, he was willing to do it.

Molly took a single circular toffee wrapped in shiny silver foil and golden cellophane from the box, and placed a reassuring hand on Anthony's shoulder as she prepared to leave. 'It's going to be okay, cariad. The doctor's going to have a nice chat with you, and I'll be back with you before you know it.'

Anthony smiled half-heartedly, and Molly persisted. 'I'll see you in an hour, cariad. Perhaps Dad will take us both for a burger later.'

'Okay, Mum.'

She gave him a nervous wave and hurried from the clinic without looking back.

Dr Galbraith followed Molly as far as the exit, and watched as she crossed the car park far too slowly for his liking… About time. The bitch was gone at last.

He locked the door, neglected to reset the alarm, and hurried back into reception… He had an hour, just an hour; but he had to stay in control, despite the pressure, despite the temptation.

'Anthony, my dear boy, I'm sorry to have kept you waiting. I think your mother's gone for a pleasant stroll in the winter sunshine. To the park I suspect. And why not, eh? It's a lovely day for it. Now then, I have a couple of things I need to get on with before we talk together. Why don't you go into the therapy room and choose a suitable video? I'm sure a clever boy like you knows how to switch the television and VCR on, don't you?'

Anthony rose to his feet and nodded.

Dr Galbraith placed his arm around his shoulder and gently guided him towards the door. 'Of course you do. Of course you do.'

The doctor went to open the door, but suddenly paused. 'There is one thing we've forgotten. What do you think that is, young man?'

Anthony looked up into the doctor's face, and shook his head anxiously.

Dr Galbraith laughed. 'The chocolates, we mustn't forget the chocolates.'

Anthony relaxed immediately and smiled.

Dr Galbraith picked up the enticing blue and red box and handed it to Anthony with a grin. 'There you go, young man. Now choose a film, put it on, and eat as many of those as you like whilst you're waiting for me.'

A half smile flickered across Anthony's face. 'Okay.'

The doctor rubbed Anthony's short red hair gently with the palm of his hand. 'I will see you in a minute or two, my dear boy. Find something you want to watch.'

Anthony unwrapped two chocolates, stuffed them both into his mouth, and sat on the floor sorting through the various videos, as Dr Galbraith removed a framed colour picture of his two daughters from a wall and watched through a small peephole drilled in the partition for the purpose.

Dr Galbraith checked the clock, cursed quietly under his breath, and grasped his head with both hands… Come on, you little bastard. Come on. Put it on. Put the fucking thing on.

Anthony quickly discarded all but the Best Goals compilation. He couldn't believe his luck… One gem amongst a pretty poor bunch.

Anthony switched the television on, took the video from its case, placed it in the VCR, and pressed the play button before moving a large navy blue corduroy beanbag nearer to the television set, and waiting for the film to start. When it eventually came onto the screen he froze and dropped the box of confectionery to the floor, but couldn't look away… That wasn't football! Why didn't the men have clothes on? Why were they wearing masks? What were they doing to that boy?

Anthony began weeping uncontrollably. 'Mummy! Mummy! I want my mummy!'

Dr Galbraith sweated, twitched, panted and salivated as his body flooded with adrenaline… That's it, you little bastard. That's it!

He checked the clock again… Give him time. Give the little bastard time; don't rush it.

He checked his watch… The hands were moving too quickly. Far too quickly! Should he go in? Was the little bastard sufficiently distressed?

Yes, yes, of course he was. Time was getting on. It was time to expedite matters.

Dr Galbraith entered the room and stood motionless for a moment without speaking.

Anthony turned towards him and continued calling for his mother.

'What on earth's wrong, my dear boy? Wasn't there a film you liked?'

'Where's Mummy? I want my mummy.'

The doctor approached the television and watched for a second or two before finally reaching down and switching it off. 'You really shouldn't have watched that film, Anthony. That's not good, it's not good at all.'

'I want my mummy.'

Dr Galbraith loomed over Anthony, proactively adopting a pensive expression, as if carefully considering his response. 'Oh dear, I've just thought of something terrible. What will your mother and father say if they ever find out what you've watched? Your father would never come home again.' He shook his head forlornly. 'Never!'

Anthony's tears became deep unmanageable sobs that caused his entire body to shake as he fought for breath. He curled up on the floor in the foetal position and began sucking his thumb.

Dr Galbraith sat on the floor next to his prone victim and began stroking his head gently. 'Your mother will be back soon. She's bound to ask why you're upset. And when she does, what shall I tell her? What do you think she'll say when she finds out what you've done?'

Anthony shook his head silently with a look of trepidation on his face.

'She's going to be very, very angry.'

Silence.

Dr Galbraith said nothing more for a few seconds, but continued stroking Anthony's head. 'I really should tell your mother, but I'm your friend. What do you think, Tony? Friends don't tell, do they?'

Anthony shook his head.

'If you promise to be a good boy, I won't tell her. It will be our secret. That's what best friends do, Anthony. They keep secrets. Now, what are we going to do until your mother returns?'

Molly sat on a park bench directly opposite the small man-made lake, and watched two mallard ducks paddle by, whilst thinking of picnics past. She smiled as she pictured the scene: ball games, smiling children, laughter, the warm sun caressing her skin, vivid green trees and multicoloured summer flowers that pleased the senses, and shimmering water, alive with wildfowl and lakeside insects… They were happier times, and the place still held fond memories.

She couldn't put her finger on why, but as she reminisced, Molly began feeling increasingly uneasy about leaving Anthony alone with the doctor… Surely there wasn't anything to worry about? He was a doctor, after all. He had an excellent reputation. The GP had said as much. Was she being stupid? He couldn't be nicer. Then, why was she worrying? Was it due to Phil's phone call? Was there something he hadn't told her? There had better not be, for his sake.

Molly began walking briskly in the direction of the clinic, covering the distance in approximately half the time she'd taken in the original direction. She stood at the entrance to the building, panting to catch her breath, and turned the door handle. But it didn't open. She turned it again, this time with more urgency, and attempted to force the door open with her shoulder… Why was it locked? Surely it shouldn't be locked.

Molly knocked and kept knocking: harder, harder, harder… Why wasn't anyone answering?

She ran around the building… There had to be another door? Surely there was a back door. Yes, there it was, thank God! She turned the handle. Locked! What was going on? What if something was wrong? Something must be wrong. There was a window. It was small. But at least it was open.

Molly paused… Should she climb through the window, or was she being stupid? Was she overreacting? She was probably overreacting. But, what if Tony needed her?

She prised the tiny window open as far as it would go, and somehow squeezed herself through the inadequate gap, tearing one leg of her jeans and grazing her left thigh in the process. She found herself in a small antiquated kitchen in a part of the building she hadn't seen before. She hurried from the room into a brightly lit corridor, and was relieved to see the familiar reception room at the other end. Molly ran the last few steps, stumbled and fell into the room, hitting the thin-carpeted floor with a resounding thud.

Dr Galbraith was towering over Anthony: attempting to ignore his impulses, fighting to stay in control, and cursing the booming in his head, when he heard the sudden unexpected thump emanating from reception… Sharon wouldn't be back for another hour or so. It had to be the bitch mother. He'd locked the door. Of course he had. How the hell had she got in?

The doctor lowered himself to the floor next to Anthony, and placed his face only inches from his. He stared into his panic-stricken eyes and whispered, 'Remember what I said, boy. If your mother and father find out, they will argue. And if they argue, they will never get back together. Do you understand? Never! It would be your fault. Do you understand that?'

Anthony nodded anxiously.

Dr Galbraith stood and helped him to his feet. 'Come on, young man, up you get. Try to stop your damn snivelling. You don't want to upset your mother, do you?'

'No!'

The doctor steered Anthony in the direction of reception, and met Molly as she hurried into his office without knocking… The bitch was suspicious. She was definitely suspicious. 'Ah, Molly my dear, I'm delighted that you're back. I'm glad to say that we've made some excellent progress. Tony did get a little upset when we talked of your marital difficulties, but that's to be expected.'

Anthony pulled away from him, rushed towards his mother, and hugged her tightly without speaking.

Molly pulled her son closer, and glared at the doctor. 'Why was the door locked?'

Focus, man, focus. This had better be good. 'As I explained at our initial appointment, it is absolutely essential that therapy sessions aren't disturbed. Sharon usually sees to that for me, of course, but she's out, as you know.'

Molly frowned… Was locking the door really necessary? Maybe it was. Someone could conceivably have walked in and disturbed Anthony's treatment session. Maybe locking the door was the best option in the circumstances.

She was swallowing it. The bitch was swallowing it. 'What on earth have you done to your leg, my dear girl? You appear to be bleeding rather badly; let me take a look at that for you.'

Molly transferred her weight uneasily from one foot to another… What on earth had she been worrying about? What was she going to say now? 'Oh, I slipped on some ice in the park, Doctor. It's nothing really.'

Dr Galbraith pointed towards his swivel chair and smiled… The bitch was on the defensive. He was back in control. 'Please allow me to be the judge of that, young lady. Take a seat, and let me examine that leg of yours.'

Molly sat as instructed, with Anthony standing close to her with a blank expression on his pallid tear-stained face.

The doctor went down on one knee as if proposing, and gently prised the torn denim from the bloody abrasion… One day the fucking bitch would pay. 'That's going to be absolutely fine, my dear. Stay there for a minute or two and I'll fetch a little damp cotton wool and a plaster from the first-aid box.'

Anthony shook his mother's arm repeatedly. 'Can we go home now, Mummy?'

'There's no need, Doctor. Honestly, I'm fine.'

One fine day, bitch. One fine day. Her time would come. 'You do as you're told, young lady. You don't want it to become infected, do you? It won't take me any time at all.'

Dr Galbraith quickly reappeared balancing a ball of cotton wool, a half-full glass of tepid water, and a large plaster on top of the appointments diary. He knelt again, and placed the items on the floor directly next to his knee… Gullible bitch. 'You try to relax, my dear girl. This may sting a little.'

'Thank you, Doctor.'

He repeatedly dabbed at the wound with the moist cotton wool. 'Right, that's nice and clean again. I'll just dry it quickly and apply the plaster.'

'Thank you.'

'There you go, young lady, all done.' He grinned. 'I can't mend your jeans for you, I'm afraid.'

Molly forced a nervous laugh. 'Thank you again, Doctor.'

Dr Galbraith stood, and placed his right hand on Anthony's shoulder. 'Let's sort out this young man's next appointment. I do have a couple of days off next week, but I think it would be a good idea if I saw Anthony at my home. What do you say, young man?'

Anthony attempted to climb onto his mother's lap.

Molly smiled weakly, and looked at the floor… This was becoming embarrassing. 'Come on now, cariad. You're far too big for that. When have you got in mind, Doctor?'

Dr Galbraith pulled up a seat, turned sideways to face her, and began turning the pages of the diary. 'How about ten o'clock on Tuesday morning? That will be February the fourth. Doesn't time fly?'

'That soon?'

'I don't want to worry you, my dear girl. I really don't. But, Anthony is one of my more urgent cases.'

'Anthony? Really?'

He took a blank sheet of paper from his desktop and wrote down his home address and telephone number in his usual flamboyant flowing copperplate script. 'I look forward to seeing you on Tuesday morning, young man. There's ample room for your mother to park in the street. Just drop him off at my home, Molly, and collect him at the end of his treatment.'

Molly stood and nodded meekly.

Dr Galbraith tapped the diary repeatedly with his pen and adopted a contemplative expression… Should he risk it? Yes, why not? The potential payoff was well worth the minimal additional risk. 'I think we had better allow two hours next time. There's still a great deal of work to do if we're to get Anthony firing on all cylinders again.'

Molly paused and then said, 'Okay. If you think that's really necessary?'

Oh, it's certainly necessary, bitch. 'I'm afraid I do, my dear.'

Dr Galbraith escorted them both as far as the car park, where Mike was waiting impatiently in the same red Citroen taxi cab. Molly struggled into the car's rear seat with Anthony clamped onto her arm like a determined limpet. As the driver manoeuvred the vehicle towards the main road they sat hugging each other tightly and silently, with Anthony's head resting on her shoulder.

Mike swivelled in his seat, peered accusingly at his wife and son, and sighed. 'Is everything all right, Mo? Tony seems upset. I can see him shaking from here. He was as happy as a sandboy when he arrived here an hour ago. What's that about?'

Molly squeezed Anthony's knee and smiled half-heartedly… Mike had a point. She needed time to think. Perhaps she'd been wrong, and therapy wasn't such a good idea after all? 'I don't know what to say to be honest, Mike. Let's leave it for now and have a chat later when we get back to the cottage.'

Anthony pressed his head against Molly's shoulder and began crying again. 'I w-want to go home.'

'What's wrong, cariad?'

'I want to go h-home please, Mum. My tummy's really hurting!'

'Don't you want to go for a burger?'

'I just want to go home, Mummy.'

'All right, cariad. Home it is.'

Chapter 20

'I need to have a private chat with Dad, cariad. Go and play in your bedroom for a while. I'll bring you up a nice mug of hot chocolate and some Jammy Dodgers in a couple of minutes. Do you want a hot-water bottle for your tummy?'

Anthony began slowly ascending the stairs. 'Yes, please, Mum.'

'Get a move on, cariad. I'll be up before you know it.'

Anthony checked for potential intruders under his bed and in the wardrobe before eventually taking a football sticker album from his bedside drawer and opening it on top of his quilt. But he just couldn't concentrate despite the collection's usual fascination… It was good to have Dad home, for sure. But what were they going to talk about?

He hung his head and salty tears began falling on the open pages… What if they'd found out what he saw? The doctor said Dad would never come home again. What if that happened? It would be his fault.

Anthony pushed the album to the floor, and curled up on the bed to await his mother.

Molly appeared at his bedroom door a few minutes later, holding a black and white Swansea City supporters mug full to the brim with hot sweet cocoa and a generous plate of Anthony's favourite sugary biscuits. She placed them carefully on the bedside cabinet, retrieved the discarded album and several loose stickers from the carpet, and sat on the single bed next to her son. 'What is it, cariad? You were in such a good mood this morning. Is it something you talked about at the clinic? Did the doctor say something that upset you?'

'No!'

'What is it then? Something must have upset you?'

'My tummy hurts.'

She rubbed his shoulder affectionately. 'Come on, cariad, into bed with you. Drink your cocoa, and I'll be back up again with the hot-water bottle as soon as I've talked to Dad. Now, stop those tears. I'll get you some extra pillows so you can sit up properly and enjoy your snack.'

Anthony forced a fleeting smile and nodded his reluctant agreement.

Molly made a strong coffee for Mike and a peppermint tea for herself, before joining him in the lounge, where he was watching a daytime property programme on an ageing Bush television set that was well past its best. She handed him his mug, switched the television off pointedly, and sat next to him on the three-seater settee.

'How's he doing up there?'

'Not too great to be honest, Mike. I'm beginning to wonder if Phil was right after all. Perhaps the therapy isn't such a good idea.'

Mike took a sip of coffee and wiped the milky moustache from his top lip with the back of his hand. 'What happened to your knee?'

'Don't change the subject, Mike. I want to know what you really think. None of your usual avoidance bullshit.'

Mike shifted uneasily in his seat… He couldn't avoid answering, however tempting it was to try.

'I've had my doubts from the start, to be candid, Mo. I'm certain Phil's right. What Anthony needs is for us two to stop arguing and get back together as soon as possible.'

She glared at him, and said, 'Really?'

'I know this is all down to me, Mo. Please give me the chance to put it right.'

'Now really isn't the time for this, Mike. When you've actually left that tart, instead of just talking about it, we may be able to talk about us getting back together, but not before. Get that into your thick head. Let's concentrate on Tony's treatment for now, please. He's got another appointment in a few days, and we need to make a decision one way or the other. Do you think I should cancel Tuesday's appointment or not?'

Mike appeared perplexed. 'Tuesday? Why so soon?'

'The doctor seems to think it's urgent.'

'I don't know what to say for the best, Mo. You seemed really keen after the first appointment.'

'Man up, Mike, grow a pair of balls, and say what you really think for once in your life.'

He averted his eyes and drained his mug, stalling for time… Here goes. 'I don't think the therapy's a good idea, Mo. As I said, I've thought that from the start. I don't like psychiatry, you know that. Look at the state the poor boy's in today. That should tell us something, shouldn't it?'

'We have to be absolutely certain, Mike. Tony seemed so much better after the first appointment. It's not a decision we can afford to get wrong. I was so sure the therapy was helping him. The doctor's a nice man, and he means well. I know that. And he did tell us that things may get worse before they get better. You have to admit that.'

'Yeah, he did, but I'm still not convinced, Mo.'

'We could just be at that stage, I guess. But I didn't anticipate him being as upset as he obviously is. Maybe we could cancel and then rearrange another appointment if it proves necessary.'

'I'm sure you're right, Mo. Do you want me to talk to Phil again?'

'No thanks, Mike. What's the point? We already know exactly what he thinks. He made his views perfectly clear to both of us. I'll give it some more thought over the weekend and ring the clinic on Monday if I decide to cancel.'

'That makes sense, love. I'll head up and see Tony before getting off, if that's all right with you?'

'Yeah, no problem, he wouldn't want you to go without saying goodbye.'

'Thanks, Mo. I'll give you a ring over the weekend to see how things are going.'

'Okay, Mike. Thanks for today. I'll speak to you soon.'

As Mike walked away from the cottage, he finally decided it was time to stop prevaricating… Molly was right. He had to man up. His relationship with Tina had run its course. It was time to leave her and put his family first for a change. It was what they wanted. It was what *he* wanted. Why not do something about it? Tina was all looks and little substance. Was he really that stupid? How had a drunken shag in the back of his car ended up as a full blown affair?

He giggled quietly to himself… What was it that Phil had said on the subject? He'd been thinking with his dick. He'd never said a truer word.

Mike did his best to avoid Tina when he eventually arrived at work, and left early for a nonexistent dental appointment, after arranging for a local garage to collect the XR3 and fit four new, costly, high-performance tyres. By the time his taxi arrived at Highgrove garage, the Escort was already on the ramp, and he only had to wait for half an hour or so before paying the unwelcome bill and driving off with a heavy heart.

Mike checked his Seiko… Only about twenty minutes before Tina arrived back at the flat.

He dashed from room to room, frantically stuffing his meagre belongings into a red Puma sports bag and two large black plastic bin bags taken from a kitchen drawer. He threw all three bags into the back seat of the convertible and rushed back into the flat to double-check that he had everything, and to write Tina a hurried note of explanation… He was being cowardly; he was taking the easy option yet again, he knew that full well. But there had already been more than enough drama for one day.

He wrote a short scribbled message to the effect that he missed his children, didn't love her and still loved his wife, and left it in the narrow galley kitchen propped up against the kettle, before making his urgent escape.

As he drove away with the accelerator pressed to the floor, the convertible's tyres screeched loudly, leaving black rubber fragments on the dark tarmac. He sped down two fast darkening streets lined with modest terraced houses, and turned off into a quiet side street that he knew Tina was unlikely to drive through on her journey home. He pulled the car up next to a faded red phone box, and tried to ignore the stench of stale urine permeating the air as he dialled Molly's number. She answered within seconds, but before she could even say hello, Mike was shouting into the receiver, 'I've done it, Mo. I've left her. Can I come home, love?'

Molly punched the air in silent triumph, but immediately cautioned herself and actively adopted a sombre tone. 'Do you really think it's going to be that easy, Mike? Have you really thought about what you've put me and the kids through? Do I need to jog your memory for you? You shat on us from a great height. There were times I would have been quite happy never to see your ugly face again. I need you to understand that.'

'I'm sorry, Mo. Really I am, but where do you expect me to go.'

'That's not my problem, Mike, but if you ever go near that tart again, that's the end for us. No more chances. If you can get that into your thick skull, come over tomorrow evening and we can talk about the future.'

'That's great, Mo, what time?'

'About sevenish, we need to set some ground rules if there's any chance of this working.'

'Thanks, Mo, it's appreciated. See you tomorrow. I love you, Mo. Give my best to the kids.'

She wiped a tear from her cheek. 'If you so much as look at another woman again, I'll take a Stanley knife and slice your balls off.'

Chapter 21

Mike arrived at his mother's semi-detached 1950s council house just as the temperature was dropping to freezing point. The old lady shook her head repeatedly when she met him at the door holding his paltry possessions, but she chose to hold her counsel… He knew her well enough to know she disapproved. Why bother with words? There would be plenty of time for talking.

Mike carried his things up to the small boxroom that had once been his childhood bedroom, and sat on the single divan bed… Life really had gone full circle.

He decided not to bother unpacking, and went straight back downstairs to have a cup of tea, and to let his mother have her inevitable say… It was best to get it over with.

They sat in her dated, cheaply furnished but immaculate sitting room for about ten minutes before June Mailer finally looked away from the television, and gave him a look of utter exasperation. 'Sort it out with Molly, Mikey, for the kids' sake, if nothing else.'

'I am doing, Mum.'

'I'm glad to hear it, son. Put the kettle on. A nice cup of Rosie will cheer us both up a bit.'

For the next twenty minutes or so they sat in virtual silence, drinking tea from porcelain cups and watching a familiar, engaging, but ultimately pointless game show on HTV. Mike rose to his feet as soon as the early evening news started, and turned to face his mother. 'Is it all right if I use the phone, Mum? It's after six and it's a local call.'

June checked her aged gold-plated Rotary dress watch and relaxed. 'Of course you can, Mikey. There's no need to ask.'

Phillip Beringer answered after about thirty seconds. 'Hello?'

'Hi, Phil, it's Mike. Fancy a couple of pints?'

'Yeah, why not? Rugby club, eight o'clock? Should be relatively quiet tonight; there's an away game in the morning.'

‘Sounds like a plan. I’ll give you another hammering at darts, if you think you’re up to it?’

‘Yeah, yeah, in your dreams. I’ll see you there.’

Beringer was standing at the bar engaged in animated conversation with an overweight but shapely, heavily made-up, middle-aged, bottle blonde barmaid, when Mike entered the unusually quiet rugby club bar. He ordered two pints: one Buckleys Bitter and one Guinness, and asked for the house darts, before finally bothering to say a belated, ‘Hello.’ Beringer reciprocated, accepted his pint gratefully, and took a seat in a quiet spot at the far side of the room behind the worn-out pool table. Mike placed the three tungsten darts on a sodden Babysham beer mat and proactively chose a seat with a good view of the barmaid and her overflowing low-cut blouse.

Beringer stared at his friend and snorted. ‘For fuck’s sake, Mike. You don’t change do you? Do you think you can actually concentrate on something else for a few minutes and tell me how Anthony’s doing?’ His expression became more serious. ‘What did Molly decide about the clinic?’

‘He’s been to another appointment, but she’s talking about cancelling the next one.’

‘What? I thought you said your car was out of action?’

‘Molly insisted I arrange a taxi.’

Beringer frowned uneasily. ‘How’s Anthony doing?’

‘Like I told you, he was in a cracking mood after the first appointment, but this time he came out in one hell of a state.’

‘Was Molly with him the entire time?’

‘No, it was just Tony and the doctor this time. But why the hell are you asking that? There had better not be more to this than you’re letting on, Phil.’

Beringer drained his pint and struggled to maintain eye contact. ‘No, I told you, it’s nothing like that. I just don’t think it’s a good idea, Mike. That’s all! Do you want me to have another word with Molly for you?’

‘No, there’s no need for that, Phil. I can tell her myself. I think she’s come to the same conclusion herself anyway. I haven’t told you… we’re going to be getting back together.’

Beringer felt a weight lift off his shoulders… It may already be too late, but hopefully not. ‘Does Molly know about this arrangement?’

‘Of course she does, you prat. I’m back living at my mum’s house for the time being.’

Beringer laughed until his chest hurt and tears ran down his craggy face. ‘How’s that working for you?’

‘I was hoping I could kip at your place for a while, to be honest.’

‘You have got to be kidding.’ He picked up the two empty pint glasses and grinned. ‘On a positive note, I suppose your mum’s pleased to have her little boy back home again. Suck it up, Mike. You deserve all you’re getting.’

‘Yeah, you’re probably right, Phil. Get the beer in.’

Chapter 22

Molly spent a minute or two searching for Anthony's soiled pyjamas and bedclothes, before eventually finding them hidden in one corner of his wardrobe under a Scalextric box. She gathered them up in her arms along with several other items of clothing and a pair of trainers contaminated by the urine, and fought back her tears as she descended the stairs towards the similarly overburdened washing machine.

Molly bundled everything with the exception of the trainers into the front loader, sprinkled in the powder from a half-empty box of Daz, and washed her hands thoroughly, before making a hot drink and slumping at the kitchen table for a brief, but necessary reprieve. She sipped the hot liquid and sighed… Life appeared to be mocking her. It was as if some great puppet master in the sky were pulling the strings and toying with her fragile emotions for his own amusement. One step forward and two backwards. That seemed to be the way of things these days. Tony had been great after the initial appointment, but how long had that lasted? He'd been clingy and prone to tears over the weekend. And now he was wetting the bed again. Things were just as bad as ever. Worse if anything! If she was going to cancel the next appointment, she needed to get on with it. The doctor was a busy man. He'd probably want to fit in another patient.

Molly turned up the radio to drown out the incessant vibrating drone of the washing machine, and made herself another mug of mint tea. As she stirred in a large spoonful of clear cold-pressed honey, she silently acknowledged that she was simply putting off the inevitable… The decision was made. Maybe she should have listened to Phil in the first place.

Molly dialled the clinic's number and only had to wait a few seconds before hearing Sharon's cheery, instantly recognisable phone voice say, 'Good morning, Dr Galbraith's secretary. How can I help you?'

'Hello Sharon, it's Mrs Mailer, Molly Mailer, Anthony's mother.'

'What can I do for you, Mrs Mailer?'

‘I’d like to cancel Anthony’s appointment please.’

‘If the appointment isn’t convenient, I can look in the diary for another time that suits you.’

‘Please thank the doctor for me, but Anthony won’t be seeing him again.’

‘Really? Are you sure that’s wise? Dr Galbraith’s at a Welsh Office conference in Llandrindod Wells all day today, but I’ll give him a ring at home first thing in the morning and let him know. I suspect he may want to speak to you in person.’

‘There really is no need for that. I wouldn’t want to waste any more of his time.’

Molly put the phone down as quickly as possible, before Sharon had the opportunity to argue the point any further… Anthony wouldn’t be going again. It really was as simple as that.

Chapter 23

Dr Galbraith was back in his study at 7:15 a.m. on Tuesday 4, February, updating Anthony's file, repeatedly checking his wrist watch, and trying to contain his burgeoning excitement. His head was already feeling a little better. Today was the day. It had finally arrived, and the agonising waiting would soon be over. What should he do first? Should he take the little bastard straight to the cellar? Yes, why not? Why not make full use of the time? He'd have to ensure he left no marks, of course. That wouldn't be easy. It would mean some unfortunate restrictions. But, like it or not, such things were necessary. Was everything ready? Had he put a new tape in the video camera?

He grimaced as a stabbing pain cut through his brain… He shouldn't have to deal with the damned minutia. Such things were for the Sherwoods of this world. For lesser men! He should be able to focus on the bigger picture. Maybe he should have allowed Sherwood to live despite his many failings.

He screwed his face up… Get a grip, man. It was utterly pointless pondering such matters. Sherwood was dead for good reason, and time was getting on.

He rose to his feet and punched the oak-panelled wall hard with a clenched fist, grazing his knuckles… He had to check things himself. What other option was there?

The phone sounded just as Dr Galbraith was leaving his study and walking in the direction of the kitchen. Cynthia reached it before him, and recognised Sharon's voice immediately. She held out the phone at arm's-length, and spoke quickly before he reached her. 'It's Sharon, she needs to speak to you.'

He took the phone from her without comment… What did the obnoxious bitch want now? 'Sharon, lovely to hear from you, my dear girl. Now then, how can I help you?'

'I didn't want to bother you while you were at the conference, Doctor. Mrs Mailer rang yesterday. Anthony won't be attending his appointment this morning.'

Dr Galbraith gripped the phone table tightly with both hands, and lowered himself slowly to the hall floor before speaking again. 'Did she say why? Did she arrange another appointment? Will I see him again?'

'Are you all right, Doctor? You sound upset.'

His head pounded… Could she hear it? Surely the bitch could hear it.

Dr Galbraith closed his eyes, and began twitching uncontrollably.

'Are you still there, Doctor?'

'Another appointment? Did she make another appointment?'

'No, she didn't, Doctor. I did say…'

Dr Galbraith was very close to tears. 'The number?'

'I'm sorry, Doctor?'

'The Mailers' number; give me the damn number.'

It took Dr Galbraith three attempts to dial the correct number with a trembling finger… Answer, bitch. Answer the fucking phone.

'Hello, Molly Mailer.'

'Good morning, Molly, my dear girl! It's Dr Galbraith. I was somewhat surprised to hear that you've cancelled Anthony's appointment.'

'We appreciate your help, Doctor. We really do. But I really don't think the treatment is helping Tony.'

Fucking mothers, why did they always feel the need to interfere? Choose your words carefully, man. Choose them carefully… 'You urgently need to reconsider, my dear. As I explained, it is essential that Anthony completes the course of treatment. You may recall that you signed an agreement to that effect.'

'I've talked it through with my husband, Doctor. It's not a decision we've taken lightly. We both agree that it's best if Tony doesn't attend again. I'm very sorry if we've wasted your time.'

'Are you an expert in these matters, Mrs Mailer?'

‘No, of course not, but…’

‘Is your husband a childcare expert, Mrs Mailer?’

Molly silently scowled… This was starting to get irritating.

‘Please listen to me very carefully, Mrs Mailer. It is crucially important that you recognise that despite appearances to the contrary, Anthony has made some significant progress. You may recall my shaking the bottle analogy: if he continues therapy his emotional trauma will eventually subside, and his behaviour will dramatically improve. He’ll be a happy child again. You do want that for your son, don’t you, Molly?’

‘I suppose so, but…’

‘Now, now Molly, there is no room for doubts where a child’s wellbeing is concerned. I will ask Sharon to send you another appointment at the earliest opportunity.’

‘I’d like to think about it, Doctor. I’ll talk it through with Mike again, but please don’t send another appointment letter at this stage. I wouldn’t want to waste even more of your valuable time. If we decide Anthony needs to see you again I’ll speak to Dr Procter.’

‘You’re making a grave error of judgement, Mrs Mailer.’

‘I’m sorry, Doctor. I will think about it, but I’ve got nothing more to say.’

Chapter 24

Dr Galbraith awoke in surprisingly positive mood on Wednesday 5, February, despite the bitter disappointment of the previous day… It was time for action. Time for a different, more radical approach. There was no time for dwelling on past failures. His ultimate goal was far too important for that.

He forwent his usual morning exercise routine in favour of an early breakfast, which he enjoyed without interacting with Cynthia on any level whatsoever… There were more important things to do with his time. Significant things that required his total undistracted attention.

The doctor phoned Sharon at 8:45 a.m. precisely, and engaged in a lengthy, somewhat inconsistent apology in which he cited various reasons for the previous day's aberration, as he put it. He informed her that he'd be taking a few days sick leave by unfortunate necessity, and instructed her to cancel his various professional commitments. Sharon concluded that illness, or to be more specific fever, best explained his shocking outburst of the previous day… It was so out of character. What other explanation was there?

Dr Galbraith made one further call, ordering a large bunch of red and white roses from a local florist, which would be delivered to Sharon at the clinic later in the day. They would have a simple message of apology and affection attached. He smiled in response to his largess… It was well worth spending a few miserable pounds to keep the obnoxious bitch onside.

After an hour or more spent watching videos and fondly reminiscing, he turned his attention to planning Anthony's abduction with what he considered military precision. He took a notepad and a fountain pen from a desk drawer, and began exploring his thoughts on paper: firstly, when the time was right, he would borrow a suitable vehicle from a paedophile acquaintance.

Next, he'd dedicate as much time as was required to observe the Mailer family in order to determine the optimum time and place to seize his prey.

Once Anthony was imprisoned in the cellar he'd take his time to chronicle every moment on film and paper.

Finally, when the little bastard had served his purpose and was of no further use to him, he would maximise the bitch mother's suffering by sending her copies of the videos.

Dr Galbraith linked his fingers behind his nape, pictured the scene, and relaxed. When he was finally ready to let go of the fantasy, he placed his completed plans in Anthony's case file for safekeeping and future reference.

The doctor suddenly sat bolt upright… Who the hell would assist him with the practicalities? Sherwood had occasionally served a useful purpose: fetching and carrying, assisting with filming, and doing the cleaning up that invariably followed their activities. At some point in the near future he'd require another like-minded, malleable accomplice to do his bidding. What about Gary Davies? Davies owed him. That was true. But, was he too risky? Should he be ruled out on the basis of recent police attention? Why the hell was he finding it so much harder to reach definitive decisions than he had over the years? Why did thinking make his head ache? What the hell! Davies would have to do. Davies was the obvious choice.

Chapter 25

At 8:00 a.m. the next morning, Dr Galbraith was sitting outside the Mailer family cottage in an old white Ford Transit van borrowed from a sex offender contact, who owned a local scrapyard located in the neighbouring industrial town. The man was a member of the ring, and happy to assist without asking too many unwelcome questions.

The doctor lifted his Zeiss Jena DF 7x40 military binoculars to his eyes, and stared into each room in turn. His eyes darted from window to window: ground floor to first floor, right to left, left to right, and then back again. He watched, and waited, constantly repeating the process, until he finally saw Anthony leave the cottage approximately half an hour later… Come on, you little bastard. Out you come. Out you come.

Anthony walked down the path hand in hand with Molly, boarded the bus, and sat at the front rather than join the other boys of his age, who considered it cool to sit at the back. Molly waved with exaggerated enthusiasm until the bus left her sight.

Dr Galbraith silently cursed Molly's existence, started the van's ill-kept diesel engine on the third turn of the key, and followed cautiously at a discreet distance, adhering slavishly to the speed limits and actively avoiding any ill-considered manoeuvre that could potentially draw the attention of the police, or anybody else, to the van.

Clouds of choking black smoke poured from the Transit's fractured exhaust, as he overtook the bus on reaching its ultimate destination approximately fifteen minutes later. He applied the brakes, turned off the engine, and parked about fifty yards or so further down the road to watch the children disembarking in his passenger side rear-view mirror… It wasn't good. It wasn't good at all.

The doctor gripped the steering wheel tightly with both hands, lurched forwards, and head-butted the windscreen… A bitch crossing attendant was helping the little bastards cross the road. A moronic male teacher was watching from the school's entrance. It was fucking hopeless.

Dr Galbraith was back outside the school at 3:20 p.m. having concluded that while it provided an unlikely snatch point, it was probably worth a second look before ruling the option out completely. He parked on the opposite side of the road at a place he'd chosen earlier in the day, and observed events with keen eyes… The same bitch lollipop woman, the same moronic pleb teacher; the simple system appeared to work frustratingly well.

He followed the bus on its return journey, more in hope than expectation, and pulled up behind it as Anthony disembarked directly outside the Mailers' cottage. For a glorious second or two, Dr Galbraith thought this may offer an opportunity. But, no… There the bitch mother was. Back in the doorway. Watching every move the little bastard made like an obsessive mother hen. What was it with these people?

He swore loudly and crudely, punched the steering wheel violently with a clenched fist, overtook the bus, and drove off as speedily as the spluttering engine would allow… It was high time to consider other options.

Dr Galbraith parked almost directly outside Mike Mailer's workplace at 4:44 p.m. and watched as Mike left the building approximately twenty minutes later. He was contemplating whether to follow in the van or on foot, when Mike stopped next to his convertible, unlocked the car, and got into the driver's seat. The doctor restarted the van's engine on the fourth attempt just as Mike drove off, and succeeded in keeping the car in sight despite its vastly superior performance, due to the busy rush-hour traffic.

The doctor didn't stop on reaching June Mailer's council house, but he slowed as he passed by, and watched Mike get out of the car and walk down the path towards the front door. He made a mental note of the street name and house number… It looked hopeful. One less obstacle to worry about? Probably, but he had to be sure.

Dr Galbraith pressed his foot down hard on the accelerator and headed in the direction of the Ceffyl Du public house, which he'd passed a few minutes earlier at the entrance to the council estate. He'd anticipated leaving the anonymous security of the van at some point or other during the day, and had prepared accordingly. He was wearing thick-rimmed, mock tortoiseshell glasses with brown, lightly tinted, nonprescription lenses; a dirty dark green bobble hat pulled down low over his precisely trimmed eyebrows, a pair of the scrap man's oil-stained grey overalls, and a pair of decrepit black wellingtons unnecessarily turned down at the top. He left the van and admired his reflection in one of the pub's two large ground-floor windows… It was an effective ensemble that rendered any fear of recognition virtually groundless. Even a close family member would struggle to identify him if challenged.

The Ceff, as the tavern was affectionately known locally, was a typical Welsh working-class watering hole. He pushed open the door with his foot, and waited in the doorway for a few seconds, allowing his eyes to adjust to the dim interior before entering the bar. Even in the gloomy atmosphere, through choking clouds of swirling tobacco smoke, he could see that the only customers were three dishevelled-looking elderly men holding cigarettes with yellow fingers, and a younger alcohol-ravaged drunk of indeterminate age standing unsteadily at the bar, talking to a grossly overweight landlord who couldn't have looked less interested if paid to. A pounding Rolling Stones rock track the doctor didn't recognise or appreciate was playing on the wall-mounted jukebox.

Dr Galbraith said, 'Evening,' to the proprietor in a fairly convincing Glaswegian accent on approaching the bar, and ordered a single malt whisky.

'We've only got the one brand of blended whisky, if that's any good to you?'

The doctor was used to more expensive spirits, but replied, 'No problem,' with mock enthusiasm, and gulped it down with the flick of his wrist. 'I'll have another, and have one yourself.'

'That's very kind of you, it's a rare event around here, I can tell you.'

'You're welcome.'

The landlord laughed jovially and gestured to the inebriated regulars. 'I can't remember the last time one of these mean sods bought me a drink.' He poured the spirits and smiled, revealing decaying teeth. 'I haven't seen you in here before. What brings you to our part of the world?'

The doctor leant casually on the bar, proactively portraying a relaxed demeanour. 'I'm looking for an old friend of mine: Mike, Mike Mailer. Any idea where I can find him?'

The landlord scratched his bulbous balding head and frowned. 'I should do, I've run this place for almost thirty years, but no, I can't place him.'

'I'm pretty sure he lives around here somewhere.'

The landlord thought for a few seconds before the quizzical look suddenly evaporated from his face. 'Ah, you mean Mikey, June's boy.' He laughed loudly causing his grossly protruding beer gut to wobble like a birthday jelly. 'He's back living with his mother, the silly sod. Kicked out by his missus after screwing some slapper or other.'

Dr Galbraith laughed along with his jovial host. 'What, he's not with that Tina he left his wife and kids for?'

'No, I was talking to June only yesterday, as it happens. It's all over, but his wife won't have him back.' He laughed again and added, 'Silly sod, June's gutted' before turning away and pouring the drunk another pint of strong German lager.

'So he's definitely back living with June?'

'Yeah, definitely, she said so much herself.'

The doctor said his goodbyes and started for home… It was a minor victory, but a victory nonetheless. Things were looking up at last.

That evening Dr Galbraith sat in his study sanctuary, reviewing his progress, or rather the lack of it… In all, Mike Mailer's living arrangements apart, it was disappointing. He had to acknowledge that reality. No wonder his damned head was aching so badly. It was to his credit that he could function at all. He'd ruled things out, but nothing in, and that simply wasn't good enough. He had to do something proactive to progress matters. Invading the Mailers' home was an option, he'd already accepted that, but it was perilous. Was it too perilous despite the pleb father being off the scene? Surely such an approach should be a last resort to be kept in reserve if all else failed.

The doctor perused Anthony's file for the umpteenth time, searching desperately for much-needed inspiration… *Rugby training.* What about rugby training? Hadn't the bitch mother said that the little bastard went to rugby training on Fridays?

Dr Galbraith checked his notes: six thirty on Fridays; but he hadn't been for a while. Was it still worth considering? The bitch was encouraging him to attend. She'd made that perfectly clear.

The pounding in his head eased slightly, and he sat back in his seat with his eyes closed, attempting to unwind… The possibility had to be worth exploring.

The doctor stood and paced the floor… He'd done well. Of course he had. He deserved a reward. He took a video from a desk drawer, unzipped his trousers, and switched on the VCR.

Chapter 26

Dr Galbraith watched from the anonymity of the Transit van as three boys of about Anthony's age dressed in brightly coloured sports clothes approached the Mailers' front door at 6:16 p.m. on Friday 7, February. Molly answered the door and immediately disappeared back into the cottage, whilst the boys, who had unwisely declined her invite to wait in the warm, stood and shivered on the doorstep.

The doctor stared at each boy in turn, looking them up and down, and considering their potential as future projects. But he quickly ruled it out as the pressure in his head began building… What the hell was wrong with him? He had to focus on one project at a time if unforeseen mistakes were to be avoided.

He forced himself to stare at the door and nothing else… Come out, you little bastard. Out you come. Out you come.

Molly placed an open hand on each of Anthony's shoulders and tried not to let her increasing frustration show on her face. 'Come on now, Tony, your friends are waiting for you. You've got your kit on. I've cleaned your boots for you. Go on now, you'll enjoy yourself once you're there.'

'I'll go next week, Mum.'

'The longer you leave it before starting back, the harder it's going to be, cariad. Dad will be really proud of you if you go tonight.'

'Will he?'

'Yes, of course he will. Off you go now. I'll have your supper waiting for you as soon as you arrive back home.'

Anthony made his way towards the front door as if he were approaching the gallows, but his mood raised immediately and he smiled on joining his friends outside in the semi-darkness. Molly sighed with relief as she watched the four boys walk down the path towards the pavement, and finally closed the door once they left her sight.

Dr Galbraith left the van and followed the boys at a discreet distance with his head bowed low to avoid his face being seen by any potential onlookers or passers-by, until they eventually reached the sports field about fifteen minutes later. Several other lads were already playing touch rugby under the bright electric glare of the floodlights, and the four new arrivals joined in the impromptu game without waiting to be invited. Two men in casual clothes, who the doctor assumed to be overattentive fathers, and a third man in a red tracksuit, who turned out to be the youth coach, were talking animatedly on the touchline near to the twenty-two line. Dr Galbraith walked around the edge of the gradually hardening pitch, and stood on the opposite side of the field with his woolly hat pulled low to cover as much of his face as possible.

The man in the tracksuit ended his conversation, jogged easily onto the pitch, and blew a shrill whistle loudly three times. Past experience had taught the boys to react quickly when summoned, and they immediately gathered around the coach in a semicircle eagerly awaiting his instructions. The coach picked up the oval ball and began shouting, while repeatedly throwing it high into the air and catching it casually with one hand. 'Where were you last week, Mailer, you dickhead?'

Anthony grimaced as all the other boys burst out laughing. They were well used to the coach's unconventional methods, and relieved not to be in the firing line themselves. The two fathers standing on the touchline appeared to find the coach's actions as hilarious as the boys had, and guffawed loudly. The coach was a popular, well-respected, retired first-class rugby player, who had once played for Wales against the old enemy England in the annual five nations' tournament, giving him a status just a fraction below God in the eyes of the locals.

Dr Galbraith watched the training session attentively until the coach brought it to a timely end an hour later. The boys left the field chatting and laughing en masse, to begin their respective journeys home, with Dr Galbraith shadowing Anthony's every step. Anthony and his companions were aware of the man walking some distance behind them, but gave him little, if any, thought. Anthony glanced back at one point and thought he recognised the man from somewhere, but he couldn't think where.

The doctor watched intently, and waited for an opportunity that didn't materialise. Anthony wasn't left alone at any stage of his journey, and was predictably met on arrival home by his mother, who opened the cottage door before he had the opportunity to knock.

Dr Galbraith retreated to the anonymity of the van and started the tired engine. As he manoeuvred into the quiet street to head for Eden Road, he cursed Anthony's friends, he cursed Molly Mailer, and he cursed the repetitive diesel throb of the engine, which appeared to mock the pounding in his mind.

Chapter 27

Dr Galbraith yelled, 'Coffee,' at the top of his voice, and slammed his study door shut with such force that the sound reverberated throughout the large Georgian town house. Cynthia made her husband's drink as fast as humanly possible, but as she carried it through the house, her shaking hand caused a small amount of the sweet black liquid to spill over the top of the china cup, and into the white saucer… What to do? Should she return to the kitchen and wash the saucer, or pour the coffee from the saucer back into the cup? She had to make a decision. Keeping him waiting was never a good idea.

Cynthia poured the coffee from the saucer into the cup and wiped the saucer clean with the sleeve of her powder-blue cashmere cardigan as she walked. She knocked reticently on the study door and waited with bated breath for her husband's next command. When he screamed, 'Don't come in, leave it outside the door,' she placed the cup and saucer carefully on the hall tiles, moved it an inch or two, and then back again, before quickly retreating upstairs to change… It was important to look her best.

Dr Galbraith sat at his desk, sipping his fine Columbian coffee, and carefully considering his next move… It was time for decisive action, high-risk or not.

The doctor sucked the air deep into his lungs and focused his mind… He would snatch Anthony from his home, that was a given, but when and how? He had to get it right first time, and had to prepare accordingly. There were things to sort out. And he'd need help, of course. That was a certainty. But such things could be achieved quickly, couldn't they? Yes, yes, of course they could. Why wait? He'd only need a day to prepare. The early hours of Sunday morning would be as good a time as any.

He took a notepad from a drawer and poised the gold nib of his fountain pen over the handmade paper for a few seconds, pondering the best approach before eventually elucidating his thoughts in writing… He'd need to find a suitable access point out of sight to potentially prying eyes, and break in silently.

The doctor felt as if a vice were gripping his head, squeezing, squeezing, tighter and tighter, attempting to crush his skull… The bitch mother would summon help if given the opportunity. Silence was a prerequisite for success.

He'd need to find the little bastard's bedroom quickly and render him unconscious before he made even the slightest sound. But how best to do it? An injection of ketamine possibly. It was fast-acting and could be administered through pyjamas and the like. Yes, that made sense. The van would provide a suitable means of transportation, that was obvious, but should he carry the little bastard from the cottage to the vehicle unaided? What the hell was he thinking? He was the brains not the brawn.

He shook his head repeatedly… Why not contact Gary Davies in the morning? Davies was something of an unknown quantity, certainly. He wasn't the old reliable Sherwood, which was somewhat regrettable given the particular circumstances. But he'd have to do. Like it or not, he'd have to do.

The doctor tapped his fountain pen on the desktop and frowned… What would they need to accomplish the plan? It made sense to comprise a list, didn't it? Yes, yes, a list was essential to ultimate success. There were practical things they couldn't do without.

He nodded his head confirming his conclusion, and began writing:

two disposable paper overalls with hoods;
two pairs of surgical gloves;
an implement for cutting glass;
a high-powered rubber torch;
a syringe and needle;
and three vials of ketamine.

He placed his pen down on the desktop and examined the results of his ruminations... Anything else? There had to be something else. Ah, yes, he'd need to ensure there was adequate diesel in the van beforehand. No problem at all; that was easily done. He'd covered all the angles, hadn't he? How could the plan fail?

Dr Galbraith closed his eyes, visualised the process from beginning to end, and smiled... Surely he'd thought of everything? Yes, yes, of course he had. The plan was nothing if not inspired.

He pushed his notes casually to one side and relaxed... Soon his fantasies would become a much anticipated reality.

Chapter 28

Gary Davies left the phone ring for several minutes on Saturday 8, February, before finally accepting that the early morning caller wasn't inclined to give up easily. He threw back the bedclothes and swore gratuitously, before making his way downstairs and picking up the phone in his partner's shabby, ill-kept lounge. 'What the fuck do you want at this time of the morning?'

'Davies? Is that you?'

'Who's asking?'

'It's Dr Galbraith.'

'Oh, Doctor, I'm sorry, I had no idea…'

'What the hell are you trying to say, man?'

'I haven't had the opportunity to speak to you since the day of the case conference. I wanted to thank you for all you did. I can't stress enough how much your help was appreciated.'

'It's not your thanks I require, man. You owe your freedom to me. Do you hear me, Gary? You owe me. You would be wise to remember that.'

'There's no need for that, Doctor. If there's anything I can do to repay you, all you have to do is ask.'

'Those had better not be empty words, Gary. I require your assistance with a small task I have planned.'

'Just tell me what to do, and I'll do it if I can.'

'If you can? I hope you're not trying to worm your way out of assisting me, Davies? That would not be a good idea.'

'Not at all, Doctor! Just say the word.'

'Are you whimpering, Gary?'

'Please, Doctor, just tell me what you want me to do.'

'Get a grip, man! Have you got a pen and paper?'

'Give me a second.'

'Davies? Are you ready, man?'

'Yes, Doctor, please go ahead.'

'Right, buy a rubber torch; a suitable tool for cutting glass, and two pairs of disposable overalls with hoods, later today. Make certain they are all of good quality, and pay cash. Do you hear me, Gary? Cash! Be at my house at two o'clock this morning. That's two o'clock. Not five to, not five past, two o'clock! Make damn sure you've got everything. You still have my address I presume?'

'Yes, Doctor, but why?'

'You sound somewhat anxious, old man. There's no need for that. If you do as you're told, you have nothing whatsoever to worry about. I'll see you at two sharp. Make damn sure you're wearing soft-soled shoes. Nothing that makes even the slightest sound on walking.'

Gary Davies knocked reticently on the Galbraiths' imposing black gloss front door at 1:57 a.m. on Sunday, 9, February. A big part of him was hoping he wouldn't receive an answer, but the doctor opened the door on the fourth knock, and shepherded him into the hall with an exuberant hand gesture after checking the street for potential witnesses.

'Did you see anyone on your way in?'

'I don't think so.'

'For fuck's sake Davies, get a grip, man.'

Davies glanced behind him. 'No, no, I didn't see anybody.'

'That's a good omen, Gary, I assume you've got everything?'

Davies held up the black and white Adidas sports bag he was clutching tightly in one hand and replied, 'Yes, Doctor, as per your instructions. Can I ask what they're for?'

'All in good time, old man. All in good time.'

Dr Galbraith confirmed the contents of the bag, indicated his whole-hearted approval, and steered his newfound accomplice towards the kitchen.

The doctor sat at the kitchen table and gestured to Davies to take a seat next to him. Davies sat immediately like an obedient puppy, and managed a thin smile as he waited for the doctor to fill the increasingly unnerving silence. He watched apprehensively as Dr Galbraith opened a cardboard file on the table in front of him, but his inquisitiveness suddenly overrode his reticence. 'What's this about, Doctor? Why am I here?'

Dr Galbraith grimaced angrily and growled, 'Be patient man,' before turning the pages, and explaining every aspect of his scheme in simple language, that he thought even a man of inferior intellect such as Davies could comprehend.

Davies listened intently, becoming increasingly anxious with each new detail the doctor chose to share… He had no qualms about assaulting children, there was no problem there. But, it sounded risky. What if they were caught in the act? The chances of detection and arrest seemed high, and abducting a child carried a very lengthy potential prison sentence.

Davies desperately wanted to say, no. He wanted to *shout*, no. But, he couldn't bring himself to utter the word. He looked down at the table, avoiding the doctor's gaze, and mumbled, 'It sounds risky to be honest, Doctor.'

Dr Galbraith closed his eyes for a moment's silent reflection… Was that implied criticism? Was the pleb being critical? Would he dare?

The doctor jumped to his feet, and began shouting manically, spraying a myriad tiny globules of saliva onto Davies' horrified face. 'You are going to do exactly what I tell you to do, you ungrateful low life. Do you hear me, man? Everything I tell you. You owe me, Davies. You would be well-advised to remember that.'

Davies saw a reptile-like coldness in the doctor's eyes that left him trembling.

He urgently pulled away from the table, almost losing his balance in the process, and blurted out the words he was certain Dr Galbraith wanted to hear. 'Okay, no problem. It's a crazy idea, but I'll do it.'

The doctor visibly relaxed, sat back down in his seat, and smiled contentedly. 'That's good to hear, Gary. You've made a wise decision, old man.'

Davies' relief was almost tangible. 'When it's done, we're quits, right?'

The doctor looked him in the eye and nodded assuredly. In reality he had no intention whatsoever of honouring the agreement.

Doctor Galbraith marshalled his increasingly reluctant co-conspirator down the concrete steps and into the cellar a few minutes later. Davies couldn't quite believe what he was seeing… The secret entrance, the heavy steel security door, the glaringly white room with its torture equipment and video apparatus—like a scene from a Hammer horror movie.

There were numerous questions Gary Davies would have loved to ask, but he instinctively knew that any such inquiries would be extremely unwelcome and potentially detrimental to his safety.

Dr Galbraith saw the uncertainty in Davies' eyes and laughed. 'Your assistance is appreciated, Gary. All will become clear, my dear boy. All will become clear. But, there is insufficient time for that now.' He checked his Cartier wristwatch and scowled. 'We're running late, old man. We need to get on.'

Dr Galbraith instructed Davies to don an overall and a pair of thin latex gloves before doing likewise, and rechecking the various implements against his list… Everything was ready.

Davies followed the doctor back up the cellar's grey concrete steps, through the family kitchen, down the long hall and out of the front door into the cold, dank, Welsh winter night. Dr Galbraith unlocked the van and jumped into the driver's seat, keen to avoid the intermittent icy drizzle that seemed to emanate from every direction at once. They were running slightly late despite his earlier prompting, and he drove rapidly despite the fast-deteriorating driving conditions. The journey took place in almost total silence, but the nearer they got to the Mailers' address, the more animated the doctor became. He hadn't spoken, but his eyes appeared to bulge alarmingly, multiple beads of sweat formed on his forehead despite the winter chill, and his whole body began to twitch violently every few seconds, as if he were experiencing severe drug withdrawal. Davies began to think that the psychiatrist may himself be insane… Was he mad or bad? It was hard to tell. Maybe a bit of both.

It took the two men about fifteen minutes or so to drive the eleven miles through the dark February streets to the Mailers' home. They arrived at their destination just as the wintry drizzle began to freeze and form thin sheets of ice in the many puddles. Dr Galbraith switched off the engine two hundred yards or more from their destination, and glided the remainder of the way, avoiding any unnecessary noise that may wake the Mailer family, or draw the attention of potential witnesses in neighbouring houses. He judged it rather well, and the van came to a natural halt almost directly alongside the cottage's front path. He urgently applied the handbrake, and turned to look directly at Davies… If only Sherwood were still alive and assisting him in place of this unknown quantity: a man who he barely knew and didn't trust! But, such thoughts were utterly pointless. Richard Sherwood was dead. It was time to get on with the night's work.

Dr Galbraith spoke to Davies in hushed tones. 'Do only as I say. Stay behind me unless I tell you otherwise, and await my instructions. Do not speak until we have the little bastard secured safely in the vehicle and have driven away. Do you understand my instructions?'

As Davies nodded his reticent agreement, Dr Galbraith gripped his face tightly between the thumb and fingers of one hand. 'Right, Davies. Time to go, old man. Do everything quietly. Do you hear me?'

'Yes, Doctor.'

Dr Galbraith glared directly into his hesitant accomplice's eyes, and lowered his tone still further from a whisper to a hiss. 'This is important to me, Gary. It couldn't be more important. Be in no doubt, if you do anything at all to cock this up, I will kill you.'

The doctor left the van first, with Davies close on his heels, and made his way down the fragmented concrete path towards the Mailers' front door. On reaching the cottage he walked rapidly to the right side of the building, which had the obvious advantage of being less visible from the road, but had no viable access point. He moved on quickly, with Davies in close attendance, and discovered a narrow path running along the entire length of the back wall. The cottage had been built against a high stone and earth bank covered in various shrubs and small trees of varying sizes, with only a two- to three-foot gap between the bank and the rear wall of the stone building. The doctor swore silently under his breath as he squeezed his muscular frame along the path in the intermittent light of the half-moon breaking through the gradually dispersing rain clouds, until he reached an opaque window located halfway along the wall at ground-floor level. He paused briefly, carefully surveying the scene, before looking back at Davies and repeatedly pointing at the window with a jabbing digit. He leant his head close to his accomplice's right ear and whispered, 'Open it,' with obvious urgency.

Davies was in reasonably good physical shape for a man in his late forties, but increasingly close to panic. He pulled himself together as best he could, and got to work. The window was a badly designed double-glazed type, in which the glass was secured in the white PVC frame by external beading. Davies immediately realised that he wasn't going to need the glass-cutter after all. He dropped the sports bag to the damp semi-frozen earth, and tore a hole in his paper overalls big enough to take a red multitool Swiss Army penknife from a front pocket of his faded jeans. He unfolded the longest blade and triumphantly prised the black rubber beading from one corner of the frame, before taking hold of the double-glazed unit and removing it completely, leaving ample room for the two men to climb through the resulting gap into the cottage's little ground-floor bathroom.

Dr Galbraith tapped Davies on one shoulder, and pointed to the various cosmetics and toiletries on the narrow white-tiled sill, and then to the path at the far side of the gaping opening. Davies understood immediately, and picked up each item in turn with increasingly cold, numb fingers, while simultaneously reaching for a chrome freestanding shaving mirror located on the far corner of the sill. His triumph was short-lived, however. Davies misjudged his grip, causing the mirror to topple forward into the sink located directly below the window, with a resounding clang. Dr Galbraith somehow managed to maintain his silence, but he grabbed Davies' shoulder aggressively, and glared at him with an expression that left him in absolutely no doubt that he had failed miserably. Davies mouthed the word, 'Sorry,' in an attempt to appease his antagonist, and waited anxiously for his next instruction.

Dr Galbraith rushed forward and pushed Davies roughly aside, before placing his head through the open frame. He listened intently for a full minute before his initial alarm abated… There was no sound of stirring. Just silence, glorious silence. It was time to continue with the night's work.

The doctor took a brown leather case containing the sedative drug, syringe and needle from the sports bag, and unzipped his paper overalls to tuck the case into the rear waistband of his tailored trousers. He climbed head first onto the windowsill, and pulled his body through the open gap: inch by cautious inch. He placed his hands firmly around the sink, and levered himself forwards until his weight suddenly acted as a fulcrum, and he fell forward, landing heavily on the hard quarry tiled-floor of the tiny room. He hurriedly pulled himself to his feet with the aid of a stainless steel heated towel rail, and listened anxiously for the second time. To his relief, no one stirred.

Dr Galbraith pointed to the sports bag outside on the increasingly freezing ground and silently mouthed the word, 'Torch.' Once Davies handed it over, the doctor motioned to him to enter the cottage as he had. Davies climbed through with apparent ease, and was soon standing closely behind the doctor in the cramped room.

As Dr Galbraith's eyesight gradually adjusted to the semi-darkness, he picked up a white facecloth that had fallen to the floor next to the sink, and used it to mask the torch, before switching it on and smiling… It offered sufficient light to navigate without the risk of drawing unwanted attention from neighbours or unlikely early hour passers-by.

Dr Galbraith opened the bathroom door gingerly, and slowly made his way into the short corridor that led to a dated oak-veneered family kitchen. Davies followed tentatively, fearing that he might throw up at any moment as he reluctantly urged himself onwards.

The doctor pointed the torch down at an approximate forty-five-degree angle, and led the way through the kitchen and dining room, and into the red-tiled hall, from where the ancient wooden staircase led to a landing, three bedrooms and a second larger family bathroom. He placed one foot onto the first step causing it to creak alarmingly, and pulled his leg back expeditiously, relieved to hear no sound of movement from any of the bedrooms. He moved his right foot back onto the first step, but this time he placed it precisely to the far side, so that it was almost touching the white-painted bannister. Slowly but surely he proceeded to silently climb the stairs, utilising the impromptu but effective method all the way to the top.

Davies waited apprehensively at the bottom of the staircase until Dr Galbraith finally reached the landing. He stood in a quandary, staring at the steps… Should he go up? Should he follow the doctor? Or should he stay where he was and wait?

The doctor made increasingly frenzied hand gestures directing Davies to join him on the landing. As Davies ascended the stairs with exaggerated care, he experienced heights of anxiety that were entirely new to him. The doctor saw the signs of panic in his eyes, and fearing his accomplice may compromise the operation, urgently pointed at the edge of each step with outstretched arms, in the style of a flight attendant indicating the location of escape routes during a preflight safety briefing. To his relief it had the desired effect. Davies lifted seemingly leaden legs, slowly, one step at a time, until he eventually reached the landing with the comparative relief of a climber who had reached the summit of Everest. He stood at the top of the stairs, staring at the floor and unable to move an inch. When the doctor gave a further hand signal, this time indicating it was high time to search the first bedroom, Davies remained static with tears running down his morose face. He had lost control of his bowel like many criminals before him, and could feel the warm loose faeces running down both legs and into one shoe. He sank to his knees as the rancid smell of human excrement permeated the air.

Dr Galbraith bit his lower lip hard, with sufficient force to cut the skin. He leant down urgently, fought the virtually overwhelming temptation to strike his accomplice in the interest of the mission, and placed his mouth immediately next to Davies' ear. 'Get a grip on yourself, Gary. Get a fucking grip! Only ten more minutes, and this will all be over. Now get the fuck up.'

Davies, who was temporarily incapable of independent thought, was extremely relieved to be told what to do… All he had to do was follow orders. Just follow orders.

He rose to his feet and followed, as the doctor approached a bedroom door and pushed it gently, providing them both with a panoramic view of the entire room. As Molly tossed and turned under her heavy winterweight quilt, dreaming of happier times, she was totally oblivious to the strangely dressed men who had invaded her home. Dr Galbraith resisted the temptation to attack; he fought the impulse to inflict terrible suffering… He had to maintain his focus on the night's primary purpose. Stay in control, man. Focus. When the time was right her time would come.

The doctor turned away and crossed the landing towards the second of the three bedrooms. The door was already slightly ajar, allowing a relatively unobstructed view of the room. As he directed the torch beam around the bedroom in a gradual sweeping arc, his chest suddenly tightened and his head began to pound… The bed was empty. The fucking bed was empty.

He looked again, more carefully this time, his eyes darting from place to place… Focus, man, focus. There were no boys' toys! The quilt cover was pink. There was a denim dress draped across a chair. All was not lost. It clearly wasn't the little bastard's room. Everything was going to be fine, just fine.

Dr Galbraith stood perfectly still for an instant, controlling his increasingly heavy breathing, and then turned to approach the third and final bedroom… Would he be there? Would the little bastard be there? He just *had* to be there.

The doctor peered into the darkness with Davies standing at his shoulder, again taking the precautionary measure of masking the otherwise powerful torch beam with the facecloth… The Swansea City lampshade, the posters of sports stars covering the walls. It had to be the little bastard's room. Didn't all seven-year-old boys love sport? Yes, there he was. There he was!

The pounding in his head subsided immediately, and his breathing became easier… Almost there. But, he had to be careful. There was no room for errors. Not when he was so very close to achieving his goal.

Davies watched from the virtual darkness of the landing as Dr Galbraith crossed the single bedroom in two strides, moved a plastic box containing several Dinky toys and an Action Man dressed in deep-sea diving equipment to one side with the edge of his foot, and stood triumphantly at Anthony's side. The doctor smiled and resisted the impulse to laugh… Now he was in control. Where was the bitch mother when her son most needed her? The little bastard was finally at his mercy.

Dr Galbraith unzipped the front of his overalls and took the case containing the sedative from his rear waistband. He placed the syringe on top of the quilt at the bottom of the bed, tore open the paper packaging covering the needle, and picked the syringe up again to fix the needle carefully in place. While holding the injection in one hand, he took a glass vial containing the strong drug from the case, and broke off its top with a barely audible snap that made him flinch. He inserted the needle precisely through the mouth of the vial, and slowly drew the clear liquid into the syringe chamber. Finally, he pressed the plunger gently with his thumb, forcing out the air, until a tiny drop of the clear liquid squirted reassuringly from the tip of the needle… He was ready.

The doctor took a deep breath, and cautiously lifted back one corner of Anthony's black and white quilt, so that the left side of his body was uncovered. As Davies looked on open-mouthed, Dr Galbraith plunged the needle through Anthony's pyjama trousers and deep into his thigh, administering the adult dose of the drug to be certain of rapid results. The sudden sharp pain of the injection woke Anthony for an instant, but almost immediately he was unconscious.

Dr Galbraith pulled Anthony's quilt from his comatose body, and threw it to the floor on top of a box of red and white Lego at the far end of the single bed. He turned to his accomplice and mimed an urgent instruction to pick their victim up in a fireman's lift. For a second Davies hesitated, as if frozen to the spot with the fear of it all, but the doctor wasn't about to let him jeopardise the abduction when they were so very close to success. He stepped forward and jabbed Davies hard in the chest, before pointing repeatedly at the seven-year-old boy with an urgent index finger. Davies suddenly tensed, took a gulp of air, and gave a thumbs up gesture… The quicker he was out of the cottage, the happier he'd be.

As Dr Galbraith stood aside to allow him sufficient space, Davies lifted Anthony's insensate body effortlessly from his bed despite his dead weight, and held him easily over one shoulder. The doctor pointed to the bedroom door and followed Davies onto the landing. He tapped him on his free shoulder, pointed to the stairs and cautioned continued silence by putting a finger to his lips and holding it there until he was certain that Davies had taken on board the instruction.

Davies had no problem descending the stairs, despite adopting the same cautionary technique utilised when ascending. The doctor sensed imminent success and was about to follow, when he glanced in at Molly on passing her bedroom door. He felt his entire body tense; his heart rate increased sharply, his blood pressure suddenly soared, and his face took on an angry animalistic snarl that contorted his otherwise handsome features… Should he punish the bitch? Surely he should punish the bitch. She'd placed obstacles in his way time and time again.

Molly woke with an unexpected start, and was about to scream at the sight of the strangely dressed intruder looming above her, when the doctor abandoned all thoughts of caution and lifted the heavy torch high above his head. He smashed it down onto Molly's forehead, using all of his strength and weight to maximise the impact. The first blow left her dazed and close to unconsciousness. The second shattered her nasal bones, causing blood to spray from broken skin and pour from distorted nostrils. The doctor hit her repeatedly: time and time and time again. He kept raining down blow after blow until Molly's face was an unrecognisable bloody mess.

Davies stood at the bottom of the stairs, listening aghast to the sounds emanating from upstairs… Murder was never a part of the plan.

Despite Davies' escalating fear, he somehow summoned sufficient courage to yell, 'What the fuck's going on up there? We need to get out of here.'

Dr Galbraith froze, as if suddenly awoken from a trance, and walked away from the bloody scene as if nothing at all had happened. He was out of breath, panting hard, and sweating profusely, but he had a broad grin on his face. Noise was no longer an issue, and with adrenaline surging through his veins he bounded energetically down the stairs, two or three at a time, before tripping on the last step and crashing heavily onto the hard red tiles. The mix of dopamine and endorphin in his system acted as an extremely effective painkiller, and he lifted himself off the floor with apparent ease, before unlocking the front door with a key left in the Yale lock.

Dr Galbraith moved to one side to allow Davies to exit first. He pushed his accomplice repeatedly in the back to hurry him down the path towards the van as he went. Davies got the message immediately, and moved as rapidly as he could, with the doctor following close behind, staring at their unconscious captive while drooling like a rabid dog.

Davies kicked open the rusty black metal gate leading from path to pavement and hurried to the back of the van, where he stood waiting for a brief moment until the doctor opened the rear doors. Davies was in the process of gently lowering Anthony onto the floor of the vehicle when the doctor snarled, 'Throw the little bastard in, Gary. Throw the bastard in! We haven't got time to piss about. It's time to go, man.'

Dr Galbraith was already in the driver's seat when Davies opened the passenger door and got in next to him. He turned the ignition key; the engine turned over but didn't start. He pounded the dashboard with the side of his right fist... Start you bastard, come on, start!

He tried for a second time, and this time the engine reluctantly spluttered into life. He quickly executed a proficient three-point turn in the quiet road before pushing the accelerator to the floor and heading back in the direction of Eden Road.

Dr Galbraith broke into a broad smile, but kept his eyes firmly focused on the road rather than turn to face his companion. 'I've waited a long time for this moment, Gary. A long time. The job's nearly done, but now isn't the time to take your eye off the ball. You need to stay focused. Do you hear me?' He banged the dashboard hard with the palm of one hand to emphasise his point. 'There's more work to do. Once we've got the little bastard safely in his new home, then you can relax. Not before!'

Davies began whimpering like a young puppy separated from its mother, but didn't say anything in response.

The doctor gritted his teeth and resisted the temptation to hit out… The man was fucking pathetic. 'Come on now, Gary. You've done well, man. Try not to worry. You'll be able to head home as soon as we get the little bastard safely back to the house.'

Davies felt slightly better for a time. But mere words were never going to be enough.

There was very little traffic on the streets at that time of the morning, and they made good progress despite occasional patches of perilous black ice which the doctor chose to ignore. Davies hadn't spoken since leaving the cottage, but he now asked if he could put the radio on. He felt ridiculously, disproportionately pleased when Dr Galbraith acceded.

Davies broke his silence for a second time as Dr Galbraith turned into Eden Road, this time by urgent necessity. His voice broke with trepidation as he hissed, 'There's a fucking police car behind us.'

Waves of vicious stabbing pain fired through the doctor's head like recurrent bolts of electricity, and cymbals crashed in his mind as if trying to drown out his thoughts. He clawed at his scalp with one hand… Come on, man. Focus, Focus. Davies was incapable of holding things together. That was blatantly obvious. The man was a slug, a rodent, an intellectual sub-human. He had to rescue the situation himself. No one else was going to do it.

The panda car was driven by a young probationary constable only eighteen months into his journey from comparative innocence to experience, after leaving a polytechnic degree course prematurely to join the local force. It had been a quiet night, and PC 143 Kieran Harris was looking for almost anything to do to break the potentially mind-numbing monotony of early hours rural policing. He contacted his control room on the car's two-way radio, requested a police national computer check on the van's index number, and pondered whether or not to stop the vehicle in order to examine the driver's documents before receiving a response.

He toyed with the idea of allowing the driver to continue his journey unencumbered, but he was still at the stage of his career when exercising his legal authority remained something of a novelty. He flicked on the blue lights, and signalled to overtake without giving the matter any further thought.

As the police car pulled alongside the Transit van, both Dr Galbraith and Davies were frantically pulling off their surgical gloves and tearing at their paper overalls. Dr Galbraith had just thrown his over the back of the seat into the rear, when PC Harris parked the police car directly in front of the van.

Dr Galbraith braked hard, pulled up next to the curb, retrieved the syringe, attached the needle and rapidly prepared the injection. 'If the pleb goes anywhere near the back of the van, get out and keep him talking. Distract him, and leave the rest to me. Do not fuck this up for me, Gary. Any slip ups, and death will be the least of your worries.'

Davies was nodding yes, but his eyes were screaming no… He meant it. The maniac meant it. Perhaps being arrested wasn't such a bad option in the circumstances. At least it would be over. He'd be alive. Maybe he could warn the pig in some way? That would go down well in court. But hold on, what if Galbraith still managed to stick him with the needle?

PC Harris turned off the engine, put his cap on, and approached the van driver's side door just as the doctor was winding his window down to receive him.

'Evening, Constable, what can I do for you?'

'Name, please?'

The doctor replied, 'Wayne Fisher,' without turning his head to face the officer.

'What's the purpose of your journey, Mr Fisher?'

'That's not really your business, is it Constable?'

'Driver's licence, insurance, and MOT certificate, please.'

Dr Galbraith tightened his grip of the steering wheel. 'I keep my documents at my home.'

'Control room to PC 143, come in, please.'

The young constable took a step forward, leant against the van door, and placed his head partially through the open window. 'I need to speak to my control room, please stay in the van.'

'PC 143 to base, go ahead please.'

'The registered keeper is a Wayne Fisher. He's known, but not currently wanted. The van is not reported stolen. I repeat, not reported stolen.'

PC Harris placed the radio back in the top pocket of his navy tunic, and took out a pen and a small beige booklet of forms. 'I'm going to issue you with a HORT1, Mr Fisher. It requires you to produce your documents at a police station of your choice within five days. Failing to produce them within that timescale is an offence under the Road Traffic Act.'

The doctor took the newly completed form from the officer's outstretched hand. 'Is there anything else I can do for you, Constable?'

'You can go on your way, Mr Fisher. But, don't forget those documents.'

Dr Galbraith and his quivering collaborator sat in stunned silence as they watched the young officer drive away. The doctor concluded that fate had intervened to enable him to continue his important work. Davies, in contrast, was conflicted. And part of him was relieved... But on the other hand, a cell may have been preferable to an ongoing relationship with the doctor.

Dr Galbraith drove on and parked directly outside his impressive three-storey home... The convenience seemed to outweigh any potential risk given the early hour and the police car's recent departure.

Davies pulled Anthony's unconscious body from the rear of the van by his feet, lifted him onto one shoulder, walked up the granite steps, and waited by the front door while the doctor scrambled into the back of the van collecting the gloves, pieces of overall and everything else they'd taken with them. Dr Galbraith lowered himself onto the road with the bag in one hand and the front door key in the other.

Cynthia Galbraith had been abruptly awoken by the commotion, and was peering out from behind her bedroom curtains as Dr Galbraith unlocked the front door, enabling Davies to carry Anthony into the Georgian house… Wasn't that a boy the man was carrying? Why would they be bringing a child into the house? Perhaps he'd been involved in an accident? She really should go downstairs to help, shouldn't she? No, if he was hurt he was in good hands. And her husband certainly wouldn't welcome her interference.

Cynthia returned to bed and lay perfectly still, listening intently for any clues that may explain why a young boy with short cropped hair and wearing pyjamas, had been carried into her house by a man she didn't know in the early hours of the morning. Her confusion intensified still further when she heard the unmistakable sound of the Welsh dresser being pushed aside in the kitchen… Was the boy something to do with her husband's work? Surely he must be. What other explanation was there?

She lay there, unable to sleep, and began to sob quietly into her pillow, muffling the sound, and trying to ignore the increasingly insidious thoughts invading her troubled mind.

Dr Galbraith was in jubilant mood as he skipped down the grey concrete steps and into his spacious white basement. Davies followed, a lot less enthusiastically, with the doctor's constant encouragement ringing in his ears: 'Come on, come on, man. Bring him in. Bring the little bastard in. Throw him to the floor.'

Davies followed instructions and paced the floor, anxiously awaiting his next instruction. Dr Galbraith stripped off his bloodstained garments and discarded them by the sink, before scrubbing his soiled hands and nails clean as best he could. Once satisfied with his efforts he refocused on Anthony, who was breathing shallowly, but hadn't moved an inch. The doctor administered a second dose of the sedative drug to ensure that his captive didn't wake prematurely, and kicked him hard in the ribs to confirm he remained unconscious. Anthony's entire body visibly shook with the force of the blow, but he didn't respond.

Dr Galbraith casually tossed the syringe to the floor and instructed Davies to put it in the sports bag along with his soiled clothing for subsequent disposal. Davies sought reassurance with fawning respect born of fear while clearing up, and hoped the doctor wouldn't decide he too formed part of the evidence requiring destruction.

Davies was worrying unnecessarily, at least for the moment. Doctor Galbraith had concluded that despite his undoubted limitations, Davies had his uses… The protocol established following the previous little bastard's death, required a good deal of physical effort. Why not make continued use of the moron?

Within twenty minutes, Anthony's senseless body hung from the same steel shackles that had once secured the cellar's previous victim. As Dr Galbraith set up Anthony's feeding tube, he became acutely aware that he was totally exhausted after the night's labours… He badly needed sleep.

Dr Galbraith turned to Davies with a look of sincere regret. 'I'm sorry to say that the little bastard is going to have to wait until tomorrow, Gary. He's going to need time to come around from the anaesthetic. What use is an unconscious child, eh? What do you say, old man? No use at all. The little bastard should be wide awake by morning. You can come over at eleven, when I've had some time to entertain our guest alone. I'm sure you won't deny me that particular pleasure. You'll have your opportunity; don't concern yourself in that regard. We're in this together, Gary.' He paused, looking at Anthony, admiring his work, and then suddenly looked away. 'We still have essential tasks to address before you go home, old man. Bring the bag.'

As Davies followed the doctor out of the cellar and into the comparative normality of the family kitchen, he was struggling with the violent severity of his new master's crimes, as Sherwood had before him… Having a bit of fun was one thing, but things had gone too far. Should he say something? It wasn't too late, was it? The boy was still alive, after all. He hadn't seen anything. How could he have? Surely they could let him go and get away with it.

He paused, pondering whether or not to act on his misgivings… But hang on a minute, he had to be cautious. How would the doctor react if he suggested freeing the boy after all his efforts? He'd very probably go absolutely berserk.

Davies shook his head thoughtfully… It really wasn't worth the risk.

He put Anthony's situation out of his mind and focused on drinking the hot, sweet instant coffee and eating the warm buttered toast the doctor had provided.

Dr Galbraith suddenly slammed down his empty coffee cup with a bang that shattered the pervasive silence. 'It's time to get back to work, Davies.'

'Yes, Doctor.'

The doctor strode towards the double-glazed double door that lead from the kitchen to the conservatory and garden beyond. 'Right, Gary, my boy, bring that bag. I'll fetch some paraffin and matches.'

Davies followed Dr Galbraith into the shadowy walled-garden at the rear of the property, glad that the night was finally close to an end. The doctor checked his watch and concluded that it was still early enough to burn the evidence of their crimes without the undue risk of curtain-twitching prying eyes looking on quizzically from other nearby dwellings. He told Davies to empty the bag into a large, battered, metal refuse bin located in one corner of an immaculate manicured lawn out of sight of other adjacent houses, and poured half the bottle of accelerant over the contents. He struck a match and threw it into the bin, causing flames to instantly burst into seemingly enthusiastic life. He picked up the sports bag, fed it to the fire, and watched mesmerised for several minutes as the flames leapt and danced, before finally reducing to an intense orange glow that fed acrid black smoke into the early morning air.

Dr Galbraith turned away from the spectacle, suddenly aware that Davies was still standing close behind him. 'You'll no doubt be glad to hear that we're done for tonight, Gary. You can get on home. I'll contact you again if and when I need you. Await my call. Oh, and one last thing: make certain, absolutely certain that you put all your clothes in the washing machine as soon as you arrive home. You fucking stink, man! Burn the shoes. Now go. Do you hear me, Gary? Go.'

'I thought you said I should come over in the morning?'

'Are you experiencing hearing problems, Davies? I've just said I'll contact you if and when I need you. I do not appreciate having to repeat myself.'

Gary Davies nodded his confused agreement. He looked quizzically and asked, 'What about the glass cutters?'

'Leave them to me, Gary. I want you gone. And make damn sure you're not seen as you leave.'

As Davies walked away, the doctor jolted him back by the right shoulder. 'Keep tonight's events entirely secret. Do you hear me, man? Secret! Remember, you are as guilty as I am.' He prodded him aggressively in the chest. 'If you ever bring the police to my door, you will pay an extremely heavy price. That I can guarantee you.'

Davies hurried back through the now familiar house, and obediently checked the street with nervous darting eyes in the style of a young child following the Green Cross Code for the first time… All was quiet. No one stirred. The outside world seemed oblivious to his existence.

Once alone, Dr Galbraith hurried directly to his bedroom and set his alarm for 10:00 a.m. before getting into bed… Sleep was a necessary inconvenience interrupting his work, but essential if he were to perform at his very best.

As he drifted off, he pictured himself burying the glass cutters under a favoured rose bush and gleefully anticipated waking Anthony from his chemically induced slumber.

Dr Galbraith was awoken by the shrill tone of his alarm clock as planned on Sunday, 9, February, and leapt from bed with the energy and exuberance of a much younger man. He salivated at the thought of what the day would bring… It was going to be an important day. A momentous day! Soon he'd introduce the little bastard to his new home.

He visited the bathroom, forwent his regular physical exercise routine, pulled on some casual clothes and rushed down to the cellar, keenly anticipating what would inevitably follow.

The doctor entered the cellar brimming with burgeoning enthusiasm, and approached Anthony, fully expecting to savour the terror in his eyes. But instead, he stopped and stared at his captive… He should be awake. Why wasn't he awake? Why the hell wasn't the little bastard awake?

Dr Galbraith slapped Anthony hard in the face, but nothing, not a flicker of life. He rushed to the sink, filled a mug with bitterly cold water, and hurled it in the boy's face. 'Wake up, you little bastard. Wake the fuck up!'

The doctor grasped at his head as the cymbals in his mind became crashing, ear-splitting explosions of sound that he momentarily feared may shatter his skull… Why wasn't he awake? The little bastard should be awake?

Dr Galbraith began to weep and a steady stream of salty tears ran down his morose face… It was suffering that most excited him. What use was an insentient child?

He shook his head violently, desperately attempting to silence the reverberating pounding pressure hammering every inch of his brain… Focus, man, focus! No need to panic. No need to panic. It was too soon for that.

He collected his thoughts, and approached the wall-mounted glass-fronted medical cabinet at the far side of the room. He returned to his victim's side, and hurriedly administered an opioid antagonist… It should do the job. Surely it would do the job.

He fell to his knees… It wasn't working. It had never failed before. Why the hell wasn't it working?

Dr Galbraith slumped to the floor, sobbing uncontrollably, and curled up in a ball with his hands clutched tightly over his ears. He began screaming: louder and louder and louder, until his throat ached… It was the lowest point of his entire life.

Chapter 29

Never again! She'd said it before, but this time she meant it. It hurt to move, it hurt to breathe. There was an unpleasant lingering acidic taste of last night's vomit in her mouth, and her throat felt as if she'd drunk a barbed-wire cocktail. It was like having the flu, but self-inflicted. One thing was certain: she'd get no sympathy whatsoever from her mother if and when she spotted the telltale signs of a very heavy night.

Siân Mailer tried the side door, hoping to sneak into the cottage undetected, and lock herself in the downstairs bathroom for a quick shower, before retreating to her teenage bedroom to sleep off her hangover… It was locked. Why was it locked? Her mum usually opened it first thing to let the cat out.

She made her way back around to the front of the cottage, shielding her eyes from the bright sunrays piercing the grey clouds, and knocked reticently on the door… No reply. What a stroke of luck; her mum must have gone out.

Siân bent down stiffly to search for the house key under the black rubber doormat… It wasn't there. That was strange. Mum usually left a key these days.

She pushed the door hard with the palm of one hand in frustration, fully expecting it to remain shut, but instead it flew open.

Siân paused momentarily before entering the hall, and wondered if her mother would suddenly appear from one direction or another with a predictably disapproving expression on her face. Siân shouted, 'Mum,' at the top of her voice, but received no reply… It looked as if she had the house to herself. Why not make the most of it? Maybe a shower would make her feel a little better. It couldn't make her feel any worse—that was certain.

She headed for the downstairs bathroom, stopping briefly in the kitchen to switch on the radio and swallow two dispersible aspirins en route. Siân was singing along to a melodic Culture Club hit as she opened the bathroom door, but she was suddenly silenced when she saw the windowless frame. Her initial surprise quickly turned to concern, and then to fear.

Siân hurried through all the other downstairs rooms, calling repeatedly for her mother and brother... Where were they? Where on earth were they? Why had she stayed out? She shouldn't have stayed out.

She stood in the hall staring at the stairs, then at the front door, and then the stairs again... Should she go up? What would she find? What if there was someone up there? She had to find her family.

Siân paused time and time again as she ascended the stairs, but she eventually reached the top. She slowly crossed the landing, ignoring the stench of excrement, and pushed open the bathroom door with a trembling hand... Empty. Don't run, Siân. Don't run.

She steadied herself, and slowly approached her mother's bedroom. As she looked through the open door she couldn't quite believe what she was seeing. Siân's knees buckled, and she sank to the floor holding her head in both hands, as she realised that the bloody mess she was witnessing was her mother's face. She pulled herself to her feet, spat out a mouthful of bile, and blew her nose onto the carpet before forcing herself to walk across the room, one small step at a time, to her mother's side. .. Don't be dead, Mum. Please don't be dead.

Siân studied her mother's obliterated features and feared the worst. Her entire face was swollen, badly bruised and caked in dark congealed blood. Her nose was severely fractured, with a startlingly white bone breaking the skin, the area directly below her left eye was depressed, crater like, due to a shattered cheek bone, her bottom lip was torn and hanging onto her chin, and three of her front teeth were laying on the multicoloured wool-mix carpet next to the double bed. Molly was virtually unrecognisable as the woman she knew... Please don't be dead, Mum. Please God, don't let her be dead. I'll never stay out again if you let her live. Please let her live.

Siân leant close to her mother's face with warm tears streaming down her pretty face. She placed her right hand ever so tenderly on her mother's left shoulder, and gently shook her. 'Mum! Mum! Wake up, Mum. Please wake up.'

Siân wiped away her tears… Her chest was moving. It was, wasn't it? Yes, it was definitely moving. She was breathing. Mum was breathing. Thank you, God. She was breathing.

Molly groaned softly, causing bubbles of crimson blood and pink saliva to emanate from her horribly misshapen mouth, but she was physically incapable of speech. She was barely conscious, but she fought to communicate. Molly's mouth moved, but no words materialised. Inside her head she was screaming: *Anthony!*

Siân stared at her mother's bloody mouth… Mum was trying to say something. Yes, she was definitely trying to say something. What was she trying to say?

She stood for a second or two, as if attempting to read her mother's mind, and then sprang into life, running towards her younger brother's bedroom… He wasn't there. Why wasn't he there? There wasn't any blood. That must be a good thing. But where was he?

Siân began weeping… Could he be hiding? Yes, that was it. He was very probably hiding.

She flung open the wardrobe door, and then fell to the floor, peering under the single bed… Where was he? Please be safe, Tony. Please be safe. Please, God, let him be safe.

Her chest tightened and she struggled for breath… She had to get help. It was time to get help.

Siân shouted, 'I won't be long, Mum,' as she ran down the stairs and into the hall to use the phone… nine-nine-nine, that was it, nine-nine-nine. Answer. Please hurry. Please hurry.

'Emergency, what service do you require?'

Oh, thank God. 'I need an ambulance and the police. It's very urgent. My mum's been attacked, and I can't find my little brother anywhere. He's missing.'

'What's your name and address please?'

Siân provided the required information and other pertinent details on being prompted by the emergency room operator.

'And you're at that address now?'

'Yes, yes, please hurry.'

'Help is already on the way, Siân. I know it's easier said than done, but please try to remain calm. Do you want me to stay on the line until the police or an ambulance arrive?'

Siân remained silent for a few seconds, considering her options... It was a tempting offer. And what if the attacker came back? But, no, her mother needed her.

'Are you still there, Siân? I can stay on the line if you want me to?'

'No thanks, I have to go back upstairs. My mum's on her own. Please don't let them be too long.'

'Help's already on the way; your mother's going to be very proud of you.'

Siân sat on the bloodstained carpet next to her mother's bed and tried her best to smile. 'Help's on the way, Mum; they won't be too long. Everything's going to be all right. Promise it is. Hold on, Mum. Please hold on.'

An ambulance arrived outside the cottage with its siren blaring and blue lights flashing within ten minutes of Siân's emergency call. She watched, relieved, from the bedroom window as a middle-aged paramedic and his much younger assistant hurried up the path. Siân was already halfway down the stairs to greet them when the first of the two men knocked heavily on the front door, and shouted, 'Hello, ambulance,' as loudly as he could through the letter box. Siân opened the door almost immediately and yelled, 'Up here,' as she turned and ran back up the stairs.

Both men struggled to hide their shock on first sight of Molly's severe facial injuries, despite their extensive experience of dealing with all manner of medical emergencies. While the paramedic reassured Siân that things were going to be okay despite his unspoken doubts, his assistant followed his senior colleague's instructions and rushed back and forth to the ambulance, fetching a neck collar, stretcher, oxygen cylinder and mask.

The paramedic rested his hand very briefly on Siân's shoulder. 'I'm Dai. Is it okay if I call you Siân?'

'Yes, of course.'

'I'm going to need your help, Siân. Do you think you can do that for me?'

'Just tell me what to do.'

He smiled reassuringly. 'Sit on the bed, Siân, as gently as you can, and hold your mum's head absolutely still.'

'But, won't that hurt her?'

'I'm not going to lie to you, Siân, it may hurt a little, but it's important. We have to be extra careful in case your mum's suffered a spinal injury. Do you think you can do it for me?'

Siân sat on the bed next to her mother and followed instructions.

'That's great, Siân, you're doing well. I'm just going to check your mum's breathing, pulse and blood pressure.'

'She is going to be all right, isn't she?'

'We need to get your mum to hospital as soon as possible, love. But she's going to be just fine...' He sounded a lot more certain than he felt.

The second of the two men suddenly reappeared carrying a stretcher. 'Who the hell did this?'

'I don't know. There was no one else here when I found her. Are you sure my mum's going to be all right?'

Dai Rees considered his next words carefully, and then said, 'We'll make sure that your mum's as comfortable as possible, and then get her off to hospital as soon as we can,' in gentle, reassuring West Wallian tones... He shouldn't make promises he couldn't keep. He knew that. But sometimes the temptation was just too great to resist. 'Your mum's going to be just fine. What's her name, Siân?'

'Molly, her name's Molly!'

The paramedic smiled down at Molly, masking his horror at what had been done to her as best he could. He wasn't entirely sure if she could hear him, but he spoke on the assumption she could. 'I'm just going to put a neck collar on you now, Molly. It's purely precautionary. Nothing to worry about. You're in good hands. We'll have you in hospital before you know it.'

Molly had some limited dream-like awareness of what was going on and tried to smile in response to his kindness, but her face barely moved. She began crying silent tears.

Siân began to shake violently as she watched the two men lift her mother onto one side at an approximate forty-five-degree angle, and carefully slide the stretcher under her traumatised body. As they lifted Molly off the bed, Siân finally lost control and shouted, 'My brother's missing.'

Dai Rees, who had two teenage daughters of his own, wanted to help... But what could he say? If the boy was missing, he was missing. Nothing he said was going to change that fact.

He forced another weary smile and said, 'Is there someone you can call, Siân? Your dad, perhaps?'

Before she could answer, Siân's dark thoughts were suddenly interrupted by a female voice shouting, 'Hello, police,' from the hall. WPC Bethan Williams reached the top of the stairs just as the two men were carrying Molly out of the bedroom strapped securely to the stretcher. She took one look at Molly's face and urgently stood to one side to allow them to pass... There were important questions to ask, but any thoughts of an interview were going to have to wait.

As the ambulance men carried their patient down the stairs, the WPC shouted after them, 'Where are you taking her, boys?'

The paramedic replied, 'South Wales General,' without looking back.

'Thanks, boys, I'll follow you there as soon as I can.'

Siân looked at the officer with pleading eyes. 'I want to go with my mum, but my brother...'

'You must be Siân Mailer, you dialled nine-nine-nine?'

'Yes.'

'Your mother's in good hands. I'll need to ask you a few questions, if that's all right with you?'

Siân nodded. 'The downstairs bathroom window's broken and he's missing.'

'Missing? Who's missing?'

Siân began sobbing. 'My b-b-brother, Anthony, he's only seven. Please, you have to f-find him.'

Oh shit, that was not good news. Why the hell hadn't she been told that before? 'Every effort will be made to find your brother as quickly as humanly possible, Siân. Let's go downstairs to wait for the CID officers. They shouldn't be too long. I'll take you to the hospital to see your mum as soon as they arrive. Come on, I'll make you a quick cup of tea, and we can talk in the lounge. It'll be more comfortable.'

'Okay.'

The officer switched the kettle on and waited for it to come to the boil. 'How do you like your tea, Siân?'

'I don't really care at the moment.'

'Milk and sugar?'

'Just milk.'

She handed Siân her mug. 'Come on, let's take a seat in the lounge. It's important I establish the facts as soon as possible. It'll help us find your brother. Do you understand what I'm saying?'

Siân took a seat and sipped her hot tea. 'I suppose so.'

'When did you last see your mother and brother before finding your mother this morning?'

Siân took a deep breath before responding… This really mattered; she had to get it right. 'I had some t-tea with mum and Tony at about f-four yesterday afternoon. They were in the l-lounge watching something on the telly when I went out to meet some friends at about half past four.'

The officer smiled. 'Did you actually see them before you left?'

Siân stared into her tea. 'No, I was in a h-hurry to get to my friend's house. Mum called me from the l-lounge when I was about t-to leave, asking when I'd be b-back, but I didn't answer. I really wish I had now.'

'Hindsight is an exact science.'

Siân raised her eyes with a baffled expression on her face, but didn't respond.

The WPC winced… How could she be so stupid? 'You couldn't have known what would happen, Siân. I'm sure your mum will understand. Now then, just so I'm clear, you left the cottage at about four thirty yesterday afternoon, and your mother and brother were absolutely fine. Correct?'

Siân nodded and said, 'Yes.'

'And you didn't see either of them until you found your mum at approximately half past eleven this morning?'

'Y-yes, yes, I told the woman on the phone. The front door was open when I arrived, and the bathroom window was broken. I searched for my mum and Tony, and found Mum upstairs. When are you going to start looking for T-tony? Surely you should be looking for Tony?'

'Detectives are already on the way here, Siân. They'll arrive at any minute. This information is really, really important. The more I can tell them when they get here, the better. It will help us find your brother. Do you understand?'

'Yes, of course I do.'

'I'll have a quick look at the bathroom later. Now then, what's your brother's full name and date of birth?'

'Anthony Mailer, he was s-seven in December.'

'What date in December?'

'The s-second, we had a birthday tea with a cake, and some of his friends came.'

'That must have been nice. Does anyone else live at the house?'

'Dad used to l-live with us, but he met another woman a few months ago and l-left.'

'Do you and your brother still see him?'

'Yeah, Dad came to see the child psychiatrist with us. I think Mum and Dad may be getting back together. Mum seems to think so anyway.'

'Your mum must have been extremely angry when she first found out about the affair.' It was a statement rather than a question, and she continued without waiting for a response. 'Did your parents argue a lot?'

'I s-suppose so.'

'Does your father ever hit you, Anthony, or your mum?'

'No, never! He's not like that.'

'Okay, I'm sorry, Siân. I had to ask. Do you think Anthony could be with him?'

'I suppose it's possible, b-but I doubt it. I think Dad was supposed to be coming over to see us this evening.'

WPC Williams made a note of Mike Mailer's new temporary address and said, 'Can you think of anywhere else Anthony may be, at a friend's house, for instance?'

'I d-don't think so. Tony hasn't been seeing much of his friends since Dad left.' She frowned. 'Can w-we go to the hospital soon please?'

'We will, Siân, I promise, but this is important. Give me a list of all Anthony's friends. It may help us find him.'

Siân provided what information she could.

'That's great, thanks, Siân. Have you got a recent photograph of your brother?'

Siân fetched an unframed portrait taken at school a few weeks previously, and handed it over. Anthony was smiling in the picture, but there was an unmistakable sadness about him.

'Thanks, Siân. That's really helpful! Now show me the bathroom.'

WPC Williams heard the Vauxhall Cavalier that served as one of the force's inconspicuous CID cars pull up outside the cottage a few minutes later, and acknowledged her two plain clothes colleagues from the lounge window as they walked down the path. She instructed Siân to wait in the lounge and met the two detectives at the front door. 'DI Gravel, DS Rankin, I'm very glad to see you both.'

She showed them the obvious access point, succinctly outlined the information collated prior to their arrival, and introduced them to Siân, who was still sitting in the lounge waiting anxiously for some positive development.

Detective Inspector Gravel acknowledged Siân with a cursory nod of his head, but nothing more… There was no time for pleasantries when a child's life was at stake.

'Let's talk outside, Bethan. Rankin, you stay with the girl. See if she's got anything useful to tell us.'

WPC Williams closed the front door and looked at the DI quizzically. 'What is it, sir?'

'I want you to take the young girl along to see her mother. Contact me as soon as Mrs Mailer can be interviewed. Speed is of the essence. The chances of finding the boy alive diminish with every hour that passes. As soon as she's conscious, talk to whoever's in charge, and don't take no for an answer. Do not contact Mr Mailer under any circumstances. Which goes for the girl as well, by the way. Leave that to me. I need to be certain what we are dealing with before approaching him.'

'That's going to be tough on Siân, sir.'

'I'm fully aware of that, thank you, Constable. The father could be involved. There's no room for assumptions in this job. As soon as I rule him out, you'll be the first to know. Is that all right with you?'

WPC Williams swallowed hard. 'Yes, sir!'

'You've been in the job long enough to know that, Bethan. You're a police officer not a social worker, for fuck's sake.'

Bethan Williams returned to the lounge, glared at Rankin with a look that said a thousand words, placed a supportive arm around Siân's shoulder, and guided her towards the panda car. 'Come on, Siân, let's go and see how your mum's doing.'

DI Gravel and his experienced sergeant made a thorough search of the property as soon as WPC Williams and the teenager left the building. It was a long shot, but the inspector had once found a baby's body in a kitchen drawer, and it was a painful lesson he would never forget. They searched every room: looking in cupboards, wardrobes, under beds and in the attic, but found nothing out of the ordinary, except for a small piece of glass on Anthony's bedroom floor. It puzzled them for a time… But could it really be of any significance?

They discussed it briefly, and concluded that the answer was almost certainly *no.*

Chapter 30

Molly was still in the hospital's busy casualty department awaiting admission to the major trauma ward for assessment by a surgeon specialising in facial reconstructive surgery, when WPC Williams and her charge arrived at South Wales General. There was, however, going to be an unavoidable delay as the surgeon had to be contacted at home, where he was enjoying his Sunday lunch with his family.

Both WPC Williams and Siân were motivated to speak to Molly for their own very different reasons. They tried repeatedly to engage her in conversation, but the combination of her injuries and the pain-killing morphine in her system meant that her responses were limited to incomprehensible noises rather than words. They eventually gave up trying to communicate with her, and waited in hushed contemplative silence.

Within fifteen minutes or so a thin young porter, seemingly covered with multiple poor-quality tattoos that appeared self-inflicted, arrived to transfer Molly to the ward, with WPC Williams and Siân following close behind. Siân was increasingly desperate to contact her father, and was finding the police officer's predictable explanations as to why this wasn't currently possible difficult to comprehend… She didn't even seem convinced by her own arguments.

On reaching the ward Molly was transferred from trolley to bed by two concerned state registered staff nurses in light blue uniforms, while the porter stood by and watched. The ward sister made a second urgent request for a prompt assessment by the appropriate surgeon, and ensured that Molly was as comfortable as circumstances allowed. The surgeon arrived surprisingly quickly and predictably concluded that urgent reconstructive surgery was essential. The complex operation was arranged for later that afternoon. All WPC Williams and Siân could do was wait, watch the minutes tick by on the clock on the wall opposite Molly's bed, and hope for the best.

Chapter 31

DI Gravel kicked his filing cabinet drawer shut in frustration, and slumped back into his office chair with his broad fingers linked tightly behind his head… He'd done what needed to be done, he'd followed the relevant standing orders, he'd written them, for fuck's sake. But what had been achieved? Fuck all, that's what.

The inspector closed his eyes, released his hands, bowed his head, and tapped his forehead gently with the first two fingers of his right hand… Had he missed something? Was there anything he hadn't thought of? Anything he hadn't covered?

He opened his bloodshot eyes, rubbed them with the back of his hand, took a generous gulp of tepid coffee, and reviewed progress, or rather the lack of it, in his analytical mind… He'd arranged for a scenes of crime officer to check the cottage for potential evidence, basic good practice in complex cases, but nothing of use had been found except for a number of faint but discernible footprints in the semi-frozen earth at the rear of the stone building.

He smiled half-heartedly… It wasn't much to go on, but it was a lot better than nothing. He'd liaised with the top brass and negotiated what additional resources he could, but they were never sufficient. Rankin was contacting local hospitals and Anthony's friends and relatives. He'd get on with it quickly and efficiently, as he always did. DC Hawkins was collating information relating to all known criminals in the area who posed a threat to children, or had a relevant history of violence. That would take a bit of time. All available officers were making door-to-door enquiries and searching the immediate area. He'd told them where to look: outbuildings such as garages and sheds, any containers such as bins and water tanks, and any other place Anthony could potentially hide, or, God forbid, a perpetrator could conceal a child's body. They were reporting back at seven that evening. It was a case of fingers crossed. Anthony's description had been circulated to all operational officers in the force area. He'd covered all the bases; what he needed now was a break.

DI Gravel loosened his paisley tie, and undid the top button of his increasingly grimy shirt… He'd have to let the team do their jobs and hope someone came up with something worthwhile. They had to do their jobs, and he needed to concentrate on his. He was their inspector not their baby-sitter, for fuck's sake. He'd interview the boy's father later in the day. The background checks hadn't come up with anything significant. Mike Mailer's only prior conviction was for cannabis use at the age of nineteen, when a student at Cardiff University. That was it: no history of violence, no domestics, nothing.

The inspector sighed… It was probably a waste of his time. The father was an unlikely suspect at best, but child abductions by strangers were rare. He couldn't rule anything out prematurely. Such things had a habit of coming back to bite you in the arse. The interview needed to be done. Why not get on with it?

DI Gravel took his warrant card from an inside pocket of his ancient, but much-loved grey Harris Tweed jacket, before knocking hard on June Mailer's front door. Both June and her son were upstairs: June rearranging her meagre wardrobe, everything in its place, everything coordinated, an invariably lengthy process, and Mike getting changed in his childhood bedroom in preparation for a much-anticipated meal with his family at the cottage later that evening. Mike pulled up and fastened a clean pair of faded blue Levis 501 jeans, and rushed downstairs to answer the door.

Mike stood staring into the stranger's face… He exuded an undoubted air of authority, he looked important somehow, despite his slightly dishevelled appearance and the unmistakable smell of body odour. And he looked concerned. Above all, he looked concerned.

DI Gravel held up his warrant card in clear view. 'Detective Inspector Gravel, local police. Mr Mailer? Mr Mike Mailer?'

Mike experienced a sudden pain in his gut as his intestines cramped and twisted… What the hell was this about? Something must be amiss? Surely detective inspectors didn't call at your home unless it was something serious?

'What's this about, Inspector? Has something happened?'

'It's better we talk inside, Mr Mailer. I need to ask you some questions.'

Mike fought to control his emotions. 'Has something happened to one of my family?'

DI Gravel's face took on a steely expression. 'Let's go inside, Mr Mailer. We can talk here or at the police station. It's your choice.'

Mike wanted to protest, but the inspector's self-confident assertiveness negated his natural instincts. He actively calmed himself… Arguing didn't seem like a good idea. 'Come in, Inspector, we can talk in the lounge. Can I get you a tea or coffee…?' Why the hell did he ask that?

'No thanks, Mr Mailer. Just sit down and we can make a start.'

Mike sat as instructed.

'Mr Mailer, where were you between four thirty yesterday afternoon and eleven thirty this morning? Be precise please.'

'I'm starting to get seriously worried here, Inspector. Is there something I should know?'

'Just answer the question, Mr Mailer. The quicker we do this, the quicker I can tell you why I'm here.'

'Okay, message received. I was in the house all afternoon, retiling the kitchen for my mother, and then I met a mate for a few pints at about half seven.'

June Mailer began her slow journey downstairs just as DI Gravel was about to ask another question. 'Is that your mother I can hear, Mr Mailer?'

Mike nodded.

'Can she confirm your alibi?'

Mike looked incredulous. 'Alibi? Why would I need an alibi?'

'Just answer the question, Mr Mailer.'

Mike took a deep breath and said, 'Yes,' just as June Mailer opened the lounge door, and looked at him with a quizzical expression on her heavily wrinkled face.

'This is Detective Inspector Gravel, Mum. He wants to ask you some questions.'

'Me?'

'Yes, Mum.'

She remained static in the doorway, her mouth gaping, but saying nothing more until DI Gravel broke the brief silence. 'Mrs Mailer, where were you from four thirty onwards yesterday afternoon?'

'I stayed in all day.'

'Were you alone, Mrs Mailer?'

'No, Mikey was in all day doing the tiling for me. He did a lovely job. You're welcome to have a look, if you like.'

'Did he go out at all?'

June Mailer looked at her son, meeting his eyes in a search for guidance.

'Just be honest, Mum. I've got nothing to hide.'

She smiled... Of course he didn't. 'He went out for a pint about sevenish. That's right, isn't it, Mikey?'

Mike nodded his agreement.

'Thank you, Mrs Mailer, that's very helpful. What time did he get back?'

June Mailer thought for a second or two. 'I went to bed after the ten o'clock news. Mikey wasn't back then, and I didn't hear him come in, to be honest.'

'Thank you again, Mrs Mailer. If you can leave us now, I'd like to speak to your son alone. Close the lounge door on your way out please.'

She reluctantly retreated into her newly tiled kitchen with its tired units, to worry about her son and enjoy her umpteenth cup of tea of the day.

'Mr Mailer, you went out at approximately seven o'clock?'

'Yeah, about ten past to be exact. I met a mate at the rugby club at about half past.'

'Your friend will confirm that?'

Mike nodded. 'Yeah, no problem!'

'His name, address and contact details, please?'

'Phillip Beringer, Flat three, eight Glan Yr Ystrad. I can fetch you his telephone number, if that helps?'

'Phillip Beringer, the social work manager?'

Mike nodded.

'Small world, I've got his number. What time exactly did you leave the club? I couldn't give a toss about any after-hours drinking. You need to be honest with me.'

'We shared a taxi at about twenty to two. The driver dropped me off here about twoish before taking Phil home.'

'The taxi dropped you off first?'

'Yeah, as I said.'

'And what did you do then?'

'I was seriously pissed, to be honest. I just crashed into bed and got up this morning at about tenish for a glass of water and a bacon sandwich.'

'Your mother can confirm that?'

'Like she said, she was already asleep when I got in. But she was up and about when I finally came downstairs this morning.'

'Where's your car, Mr Mailer?'

'It's still at the club. I'm planning to pick it up later, on the way to see my wife and kids.'

Detective Inspector Gravel had heard enough… Mike Mailer wasn't the man he was looking for. 'Mr Mailer, I'm afraid I've got some extremely unwelcome news for you. There's no easy way of saying this: your wife was attacked at the cottage. She's been taken to South Wales General. Your daughter is already there with one of our female constables.'

Mike's face crumpled. 'What? Attacked? When? Is she going to be all right?'

'She's suffered some serious head injuries, Mr Mailer. You'll get a much better picture when you talk to the doctors. Your car is in the rugby club car park, correct?'

Mike nodded with an angst expression on his face.

DI Gravel stood and approached the door. 'I'll run you to the hospital. I don't think it would be a good idea for you to drive at the moment. Best leave your car where it is for now.'

'Thanks.'

'Do you know where your son is, Mr Mailer?'

Mike was trying hard to hold it together, but he was increasingly close to falling apart. 'Anthony? No, what are you saying? Where the hell is he?'

The inspector unlocked the car doors. 'There's no way of sugar-coating this, Mike. We don't know of your son's whereabouts since late yesterday afternoon. Could he be with friends or relatives?'

Mike's legs buckled and he hit the pavement.

DI Gravel took his arm and assisted him into the front passenger seat. 'I've got every officer in the force looking for your son as we speak, Mike. Let's get you to the hospital. We can talk on the way.'

'I spoke to him last night on the phone at about sixish. We talked about the football results. He was chuffed Swansea'd won. He was absolutely fine. Are you sure you've got this right?'

'I'm sorry, Mike. As of now, your son is missing. Friends and family?'

'My father died a few years back, and Molly's parents live in Spain. I n-need to contact his friends…'

'One of my best officers is already doing that, Mike. I promise you, we are doing all we can.'

'I can't see him being with friends anyway, to be honest. He's not been going out much lately, and he knew I was going around this evening. We're close, you see? He was looking forward to seeing me. He wanted me to play Monopoly with him.' His face looked suddenly paler. 'I should have been there. I should have been there to protect him.'

‘Let’s focus on finding him for now, Mike. There’ll be plenty of time for soul-searching when he’s safe. Any questions?’

‘There’s no news?’ He knew he was clutching at straws.

‘We are doing all we can. It’s just a matter of time.’

‘Any idea who did this? If the bastard hurts Tony, I’ll fucking kill him.’

‘Not as yet, but I will get to the bottom of this, I give you my word. Come on, Mike, let’s find out how your wife’s doing.’

As the two men trotted across the hospital’s busy car park in a hopeless attempt to avoid the driving rain, Mike had little if any control of his racing thoughts, and he didn’t slow down until he reached Cilgeran ward on the second floor of the modernist concrete edifice.

Siân jumped to her feet the instant she saw her father entering the dayroom, and rushed into his open arms, hugging him tightly and almost knocking him over in the process. They held each other as if their very lives depended on it.

After about thirty seconds, Mike freed himself from her desperate embrace and said, ‘Hello love. I’m here now. Things are going to be just fine. Have you met the inspector?’

Siân nodded. ‘He was at the cottage earlier.’

‘Have the doctors told you anything yet, love?’

‘Not really, Dad. Mum’s having an operation, that’s as much as I know. Who would do that to her?’ Her eyes filled with tears. ‘I thought she was dead. When I found her, I mean. She will be all right, won’t she?’

Mike faced his daughter, placed an open hand on each of her shoulders, and looked deep into her eyes… He had no idea if Molly was going to be all right, or even if she’d survive, but his daughter didn’t need to hear his doubts or concerns. He had to be strong for once in his miserable life. How would Mo put it? He had to man up. That was it. ‘Of course she is, love. Mum’s a fighter! You know that as well as I do.’

Siân hugged him again, even more tightly this time, and then suddenly pulled away. 'Dad!'

'Yes, love?'

'What about Tony?'

Mike attempted to remain stoic, but he couldn't prevent his anxiety showing. 'I'm so sorry, love. The police haven't found him as yet, but they will soon. That's right, isn't it, Inspector?'

DI Gravel nodded unconvincingly. 'We're doing all we can to find your brother, Siân. Every available officer is on the case.'

It wasn't exactly what Mike had hoped for... But perhaps it was the best the inspector could offer in the circumstances.

'You stay with the officers for a while, love. I need to find out how your mum's doing. I'll be back with you as soon as I can.'

Mike found the senior ward sister working on staff rosters in a small office she shared with a colleague. He stood in the doorway and waited with increasing impatience until she eventually raised her eyes from her paperwork and acknowledged his presence. 'Can I talk to you please, Sister? I'm Molly Mailer's husband. She was brought in this afternoon.'

'I was here when she arrived, Mr Mailer. What would you like to know?'

Mike took a deep breath, and hoped he could hold it together long enough to ask the necessary questions. 'How serious is it, Sister? Is my wife going to come through this?'

Sister Thomas frowned. 'She was badly concussed and had some extremely severe facial injuries, Mr Mailer. She's already been in theatre for about an hour, and I would expect it will be a while yet. Mr Faulks really is an excellent surgeon, but it's difficult work, and the operation may take some time. We'll have a much better idea of how things are, once Mrs Mailer's back on the ward.'

'Thank you for your honesty, Sister. It's appreciated. Can you give me any idea how long it's likely to be before I can see her?'

'Your wife will be taken straight to recovery after surgery, Mr Mailer. I wouldn't expect her back on the ward for at least another two hours, if I were you. There's a canteen on the ground floor, if that helps at all? I'm sorry, but there really is nothing more I can tell you at this stage.'

Mike just stood there, staring into space and hoping she may suddenly say something more positive.

Sister Thomas looked down at the papers on her desk… Why wasn't he going? Relatives always seemed to want more information than she was in a position to provide.

She raised her head and looked at him with a blank expression on her face. 'Is there anything else I can do for you, Mr Mailer?'

'I'll be waiting in the dayroom with my daughter. Will you let us know as soon as we can see Molly please?'

'I will, Mr Mailer. Now, I must get on. These rosters aren't going to write themselves.'

Mike paused before re-entering the dayroom… Man up, Mike, man up. He'd already left his daughter down enough for one lifetime.

Siân hurried towards him as soon as he opened the door. 'Any news, Dad?'

Mike took her hand in his before replying. 'She'll be back on the ward in about two hours, love. All we can do is wait.'

DI Gravel rose to his feet. 'I'll make a move. There are things I need to get on with. I very much hope Mrs Mailer makes a good recovery. I'll keep you informed of any significant developments as and when they happen. As soon as we know of Anthony's whereabouts, you'll be the first to know.'

Mike nodded, and said, 'Thank you.'

The inspector shook Mike's hand firmly, acknowledged Siân with a barely discernible nod, and turned to WPC Williams. 'Contact me the second Mrs Mailer comes around, Bethan. It's essential we talk to her as soon as possible. What she has to tell us could well be crucial.'

Chapter 32

Probationary constable Kieran Harris pulled up the collar of his navy-blue police issue garbadine overcoat against the inclement weather, and knocked on the front door of the1960s semi-detached red-brick house, located almost directly opposite the Mailers' cottage... So far his enquiries hadn't resulted in anything useful. Hopefully his luck was about to change.

PC Harris knocked again and waited... There was a light on. He could hear what sounded like Radio 4 somewhere in the house. Why the delay? He was cold, he was wet, and he was shivering. Should he walk away and try next door? No, he had a job to do. It mattered. He had to do it properly.

He stamped his feet, clapped his black leather-gloved hands together vigorously in an attempt to warm them, and knocked forcefully for the third time.

Eighty-seven-year-old Rachel Evans was not nearly as mobile as she'd once been. She was heavily reliant on a walking frame, and very much hoping that her visitor was still in situ when she finally reached her front door and opened it... Thankfully he was. 'Oh, hello, dear. I wasn't expecting the police.' She smiled revealing stained broken teeth that were at least her own. 'You're not going to arrest me, are you, dear?'

PC Harris had heard the joke what felt like a thousand times before, but he smiled anyway. 'We're undertaking enquiries in the area, and are speaking to all potential witnesses. I'd just like to ask you a few questions if that's all right? Would you like to see my warrant card?'

Mrs Evans declined with a mischievous grin. 'That's all right, my dear, I can see you're a police officer, even if you do look young enough to be my grandson. Why don't you come in for a nice cup of tea in the warm? You look as if you could do with it.'

He reciprocated her friendly smile, thinking that the old lady reminded him of his maternal grandmother. 'I haven't got time for a cuppa now, sorry, but maybe another time. I want you to tell me if you saw anything suspicious or unusual between approximately four thirty yesterday afternoon and about eleven thirty this morning. Think carefully please; anything you can tell me may be important.'

'Oh, I don't think so, dear. Are you sure you won't come in for a nice cup of tea and a piece of sponge? It's home-made.'

PC Harris made a mental commitment to call again when he had more time. 'I'm really sorry; I would like to, honestly, but I must get on. I've got a lot more houses to visit.'

Mrs Evans looked crestfallen. 'Oh, all right, dear, you must visit again you know.'

'I will. Goodbye for now.'

'Goodbye, dear! Don't forget to call.'

As he walked away, pulling his coat around himself against the stinging rain, the old woman called after him in a faltering voice: 'Oh, there was one thing, dear. There was an old van outside the Mailers' cottage. It was the middle of the night. I thought that was a bit odd.'

PC Harris felt as if a bolt of electricity were passing through his body. 'I think I will have that cup of tea after all.'

Kieran Harris followed the old lady as she slowly manoeuvred herself towards her lounge, every item of ageing furniture a seeming obstacle. When they eventually reached their destination Mrs Evans gave him a beaming smile. 'You sit yourself down there on the sofa, dear, and I'll get you that cuppa and a lovely piece of fresh sponge. I made it yesterday morning with plenty of strawberry jam.'

Could he get away with saying no? Probably not, and a hot drink and a bite to eat wouldn't do any harm. 'That would be lovely, thank you.'

'Milk and sugar, dear?'

'Just a drop of milk, please.'

As she ambled unsteadily towards her kitchen, he was on pins… Would he, an inexperienced junior officer, be the one to break this high profile case? How good would that be? He may not have fitted in too well at the police station, but this could be a game changer. Zero to hero in one dramatic bound.

As he sat there, surrounded by woodchip wallpaper, brown furniture and fading memories, impatiently awaiting the old lady's imminent return, he pictured himself providing DI Gravel with the vital information that lead to the violent perpetrator's arrest and Anthony Mailer's dramatic life-saving rescue… It was a nice thought. Maybe, just maybe, it would become more than an ego-boosting fantasy.

To the young constable's relief, Mrs Evans reappeared from her kitchen balancing perilously with a hospital-issue aluminium walking stick in one hand and a cup and saucer in the other. She smiled anxiously. 'Nearly there, dear.'

PC Harris rose from his seat… Was she going to fall? She may well do.

He rushed towards her. 'Let me take that from you!'

'Oh, all right, dear. I'm not getting any younger, you know. I'll be eighty-eight in July. Fancy that. Life passes by so very quickly. Put your tea down on the coffee table, dear, and you can fetch my tea and the sponge from the kitchen. You'll find some plates in the cupboard above the fridge.'

PC Harris returned carrying a heavily laden tray a minute or two later.

'Oh, that's lovely, dear! Now, put the tray down here, and we can enjoy ourselves. Oh look, dear, you've forgotten a knife for the sponge.'

He returned to the kitchen… Count to ten, Kieran. Count to ten.

'Thank you, dear. Why don't I cut you a nice big slice, and tell you what I saw?'

He took his pocket book and a yellow plastic ballpoint pen from a uniform pocket. 'Tell me exactly what you saw, Mrs Evans, take your time please. Anything you can tell me could be very important.'

Mrs Evans placed her cup back on its saucer and looked up at the young officer with obvious pride. 'I will, dear. Where shall I start? Now, let me think. I went to bed at about nine o'clock. There's nothing worth watching on the telly these days. I couldn't sleep, dear, so I took a sleeping tablet, just the one. I do sometimes. In the middle of the night, I'm not really sure what time it was, I woke up needing the bathroom. It was very cold, dear. I looked out of my bedroom window to see if it was snowing. That nice weather man with the beard said it might.'

Come to the point. Please come to the point. 'What did you actually see, Mrs Evans?'

'Well, it was very strange, dear. Like I said, I looked out of the window—my bedroom is in the front of the house, you know—and there was a big white van just outside that nice Mr and Mrs Mailer's cottage. I thought it rather odd. Well, you would, wouldn't you, dear, in the middle of the night?'

'Why did you think it was unusual?'

'I'd never seen that van in the street before, and then things became even stranger. Two men came out of the cottage. Dressed all in white they were. They walked up the path as bold as brass. Eat your sponge dear, there's plenty more where that came from.'

PC Harris took another large bite and washed it down with a gulp of tea.

'What's your sponge like, dear?'

'Very nice, thanks, Mrs Evans.'

The old lady beamed. 'Would you like another piece, dear?'

'Not just now thanks, Mrs Evans. I really would love to, but I must get on or I'll be in trouble with my boss.'

'Oh, I wouldn't want that, dear. Now then, what was it you wanted to ask me?'

About time. 'Can you describe the van for me, Mrs Evans? This really is very important.'

The old lady looked troubled initially, but after a few seconds' thought she smiled. 'I'll try my best, dear.'

PC Harris strongly suspected that he wasn't going to like the answer, but he asked the question anyway. 'Do you know the make of the van, Mrs Evans?'

'Oh no, no, no, dear! I don't know much about vans and the like. Does it matter, dear?'

'That's all right, Mrs Evans, you're being very helpful.'

'Oh, thank you, dear.'

This was going to be a long shot. 'Did you see the number plate?'

'No, sorry, I'm not being very helpful, am I? Would you like another cup of tea, dear?'

'I won't have anything more now, thanks. Can you tell me anything else about the van? Anything at all?'

'Oh, now let me think. I don't know, dear. It was very rusty. I don't suppose that matters?'

PC Harris felt the adrenaline flood through his body… He'd stopped a van meeting that description. He'd requested a PNC check. It could be the same vehicle, couldn't it? Was that too much to hope for?

He composed himself and continued. 'What about the two men, Mrs Evans? Can you describe them for me?'

'Oh, I'll do my best, dear. But, it was very dark, you know. As I said before, there were two of them, one was quite tall and well-built, and the other one was a little bit on the short side. I don't mean to be unkind, dear. And the strangest thing: they were dressed from head to foot in white.'

'White? Are you sure?'

'Yes, dear.'

'That really is very helpful, Mrs Evans. Did you see their faces, by any chance?'

The old lady looked crestfallen. 'Oh, no, dear, they were too far away for that. And I didn't have my glasses on. I am sorry. Have I helped at all, dear?'

PC Harris smiled warmly. 'You have been extremely helpful, Mrs Evans. Now, think hard. Is there anything else you can tell me? Anything at all?'

'Now let me think. There was one thing, dear. The shorter one was carrying something on his shoulder. A rug perhaps. Or something like that anyway. He threw it in the back of the van before they drove off. Were they stealing, dear?'

It had to be worth asking. 'Could he have been carrying a child, Mrs Evans?'

'A child, dear? Surely not!' She paused, 'Well, it could have been a child, I suppose.'

PC Harris nodded. 'Thank you very, very much, Mrs Evans. You've been extremely helpful. Someone from CID will want to talk to you and take a full statement. Will that be all right?'

She hadn't felt useful in a long, long time, and it felt good. 'That will be lovely, dear. I'm very happy to help. Now, will you have one last cup of tea or something else to eat before you go back out into the cold? You could do with a bit of feeding up, young man.'

PC Harris stood up to leave. 'I would like to, Mrs Evans, but I really do have to leave now. Thank you again for your assistance.'

What a shame! Still, she'd be receiving another visitor soon. That was something to look forward to. 'You will call again, won't you, dear?'

He looked back and said that he would… He planned to keep his promise.

As he walked the short distance to the adjoining house, PC Harris had an unmistakable skip in his step… Maybe he'd won the investigative lottery. His information was potentially important, that was definite. But, should he use his radio to contact the inspector? Maybe yes, maybe no. His information would have a greater impact at the feedback meeting, wouldn't it?

He pictured himself receiving the glowing plaudits of his previously dismissive colleagues… It could wait until seven o'clock, couldn't it? Of course it could. Where was the harm in that?

Chapter 33

Sister Thomas appeared at the dayroom door with a fleeting smile that hardened as she entered the room. Mike squeezed Siân's hand, expecting the worst, but hoping for the best… A look could sometimes do that.

In a faltering voice resonating with disquiet emotion he asked, 'How is she, Sister?'

'If you come to my office, Mr Mailer, I'll tell you what I can.'

Mike stood to follow her, but stopped abruptly when Siân said, 'I want to hear what she has to say, Dad. She's my mother. I'm old enough.'

'All right, love, fair comment.' He met the sister's eyes and nodded his agreement… Siân had the right to know the truth, however potentially painful. And at least someone else would be doing the telling.

The sister returned his nod, and chose her words carefully. 'Mrs Mailer is in intensive care. The operation to repair her facial injuries went relatively well, but I'm afraid there were complications. Mr Faulks will be along to speak to you as soon as he can.'

Mike and Siân responded in unison as WPC Williams looked on, acutely aware that she was trespassing on the family's grief. 'Complications? What sort of complications?'

Sister Thomas appeared suddenly flustered. 'I really can't tell you any more at the moment. I'll try and find out how quickly Mr Faulks can speak to you.'

Mike placed a mutually supportive arm around Siân's shoulder… Why was the nurse being so evasive? So cautious? She was hiding something. What wasn't she saying?

He tried again. 'Surely you can tell us something more, Sister?'

She mumbled her virtually incomprehensible apologies, and hurried from the room without saying anything more.

Time passed frustratingly slowly as they waited for the consultant surgeon to make an appearance. When he did finally appear, he stood just inside the door a good ten feet from Mike, Siân and the WPC, and looked past them into the distance, rather than meet their anxious gaze. When he began speaking, Mike noted it was in what he considered a predictably privileged, privately educated south of England accent.

'Mr Mailer, I am sure you will be pleased to hear that the operation went relatively well given the severity of your wife's injuries. As the weeks pass the physical scars will heal, and her features will appear much as they did prior to the attack. There were, however, some difficulties during the operation, and we will just have to wait and see how she is when she eventually comes around from the anaesthetic.' And with that said, he turned to leave.

Mike took a deep breath… Was that it? Difficulties? What the fuck did he mean by difficulties? Did the patronising prat really think the information he'd provided was adequate?

He stood up, shouted, 'Hold on a minute,' and walked towards the surgeon, who appeared genuinely surprised at what he interpreted as Mike's audacity.

'What the hell do you mean by difficulties?'

Mr Faulks steadied himself. 'As I said, Mrs Mailer's facial injuries will heal given sufficient time. She did though receive several heavy blows to the head during the assault, which will almost certainly have caused some degree of injury to her brain. Patients do usually recover from such injuries as the swelling recedes. But I'm afraid in Mrs Mailer's case the picture is rather more complex.'

Mike returned to his seat to comfort his daughter… Here we go again. 'Complex? What's that supposed to mean?'

The surgeon stared at the ceiling, shifted his weight uneasily from one foot to the other, and cleared his throat noisily before responding. 'Mrs Mailer suffered a cardiac event during the surgery. It's regrettable, but it sometimes happens.'

Mike shook his head incredulously. 'Cardiac event? Do you mean a heart attack?'

'Yes, I'm afraid I do, Mr Mailer. Mrs Mailer was successfully resuscitated, but she stopped breathing for a time. Her brain was deprived of oxygen, and may have been irrevocably damaged as a consequence. One can't say with any certainty in such cases. As I said, we will just have to wait and see. I will assess her again along with my neurological colleagues in due course.'

'Are you saying she died?'

'Her heart stopped for almost three minutes, Mr Mailer. Let's wait and see how things progress.'

Please get better, Mo. Please God, make her better. 'C-can we see her now, Doctor?'

'I really can't see any reason why not, Mr Mailer. You will find her on the intensive care ward. But please don't expect too much. It's far too soon to expect her to speak. Now, I really must get on, I have other patients to think of. Any final questions?'

Mike shook his head wearily, and nothing more was said.

WPC Williams had heard enough to know it was pointless asking when interviewing Molly would be feasible… It was going to be a long wait, if it happened at all.

As Mike watched the surgeon walk away, a thousand questions invaded his troubled mind. He wanted to stamp and shout like a petulant child… But what purpose would it serve. One thing at a time, bite-sized chunks. That was how to deal with the situation. Go and see Mo, and then think about Tony. Man up, Mike. For Siân's sake, man up. 'Come on, love. Let's go and see your mum.'

Chapter 34

DI Gravel drained his much-favoured black and white Neath rugby club mug, pulled up the sleeve of his jacket, and checked his Casio… Only ten minutes before the feedback meeting and he had fuck all of note to tell the troops.

He evaluated the relevant facts in his mind for the umpteenth time, searching for a positive… Was there something he'd missed? Was there anything he hadn't done? If only it were that simple! Stranger abductions were rare, but it looked as if this was one of those cases. There just wasn't much to go on unless they came up with something and quickly. Fuck it! Things were not looking good. The chances of finding Anthony Mailer alive were diminishing with every minute that passed.

He picked up a pencil, and snapped it in half before hurling the pieces at the wall… Raising the team's morale wasn't going to be easy.

When DI Gravel entered the incident room a few minutes later, he was attempting to exude an air of confidence he didn't feel. He looked around the room, gratified that all relevant officers were ready and waiting, with the exception of Bethan Williams, whom he wasn't expecting to attend.

The loud chatter stopped abruptly when the inspector stood at the front of the room and raised a hand high above his head. He casually surveyed the limited resources under his command and swore silently under his breath… They were inadequate, but would have to do. The curse of small rural forces.

You could have heard a pin drop as he began speaking. 'Right people, listen carefully.' And then a joke to reduce the tension: 'I'll be asking questions later.' Everyone laughed. They felt they had to.

He raised his open hand in the air for a second time, effectively silencing the room. 'Listen up, everyone. Time to get serious. Siân Mailer found her injured mother and discovered that her brother was missing approximately seven and a half hours ago. Time is moving on, people. In this type of investigation rapid results are essential for a successful outcome. Molly Mailer is in South Wales General. She's had surgery, and Bethan will let me know if and when she can be interviewed. But I'm not holding my breath. It's not going to be anytime soon. So I hope you lot can offer me something. Anthony Mailer is still missing. Mrs Mailer's attack was a vicious, sustained assault. It is highly likely that the same perpetrator, or perpetrators, snatched Anthony. I do not need to tell you what that could mean. We need to find him, and fast.' He paused for breath and then continued. 'Let's hear what you've got. Clive, you kick off. Anything from the hospitals or the boy's known contacts?'

DS Rankin shook his head. 'Nothing, sorry, boss.'

'What, nothing at all?'

'Nothing, boss.'

'DC Hawkins, what of the nonces?'

'I've made a good start, sir, but we're talking over three hundred known paedophiles in this county alone. I'm looking at MOs and putting a shortlist together, but as you know it takes time. Up to this point there are no standout suspects. And there are the robbers as well, of course. A few housebreakers have attacked householders in recent years. They'll have to be looked at.'

'Thanks, George, concentrate on the nonces for now, and get the shortlist completed by nine tomorrow morning. We'll talk and see what we've got then.'

DC Hawkins nodded… It was going to be a long night.

DI Gravel turned to the scenes of crime officer. 'Anything useful?'

'Nothing new to report I'm afraid, sir. I think we can safely say that whoever did this was forensically aware.'

'Okay, we know what you didn't find; now tell everyone the good news.'

'Will do, sir. As you know, we did find several faint footprints at the back of the building. We're talking about what appear to be fresh prints leading to and at the obvious access point. They exited the building somewhere else, probably the front door. There are two different size prints: one pair of size eight and the other size ten. The prints strongly suggest that the perpetrator with the size eight feet is significantly heavier than the other. That's as good as it gets, I'm afraid.'

DI Gravel nodded. 'It doesn't give us a suspect, but it's a start. If you're left with any interesting prints after the obvious are excluded let me know immediately. Thanks Ben.'

'You're welcome, sir.'

'Right, let's move on. The search team, what have you got for me?'

The search officers glanced furtively in each other's direction, but nobody responded.

'Come on, let's hear it.'

A long-serving career constable seated at the back finally spoke up. 'Nothing, sir.'

'What, nothing at all?'

'No, sir, the dog did pick up on something at the back of the building, but he lost the scent on the road just outside the cottage.'

'Right, we'll widen the search at first light. I want you all back here at five a.m. sharp. I'll talk to the uniform chief super and make sure additional officers are available to help you. Let's move on. Door-to-door, anything to report?'

PC Kieran Harris moved closer to the edge of his seat… This was it. This was his moment in the sun.

He cleared his throat theatrically, and held his hand up like an enthusiastic child in a classroom; but he lowered it quickly when the room erupted in laughter… This wasn't how it was supposed to be.

DI Gravel guffawed along with the others… But enough was enough. The young constable had experienced some difficulties settling in, but he showed significant promise that was worthy of encouragement.

He clapped his hands together hard. 'Back to business, people. We need to get on. Right, son, what have you got to say for yourself?'

PC Harris swallowed hard.

'Come on, son, don't be shy. We're all on the same side.'

This is it, Kieran. This is your moment. 'Sir, I've got something to report…' Glory was imminent. They wouldn't be laughing after this.

He took his pocket book from the top right-hand pocket of his tunic and turned dramatically to the relevant page, which he'd earlier marked with an oversized paper clip. He made an unnecessary show of referring to his notes, cleared his throat loudly, and began. 'Sir, at seventeen thirty hours I interviewed eighty-seven-year-old Mrs Rachel Evans at her home, Rose house, located almost exactly opposite the Mailers' cottage.'

'Come on, son, you're not in court now. Get on with it, for fuck's sake. What did the old dear have to say for herself?'

PC Harris took a deep intake of breath, puffed out his chest and continued. 'Mrs Evans informed me that during the early hours of this morning she saw a large white van, which was covered in rust, parked directly outside the Mailers' home. She couldn't give an exact time, and she didn't know the make of the vehicle.'

DI Gravel knew the answer was going to be 'no' before asking the question. 'Did she see the number plate, son?'

'No, sir, I did ask, but no.'

'I suppose that would have been too much to ask for. Right son, anything else?'

'Mrs Evans saw two men leave the cottage and drive off in the van. One of the men was carrying something on his shoulder. She said it could have been a child.'

'Description, son, did you get a description?'

How could he forget the description? He swallowed hard. 'That's the strange thing, sir, she said they were dressed from head to foot in white, even their heads.'

The inspector looked perplexed. 'Right son, is that it?'

'She said one man was tall and muscular and the other shorter and slightly overweight. The shorter one was carrying what could have been the boy.'

PC Harris sat back in his seat and awaited his plaudits.

'That's great, son, but why the fuck didn't you tell me all this earlier? Every minute matters, son. You've got a fucking radio, haven't you? Use the fucking thing.'

The DI paused briefly to collect his thoughts. 'Right, Clive, you heard what the boy had to say for himself. Get yourself over to the old dear's house and take a full statement from her. Hawkins, check the system, find out if any of the local nonces own or have access to a white van meeting the description. This could be the break we need. I'm going to be in the station for another hour or two and then you can get me at home if you need to.'

He focused on PC Harris, who actively avoided his accusing gaze. 'I don't want anyone else making the same mistake as the boy here. Pick up the fucking phone or use your radio immediately if you find out anything useful.'

There was a chorus of, 'Yes, sir!' from every corner of the room.

DI Gravel was about to bring the meeting to a timely close when PC Harris put his hand up for a second time. This time nobody laughed. 'Sir, there is one more thing. I don't know if it's significant.'

This had better be good. 'Come on, son, let's hear it.'

PC Harris reopened his pocket book and frantically searched for the relevant page. 'Sir, at ten to four this morning I stopped a van meeting the description given by Mrs Evans in Eden Road.'

'Oh, for fuck's sake, son, you have to tell me this stuff. Right, bollocking over. Did you by any chance get the index number?'

'I requested a PNC check, sir. The registered keeper has a history of dishonesty offences, but he's not currently wanted.'

'What's his name, son?'

'Fisher, Wayne Fisher! I issued him with a HORT1.'

'Did you look in the van, son?'

PC Harris looked suddenly paler. 'I didn't give it any thought to be honest, sir.'

'No worries, son, you've done well.'

The thin smile that crossed the young constable's face quickly became a frown… This wasn't going to go down well. 'Sir, I need to inform you that there was a second man in the van with Fisher.'

'A second man?'

'Yes, sir!

DI Gravel shook his head discontentedly. 'I'm assuming they weren't dressed in white?'

'The young constable's face reddened. 'No, sir.'

'Did you get the second man's details?'

'No, sir.'

'Did you get a look at him, son?'

'I'm sorry, sir, it was dark, and the passenger didn't turn to face me. I was focused on checking the driver's documents. I just didn't think it mattered at the time.'

'Don't beat yourself up, son. You couldn't have known it could be important. Things seem a lot clearer after the event. You've done well, keep up the good work.'

Chapter 35

DI Gravel handed Rankin a chipped mug containing a generous tot of cheap-blended corner shop whisky. 'Well, Clive, my boy, we've been friends a long time; tell me what you think?'

The DS took a swig of whisky and grimaced as the malty spirit burned his throat. 'It's a long shot, boss, but you never know your luck. It is one hell of a coincidence: same description, same night, small town, not much traffic? It's possible, I guess.'

The inspector refilled both mugs and shook his head. 'What the fuck was Wayne Fisher doing in Eden Road at that time of the morning? You've had recent dealings with him, Clive. What do you make of it?'

'I'm not sure, boss, he's got a long history of theft, burglary, receiving, that sort of thing, but no history of violence or anything involving kids, as far as I'm aware. It's got to be worth a look I guess, but I can't see it to be honest.'

DI Gravel leant back in his seat and rested his feet on the desk. 'Right, Clive, I've got one or two things to mull over, but no doubt we'll be paying our friend Mr Fisher a visit in the morning. The way I look at it, we've got fuck all to lose. Sort out a search warrant and I'll see you at five. Now, piss off home and get some sleep.'

DS Rankin got up to leave, glad of the opportunity to finally see his family… Police work could be extremely hard on relationships.

He turned to the inspector as he left and casually touched his head with the side of one hand in reflexive salute. 'Will do, boss, see you in the morning.'

The second Rankin left the office, DI Gravel poured the remainder of his whisky into a plant pot, kicked his office door shut, and picked up the phone… What the hell was Trevor Simpson's home number?

He flicked through his contacts book… Trevor Simpson? Trevor Simpson? Yes, there it was.

He dialled the number… Get a move on, Trevor, answer the fucking thing.

'DI Simpson,'

'Hello, Trevor, it's Grav. About fucking time. Sorry to bother you at home, mate, but you know how it is.'

'I certainly do, Grav, no peace for the wicked, eh? What can I do for you?'

'I could be wrong, Trevor, but am I right in thinking that Wayne Fisher has been mentioned as part of your paedophile ring investigation?'

'It was all a bit vague to be honest, Grav. He's only been mentioned by the one child, and she couldn't be certain of his identity. The description she gave doesn't match aspects of his appearance. He may or may not be involved. I've got my doubts. We'd need a lot more before pulling him in.'

'But it's a possibility?'

'Well, I guess it's a possibility. I haven't ruled it out completely. Why do you ask?'

'It's a long shot to be honest, Trevor. You know this Mailer case I'm working on, GBH to the mother, and a missing seven-year-old boy?'

'Yeah, of course, Grav. But where does Fisher fit in?'

'I doubt if he does to be honest, Trevor. But it's worth considering. I've got fuck all else at the moment. An old dear living opposite the crime scene is saying she saw a white van matching the description of Fisher's vehicle parked outside the house on the night of the abduction.'

DI Simpson laughed loudly. 'There are a lot of white vans about, Grav. You're not getting desperate are you?'

'One of our young probationers ran a PNC check on Fisher's van in Eden Road in the early hours. It meets the description: large white van, rusty, right sort of time, and there was someone else in the vehicle.'

'Any idea who?'

'No'

'Got a description?'

'Nothing of any use.'

'Eden Road? That's well out of Fisher's usual stomping ground. Eden Road? Eden Road? It does ring a bell.'

'Come on, Trevor, get a grip for fuck's sake. Spit it out, I've got a bed to go to.'

There was a few seconds' silence before DI Simpson responded. 'It's probably nothing, Grav, but Galbraith lives there, the psychiatrist.'

'I don't like coincidences, Trevor.'

'Oh, come on, Grav, I don't see Fisher and Galbraith as friends, do you?'

Grav laughed. 'No, you've got a point there, Trevor. I can't see them having too much in common.'

'Look Grav, the ring investigation's making surprisingly good progress. Things have moved on a lot quicker than I could have hoped for. I talked to the CPS this afternoon as it happens. We've got enough to arrest five of the suspects as of now: four men and one woman. Fisher isn't on the list at the moment, and he isn't likely to be unless additional evidence surfaces, but Galbraith is. There are still a few outstanding video interviews with child witnesses arranged for tomorrow, which with a bit of luck may give us enough for more arrests. It's a game in progress, Grav. I'm only going to know the situation for certain when I review the joint investigation tapes and see what we've got. There's a planning meeting arranged at the social services resource centre at two on Tuesday to agree the timing of arrests *etcetera*. Can you hold off any action on Fisher until after that? In the unlikely event he's involved, I wouldn't want any of the suspects getting the idea we're on to them any sooner than they need to know.'

'Oh, for fuck's sake! I don't like it to be honest, Trevor. I know it's a long shot, but if Fisher played any part in abducting the boy and I do fuck all for a couple of days, it's not going to look too good is it? That's a rhetorical question by the way; the mother's in one hell of a state.'

'All right, Grav, point taken, but we're not going to agree on this one. Look, how about we talk to the chief super in the morning? He's always in by about half eight. He can make the decision, privilege of rank and all that. It's what he's paid for after all.'

'I've got a fucking briefing arranged for five in the morning, Trevor. I was planning on giving our Mr Fisher an early morning wake-up call straight after that.'

'I'm afraid it's going to have to wait, Grav, tempting as it is. Let's see what the super thinks and take it from there. Is that all right with you?'

DI Gravel shook his head. 'I suppose it's going to have to be, Trevor. You owe me a fucking pint.'

DI Simpson chuckled to himself. 'Fair enough, Grav.' He paused momentarily. 'Your language hasn't got any better over the years, has it? Didn't your mother ever wash your mouth out with soap and water?'

'Fuck off, Trevor. I'll see you in the morning.'

DI Gravel slammed the phone down and kicked his wastepaper bin across the room with such force that it crashed into the opposite wall almost six feet from the floor. He sat back in his swivel chair, sighed despondently, and picked up a pile of papers from his desk, full of good intentions. But he put them back in the orange plastic in-tray almost immediately… He needed a shower. He needed sleep. The papers could wait.

He stood up to head for home, but then decided to make one last call before leaving. The hospital switchboard answered after a surprisingly short wait and a chirpy female voice said, 'Hello, South Wales General.'

'Evening, intensive care please.' This time the phone rang and rang before finally being answered. 'Staff speaking?'

'Good evening, this is Detective Inspector Gravel, local police. You've got one of my uniform officers there somewhere. Can I speak to her please?'

'The last time I saw her she was in the dayroom. Shall I ask her to give you a ring?'

'I'll hold on, ta.'

After approximately five minutes he heard WPC Williams' familiar voice saying, 'Hello, sir.'

'Hi, Bethan, any news for me?'

'It's good news I suppose, sir. I was about to ring you. Mrs Mailer came around very briefly about fifteen minutes ago. The doctors seem more optimistic than they were earlier, but what with the drugs and her injuries she was drifting in and out of consciousness.'

'Did you get the chance to talk to her?'

'Very briefly, sir, before the sister stopped me. It wasn't easy to understand her, but I think she may have asked about Anthony. To be honest I couldn't bring myself to tell her the truth. She's got enough to deal with at the moment.'

'She's going to have to know at some point, Constable, but I guess it can wait for the moment. Did she say anything useful?'

He'd used her rank rather than her name. He wasn't happy. It was a no win situation. 'There is something else, sir, but it doesn't make a lot of sense.'

'Spit it out, Bethan. It's been a long day.'

'Mrs Mailer wasn't making a lot of sense, sir. I don't know if it's even worth telling you this, but here goes. Her words were garbled and disjointed, but she seemed to be trying to tell me that she woke up for a fraction of a second just before the attack. She thinks she looked directly into her attacker's face before passing out.'

The inspector's heart was racing. 'Could she describe him?'

'This is where things get strange, sir. She appeared to repeat the same name several times before drifting back into unconsciousness. I think she must have been confused or dreaming.'

'For fuck's sake, Bethan! What was the name?'

'Dr David Galbraith! You know, sir, it's a Scottish name.'

'Yes, I do know that, Bethan. I'm not a complete ignoramus despite the rumours.'

'Sorry, sir, I didn't mean to imply….'

'I'd stop digging if I were you, Constable. Right, you stay where you are tonight. I'll send someone over to relieve you in the morning, so you can get a bite to eat and a change of clothes before going back. If Mrs Mailer says anything else, anything at all, ring me at home whatever the time is. Have you got my number?'

'Yes, sir.'

'Keep what Mrs Mailer said to you to yourself for now, Bethan. It may not be as crazy as it sounds.'

Chapter 36

'Good morning to you all! Nice to see that everyone's on time, even if most of you do look like shit.' DI Gravel waited for a response, but it was limited to a few half-hearted groans… It was too early in the morning for banter, however well-intentioned and senior the source.

The inspector smiled nonetheless, and continued. 'You will no doubt be pleased to hear that there have been a number of potentially positive developments in the case. That said, Anthony Mailer is still missing. Finding him, hopefully finding him alive, remains our first priority. This is very important work, people. A child's life is at stake. We haven't got time to piss about, so listen carefully. You all need to be crystal clear what your duties are.'

The DI pointed to a map of the area he'd prepared in advance of the meeting. He tapped his forefinger repeatedly on a large black X marked close to the centre of the map in bold indelible felt pen. 'This is the exact location of the Mailers' cottage. The crime scene, if you like.' He tapped the map again. 'This first circle, the red one, indicates the area we searched yesterday. I'm sure that you are all very well aware that nothing of significance was found. That makes it all the more important that we search again today. We will keep looking until we find something. This work is not glamorous or exciting, but it is essential. We are going through a well-established methodical process that gets results. Remember that.'

He turned his attention back to the map on the wall behind him. 'This bigger circle, the blue one, marks the boundary of the additional area that those of you allocated the task will search today. To be clear, we are going to search the area we searched yesterday again, and then extend the search to the area within the blue line. Familiarise yourselves with the map before you leave. Sergeant Thomas here will be responsible for supervising the search officers on the ground. If we don't find anything today, we will do the same thing again tomorrow and the day after that, and the day after that until we do. You will be glad to know that I have arranged transport for you lucky people.' He grinned in response to the sarcastic cheer and waited impatiently for the search officers to peruse the map and leave. The process was taking too long, however, and he gestured to the uniform sergeant.

'Yes, sir?'

'Take that fucking map, Sergeant, and piss off somewhere else to look at it. I need to get on.'

'Yes, sir!'

'Right, you lot will be making further house-to-house enquiries. DS Rankin here will give you your specific orders once I've concluded the briefing. Young PC Harris obtained some useful evidence yesterday. Let's hope we can do the same today. If a probationer can do it, anyone can.' He paused for the inevitable laughter. 'Clive, if you do what needs to be done here, I'll speak to you later in the day. Remember everybody, if you discover anything potentially significant, anything at all, report it to DS Rankin who will in turn talk to me. Right, that's me done. Any questions? No, then piss off and find Anthony Mailer.'

DS Rankin looked at him with a perplexed expression on his face. 'Can I speak to you in private, boss?'

DI Gravel nodded. 'Let's go to my office, Clive. The rest of you get yourselves a quick coffee in the canteen. It's going to be a long day.'

'Don't bother sitting down, Clive. We need to make a move soon.'

'What about Fisher, boss? I've sorted the warrant.'

As the DI outlined the previous evening's events, Rankin shook his head incredulously… He'd been in the job long enough to know that investigations could change directions quickly, but this seemed to be a case of one investigation getting in the way of another with potentially serious consequences. 'I know it's a long shot, Grav, but what if Fisher's got the boy? If we delay and it goes pear-shaped, where the hell does that leave us?'

'I'm not happy with the situation either, to be honest, Clive. But, there's fuck all I can do about it. I'll know more when I've seen the chief super. Now piss off and get on with those house-to-house enquiries.'

'Okay, boss, I'll give you a shout if we come up with anything useful.'

DI Gravel got on with some paperwork and kept his eye on the clock. At 8:15 a.m. precisely he picked up the phone. 'Trevor, it's Grav. Have you given any further thought to last night's discussion?'

'I haven't revised my position, Grav.'

'I'll see you outside the super's office in ten minutes.'

The two experienced detective inspectors stood outside their head of department's door like apprehensive schoolboys awaiting their head teacher. DI Gravel knocked reticently, and waited respectfully for the chief super's response.

Detective Chief Superintendent Graham Chapman had arrived in work unusually early. He had his in-laws staying for a week's holiday from Devon, and had used work as a transparent excuse to escape the house. He knew his wife would make him pay at some later date, but he told himself it was probably worth it. He smiled when he heard the knock on the door… It was a good day to be in work. 'Come in and take a seat, boys. I'm assuming this has got to be important or you'd have made an appointment. No worries, what can I do for you both?'

The two men glanced in each other's direction, waiting for the other to reveal his cards.

'Come on, boys, for Pete's sake. What's the delay? Trevor, you make a start.'

DI Simpson began outlining the salient facts and the potentially conflicting priorities of the two overlapping investigations. But, before he had the chance to say very much at all, the chief super intervened, as he often did. It was uncanny. His efficiency and total dedication to his role meant that almost nothing that happened in the division was ever a surprise to him. 'Trevor, let me stop you there. I'm already fully conversant with the facts. I've read the relevant paperwork and seen the computer records. Let me summarise. Interrupt me if I get anything wrong.' All three men knew that wasn't going to happen. 'Firstly, the paedophile ring is a top priority investigation that's going to be high profile: in the papers, on TV, that sort of thing. There's inevitably going to be a great deal of unwelcome media interest from the gutter press. You know what the parasites are like. If there's a potential criticism to make, they'll make it. We have to get it right, and be seen to get it right. We have enough solid evidence to arrest and charge five suspects as of now. I believe that's how the CPS put it, Trevor?'

'That's correct, sir.'

'The situation may well improve as things progress. Or at least, let's hope so. You seem to be well on top of it. We can't jeopardise the enquiry; there's far too much to lose. The chief constable would not be a happy man. All arrests need to be carefully coordinated so as not to give any potential for the destruction of evidence or interference with witnesses. I shouldn't need to tell you that. It's bloody obvious.'

'Yes, sir!'

'Secondly, we have the missing seven-year-old lad and the attempted murder of his mother. It goes without saying: another high-priority case. A child's life may well be on the line. I see your dilemma, Grav. But, this business with Fisher, it's speculative at best. The witness is old with poor eyesight, it was dark, and she'd taken a sleeping tablet. Not exactly the most reliable witness, I'm sure you'd agree. Any half-decent defence barrister would tear it apart. You know that. On the other hand, we know that Fisher's van was seen in Eden Road the same night. Fisher has been named by one child as part of the ring investigation, albeit her description was less than accurate, and there's nothing to corroborate her allegations. It's far from certain. As of now there isn't enough to arrest him as part of the first wave. That situation could change, of course, as the investigation progresses. But we can't base our plans on possibilities.'

DI Gravel shook his head discontentedly, but the chief super wasn't finished.

'Don't lose the will to live just yet, Grav. There may be a way around this if we use some imagination. I realise Galbraith lives in Eden Road and that both men are implicated to varying degrees in the ring. Could be significant, but probably not. As of now there's nothing to suggest either man has, or ever had, Anthony Mailer. At this stage we don't know the identity of the second man in Fisher's van, but I'm sure you'll both agree that Fisher and Galbraith seem highly unlikely bedfellows. That said, it's a remote possibility we can't afford to ignore. What I suggest is this: Dr Galbraith will be arrested along with the other primary suspects at a time to be agreed by tomorrow's planning meeting. I propose that the time will be early on Thursday morning.' He checked his desk diary. 'That'll be the thirteenth. Each arrest team will be accompanied by trained search officers, with dogs where available. We'll go through each house with a fine-tooth comb. That takes care of Galbraith. Now for Fisher! As I've already made clear, there isn't enough on Fisher to justify arresting him as part of the first wave. I don't want the bastard arrested and then released without charge. That doesn't help anyone. Agreed?'

The two inspectors nodded their agreement as the chief superintendent continued his soliloquy. 'Fisher does, however, have a long history of dishonesty offences that is well known to you both. I'm sure there has to be some outstanding matters that would give reasonable grounds for paying him a visit. Searching his property and any vehicles he may own would be entirely justified. Get it done today, Grav. Even if you find nothing to charge him with, you can at least have a good look around and establish what he was doing in Eden Road at that time of the morning. Make no mention of any allegations relating to children at this stage. Do you understand where I'm coming from?'

'I do, sir.'

'Before we finish, boys, this conversation didn't happen. Understand?'

Both men nodded in unison.

'Off you go, boys. Best if you both go to tomorrow's meeting. Keep me informed of all developments. Like it or not, the next few days could decide our professional futures. Close the door on your way out.'

'What do you make of that, Grav?'

'Could be a lot worse, Trevor. How the fuck does he do it? He knows what I'm thinking before I do sometimes.'
'Beats me, Grav. I'll see you tomorrow.'
'Cheers, Trevor.'

'Clive, I'm back in the office. Fisher's back on. We're looking for stolen goods.'
'Receiving? What the…?'
'I know, Clive. Ask me no questions and I'll tell you no lies. Be back here at ten, and we'll pay our Mr Fisher a visit.'

'Morning, boss, have we got time for a hot drink before we go? It's bloody freezing out there.'
'I don't see why not, Clive. I'll put the kettle on. You've got the warrant I presume.'
Rankin tapped a jacket pocket and nodded.
DI Gravel poured the boiling water and added milk and sugar. 'There you go, Clive, my boy, get it down. We need to make a move in five minutes. Any developments I don't know about?'
'Nothing as yet, boss. Maybe we'll have more luck this morning.'
The DI finished his coffee, placed the mug down on his desktop, and stood up to leave. 'Let's hope so, Clive. Let's hope so.'
The inspector took a bunch of keys from a desk drawer and threw them to Rankin. 'I'm knackered, Clive. You can do the driving.'

Clive Rankin manoeuvred the unmarked police car through the large grey-painted wooden gates that lead into Wayne Fisher's shambolic scrapyard about twenty minutes later. There were mangled vehicles of every kind piled high on either side of the enclosure, and a large black and rust corrugated iron building which served as an office and workshop at the far end, where metal was weighed and cash changed hands. Fisher's white Ford Transit van was parked directly in front of the structure.
Fisher identified the car as a police vehicle long before recognising the two officers in the front seats. He swore loudly, but was ultimately

resigned to what he saw as a regrettable occupational hazard… Regular visits from the police were inconvenient, but an unavoidable part of the job.

He looked around his yard and grinned… As it happened, on this occasion, unusually for him, he had no stolen goods on the premises other than various virtually indistinguishable pieces of scrap metal that would be almost impossible to identify. There was very little, if anything, to worry about.

Fisher confidently approached the police car just as Gravel and Rankin were stepping out and closing the doors. 'Mr Gravel, Mr Rankin, lovely to see you both again. What can I do for you two fine gentlemen?'

The inspector glared at him accusingly. 'You can stop taking the piss, Fisher. I am not in the mood.'

'Oh, don't be like that, Mr Gravel. I'm always happy to help the police.'

The DI turned to Rankin. 'If he's trying to wind me up, he's doing a fucking good job of it.' He strode towards Fisher and poked him hard in the chest, causing the Irishman to lose his balance and stumble backwards. 'We've received information that you have stolen items on the premises, Wayne. Anything you want to tell us before we have a look around? Wasting my time will not do you any favours.'

Fisher got back to his feet and brushed himself off. 'Stolen goods? No, nothing like that, Mr Gravel. I'm a good boy these days.'

'We'd love to stay here all day and listen to your fucking jokes, Wayne, but we've got work to do.' He stepped forward, placed his face an inch or two from Fisher's, and stared into his eyes. 'Several churches in the area have had the lead stripped from their roofs in recent days, Wayne. That makes me extremely unhappy. I fully intend to nail any bastard who played any part in it. We'll look around the yard; when we've done that we'll look at your office, and when we've done that we'll have a good look at your van. If there's anything to find, we'll find it. Anything you want to tell us, Wayne? Now would be a good time.'

All of a sudden Wayne Fisher wasn't feeling quite so confident… Constables searched, sergeants possibly, but detective inspectors didn't get their hands dirty. They had people to do that for them. What the hell was going on?

He felt his heart pounding in his chest… What were they really there for? This wasn't about scrap metal. Why the hell did Galbraith need use of the van?

Gravel and Rankin spent almost two hours searching without finding anything to suggest that Anthony Mailer, or any other child for that matter, had ever been anywhere near the scrapyard. Both men had, however, noticed that Fisher became edgy, nervous even, when they examined the Ford Transit. They looked at every inch of the vehicle but found nothing at all, which seemed significant in itself. The outside was its usual rustbucket dirty mess, but the inside was absolutely immaculate. Someone had clearly taken a great deal of care to clean it.

Fisher had no idea why Dr Galbraith had insisted he repeatedly clean the van's interior as he supervised, and he hadn't asked… It was best not to know the answer to some questions.

'Right, Wayne, we're going to impound the van so that the SOCO boys can have a good look at it.'

Fisher's stomach was doing somersaults… He really didn't need this level of police attention. 'Oh, come on, Mr Gravel. You haven't found a thing, have you? I had fuck all to do with the church jobs. I need the van to make a living, for fuck's sake.'

'What were you doing in Eden Road in the early hours of Sunday morning, Wayne? I'd think very carefully before answering, if I were you. I'm not in the mood to take any more of your shit.'

Fisher was very close to tears… What the hell could he say to that? He had to come up with something. 'There's got to be some mistake, Mr Gravel. I had a couple of drinks, watched television, and crashed into bed for the night. I didn't leave the house.'

The inspector laughed dismissively. 'Oh come on, even you can do better than that, surely? You were stopped by a police officer, Wayne.

He made a record of your index number. You were ordered to produce your fucking documents. Now try again!'

Fisher's face appeared to drain of blood… How the hell was he supposed to respond to that? He could confirm he was driving. He could invent some crap explaining where he'd been. He could try to blag it. That was one possibility. But, what the hell was Galbraith doing? The man was a total psycho. He could potentially implicate himself in something he wanted no part of. It was a no win situation. 'Look, Mr Gravel, I don't need this kind of hassle. I've got the documents in the office. You're welcome to see them whenever you want to. I can get them now if that helps.'

'What were you doing in Eden Road, Wayne?'

'I need the van for the job, Mr Gravel. Give me a break, please.'

'I'll ask you again, Fisher. What were you doing in Eden Road? You can tell us here or at the station. It's your choice.'

Fisher began trembling as his earlier bravado melted away like an ice cube in the hot summer sun… Receiving, theft or a bit of burglary were one thing, but this had to be something more serious. A lot more serious! Whatever it was, he wanted no part of it. Say nothing. That was the only option left open to him. Say nothing.

'I'm waiting, Wayne. Stop pissing me about. I am losing patience fast, you thieving bastard.'

Silence.

'There was another man in the van with you, Wayne. Who was he?'

'I don't know what the hell you're talking about.'

'There was a man in the passenger seat when you were stopped, Wayne. He was seen by an officer. Who was he?'

Silence.

DI Gravel turned and walked away for fear of striking his suspect. 'Enough! Cuff him, Clive. Let's get the bastard arrested and in the car. We'll have a final look around this shit-hole, and search the house on the way to the station. Radio through to the SOCO boys and get that fucking van collected.'

DS Rankin drove while DI Gravel sat in the back repeatedly asking Wayne Fisher the same two unanswered questions: 'What were you doing in Eden Road?' And, 'Who else was in the van?'

Fisher sat tight-lipped, and didn't speak at any point of the journey… It seemed the sensible approach.

The inspector was all too painfully aware that his was a fishing expedition with very little bait… Unless they got a lucky break, the morning's work was going to achieve fuck all that would help find Anthony Mailer or bring his mother's attacker to justice. It was possible, even probable, that they were wasting their time. It was time they just didn't have to waste.

Chapter 37

'Fisher's still asking for his call, boss. '

DI Gravel shook his head and snorted disdainfully. 'The bastard seems to understand the legal system as well as I do.'

'It seems so, boss.'

'Let him make his call, Clive. And then lock him up and let him sweat awhile.'

'Any news from DI Simpson?'

'Fuck all as yet, Clive. I'll give him a bell to see how things are progressing. Look, why don't you have a quick cup of tea in the canteen, and I'll give you a shout when I'm ready for Fisher's interrogation.'

Wayne Fisher looked behind him and then to each side of the room, before finally picking up the phone... Unless the pigs had some unlikely high-tech snooping device hidden somewhere it was safe to make the call.

His hand hovered above the dial… What the hell was Galbraith's number? Was it five-nine-six or nine-five-six? Nine-five-six! That was it. He dialled frantically and listened to the ringtone.

Cynthia Galbraith answered the phone almost immediately and was slightly out of breath when she said, 'Hello, who's speaking, please?'

'My name's Fisher, Wayne Fisher, I'm a friend of your husband. I need to speak to him.'

'I haven't heard him mention your name, Mr Fisher.'

'Is he there?'

'Yes, but he doesn't like to be disturbed, Mr Fisher.'

What the hell was wrong with the woman? 'This is urgent, lady. He would want to hear what I have to say. Just tell him who's on the phone, please.'

Cynthia was suddenly aware that her hair was sticking to her forehead… What if it was urgent? The man seemed angry for some inexplicable reason. Maybe it was a male thing. Perhaps taking a message was the preferable option. 'I really don't want to disturb him when he's working, Mr Fisher. If you know my husband as you claim to, you will understand that he wouldn't appreciate it at all. Can I take a message?'

'This can't wait, Mrs Galbraith. I don't know how I can make myself any clearer? This call is extremely urgent. I need to talk to him now please.'

'I suppose I could ask him if he wants to speak to you.'

'That would be great. Please do that.'

Cynthia stood at the entrance to her husband's secret world, staring at the forbidden grey concrete steps, and for the first time ever she dared to descend, step by slow determined step towards the white steel security-door at the bottom. She hesitated on reaching the door, solely tempted to retreat back to the comparative safety of the kitchen. But instead, after a few seconds urging herself to act, she knocked on the cold metal, softly at first, as if hoping he wouldn't hear her, and then harder, time and time again until he did.

When Dr Galbraith opened the door, the two of them stood like silent statues, intensely focused on one another for a full ten seconds before Cynthia finally looked away. As the doctor raised his right fist to punch her, she took a rapid backward step and raised both arms defensively, before blurting out, 'Wayne Fisher's on the phone. He says it's urgent. I'm sorry, he said I had to interrupt you.'

The doctor stopped dead in his tracks… Why the hell was Fisher contacting him? It had better be good.

He lowered his arm without striking, and pushed past Cynthia on his way up the steps.

Cynthia didn't move at first, but then she took a single step forward… Should she put her head through the doorframe and peep into the prohibited glaringly bright room? It would be illuminating. But, what if he came back and caught her looking? That degree of danger was unthinkable.

She turned on her heels, fled back up the steps a great deal quicker than she'd descended a minute or two earlier, and tried her best to convince herself that she'd made the correct choice… Like it or not, there was no avoiding the fact. Something was wrong. Something was very wrong.

'Fisher? It's Dr Galbraith; I was working. What the hell do you want, man?'

Wayne Fisher was beginning to wonder if contacting Dr Galbraith was such a good idea after all. 'I'm at the police station, Doctor. I've been nicked on suspicion of receiving.'

'What the hell has that got to do with me, man?'

'They've taken the van, Doctor. They've never done that before. Something's up. They're asking questions I can't answer.'

Pressure and sound exploded inside his skull… His world was unravelling. The little bastard was still unconscious and now this. He should have insisted on crushing the damn thing. Why hadn't he thought of it before? 'Keep my name out of it, Fisher, or I will kill you. Do you hear me, man?' He slammed down the phone, cracking the red plastic receiver.

Wayne Fisher's legs weakened, his head began to swim… It was no empty threat. The man was dangerous. There was no way he was telling the pigs anything at all.

Dr Galbraith returned to the cellar and sat on the tiled-floor with his legs crossed and his head bowed low… Why hadn't he punched the bitch? It would have alleviated the pressure to a degree, wouldn't it? Yes, of course it would. And he needed all the help he could get. He'd rectify his omission at some point later in the day; but that particular pleasure would have to wait. There were important decisions to make. Decisions that couldn't be delayed further.

The doctor noticed his eyes moisten as he relived recent events in his mind… He'd dedicated a great deal of time and effort to the little bastard's abduction and incarceration. He'd prepared comprehensive plans outlining his exact intentions. Now, he had to accept the awful reality that those much-cherished plans may never become reality. It was almost too much to bear.

Dr Galbraith rose to his feet and began pacing the floor, wringing his hands, and tearing intermittently at his short black hair… If the police were sniffing around as Fisher claimed, inaction was not an option. He had to be proactive. He had to retain control. He could wait for however long it took for the little bastard to regain consciousness; that was one possibility with obvious advantages. But was it sensible if the police were getting closer? Time could well be running out.

He shook his head aggressively… Perhaps it was worth waiting two, or maybe three more days maximum. Maybe that would prove sufficient to facilitate some sport. Maybe, or maybe not? All he could do was hope. Or, he could cut his losses, kill the little bastard now, and destroy the evidence. That was the sensible option, wasn't it?

Dr Galbraith clutched at his head as the pressure built and distorted his otherwise handsome features… It made sense to keep the little bastard alive for another forty-eight hours, but not a second longer. Yes, yes, that was logical. That made sense. Forty-eight hours conscious or unconscious, then he had to die.

Chapter 38

'Trevor, it's Grav. How you doing?'

'Not bad thanks, Grav. What can I do for you, mate?'

'Any developments your end?'

'Yeah, the interviews are going pretty well, as it happens. There's some useful new evidence corroborating previous allegations and establishing further offences. There may well be enough for additional charges, probably additional arrests. I'll have to review the tapes properly and sound out the CPS before coming to any final conclusions naturally, but it's looking pretty good, Grav. Galbraith's well and truly in the frame. He should be going down for a long time all being well.'

'All being well?'

'We'll have more than enough to charge him, but getting a conviction may be a different matter. He's got a good reputation, he's one devious bastard, and the witnesses are young kids. We've got no idea how they'll stand up to cross examination, and that's if they give evidence at all.'

'Yeah, I see what you're saying, Trevor. I'd nail the cunt to a tree by his balls if it were up to me. Anything new on Fisher?'

'Nothing as yet, Grav. Fisher's going to have to wait awhile. We just haven't got enough on him as things stand. Any joy your end?'

'Fuck all, Trevor. We found nothing of interest at the yard or the house, and he kept his mouth well and truly shut despite a lot of pressure, if you know what I mean. I blame those detective shows on the telly. It seems every criminal's a fucking lawyer these days. Didn't say a word.'

'I've had a lot of dealings with Fisher over the years, Grav. He was banged up for a three-year stretch for burglary on one happy occasion. He's usually an easy option merchant. Anything for an easy life; no comment's just not his style.'

‘He’s shit scared of something or someone. We gave him a seriously hard time, but he just sat there in total silence for almost two hours. None of his usual bullshit. Not a fucking word.’

‘What about the van?’

‘The SOCO boys had a good look at it this afternoon. The inside was fucking immaculate. Like new, they said. No signs of life. Not even a single fingerprint anywhere, except for mine and Rankin’s. Fuck all! Our Mr Fisher’s been up to something, but I’ve got nothing on him.’

‘You win some, you lose some, Grav.’

‘Fisher’s time will come.’

‘Let’s hope so. How’s the Mailer investigation going otherwise? Are you any nearer finding the boy?’

‘It’s going nowhere at the moment, Trevor. I’m thinking Fisher being out and about that night was purely coincidental. Like you said, there are a lot of white vans in circulation.’

‘It was always a long shot, Grav. You already knew that.’

‘You’re not wrong, Trevor. If we find the boy alive, it’ll be a fucking miracle.’

Chapter 39

After several hours of drug-induced slumber with only brief periods of confused dreamlike consciousness, the anaesthetic was at last wearing off. Molly was suddenly aware of her surroundings, but unsure if the terrifying pictures in her head were memories of real events or nightmare constructs of her subconscious mind.

Molly opened her bruised and swollen eyes and saw Mike and Siân's familiar faces smiling down at her. She tried to reciprocate, but the effort was simply too painful. She could see that Mike was weeping, and felt his warm tears fall on her face as he leant over to gently kiss her head. 'Hello, Mo, it's good to have you back with us, love. It was touch and go for a while.'

Molly's eyes flitted urgently around the ward… Tony! Where was Tony? If only she could ask. If only she could shout his name.

She tried repeatedly to speak, but no words came. Mike instinctively guessed what she was trying to say, but feared the burden reality would place on her may be too great for either of them to bear. He placed his ear close to her mouth hoping he was mistaken, but her faint garbled whisper was unmistakable, 'A-n-t-h-o-n-y?'

Mike stood upright, and looked at Siân with a look of utter desperation on his face… What was he supposed to say now? How was he supposed to tell Mo something he knew would break her heart? It would be reasonable to ignore the implied questions in the circumstances, wouldn't it?

After a moment's agonising silence, the best he could do was to say, 'Just concentrate on getting well for now, love. We can talk later when you're feeling better.'

Molly's eyes burned with anxious fury… What was the ineffectual prat trying to hide? There was definitely something. What if her dreams were memories? Anthony! Where was Anthony?

She began to wail pitifully, and then reached up despite her pain, despite her injuries, despite the ominous tightness in her chest, and grabbed Mike firmly by the front of his shirt with both hands. She pulled him close and hissed one, barely decipherable word, 'T-r-u-t-h!'

Molly released her grip and crashed back onto the bed exhausted by her exertions, as Mike staggered backwards, stunned by the intensity of her reaction… She wanted answers. She *needed* answers. But he wasn't going to be the one to provide them.

'Say something, Dad.'

Mike stared at his daughter without responding, and suddenly darted for the door just as Sister Thomas was entering the ward from the opposite direction. 'Slow down, Mr Mailer. This is a hospital ward, not a running track.'

Mike pushed past her, head down, eyes focused on the linoleum, and continued running.

WPC Williams went after him, and was soon joined by Siân, who was disappointed but not overly surprised by her father's actions. 'Stop, Mr Mailer, where are you going? Your family needs you here.'

But Mike didn't stop running until he reached the car park, where he sat on a cold wet curb and lit a cigarette, inhaling the toxic chemical soup deep into his troubled lungs… He loved Mo dearly, so why had he let her down again? And just when she most needed him. What the hell? He'd give it twenty minutes and go back to the ward. With a bit of luck Bethan or Siân would have told her the grim reality of the situation by then.

Siân gripped her mother's hand and gazed pleadingly at the police officer who was fast approaching the bed. Molly looked at one and then the other, meeting their eyes in turn… The police were there. It wasn't a dream. She'd been attacked in her bedroom. A man had attacked her. A man with blue eyes. But, what about Tony? Oh, God, what about Tony? She had to know the truth. Why weren't they telling her the truth? Surely, any reality couldn't be as bad as her own vivid imagination.

WPC Williams moved a chair closer to Molly, and smiled a half-smile which quickly left her face… Here goes. 'Mrs Mailer, we have talked before, but you were barely conscious. Do you remember anything about our conversation?'

Molly shook her head slowly and grimaced.

This was going to be truly awful for the poor woman to hear. What if it were one of her own kids? It just didn't bear thinking about. She forced another quickly vanishing smile and began. 'It's good to see you back with us, Mrs Mailer. My name's Constable Williams, Bethan Williams, please call me Bethan. I'm sure you want to know exactly what's going on.'

Molly nodded once and grimaced.

'Mrs Mailer, there's no easy way to tell you this. You were attacked in your home. You were in your bedroom at the time. Siân found you there and dialled nine-nine-nine. Can you remember anything that could help us catch the man who did this? Anything at all? Even seemingly insignificant details may prove vital.'

Molly felt panic-stricken… The images in her mind were real. They were definitely real. Where was Anthony? Why wasn't anyone talking about Anthony?

Molly tried desperately to speak, but the officer only heard mumbled distorted incomprehensible sounds: more white noise than language.

WPC Williams looked quizzically at Siân for clarification, but she shook her head ruefully. Molly's mouth had become increasingly swollen and bloody as she strained to communicate, and Siân couldn't understand her either.

WPC Williams nodded… It was time to use her imagination. 'All right, Mrs Mailer, I promise you I will tell you all I can, but please give me a minute.'

She hurried from the ward, and soon returned carrying a large notepad and a black marker pen purchased from the hospital's tiny WRVS shop. She looked Molly in the eye and held her gaze. 'I can't understand what you're trying to say to me, Molly. Do you think you could write it down?'

Molly nodded, rested the pad on one hand, and held the marker pen tightly in the other. Her hand shook wildly as she wrote the words she'd frantically tried to vocalise minutes earlier: WHERE IS ANTHONY?

Bethan Williams spoke slowly, trying desperately to prevent her voice breaking with emotion. 'Molly, there is no easy way to tell you that we don't know where your son is. I am so very sorry. I have children myself, and can only begin to imagine how truly terrible that must be to hear. But, we have officers looking for him, and we are confident we will find him soon…' She really shouldn't have said that. It may or may not be true. He may already be dead.

Molly began writing again on the second page: HAS SOMEONE TAKEN HIM?

The WPC looked directly at Molly, rather than give in to the strong temptation to look away… It was time for total honesty. The poor woman deserved to know the truth however distressing the facts. 'I know this isn't going to be easy for you to hear, Molly. But you're entitled to the truth.' She paused… How should she put it? What did it matter? There was no sugar-coating this particular pill. 'It is possible, but far from certain, that the person, or persons, who attacked you also abducted your son.'

Molly swallowed hard as she fought the impulse to vomit.

The WPC placed a reassuring hand on her left shoulder and tried to force a sympathetic smile that failed to materialise. 'Did you see or hear anything that could help us, Molly? Can you remember anything at all about the man who attacked you? How he looked, how he smelt, how he sounded, the words he used, any distinguishing marks? Anything?'

Molly hesitated… The memories seemed so real. But, surely her mind must be playing tricks on her.

After a moment's quiet contemplation she scribbled: I remember his eyes, just his eyes.

'What about his eyes?'

Molly nodded and wrote: 'Piercing blue, striking. I'm sure I've seen those eyes before.'

'Who was it, Molly? Who attacked you?'

She thought for a brief moment, fearing she may potentially misdirect the investigation; but then decided to trust her instincts. She turned to the third page of the pad and urgently wrote: DR DAVID GALBRAITH in large bold capitals. She handed it to the officer with an outstretched hand, and watched her reaction carefully… She wasn't laughing. She wasn't shaking her head. Perhaps it wasn't so ridiculous after all. Or was she a good actress, and trying to humour her? Yes, that was probably it.

'You named the same man earlier, but I needed to be certain you knew what you were saying. You were pretty drowsy at the time. I know it's going to be difficult, but please try to get some rest. I'm going to contact the officer in charge of the investigation immediately, and let him know exactly what you've told me. No doubt he'll want you to make a full statement as soon as possible.'

Molly turned to the fourth page of the notepad and wrote quickly in huge bold capital letters filling the entire page: FIND MY SON!

Chapter 40

Detective Inspector Trevor Simpson was working his way through seemingly endless piles of paper, in an admirable but ultimately hopeless attempt to keep his mind off the afternoon's multi-agency child protection planning meeting. He pushed the papers forcefully to one side and checked the clock… At least the waiting would soon be over. The case was dominating every aspect of his life. How could the bastards do what they did to children? How could the child protection officers do what they did as a full-time job? No wonder some of them liked a drink. No wonder their black humour was a little close to the edge at times. No wonder Pam was puking after interviewing the victims. And she'd refused to be taken off the case. That was dedication. Maybe he should have made it an order.

Trevor Simpson dialled Mel Nicholson's direct number and waited impatiently for an answer. Nicholson was reading through some lengthy childcare files, and pleased to be distracted. The outcomes of the morning's interviews and the intense activity that would inevitably follow the afternoon's meeting were weighing heavily on his mind, and he was glad to hear the inspector's familiar voice on the other end of the line when he picked up the phone. 'Mel, it's Trevor, how's it going in social services world? Ready for this afternoon?'

'As ready as I'll ever be, Trevor.'

'I can pick you up on the way, if that helps, mate. It might be an idea for us to have a chat about the case en route.'

'Yeah, I can't see why not, Trevor, but I need to be there about ten minutes early, if that's all right with you?'

'No problem.'

'How are the interviews going?'

'Better than expected, as it happens, Mel. We'll talk later. I'll pick you up at about twenty past one.'

'Thanks, Trevor, I'll see you then.'

Nicholson placed the phone back on its receiver and sat back in his chair with his eyes tight shut, trying to relax. He pictured a warm sun-drenched Barbadian beach with clear blue translucent water lapping on its green and sandy shore. But it didn't last. Nicholson sighed, resigned to the inevitable, as his brief fantasy faded and reality dawned once more… Maybe after the case was over he could take his family there for a couple of weeks. He'd always wanted to.

He smiled… Why not make the fantasy reality?

But the smile evaporated from his face as quickly as it appeared… Money, that was why not. His salary just didn't suffice. It would be camping in Northern France again. Like it or lump it.

Nicholson chuckled to himself, and retrieved a file from the grey steel cabinet in a corner of his office… Back to work. The afternoon's meeting was almost certainly the most important of his career. A lot rested on its outcome. The futures of a great many children would be shaped by the success or failure of the actions agreed. He had to cope with the pressure. He had to get it right.

Nicholson scratched his nose and attempted to refocus on his paperwork with wavering enthusiasm… Why did additional piles of files and forms appear on his desk almost every time he left the room?

He decided to give it another half hour before leaving to chair a child protection case conference at South Wales General… Ideally, it would have been nice to spend the morning preparing for the afternoon's meeting, but his workload just didn't allow him that luxury.

He put his head down and got on with it.

Chapter 41

DI Simpson shook his warrant card in the face of the excessively officious attendant at the entrance to the social services headquarters car park, and drove in without waiting to be asked. He was about to get out of the CID car when he saw Nicholson parking his ancient, racing green Volkswagen Golf diesel hatchback in his reserved space nearby. The social work manager had been hoping he had five minutes or so to grab a quick cup of coffee and a sandwich before his lift arrived, but he accepted defeat when he saw Trevor Simpson's head poking through the driver's side front window, and heard his gruff voice calling his name. 'Mel! Get a move on, mate. You're going to have to get in the back. You know Grav, don't you?'

Nicholson opened the door and got into the rear seat. 'All right, Grav, how's life with you?'

'Not bad thanks, Mel, keeping busy.'

DI Simpson restarted the engine on the first turn of the key, reversed out of the tight parking space, and swung the car expertly into the road.

'I appreciate the lift, Trevor. What's the news on the joint interviews? I tried to get hold of Phil for an update, but he was tied up with a case.'

'Like I said to Grav earlier, it's looking pretty good overall. There's a couple more interviews going on at the moment, and I'll need to review the tapes before coming to any final conclusions, but it seems we're making good progress. Our Dr Galbraith may well be locked up for some time by the sound of things.'

'Anything specific?'

'We already had enough to charge him, but it looks as if he's even more involved in the ring than we realised.' He paused for a second. 'The man's a cunt! Some of the children were still in nappies, for fuck's sake. Two kids described him killing animals in front of them: puppies, kittens, lambs and the like. Apparently he holds them up by the scruff and cuts them open with what sounds like a surgeon's scalpel. The bastard told the kids he'd do the same to them if they ever said anything to anyone. It's surprising any of them ever spoke again, when you think about it. They call the ring's gatherings, *pet club*. Can you believe it? Fucking *pet club*! Apparently Galbraith came up with the name. Like I said, the man's a cunt.'

Neither Nicholson nor Grav responded… What could you say in the light of such depravity?

DI Gravel eventually broke the pervasive silence. 'The investigative teams have done fucking brilliantly convincing these kids it's safe to talk. In the circumstances, you know what I'm saying. Now, it's our turn. We've got to get this exactly right: everything by the book, dot the i's cross the t's, no mistakes.'

Both men indicated their wholehearted agreement, following which conversation turned to rugby union—a comfortable, familiar subject close to each of their hearts. For the remainder of the journey they debated the selection of the Welsh team. It was a tried and tested means of staying sane, a reminder that normal everyday life carried on while, each and every day they dealt with the things society would prefer to deny. Each knew from painful experience that humanity had a seemingly unlimited capacity for evil. For a time they chose to forget.

The journey passed relatively quickly, and they arrived at their destination a few minutes earlier than anticipated. The car park was already busy, full of other keen early arrivals, and it took Trevor Simpson some time to find an adequate parking space on an area of muddy grass near to the entrance of the large Victorian building. The three men got out of the car, treading carefully to avoid the many puddles. As they reached the entrance they were met by Phillip Beringer, who Grav loudly observed, 'Looked like shit.' Beringer had spent the morning monitoring two traumatic joint investigative interviews, and such things were never easy. Other similar interviews were ongoing at a second interview suite in another part of the county. Beringer had considered asking for the afternoon's meeting to be postponed, but ultimately decided that protective action couldn't be delayed any longer… It was always useful to have more evidence, but on each and every day that passed, children were in grave danger. It was a situation that was impossible to justify for a second longer than necessary, and it was time to act.

Nicholson opened the meeting by welcoming the attendees and facilitating introductions, despite the meeting being a virtual mirror image of the previous gathering just nineteen days before... It was a familiar, comforting ritual that played a small but important part in alleviating the inevitable anxieties the role entailed.

'Trevor, I think it would be helpful if you outline exactly what we're dealing with here. I don't want anyone to be in any doubt as to the enormity of the task at hand.'

'I can do that for you, Mel.' He took a notebook from his black plastic Sampsonite briefcase and glanced at it briefly before continuing. 'A large group of predatory men and a small number of women under their influence are operating a paedophile ring in the South West Wales area. Children have described being taken at night to a remote rural location, which is so far unknown to us, in the back of a white Transit van or what sounds like a cattle truck. Approximately twenty to thirty children make the journey at any one time, crammed into the back of one vehicle or another. They've talked of being sexually and physically assaulted by their own parents, by members of their extended family, by family friends, and by strangers. Some of the adults brought other children by car, some of whom the witnesses knew, and some whom they didn't. From what we can tell it's been going on for years. Over that time we suspect hundreds of children have been victimised. For now we're focusing on the children who are currently at risk, but we will cast the net wider in due course. I'm sure you'll all agree that makes absolute sense. We've made extensive background enquiries based on information provided by various victims who are already in the care of the local authority, or who were already working with social workers. The adults come from all walks of life, ranging from unemployed and poorly educated manual workers, to professional people in positions of influence. Intelligence suggests that local sex offenders have joined the ring as a result of knowing existing members. Others have joined from all over the United Kingdom as a result of alliances developed while serving prison sentences, or paradoxically at sex offender therapy programs run by the Probation Service. Some offenders have moved to the area, and others travel to facilitate their crimes. Members of the ring abuse their own children, each other's children, and other vulnerable children in the community. They offend as individuals and in groups, sharing their victims when it suits them. The children range from toddlers to pre-pubescent boys and girls of ten and eleven years. They are manipulated into silence by misinformation, emotional pressure, threats of violence and actual violence. Some of that violence is extreme. Some of these people have been investigated previously. Some of these kids are already on the child protection register. But, none of the past investigations identified those cases as being the tip of a very large iceberg. Very few perpetrators have been successfully prosecuted for relevant offences up to this point. With your help, that's about to change.' He met Nicholson's eyes. 'The scale and nature of this is new to us all. There are going to be inevitable tensions. But, if we keep the children's interests at the forefront of our minds, we won't go far wrong. There have been some major cock-ups in other parts of the country. Let's ensure we learn from their mistakes, and get this right. A lot of children are depending on us. Any questions?'

No one said a word.

For the next hour or more Simpson and Beringer summarised the specific details of the same investigation from different but complementary perspectives. Beringer focused on the civil child protection aspects of the case, while DI Simpson concentrated primarily on criminal matters.

Nicholson was inclined to applaud when they finally concluded their well-honed presentation, but resisted the temptation. 'Thank you both. Unless anyone wants to add anything or ask any questions, I think we can move on and agree the way forward. I know Trevor and Phil have had some preliminary discussions prior to today's meeting, and have liaised with senior management as appropriate. Which one of you wants to start?'

The two men glanced at each other as DI Simpson put his notebook back in his briefcase. 'Do you want to take the lead on this one, Phil?'

Beringer nodded… Why not? 'The CPS has already sanctioned five arrests: four men and one woman. It looks as if the subsequent interviews have strengthened those cases, and elicited further credible evidence that should lead to two further arrests—both men.'

DI Simpson interrupted. 'That'll be confirmed by tonight at the latest.'

'Thanks, Trevor. The suspects will be simultaneously arrested by teams of two detectives, who will in turn be accompanied by uniform officers with specialist training in searching for physical evidence. The arrests will take place early in the morning, ensuring an element of surprise before those who work leave their homes. The suspects' own children will be interviewed at one of the county's video interview facilities by child protection police officers and social workers, following which they'll be medically examined at South Wales General by two experienced consultant paediatricians: Doctors Sue Chandra and Nick Dali. All the children will be screened for sexually transmitted diseases including HIV infection. At least one of the adults involved—a male with a long history of intravenous drug use—is known to be HIV positive. A team of social services resource centre workers will transport the children from their homes to the interview suites and for medicals as required. A number of suitable foster placements have already been identified.'

Nicholson smiled warmly. 'Thanks, Phil, succinct as always.' He looked around the room. 'Any questions anybody? No? Then we'll bring things to a close. Thank you all for your time. I know you're busy people. I'll be here all day on Thursday if any of you need to get hold of me. Don't hesitate to pick up the phone. That's what I'm here for. Whatever way you look at it, Thursday's going to be a momentous day.'

Chapter 42

Detective Inspector Gravel's phone sounded at 12:53 p.m. on Wednesday 12, February, just as he was about to leave his office for a much-anticipated bacon and fried egg roll, in the notoriously terrible police headquarters canteen. He considered ignoring the demanding ringtone for a second or two, but reluctantly capitulated and picked up the receiver on the fifth ring.

'Hello, sir, it's June on the reception desk.'

'What can I do for you, Constable? '

'Sir, I've got a young man here who wants to talk to a detective about child abuse.'

'Young man? How old?'

'How old are you, Rhodri?'

'Nineteen.'

'He's nineteen, sir.'

'Tell him to take a seat, and keep an eye on him. I'll be with him in two minutes.'

DI Gravel smiled and held out a hand in greeting as he approached the thin, alabaster-pale teenager nervously awaiting his arrival. 'Detective Inspector Gravel, please call me Grav. Good to meet you.'

The young man stood, smiled tentatively, and accepted the handshake with a surprisingly firm grip.

'Is the interview room free, June?'

'Yes, sir.'

'If you follow me, Rhodri, we can talk privately.'

'Okay thanks.'

'Take a seat.'

'Thanks.'

'Right, let's get the basics done. What's your full name, son?'

'Rhodri Griffiths.'

'No middle names?'

'No.'

'And you're nineteen?'

'Yeah.'

'Are you local, Rhodri?'

'I'm living in Florida these days, but I grew up in this part of the world.'

'So what took you to America?'

'My father's an economics professor at Florida State University; we moved to the States when I was ten.'

'Nice place?'

'Yeah, it's all right.'

DI Gravel pushed a notepad and pen across the table. 'If you write down your home address and current contact details, Rhodri, that'll speed things up a bit.'

He picked up the pen and began writing. 'Yeah, no problem.'

'So what brings you back to Wales, son?'

'We're visiting my grandparents in Tenby.'

'Okay, Rhodri, why do you need to talk to a detective?'

'I heard him on the radio.'

'Who are we talking about?'

'Galbraith!'

DI Gravel sat up in his seat. 'Who's Galbraith?'

'He's a child psychiatrist.'

'So you heard this Dr Galbraith on the radio, and decided to talk to the police?'

'Yeah, I guess it doesn't make a lot of sense when you put it like that.'

'Not really.'

'My gran was listening to Radio Wales a few days back. Galbraith was being interviewed. I recognised his voice as soon as I heard it. It was like I was seven again. I was about to switch the radio off and try to push what happened to the back of my mind like a bad dream, but then he said he was still treating children. This is probably going to sound ridiculous to you, but I hadn't considered that before. What he might do to other children, I mean. I just focused on myself and tried to get on with my life. Does that make me sound selfish?'

'Are you saying Galbraith did something to you when you were seven, son?'

'Yeah, I think it was what you'd call an indecent assault.'

'How can you be certain it was Galbraith?'

'My older brother was paralysed in a mountaineering accident in Snowdonia. I couldn't cope with the reality. My GP referred me to Galbraith.'

'Sorry to hear about your brother, son. How many times did you see Galbraith?'

'Just the twice thankfully; I told Mum and Dad I didn't want to go back, and that was the end of it.'

'Are you saying he assaulted you at his clinic?'

'Yeah, at the second appointment, after persuading Mum she didn't need to be there.'

'Did you ever see him anywhere else? Anywhere at all?'

'No.'

'Did you tell anyone at the time?'

'No.'

'Why was that?'

'I just didn't think anyone would believe me.' He paused and looked away. 'I'm surprised you haven't laughed me out of here by now, to be honest.'

'We always take these sort of allegations seriously.'

'So you believe me?'

DI Gravel nodded. 'Don't quote me on this, son, but yes, I believe you.'

'Thanks, I can't tell you how much that means to me.'

'You need to think carefully before answering my next question, Rhodri.'

'Okay.'

'Would you be prepared to make a formal statement?'

'Yes.'

'No hesitation?'

'None at all.'

'And would you be prepared to give evidence in court if Galbraith's prosecuted?'

'I had nightmares and flashbacks for years. The bastard robbed me of my childhood. I want people to know what he is.'

'You understand we're going to need to talk about the specific details of what happened to you, son.'

'Yeah, I know.'

DI Gravel rose to his feet. 'I'll fetch the statement forms and be back with you in two minutes.'

Chapter 43

DI Gravel checked his digital watch at 05:58:37 precisely on Thursday 13, February… Time to make a move.

He unzipped the padded purple coat that his subordinates secretly joked made him resemble the Michelin man on anabolic steroids, and opened the front passenger side door of the Vauxhall.

The inspector nodded to Rankin in the driver's seat as he got in, and acknowledged the two female uniform search officers sitting in the back with a half-smile. 'Morning, everyone; time to go, Clive, my boy. I want to be knocking on Galbraith's door at exactly six thirty. All the other arrest and search teams should be doing likewise. I don't want the bastard having even the slightest opportunity to destroy evidence or pick up the phone to contact other offenders. We'll break the fucking door down if we have to. What's the news on the dog?'

Rankin rubbed his tired eyes and yawned loudly. 'The dog handler's meeting us there, boss. I've told him you'll kick his ass for him if he's a second late.'

For the remainder of the journey they engaged in occasional mundane stress-busting chit-chat until Rankin eventually steered the car into Eden Road about fifteen minutes later.

The DI checked his watch again. 'This is it, Clive. Galbraith's place is about halfway down. Stop a few houses back; we've got almost five minutes yet. Any sign of the dog?'

Rankin steered the Cavalier into a tight parking space, and peered up and down the dark tree-lined street… Where the hell was he? 'Not as yet, sir.'

'He's cutting it a bit fine, Clive.'

Just as Rankin was searching for an adequate response he spotted the dog handler's white police van approaching in the rear-view mirror… Thank fuck for that. 'He's behind us, boss.'

DI Gravel exited the car, pointed to a parking space three spaces back from the Vauxhall, and tapped repeatedly on the driver's side front window.

PC Rob Lawler wound it down. 'Sorry, sir, I've been up all night with the baby.'

'No worries, Rob, you're here now. That's what matters.' He pushed up his sleeve: 06:28:59. 'Let's go, we need to get in there.'

DI Gravel pointed to the Cavalier, and then towards the house, before approaching number sixty-four Eden Road with the four officers and a white Welsh springer spaniel with dark brown markings, which was bouncing around the pavement exuding seemingly boundless energy, following close behind.

DI Gravel stared at the face of his Casio and waited for the last few seconds to pass by before knocking hard on the glossy black door with its misleading persona of prosperous middle-class respectability. He kept knocking with escalating force with the side of a clenched fist until the door was opened only seconds later by Cynthia Galbraith, who looked at him with bulging eyes and an open-mouthed guppy-like expression.

The inspector held up his warrant card in plain view. 'Mrs Galbraith? Mrs Cynthia Galbraith?'

Cynthia narrowed her eyes to virtual slits, closed her gaping mouth, and said, 'What can I do for you?'

'My name is Detective Inspector Gravel. We're here to speak to your husband, Mrs Galbraith. Where is he please?'

Cynthia didn't move an inch. She held her ground like an obstructive doorman at a nightclub, fixed DI Gravel with a determined glare, and said, 'I can't let you in. My husband won't want to be disturbed. Not at this time of the morning. I haven't even had the chance to finish preparing his breakfast as yet. You'll have to make an appointment.'

'Get out of my way, Mrs Galbraith.'

Cynthia took a step backwards, but instead of stepping aside to allow the officers to enter, she attempted to slam the door shut, connecting violently with the inspector's right knee as he stepped forward and placed his foot in the door.

DS Rankin moved forward in an instant, and pushed the door forcefully with both hands, causing Cynthia to stumble backwards and crash to the tiled-floor with a barely audible whelp that the dog appeared to find particularly interesting.

DI Gravel rubbed his leg with one hand as he manoeuvred past her and into the hall… If Galbraith was awake he was getting too much time.

The inspector turned, bent down, offered Cynthia his open hand, and lifted her to her feet as the remaining officers crowded into the hall behind them. 'You have children, Mrs Galbraith. I'm going to give you one last opportunity to tell us where he is before we search every room in the house until we find him. Now, Mrs Galbraith! Where is your husband, Mrs Galbraith?'

Sarah and Elizabeth suddenly appeared at the top of the stairs and called for their mother as Cynthia pondered her next move… Why were these unwelcome strangers in her home? Could it be something to do with the child she'd seen being carried into the house? Wasn't the dishevelled middle-aged police inspector sitting next to that disconsolate father pleading for the return of his seven-year-old son on the Welsh evening news? She looked at her daughters, then at DI Gravel, and then at her daughters again, before finally turning away from the officers and approaching the stairs. As she placed her foot on the first step she said, 'He slept in his study last night. It's the second door on the right, down the hall,' without looking back.

'Stay with the mother and kids until someone arrives from social services, Pam. Keep them well out of the way. Rankin, with me! The rest of you can start searching as soon as Galbraith's arrested.'

DI Gravel didn't knock this time. He just opened the study door and burst into the room. He stared incredulously at Dr Galbraith, who was slumped in his recliner chair with his eyes tight shut and a fine trickle of drool running down his lightly stubbled chin from one corner of his open mouth.

The inspector scowled… The television was on, there was nothing on the screen. Was he dead? No, the man was sleeping. Unbelievable! Despite all the noise, the man was sleeping.

He took hold of the doctor's upper arm in a powerful grip, shook him vigorously and yelled, 'Wake up, Galbraith, it's the police.'

The doctor woke with a start, and quickly surveyed the room as DI Gravel pulled him to his feet… Focus, man, focus. He'd been careful. Everything that mattered was back in the cellar. All was not lost. Maybe the plebs wouldn't find the little bastard.

He clutched at his head with frantic fingers… All he had to do was stay in control and take advantage of his superior intellect.

Dr Galbraith supported his full weight, and fastened his trousers before speaking. 'Please accept my sincere apologies, gentlemen. I have trouble sleeping on occasions. I sometimes take a tablet. What can I do for you?'

DI Gravel tightened his grip, causing the doctor to squeal… He was guilty. The cunt was guilty. Innocent men asked what was going on, they protested their innocence. 'You're under arrest, Galbraith.' He cautioned him, turned to Rankin and said, 'Put the cuffs on, Sergeant.'

Dr Galbraith turned his head, and looked the inspector directly in the eye.

'This has to be a mistake.'

DI Gravel held his gaze… It really would feel good to smash the dirty bastard in the teeth. 'Have you got something to say for yourself, Galbraith?'

'Do you know who I am?'

'I know exactly who you are, you smug bastard. My officers are going to search every inch of this fucking place, and you're going to be locked up, Galbraith. Still feeling quite so confident?'

The doctor looked away and blinked repeatedly as Rankin pulled each of his arms behind his back in turn, and secured the handcuffs tightly around his wrists. 'I really fail to understand the reason for your hostility. You can search for as long as you wish. There's nothing to find.'

DI Gravel looked slowly around the room with interested eyes… Had the cunt's self-confidence slipped momentarily when he mentioned the search? Just for a fraction of a second? Maybe, just maybe!

'Shall I take him to the car, boss?'

'Leave him to me, Clive.'

The DI took hold of the back of Dr Galbraith's shirt and manhandled him out of the study and down the hall with such speed that the doctor struggled to keep his footing. He rushed him down the hall, pushing him repeatedly in the back with his shoulder if he slowed.

DI Gravel stopped abruptly on reaching the front door, and shouted back into the house, 'Rankin, bring that computer for the tech boys to have a look at. Pam, you stay with Mrs Galbraith and the kids for the moment. Social services transport's on the way. I want this fucking place searched from top to bottom. Every inch of it. If you find anything of interest, anything at all, I want to hear about it immediately. Are you all clear?'

Following a chorus of, 'Yes, sir!' DI Gravel frogmarched the doctor out of the house, down the granite steps, into the quiet early morning street, and flung him into the back seat of the Vauxhall with such force that he skipped across the velour seat like a pebble on water, and bounced off the inside of the opposite door. DS Rankin placed the computer in the boot and drove, while the inspector sat immediately alongside his prisoner in the back.

Rankin took what the inspector referred to as the scenic route, and it took them almost an hour to make the relatively short journey back to Caerystwyth police station. DI Gravel squeezed up close to the doctor, speaking directly into his ear at touching distance. 'You're going down, Galbraith. You're going down for a long, long time. They are going to love you in prison, Galbraith. The guards don't protect your kind from the pack. They'll look the other way, Doctor. The inmates will tear your fucking balls off. That's correct, isn't it, Sergeant?'

'That's right, sir, they'll kick his teeth out and use his mouth as an arsehole.'

'They will, Sergeant. That's what happens to nonces if they're not protected. But we could help, couldn't we, Sergeant?'

'Well, I suppose we could, sir, if he made it worth our while? What do you say, Galbraith? Should we help you?'

The doctor jerked, and twitched, and blinked, and sweated, as he fought to retain his composure. 'I have absolutely no idea what this is about. If you really think that your predictable attempts to intimidate me into admitting to your ludicrous allegations will succeed, you are very sadly mistaken.'

The inspector swivelled in his seat, and placed his face so close to the doctor's that their foreheads touched. 'Anything you want to tell us, Galbraith? Help us, and we'll help you. We could have a word with the judge. We could make things easier for you in prison. That's correct, isn't it, Sergeant?'

'We could, sir, if he cooperates.'

'So what do you say, Doctor? Are you going to make it easier on yourself?'

Dr Galbraith closed his eyes for a moment, and then opened them slowly and deliberately. 'You two gentlemen appear to be under the misguided impression that I am something I am not. I have spent my entire career assisting children in crisis. I would have thought that was something to be applauded. I have absolutely no intention of saying another word until we are in a formal interview situation, when everything said is a matter of official record.'

DI Gravel turned away from the doctor and sat back in his seat. 'Let's get him back to the station, Clive. It seems that Dr Galbraith doesn't want to talk to us.'

DS Rankin parked in the busy police car park, and watched as his boss dragged the doctor out of the rear seat and marched him across the tarmac towards the cells. He locked the car, followed the two men into the custody suite, and held open a heavy steel door as DI Gravel pushed the doctor into a urine-soaked cell lit only by a naked forty-watt bulb that bathed the room in a depressing yellow hue. The doctor lost his balance, stumbled, and hit the wall directly opposite the door with an audible thud, before slumping to the floor. The inspector followed his prisoner into the concrete enclosure, and knelt down next to him as he moaned quietly to himself. 'Throw me the key, Clive.'

Rankin fumbled in one trouser pocket and then another, before eventually locating the small key amongst a collection of coins, and throwing it underarm to his boss, who caught it easily with one hand.

DI Gravel flipped the doctor from his side and onto his front, before unlocking the handcuffs and throwing them back across the cell to the DS, who was still standing at the cell door.

DI Gravel stared into the doctor's eyes without blinking. 'I'm going to leave you alone to think now, Doctor. This may give you some idea of what the future holds. I'd use the time wisely if I were you. Think carefully about what we've said to you. Help us, and things will well be easier for you. You can avoid answering our questions for as long as you want, but it won't do you any favours. I'm in control now, Doctor. Anything you want to say for yourself?'

'I am fully conversant with the rules of evidence, Inspector, and have already made it perfectly clear that I have absolutely no intention of saying anything further until I am formally interviewed. At that point my innocence should become clear, even to a man of your limited intellect. I will be making a formal complaint regarding my appalling treatment at your hands and that of your subordinate. You can be certain of that.'

'You're sweating, Doctor. Are you starting to feel the pressure?'

'For your information I have a slight fever. Two analgesics would be advisable, if you have them available?'

'Have it your way, Galbraith. You're not the only fucking pervert who's been arrested this morning. And someone will talk. They always do. You are going to prison, Galbraith. It's just a matter of how long for, and what happens when you get there. Think about that, Doctor. And think hard.'

The doctor struggled upright and shook his head disdainfully… Control? Who were the morons trying to kid? If they'd found the little bastard, he'd have heard about it long before now.

DI Gravel slammed the cell door shut behind him as he left. 'Come on, Clive, I fancy a bacon roll with plenty of brown sauce. I'll meet you in the canteen in about ten minutes.'

DI Gravel dialled with one hand, whilst squeezing the bridge of his nose between the thumb and index finger of the other… Come on one of you, pick up the fucking phone.

'Hello, the Galbraith residence.'

'The Galbraith's residence? Is that you, Pam?'

'Yes, sir.'

'For fuck's sake, Pam. I thought you'd got a new job as a butler for a minute there.'

'Sorry, sir, what can I do for you?'

'I'm after an update, Pam. Any joy?'

'Social services took longer to get here than expected. They're with Mrs Galbraith and the children now, sir. It looks like they're about to leave. Mrs Galbraith's putting the girls' coats on as we speak.'

'Did she say anything to you? Anything useful?'

'Give me a second, sir. They're just going through the front door.' The WPC waved and smiled as Elizabeth looked back at her on stepping out of the house.

'Okay, sir, they're gone.'

'And?'

'It's not so much what she said, sir. It's how she was. She's obviously terrified of the man.'

'Galbraith?'

'Yes, sir, I've seen it before: once confident women crushed by manipulative, dominant bullies. I don't think she's been out of the house unsupervised for years. I'll be amazed if she tells us anything at all.'

'You never know your luck, Pam. What about the girls?'

'Not a word, sir, I hate to think what they've experienced in this house.'

'How's the search going?'

'Give me a minute, sir, I'll go and ask.'

'Hello, sir, they've just finished in the study. They took everything out, even lifted the floorboards, but not a thing as yet. They're moving onto the dining room next. It's a large house, sir, it's going to take a while.'

‘You’re not wrong, Pam. Now you’ve finished your babysitting duties you can give the others a hand. Ask Rob to confirm he collected something with Anthony Mailer’s scent from the father.’

‘Rob! The inspector wants to know if you’ve collected anything from Mr Mailer?’

‘Yeah, if the boy’s here, we’ll find him.’

‘I heard all that thanks, Pam. Tell Rob I want him to let the dog loose and see if she comes up with anything. Every minute matters.’

‘Will do, sir.’

‘Straight away, Pam. I’ll be in the station canteen for the next twenty minutes or so. Make sure you get hold of me immediately if there’s any news.’

Chapter 44

The agile young spaniel sniffed every inch of the long corridor. Bursting with energy and enthusiastic, tail up, supersensitive wet nose twitching, she searched for the target scent amongst a myriad of other fascinating and potentially distracting smells.

The dog handler walked closely behind his charge issuing constant encouragement, 'Come on, girl, find.' He held up the dog's favourite yellow tennis ball, reminding her of her prospective reward should she succeed in her allocated task. 'Come on, girl, that's it, find, find.'

The dog suddenly lost interest in the ball and stood alert as if to attention in the doorway to the large family kitchen.

'What is it girl? Are you onto something?' He held the ball high above his head in his left hand and smiled. 'That's it, girl, go on, find, find!'

The dog suddenly became more interested in the ball than the scent, and jumped repeatedly against her handler's legs.

The constable cursed loudly… He'd distracted the animal just at the wrong time.

He put the ball in a trouser pocket, reached into his tunic and took Anthony's red tee-shirt from a clear plastic evidence bag, before bending down and holding it about ten inches from the floor, allowing the spaniel to sniff it repeatedly, 'That's it, girl, find, find.'

The dog turned with a new enthusiasm for the game, and entered the kitchen on full alert. She quickly circumvented the room, sniffing every nook and cranny for any sign of the relevant scent. All of a sudden she lost any interest in the room's peripheries, and focused her entire attention on the tiled-floor close to the centre of the kitchen where a single drop of Anthony's saliva had fallen from his open mouth as Gary Davies carried him towards the cellar steps.

The dog knew instantly that she'd achieved her initial goal. She sat, raised her head proudly in the air and barked once, as her search training dictated.

The handler handed the eager spaniel her reward. 'Good girl, good girl!'

He turned towards the internal door and shouted, 'The dog's picked up on something in the kitchen. Stay where you are for the moment, I need to see if she can follow the scent.'

He attached the dog's lead to her black leather collar, patted the top of her head robustly, and walked slowly around the room, allowing the keen animal to take the lead. 'That's it, girl, find, find.'

The spaniel sniffed at every cupboard, the cooker, the fridge, the pantry, the dresser, but nothing. She repeatedly tried to return towards the centre of the floor, the scene of her earlier triumph, but the handler pulled her away on each and every occasion.

One of the two female search officers appeared in the doorway, but didn't enter the room. 'What's happening, Rob? Any joy?'

'I'm sure the boy's been here, but I don't think he's here now. If you two have a good look in the cupboards and the like, I'll take the dog out into the garden. The Mailer boy may well have been carried through the house and out through the conservatory.'

'If you're right, he's probably dead.'

'You may well be right, Pam. All we can do is keep looking.'

Chapter 45

'I'll have another one of your gourmet bacon rolls please, love.'

'One bacon roll coming up. Another coffee?'

'Yeah, why not live a little?'

'I think you're wanted, Grav.'

'Sorry to interrupt you, sir.'

'What can I do for you, Constable?'

'Pam's been on the phone, sir. She wants you to ring her back urgently.'

The inspector pushed his plate to one side and jumped to his feet. 'Thank you, Constable. Nice to see you doing something useful for a change.'

'Thank you, sir.'

DI Gravel turned to Rankin, who had recently joined him and was finishing off an unappetising cheese and tomato sandwich. 'I think it's about time we had another chat with the doctor, Clive. He's got to be sweating a bit by now. Collect him from the cells and I'll see you in interview room two as soon as I've had a word with Pam.'

'Will do, boss.'

Come on, Pam. Pick the fucking phone up, girl. 'Hello, Pam, it's DI Gravel. About time! What have you got for me?'

'It's the dog, sir, she picked up a scent in the kitchen. She does this thing where she sits and barks when she finds the scent she's looking for. Clever really! Rob says he's never known the dog be wrong.'

'Anywhere else?'

'Sorry, sir?'

'The scent, anywhere else…?' He was clutching at straws.

'No, sir, just the kitchen!'

'Has Rob tried the garden?'

'He's out there now, sir, but nothing as yet.'

'Any sign of recent digging or other ground work?'

'Not really.'

'What the hell's that supposed to mean?'

'He found a DIY tool under the earth in a flower bed, but he doesn't think it's of any relevance.'

'What sort of tool?'

'Just a small thing with a plastic handle. Rob thinks it's a glass cutter.'

'Sounds like something and nothing.'

'Yeah, that's what we thought.'

'But, is Rob certain that Anthony was at the house?'

'Yes, sir, as sure as he can be.'

'Go through the place methodically, Pam: every corner, every crevice. Tear the fucking place apart if you have to. If Anthony Mailer's anywhere in that house I want him found.'

Chapter 46

Dr Galbraith stared at Gravel and Rankin across the small interview room table, meeting their eyes in turn, and waiting for one or the other to break the persuasive silence… What the hell were they waiting for? Why the delay? Why no more questions?

Suddenly the deafening white noise in the doctor's head was silenced, and his facial muscles noticeably relaxed… The fools still hadn't found the cellar. It was the only logical explanation.

He smiled with a newfound confidence. 'Have you any further questions, Inspector, or have we finally reached the conclusion of this ridiculous charade?'

DI Gravel scowled. 'Surely you aren't still insisting that you're innocent, Doctor?'

Dr Galbraith shook his head slowly. 'I find it incredible that you both consider that a man such as myself, a man who has dedicated the majority of his adult life to assisting troubled children and their families, could be guilty of such heinous criminal acts. I am entirely innocent of the crimes to which you refer. This entire process is an utter travesty. Why would I admit to something I haven't done?'

The inspector stared at him incredulously. 'You've heard the weight of evidence against you, Galbraith. Four children have given detailed video statements outlining numerous sexual offences. A fifth victim, now an adult, has made a written statement. The investigation is ongoing, and I have no doubt that other victims will be identified. And other suspects will talk. It's in your interest to cooperate. Face facts, Doctor. It's the only card you have left to play.'

'Now that I think about it, I can perhaps understand why you would think I am guilty. But, with due respect, you are looking at an extremely complex situation rather too simplistically.'

DI Gravel smiled humourlessly… The self-satisfied cunt. 'I can't wait to hear this.'

'There are a number of hypothesis that could potentially explain these ludicrous allegations. What evidence have you got at the end of the day? Four young boys talking of alleged events which sound less than credible, at an unknown location or locations sometime in the unspecified past. A young man who claims to recall an assault some years ago. A young man with a history of psychiatric problems. Hardly the most reliable witnesses, wouldn't you agree?'

'The evidence looks pretty solid to me, Galbraith.'

'When will you people ever learn? I've seen it time and time again over the years: over-zealous police officers unwisely jumping to the wrong conclusions. Innocent men being accused of unspeakable crimes. Have you people learnt nothing from events in Cleveland and the Orkneys? Well-meaning, but misguided pseudo professionals can implant false memories in vulnerable children's minds. Any knowledgeable expert in the field would tell you likewise. Leading questions can result in the acquisition of misinformation with the potential for miscarriages of justice. It is not unusual in this type of case for children to say exactly what the investigating social worker and police officer want them to say. They are simply recounting what they have gleaned as a result of ill-advised leading questions, rather than recalling real events. Your allegations are a manufactured fantasy and nothing more.'

'All five witnesses have referred to you by name, Galbraith.'

'As I've already stated more than once, I know of no white room, and I am entirely unfamiliar with the farm building you describe so unconvincingly. Have you even considered the possibility that someone with a grudge against me has stolen my identity?'

Just for a fleeting moment a shadow of doubt crossed DI Gravel's mind. 'Nice try, Galbraith, but you're not fooling anyone. All five witnesses have described you perfectly.'

'It is not unusual for victims to accuse a trusted authority figure rather than identify the actual offender, for fear of retribution.'

'You're sounding increasingly desperate, Galbraith.'

'You're making a big mistake, Inspector.'

‘Oh, I don’t think so, Doctor. We’ve got more than enough evidence to charge you. I’m going to give you one last opportunity to cooperate. Where’s the boy?’

‘Boy? I have absolutely no idea who you’re talking about. Perhaps it would be helpful if you could be more specific.’

The DI clenched his fists tightly underneath the table. ‘Anthony Mailer. Where is Anthony Mailer?’

‘Oh, Anthony Mailer? Anthony is my patient, but then you already knew that. Why would you think I know of his whereabouts? I first became aware that he was missing when I saw a report regarding his alleged abduction on the BBC Welsh evening news. Naturally, I am gravely concerned for his welfare. It’s a terrible business. Have you interviewed the father yet? Having met him during therapy, I think it’s advisable.’

‘Where is he, Galbraith?’

Dr Galbraith issued an exaggerated sigh. ‘Have I not made myself perfectly clear time and time again? It seems I need to reiterate, despite my earlier comments. I am at a complete loss as to why you think I should know the answer to your preposterous question. I think it’s you who is becoming desperate, Inspector. Is the pressure getting to you, old man?’

‘Where was he taken, Galbraith?’

‘Am I supposed to know the answer to that? Do you think I’m clairvoyant?’

‘We have reason to believe that Anthony Mailer was at your home, Galbraith.’

The doctor smirked dismissively. ‘Reason to believe? The very pretext of your question suggests a significant element of doubt in your proposition. I consider you would be well-advised to stop wasting your time interviewing an innocent man, and attempt to locate Anthony before it’s too late.’

‘Molly Mailer saw you at her home seconds before she was viciously attacked. She saw you, Galbraith. She’s made a statement to that effect. Your footprints were found at the back of the cottage.’

'Are you really that stupid, you ridiculous man? I have already explained this to you perfectly adequately; but I will try again despite your obvious limitations. Mrs Mailer has suffered a serious head injury. Most regrettable! I became quite fond of her during her son's treatment. What you need to understand, Inspector, is that our brains can play tricks on us when subjected to extreme stress. Memories tend to become confused with dreams and even hallucinations in such cases. Anaesthetic and pain control medication can produce similar complex anomalies. I can assure you that any competent neurosurgeon or psychiatrist would tell you that her allegations are extremely unreliable at best. They certainly wouldn't qualify as credible evidence in a criminal court. Oh, and the footprints, I nearly forgot about the footprints for a second.' He smiled and waited for a second or two before speaking again. 'I think you'll find that there are quite a number of people with the same feet size as me. If I were to engage in such a crime, I would possess the foresight to wear the wrong size shoes. It seems a blatantly obvious precaution. I'm very sorry to disappoint you, Inspector, but that's the way it is. Did you find any forensic evidence at my home? Anything to suggest the boy was ever there? Anything at all? I think not, or I'd have heard about it long before now.'

DI Gravel slammed the side of his right fist down hard on the table in front of him… The cunt was right. When it came to the Mailers, he had fuck all.

'You must try and calm yourself down, Inspector. Getting worked up in that manner really isn't good for a man of your advancing years and fleshy build. But, I'll tell you one thing, as a doctor you understand. If the unfortunate young man is locked up somewhere, alone in the dark, hungry and dehydrated, terrified, chained to a radiator or bedstead possibly? In some dark attic or uninhabited building for example? Well, he's not going to last very long is he. Pure conjecture you understand.'

'Is that some sort of convoluted admission, Doctor?'

The doctor felt his penis engorge with blood as he pictured the scene and magnified it in his mind. 'Why would you think that, Inspector? I am simply attempting to draw your attention to the potential consequences of failing to address Anthony's predicament with sufficient urgency. Shock tactics in my patient's interests, so to speak. How long have you got to save him, Inspector? One hour? Two hours? Three hours possibly? Or, maybe he's dead already. What a tragedy that would be, particularly when you're wasting your limited time and resources interviewing an innocent man. The clock's ticking, Inspector: tick, tock, tick, tock.' He held a cupped hand up to his ear. 'Can you hear it, Inspector?'

DS Rankin took hold of DI Gravel's arm, and held him back as he jumped to his feet and switched the tape off. 'Don't let the bastard get to you, Grav.'

Dr Galbraith grinned contemptuously. 'Temper, temper, Inspector. Given your unreasonable attitude I think it's advisable to request a lawyer after all.'

'Now you want a solicitor?'

'If it's not too much trouble.'

'We'll arrange it.'

'I think this may well be an opportune time to request refreshments. I'm sure one of you public servants can arrange that for me.'

Chapter 47

'Phillip Beringer please, it's urgent.'

'Grav?'

'Yeah.'

'It's Phil, I thought I recognised your dulcet tones. What can I do for you, mate?'

'The two Galbraith girls, have they been interviewed yet?'

'It's happening right now, Grav. Nothing much so far, to be honest.'

'Nothing?'

'They're scared of their father, that's bloody obvious, but nothing specific, nothing criminal.'

'Okay, Phil, can you do one thing for me?'

'If I can, Grav, what is it?'

'Am I right in thinking that you can speak to the interview team without actually interrupting the interview?'

'Yeah, no problem, the police officer has a small earpiece. What do you need?'

'I need to know if either of the girls saw a young boy in the house in recent days. A seven-year-old boy with short ginger hair. This is fucking important, Phil. It looks as if Anthony Mailer was at the Galbraith house.'

'I hear you, Grav. I'll get back to you straight away if we get anything useful. Before you go, I don't think we can justify having the Galbraith girls medically examined unless something else comes up? I'll talk to Mel and see what he thinks, but I doubt he'll say any different.'

'Oh, I'm not so sure, Phillip. There are some fucking serious allegations against their father.'

'I'll talk to Mel and get back to you as soon as I can.'

'I may well give him a ring myself. One last thing before I leave you in peace: I'm sending someone over there to interview Mrs Galbraith along the same lines. As a witness at this stage, although that may change as things develop.'

'No problem, Grav, I'll make sure there's a room free.'

Chapter 48

Detective Constable Myra Thomas introduced herself to Cynthia with a limp handshake, and ushered her into a small cluttered office at the social services children's resource centre. 'Have a seat, Mrs Galbraith, I'll fetch us both a hot drink before we make a start. Tea or coffee?'

Was someone really going to make tea for her? 'Tea, please, no milk or sugar.'

'Try to relax, Mrs Galbraith. I'll be back with you in two minutes.'

DC Thomas pushed the door open with her foot and handed Cynthia a cup and saucer. 'There you go, Mrs Galbraith. Let's make a start.'

Cynthia rubbed her eyes, smearing meticulously applied mascara across one cheek.

'What's wrong, Mrs Galbraith?'

'You've been so kind.'

'You've had a difficult day, Mrs Galbraith. You're bound to be feeling emotional. Anyone would be in the circumstances.'

'I saw my parents. They collected my daughters after their interviews. I hadn't seen them since my wedding day. The girls had never met them before.'

'Really? How long have you been married?'

'Over seven years!'

'Do your parents live a long way from you?'

'No, just down the road.'

The detective looked puzzled. 'Then, why haven't you seen them?'

'My husband forbade it.'

'He prevented you seeing them?'

'Yes.'

'Are you scared of your husband, Cynthia?'

Cynthia Galbraith nodded ever so subtly, but said, 'He wouldn't want me to talk to you about that.'

'Dr Galbraith is in custody, Cynthia. He can't hurt you anymore.'

Silence.

'We need your help, Cynthia.'

'Really?'

'A child is missing, Cynthia. A seven-year-old little boy called Anthony with short red hair. His mother was attacked and he was taken from his home. It was a vicious assault. We believe that your husband had something to do with his disappearance. Have you seen the boy, Cynthia? Can you help us find him?'

Cynthia closed her bleary eyes, and began repeatedly rocking back and forth in her seat… Was the nice officer asking about that child the man she didn't know had carried into the house in the middle of the night? He may have had red hair? It was short, and it could have been ginger. It was hard to tell in the orange sodium glow of the street lamps. Her husband was in attendance at the time. He must know all about it. Maybe he could tell the police what they wanted to know. Perhaps it was something to do with his work. He'd told her a thousand times how important it was. It was never to be interrupted. Never! Yes, that must be it. It was probably best not to say anything at all.

'Mrs Galbraith?'

Silence.

'We have very good reason to believe that Anthony is in extremely serious danger. We are talking about a child's life, Mrs Galbraith. Can you help us find him?'

Silence.

'Look at me, Mrs Galbraith. Open your eyes please, Mrs Galbraith.'

Cynthia opened her eyes and stared into space.

'I am going to ask you again, Mrs Galbraith. Was Anthony Mailer at your home?'

Silence.

'What is it you're afraid of, Mrs Galbraith? If you know anything, anything at all, you must tell me.'

Cynthia closed her eyes again, acutely aware of the accusing shadow of her husband hanging over her like an omnipresent malevolent spirit… Maybe she should tell the nice officer what she'd seen. She wanted to, she really wanted to. Perhaps she should follow her instincts. It would feel so good to help.

She opened her mouth and was about to speak, but then she reconsidered… What would her husband say if she did the wrong thing again? What would he do to her? Surely if he had the boy it must be for extremely good reasons. He was an important man with an important professional role. Perhaps it was better to say nothing, rather than say or do the wrong thing yet again.

'Do you know anything at all, Mrs Galbraith? Can you help us find Anthony?'

Cynthia met the officer's pleading gaze for a fleeting moment, and shook her head vigourously.

DC Thomas persevered for another twenty minutes or so before reluctantly accepting defeat… If Cynthia Galbraith knew anything, which seemed decidedly unlikely, she wasn't going to tell her about it. What was it DI Gravel had said? If she didn't want to be directing traffic for the rest of her fucking career, she had better get Cynthia to talk. Or at least, that was the gist of it. He always did have such a nice way with words. Maybe it was worth running Cynthia home. One last throw of the dice. Witnesses sometimes found it easier to talk when sitting next to, rather than opposite the interviewer. It was less formal, less intimidating. A car journey would be ideal. Eye contact could sometimes get in the way of productive conversation rather than facilitate effective communication. It had to be worth a try. There was everything to gain and nothing to lose.

DC Thomas smiled, and placed a reassuring hand on Cynthia's shoulder. 'I'm going to make a phone call to find out if my colleagues have finished searching your house. I'll take you home as soon as I can. Is that all right with you, Cynthia?'

Cynthia nodded.

DC Thomas took a red Parker pen from her black leather police issue handbag. 'What's your home number?'

Chapter 49

DI Gravel looked up and raised his hand in silent acknowledgement as DS Rankin entered his office, before returning to his call. 'So you didn't find anything at all?'

'Like I said, sir, just the dog…'

'I know all about the dog, Constable. But a dog picking up a scent isn't evidence. I can't put a fucking dog in the witness box, can I?'

'No, sir!'

'And you looked in the attic?'

'Yes, sir!'

'You're sure?'

'Yes, sir, we even had the dog up there at one point.'

The inspector exhaled loudly. 'Enough said, Pam. If the boy was there, he's been moved on. I need you to find out if Galbraith owns any other properties. Something could be in his wife's name. Give the council a ring. If I don't hear from you within the next hour, I'll assume you haven't come up with anything useful.'

'Okay, sir, I'll get on with it.'

'You do that, Pam. Oh, Pam, one more thing before you go.'

'Sir?'

'I'm going to send the SOCO boys over once you lot have finished, to see if they can find any traces of blood anywhere. How long before you finish the search?'

'It shouldn't be more than another half hour, sir. They're just putting things back together now.'

'Thanks, Pam.'

He placed the phone back on its receiver, and immediately picked it up again, listening for a dial tone. 'Give me a minute, Clive, I've got a couple more calls to make.'

DS Rankin smiled. 'The duty solicitor's arrived, boss, some snotty kid straight out of college.'

'Thank fuck for that. Give me a second.'

He dialled and waited.

'Children's resource centre.'

'Is that you, Mel? I was after Phil, but you'll do.'

'What can I do for you, Grav?'

'I was having a chat with Phil earlier about the Galbraith girls. I think they need to be medically examined, Mel. Galbraith's one evil bastard, and he's had unrestricted access to those girls all their lives, for fuck's sake.'

'I'm not arguing with you, Grav. I don't know where Phil's coming from on this one, to be honest. I'll have a chat with the maternal grandparents later today and arrange something for the morning, if that's all right with you? The girls have been through enough for one day.'

'Thanks, Mel, it's appreciated. Is Myra Thomas still with you?'

'Yeah, she's still with Mrs Galbraith as far as I know. Do you want a word with her?'

'Please!'

'I'll be with you in a second, Clive. Nearly done!'

'Hello, sir?'

'Any joy, Myra?'

'I haven't given up as yet, sir, but I really don't think she knows anything at all.'

'Keep trying, Detective. Ask her if Galbraith has access to any other properties: offices, houses, garages, even a caravan. That sort of thing. I've got Pam talking to the council along the same lines. Ring me at the station immediately if you come up with anything. I'm going to be interviewing Galbraith for the next couple of hours. If the answer's yes, make sure the message gets to me urgently.'

'Just so I'm clear, sir, you want to be interrupted?'

'That's what I said, Myra. Now get on with it.'

The inspector put the phone down and sighed. 'We're getting nowhere fast, Clive. I think we'll have one last go at Galbraith before calling it a day.'

'What have you got in mind, boss?'

'We've got more than enough to charge the cunt with his ring activities: indecent assaults, gross indecency, even a couple of rapes, yes?'

'That's the way I see it.'

'But when it comes to the Mailers, we've got fuck all, correct?'

'Seems so.'

'Let's refocus on what we can prove for now: gradually revealing the evidence against him until he finally realises his ramblings are falling on stoney ground. He may be ready to offer us something as the pressure increases and the grim reality actually dawns on him. Having the solicitor here may actually act in our favour in that respect.'

'Let's hope so, boss. I'll let his solicitor know we're about to kick off.'

Dr Galbraith gave dismissive responses to the two officers' increasingly probing questions for the first half hour or more, as his young lawyer uttered occasional words of advice and caution. As the evidence mounted, however, the doctor's contrived urbanity melted away to a degree, and he began to twitch and jerk and blink and sweat, as the increasingly distressed solicitor looked on slack-jawed and open-mouthed.

After an hour or more, DI Gravel judged that the time was right to drive home his potential advantage. He smashed an open palm onto the tabletop, stood, and pointed at the doctor with an accusing digit, as the young solicitor fought an internal battle to avoid becoming visibly emotional. 'This is your final opportunity to cooperate, Galbraith. You are going to prison. It's just a question of how long for and what happens when you get there. You would be well-advised to consider your answer to my next question very carefully. I'm sure your solicitor would agree.'

As the young solicitor nodded, DI Gravel asked his final question. 'Where is Anthony Mailer, Galbraith?'

The doctor folded his arms nonchalantly and gazed down at the table. 'How many times do I have to say this? I have repeatedly made my position perfectly clear. I have no intention whatsoever of entering into some informal agreement with you, or anybody else for that matter. I totally refute the ludicrous allegations against me, and will continue to do so to the very best of my ability. I've said it before, and I will state it again: I had nothing whatsoever to do with Anthony Mailer's disappearance.'

'Have it your way, Doctor. This interview is at an end. Let's get him charged, Clive.'

Chapter 50

'It's a quarter to, boss. Better make a move. Galbraith's up first.'

'Thanks, Clive, is my tie straight?'

'Spot on, boss. I'll meet you for a quick pint at lunchtime. It's your round.'

'I should be back well before then, Clive. Galbraith should be a formality. He'll be remanded and on his way to Swansea nick by eleven at the latest.'

DI Gravel strode confidently into the local magistrates' court just in time to see the doctor entering the dock and facing three local Justices of the Peace. He looked somewhat dishevelled and unshaven, quite different from the image of professional respectability he usually contrived to present to the world.

The inspector entered the witness box, picked up the King James Bible, swore the oath, and presented the basic facts of the case. He had never felt more relaxed in his entire life… The courtroom was familiar, the facts appeared to speak for themselves: Galbraith was a danger to the public—that seemed blatantly obvious. He'd be remanded in custody to await trial at Crown Court in Swansea or Cardiff. What other reasonable conclusion was there?

DI Gravel paid only passing interest when Dr Galbraith's previously inept solicitor applied for bail, citing the doctor's previously good character, social standing and elevated professional status… Surely the magistrates weren't going to fall for that crock of shit, not given the odious nature of the charges.

The inspector was even more surprised when the three magistrates retired to consider the application… What the fuck was there to think about?

What DI Gravel didn't know was that two of the three magistrates knew the doctor. Or to be more accurate, one actually knew him: his true nature, what he was and what he did; and the other thought she knew him, but didn't.

Reverend Jones, the chairman of the bench, was a retired vicar in his early seventies, who shared Dr Galbraith's criminal interests and was an active member of the local paedophile community. Mrs Mary Price, in contrast, was a history teacher at one of the town's two comprehensive schools. She was a well-meaning but somewhat naïve individual, who had had some minor dealings with the doctor as a result of her work… She had listened intently to the allegations, but couldn't bring herself to accept that a fine man like Dr Galbraith, such a charming, important man who always had time to chat and ask about her family, had done anything wrong, despite the alleged evidence the police claimed to have uncovered.

When the three magistrates returned to the courtroom, everyone, with the exception of Dr Galbraith, who was staring intensely at the reverend with expectant eyes, fully anticipated that he would be imprisoned while awaiting trial. The room fell silent as Reverend Jones began to speak in a quiet, monotone voice that DI Gravel strained to hear despite his excellent hearing.

'We have carefully considered the nature of the charges. The case will be referred to the Crown Court for trial. Regrettably, I have no real choice in that regard. In such cases, it is usual to remand the defendant in custody in the interests of public safety.'

DI Gravel leant forward, straining his ears… Where the fuck was this going?

Reverend Jones continued. 'However, in this case there are very exceptional considerations.'

DI Gravel moved to the very edge of his seat… Exceptional? What the fuck was he talking about?

'Dr Galbraith is a man of the most excellent character. A highly respected individual of impeccable status, who fulfils an essential role in our local community. He has served us selflessly for many years. Countless disturbed children and their unfortunate families have a great deal to thank him for. Bail is therefore granted with the condition that he report to the police on a weekly basis.'

The inspector shook his head slowly… The man was a fucking idiot.

Reverend Jones looked directly at the doctor. 'Dr Galbraith, I am obliged to tell you that you must not approach any of the witnesses, although in your case I am sure such conditions are entirely unnecessary.'

DI Gravel couldn't quite believe what he'd just heard… Over the years he'd witnessed some crazy decisions, but this took the biscuit.

He jumped up from his seat and threw both arms in the air. 'What the fuck have you just done?'

Reverend Jones glared at him with accusing eyes… Infrequently unwise defendants publicly challenged his authority, but never the police.

He fixed DI Gravel with a steely glower and snarled, 'Be very careful, Inspector. Remember whom you are addressing. One more word out of you, and I will hold you in contempt.'

DI Gravel bit the inside of his lower lip hard, and retreated towards the exit whilst mumbling crude obscenities under his breath… The decision was made, and there was fuck all he could do about it.

He chose to ignore Dr Galbraith's supercilious smirk and jovial request for a lift home as he departed.

The inspector hurried from the court building, and out into the busy market day street, bustling with keen winter bargain shoppers… He needed a drink. He badly needed a drink.

DI Gravel walked into the nearest pub, ordered a brandy, and threw it down urgently, followed by another, which he consumed in similar fashion. He placed his empty glass on the bar and hurried from the pub in the direction of Caerystwyth Post Office… He needed a phone box.

Fuck it! Someone was using the thing. But at least it was working. Should he wait? No, he didn't have the time to spare.

He rapped hard on the glass with the knuckles of one hand until the irate caller turned towards him and gave him the V sign. DI Gravel pulled the door open and glared at the teenage lad, whose bravado immediately evaporated. 'Police. Out!'

What the hell was the number? He contacted directory enquiries, hurriedly fished out some additional coins from a trouser pocket, dialled and waited… Answer, come on, answer the fucking thing.

Cynthia approached the phone apprehensively… Please don't be him. Please don't be him.

She picked up the receiver and tentatively whispered, 'Hello?'

'Mrs Galbraith, is that you?'

Silence.

'Cynthia, it's Detective Inspector Gravel, we met at your home the other morning.'

'I remember.'

'Cynthia, I'm not in the habit of doing this, but the circumstances are exceptional.'

She tightened her grip on the phone. 'Does my husband know you're calling?'

'No, Cynthia, he doesn't, and that's a good thing. He's just finished in court. He's facing some extremely serious charges. But, he was given bail.'

'Bail?'

'That means he's free to return home, Cynthia. Please listen to me carefully. You haven't got much time. You need to understand that your husband is a very dangerous man. He's been charged with truly awful crimes against children. Please get out of there while you still have the opportunity. Why not go to your parents' place? Your daughters are already there. You need to…'

Cynthia didn't hear the rest of DI Gravel's impassioned plea. She decided she'd heard enough, and put down the phone just as Dr Galbraith was entering a taxi and giving the driver his home address.

Cynthia sat at the kitchen table with her head in her hands, and stared at the Welsh dresser for almost five minutes before eventually deciding to act. She took the security door key from a drawer with trembling fingers, and placed her shoulder against the side of the dresser, using all her limited weight and strength to gradually push it aside. She stood facing the partially unencumbered door, panting hard, willing herself to move, and then she suddenly stepped forward, gripped the door handle and opened it. She stared at the foreboding concrete steps, and hesitated for a few seconds… She could still run. It was still an option, wasn't it? It wasn't too late. But what if the boy was in there and needed her help? No, not this time; there was no going back, not this time.

Cynthia took her first tentative step, paused briefly on the stairs contemplating retreat despite her newfound determination, and then descended quickly to the bottom without allowing herself sufficient time to change her mind. She held the key to the lock, dropped it to the floor, picked it up and tried again… Her hands were shaking too much. It wouldn't open. They were shaking too much.

She held the key to the lock with her right hand while steadying it with the left… It was working. It was actually working.

There was a loud metallic click as she finally turned the key in the lock… That's it, Cynthia. That's it! She'd done it. It was open. It was actually open.

A small part of her wished that the door had remained locked, but it hadn't, and she pushed it open, slowly, inch by inch, and peered into the darkness with nervous darting eyes… It was dark, far too dark to see. Maybe that wasn't such a bad thing. Maybe she should turn and run.

She shook her head determinedly… No, not this time; there'd be no running this time.

Cynthia put her hand through the doorframe and fumbled for a light switch… Yes, there it was. There it was.

She flicked the switch on at her third attempt, causing a blindingly bright fluorescent light to burst into life. Cynthia shut her eyes tightly, shielding them from the sudden intense electric glare, and then took a step forward and slowly opened them, squinting into the glaringly white space.

At first Cynthia didn't see the young boy hanging on the wall to the left of the door, or the instruments of torture, or the metal meat hook suspended from the ceiling. On first impressions it was a strange, cold, clinical space, and despite the putrid smell of human waste, she felt strangely reassured by the room's initial scientific, lab-like appearance… Perhaps people were wrong after all. Maybe her husband was simply misunderstood rather than criminal.

She took another step forward with a newfound confidence, and slowly scanned the room with blinking eyes. When she saw the emaciated young boy for the first time she just stood and stared, desperately wanting to believe that the horror before her was a product of her imagination rather than grim reality. Cynthia walked towards Anthony and touched him gently on his right cheek… He was real. This wasn't work. It wasn't science. Her husband was a monster. There was no denying the awfulness of what he'd done.

Cynthia placed her hand ever so softly on Anthony's bare chest, and held it there… Was she imagining things? Was she in denial? No, there was a heartbeat. A faint but definitive heartbeat! Thank God, he was alive. The boy was definitely alive.

In a hormone-fuelled frenzy, she urgently struggled to free him from his metal shackles until her manicured nails were broken and her fingertips bled. But her efforts were hopeless. She fell at his feet and wept… No amount of endeavour on her part would suffice, however hard she tried. And even if she did finally manage to get him down, which appeared a lost cause, she wouldn't be able to carry him to the door, let alone drag him up the steps. She just didn't have the physical strength.

Cynthia jumped to her feet… She needed help. She had to summon help.

She turned away from Anthony without looking back, and rushed for the steps… Why on earth hadn't she told the inspector what she knew when she had the opportunity? She should have told him. It seemed so obvious. Why didn't she tell him?

Cynthia heard her husband's mocking voice in her head… Stupid girl. Stupid girl! Why can't you get anything right?

She entered the kitchen, but stopped suddenly and listened intently, hoping her ears were deceiving her… The key in the lock. The front door opening! The door being slammed shut. Footsteps on the hall tiles. He was back. Oh no, he was back! She could run. She could hide. She could try to placate him. Don't panic, Cynthia, don't panic.

She took repeated deep breaths and pictured the young boy hanging from the bloody black steel shackles in that terrible place: the hell her husband had created… There would be no retreat. There would be no running; not this time. Not this time!

Cynthia listened as the doctor's footsteps got closer, closer, closer. And then he appeared: tensing and relaxing his muscles, loosening his powerful shoulders, and forming his hands into formidable weapons. He stared at her, then at the displaced dresser, and then at her again… The bitch had opened the door. Unbelievable! She'd actually opened the door.

He took a step towards her, shouting: louder, louder, louder, until she surmised the room itself may be trembling. 'What the hell have you done, you sanctimonious bitch?'

Cynthia edged along the worktop, inch by inch, inch by cautious inch… Nearly there, nearly there. Come on, Cynthia, nearly there.

And then she moved quickly, like a sprinter off the blocks, and urgently grasped a nine-inch filleting knife from a wooden knife block on the shiny black granite work surface. She moved gradually towards the cellar entrance in a sideways motion, whilst holding the knife out in front of her with both hands clutched tightly around its shaft.

Dr Galbraith narrowed his eyes, sucked in his cheeks, growled like a ferocious beast, and suddenly rushed towards her, striking her with a glancing blow to the side of her head as she thrust at him ineffectually with the blade. Cynthia stumbled backwards, lost her footing, and hit the door frame before falling forwards and slumping to the floor.

The doctor approached her, raised his right leg high behind him, and kicked her hard in the side six inches below her armpit, before stepping over her prone body and advancing towards the first of the cellar steps.

Cynthia gasped for breath, somehow raised her dazed and shaken body onto all fours despite two cracked ribs, focused on the doctor's broad muscular back with blurred eyes, crawled forwards rapidly until she reached him, lifted her right arm, and plunged the knife deep into the back of his left thigh with as much force as her bruised body could muster, striking the bone with the tip of its razor sharp blade.

The doctor screamed like a demented howler monkey, as much from the shock that Cynthia would dare to do such a thing, as from the searing pain. He kicked out mule style with his uninjured leg, landing a heavy blow on the top of her head with the heel of his shoe, as she grabbed at his legs in a further attempt to impede his progress.

Cynthia cried out. She was stunned, dazed, her head swimming, but she didn't let go. As he shook her off and raised his foot to stamp down on her head, she grabbed the cloth of his trousers, extended her free arm, and plunged the blade deep into his thigh for a second time. He swivelled and span athletically, freeing himself from her fragile grip, and kneed her hard in the face, leaving her close to unconsciousness. He looked down at her prone body and savoured the moment.

Dr Galbraith hobbled across the kitchen and fetched a white tea towel from a kitchen drawer, tied a tight tourniquet high on his thigh above his painful injuries, and limped towards the steps with blood seeping down his leg and soaking into his tailored trousers. He clutched repeatedly at his head with anxious probing fingers… It was time to kill the little bastard. Time to destroy the evidence. He'd force the interfering bitch to help him with that particular task, before he killed her.

Just as he was approaching the bottom step, Cynthia dragged herself to her feet on punch-drunk legs. She stumbled in the direction of the stairs, and took a full two minutes to reach the bottom, with the knife held tightly in her right hand.

When she finally reached the cellar she saw the doctor standing at the medicine cupboard, drawing a clear liquid into a syringe, turning away, and fast approaching Anthony with a determined expression on his face.

As Cynthia stumbled towards him with her knife hand behind her back, he stopped, suddenly aware of her presence, and surprised by her rekindled determination…. Maybe he should revisit his thesis at some future date. The bitch had spirit despite the hopelessness of her situation. Interesting, pathetic, but interesting!

Dr Galbraith refocused on the present, met Cynthia's eyes, and smiled. 'Your timing couldn't be better, my dear. You're just in time to watch the little bastard die. And then, once you've helped me dispose of the body, it will be your turn. I suspect it may well prove to be a welcome release, my dear. But, don't be under any misapprehension; you won't die easy. I'll take my time, and you will suffer. Oh yes, you'll suffer. But, not to worry, my dear, that's for later.'

Cynthia dragged one foot forwards, then another, then another, and reached her husband's side just as he was about to insert the needle deep into the boy's swollen abdomen. He seemed strangely oblivious to her presence as she took the knife in both hands, gripped it tightly, raised it high above her head, and brought it down into his upper back with all the force her eight-stone-three-pound frame would allow.

Dr Galbraith dropped the syringe, lurched forward, lost his footing on the badly soiled floor, collided with the wall immediately next to Anthony's shackled wrists, and crashed face down onto the hard white tiles, with Cynthia straddling him and clinging on for life itself. He was stunned, he was slow to react, and Cynthia seized her opportunity. She raised the knife high above her head for a second time, and plunged it down into his right shoulder muscle with all her strength, rendering the arm useless.

Cynthia pulled out the blade, rose slowly to her feet, and stood above the incapacitated body of the man who had brought so much pain and misery into her troubled world… Was he dead? He was, wasn't he? Surely he was dead.

She knelt down at his side, somehow summoned the strength to roll him over onto his back, and stared at his seemingly lifeless face for a minute or more, before reaching out nervously to feel for a heartbeat… Was it over? Was it really over? Surely it was over. But, she had to be sure. Like it or not she had to be sure.

As Cynthia bent forwards, and placed her face close to his, listening for any sign of breathing, he suddenly opened one eye, then the other, and snatched at her left earlobe with flashing white teeth. But she reacted quickly, lurching backward and causing his attack to fall fractionally short. As he reached up in an attempt to grab her throat, she jumped to her feet, lifted the knife high above her head in both hands, and brought it down forcibly, before repeating the process time and time and time again. When he was totally, utterly, unrecognisable as the man who had tormented her, she stopped, and flopped blood-soaked and exhausted next to his corpse.

As Cynthia lay there, in that awful place, that monument to evil, panting, gasping for oxygen, it dawned on her… It was over. This time it really was over.

All fear suddenly left her, and in that instant all was calm… She was safe. The child was safe. The monster was no more, and her world was a better place.

Cynthia was oblivious to her pain, and unaware of the weapon clasped tightly in her right hand as she walked back up the steps, across the family kitchen, and into the hall. The knife clattered to the tiled floor and made her jump as she picked up the phone and dialled nine-nine-nine.

She stumbled into the lounge, slumped heavily to the floor next to an old dark oak sideboard, and dared to unlock a cupboard with bloody outstretched fingers that she noted were no longer trembling. She took her favourite LP from the collection she had not seen, let alone played in years, and pulled herself unsteadily to her feet. Cynthia took the record from its colourful atmospheric sleeve, lifted the record player's clear plastic lid, placed the disc gently on the turntable, waited for the needle to make contact with the black vinyl, and turned up the volume. She sat back down on the luxurious soft carpet with a new vitality, and listened contently to the glorious sweeping medley of Bowie's visionary songs, while waiting for the emergency services to arrive.

A note to the reader

Thanks for reading White Is The Coldest Colour. I'm always interested to know what readers think, and I'd be grateful if you'd leave a review on Amazon or Goodreads.

John Nicholl

Lightning Source UK Ltd.
Milton Keynes UK
UKOW04f1115311215

265634UK00002B/53/P

9 781785 106910